Stone Arch
FAIRY TALES
volume two

Secrets, Monsters & Magic Mirrors

STONE ARCH BOOKS
a capstone imprint

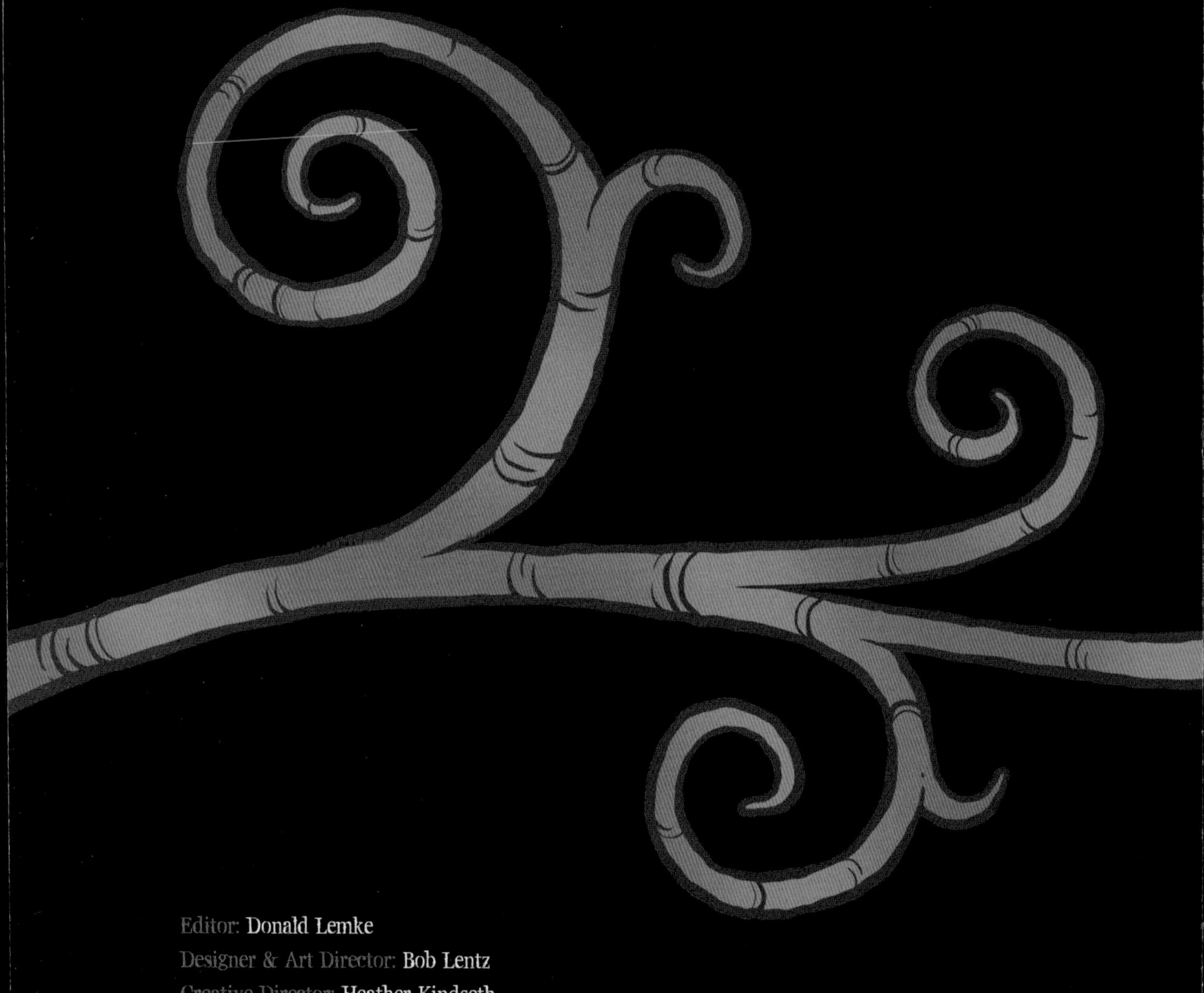

Editor: Donald Lemke
Designer & Art Director: Bob Lentz
Creative Director: Heather Kindseth
Editorial Director: Michael Dahl
Procution Specialist: Michelle Biedscheid

Graphic Spin is published by Stone Arch Books — a Capstone imprint. 151 Good Counsel Drive, P.O. Box 669 Mankato, Minnesota 56002 www.capstonepub.com. Library of Congress Cataloging-in-Publication Data is available on the Library of Congress website. Trade paperback: 978-1-4342-3456-8
The contents of this book were originally published by Stone Arch Books as library bound and paperback editions in 2008 and 2009 as: *Beauty and the Beast*, *The Princess and the Pea*, *Rapunzel*, *Snow White*, and *Thumbelina*.

Printed in China.
072011
006241

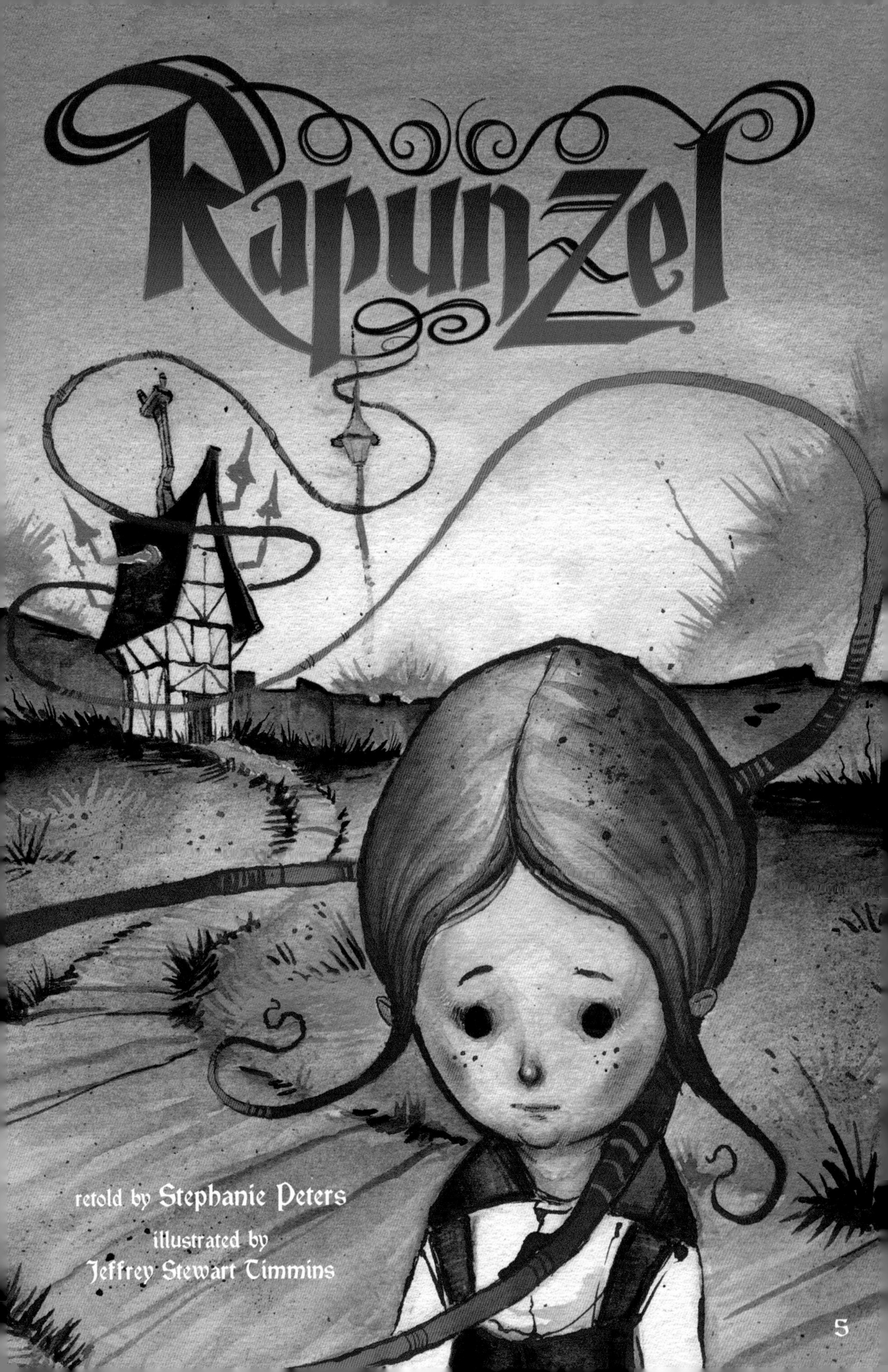
Rapunzel
retold by Stephanie Peters
illustrated by
Jeffrey Stewart Timmins

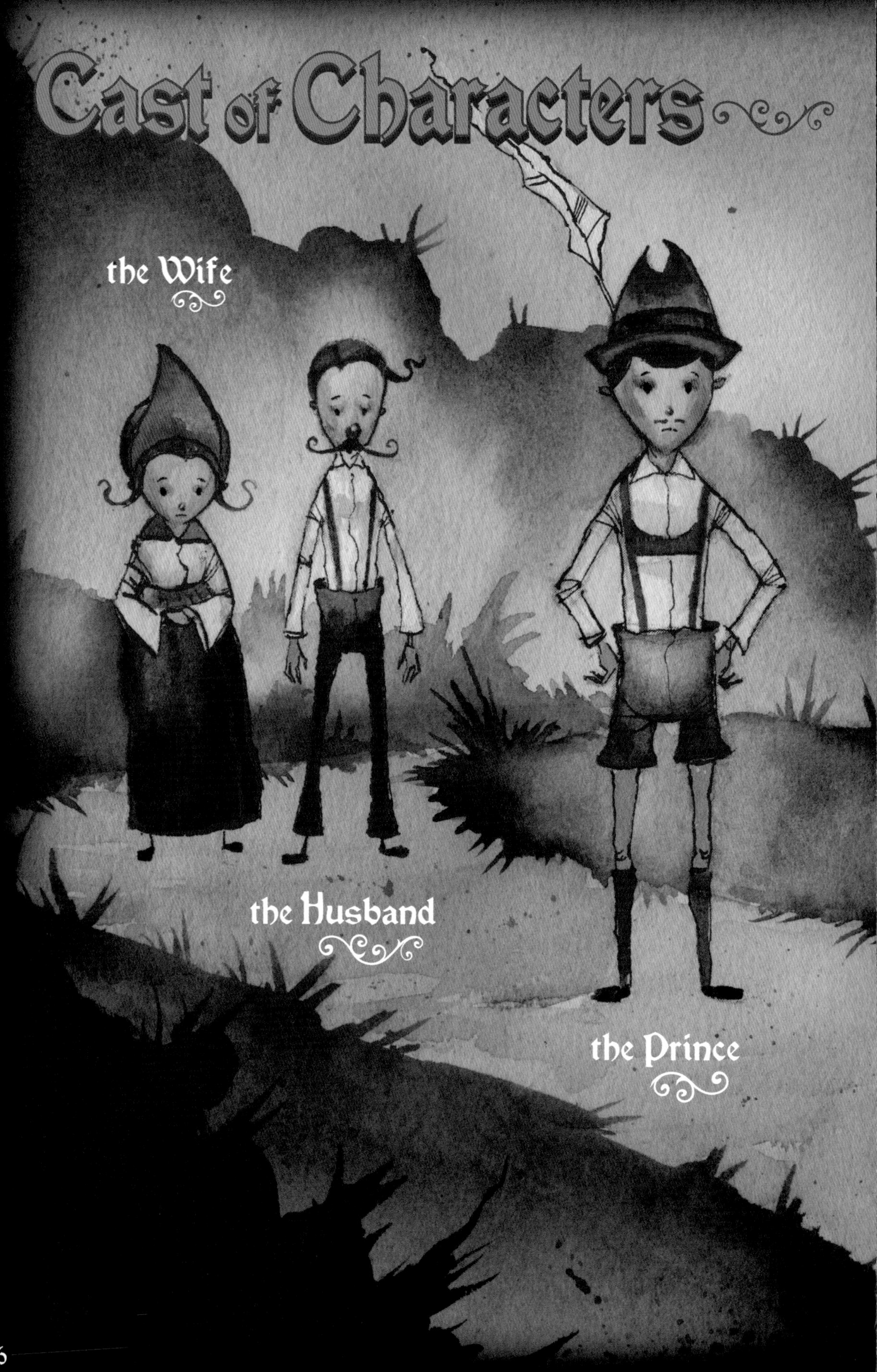
Cast of Characters
the Wife
the Husband
the Prince

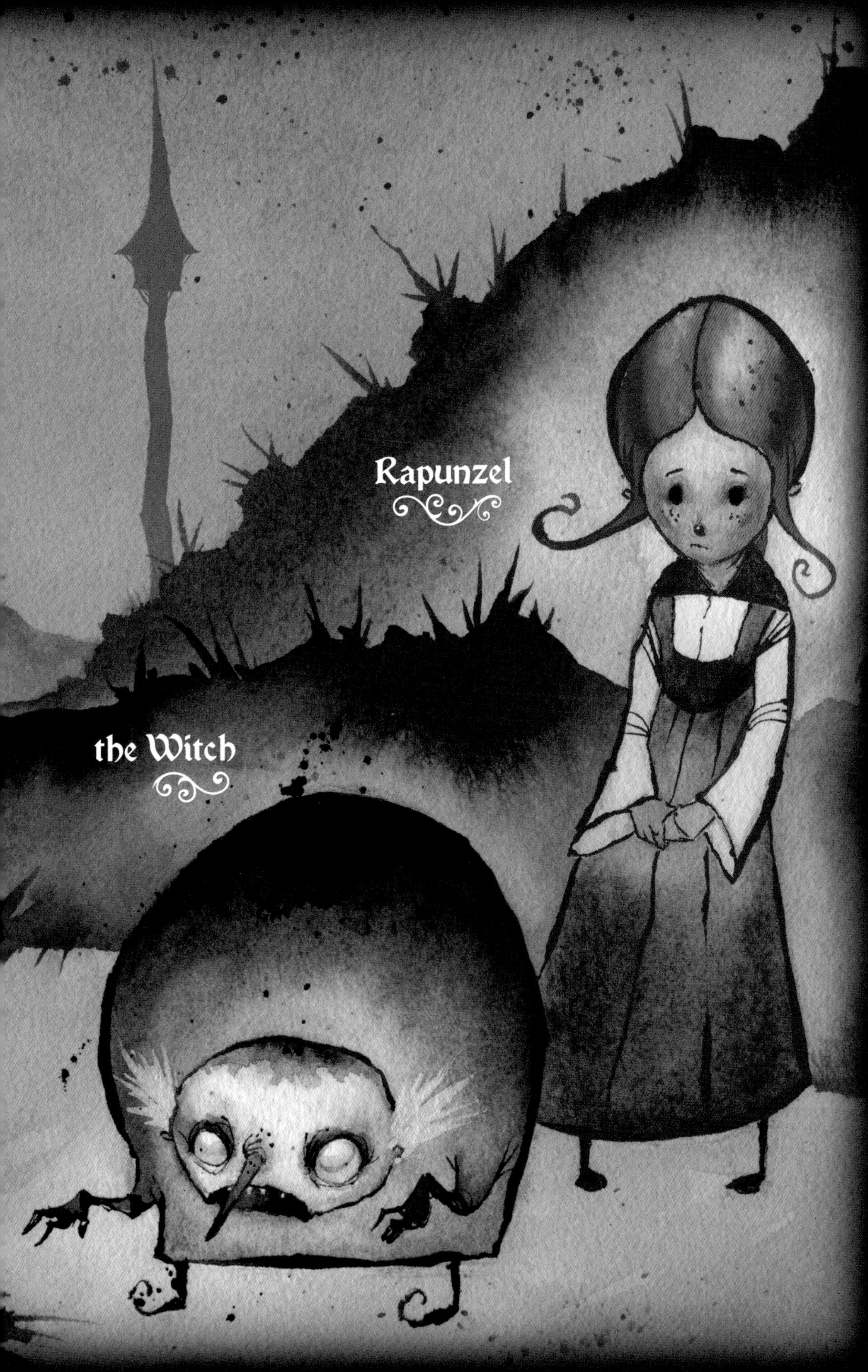
Rapunzel
the Witch

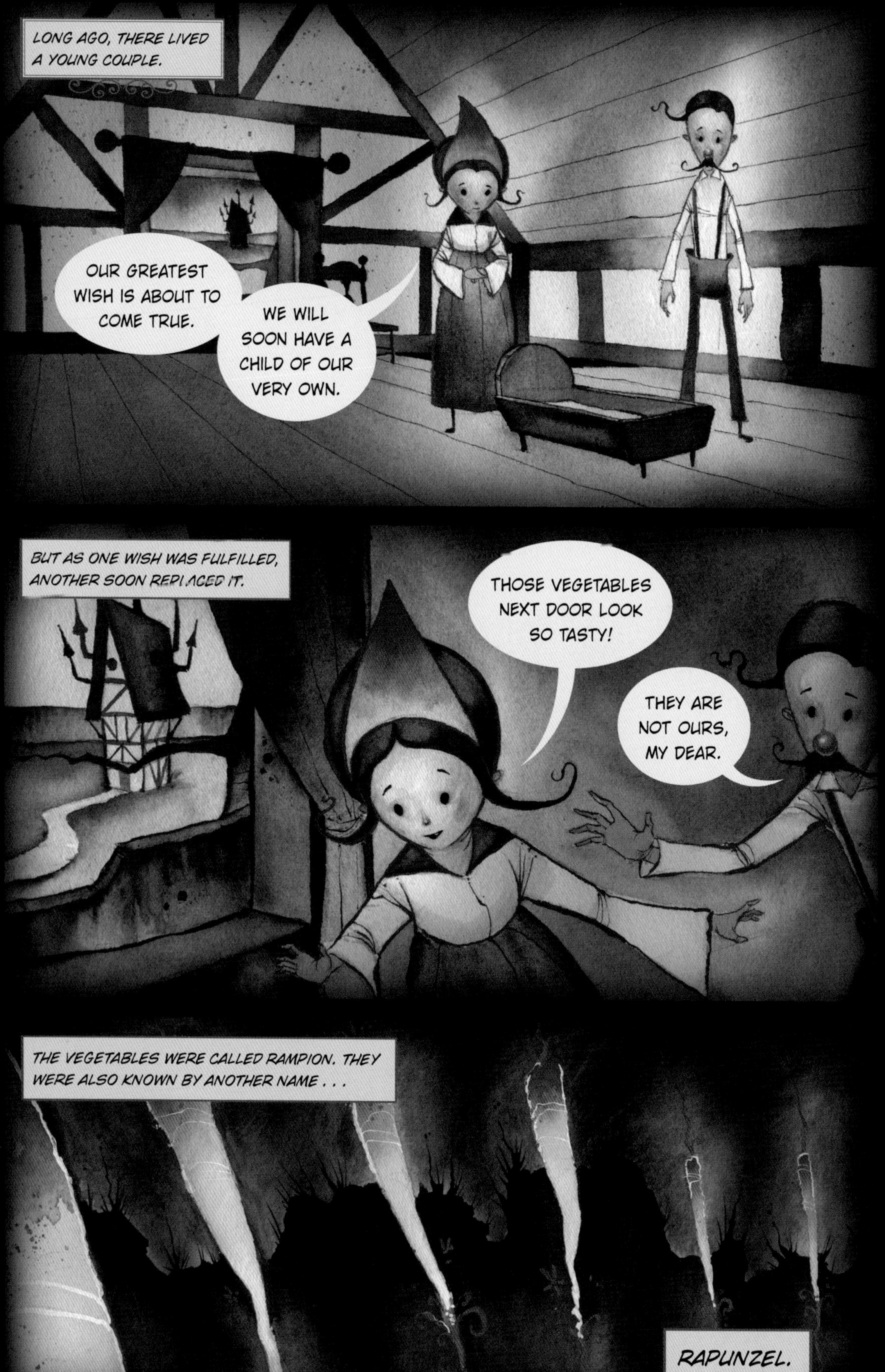
LONG AGO, THERE LIVED A YOUNG COUPLE.
OUR GREATEST WISH IS ABOUT TO COME TRUE.
WE WILL SOON HAVE A CHILD OF OUR VERY OWN.
BUT AS ONE WISH WAS FULFILLED, ANOTHER SOON REPLACED IT.
THOSE VEGETABLES NEXT DOOR LOOK SO TASTY!
THEY ARE NOT OURS, MY DEAR.
THE VEGETABLES WERE CALLED RAMPION. THEY WERE ALSO KNOWN BY ANOTHER NAME . . .
RAPUNZEL.

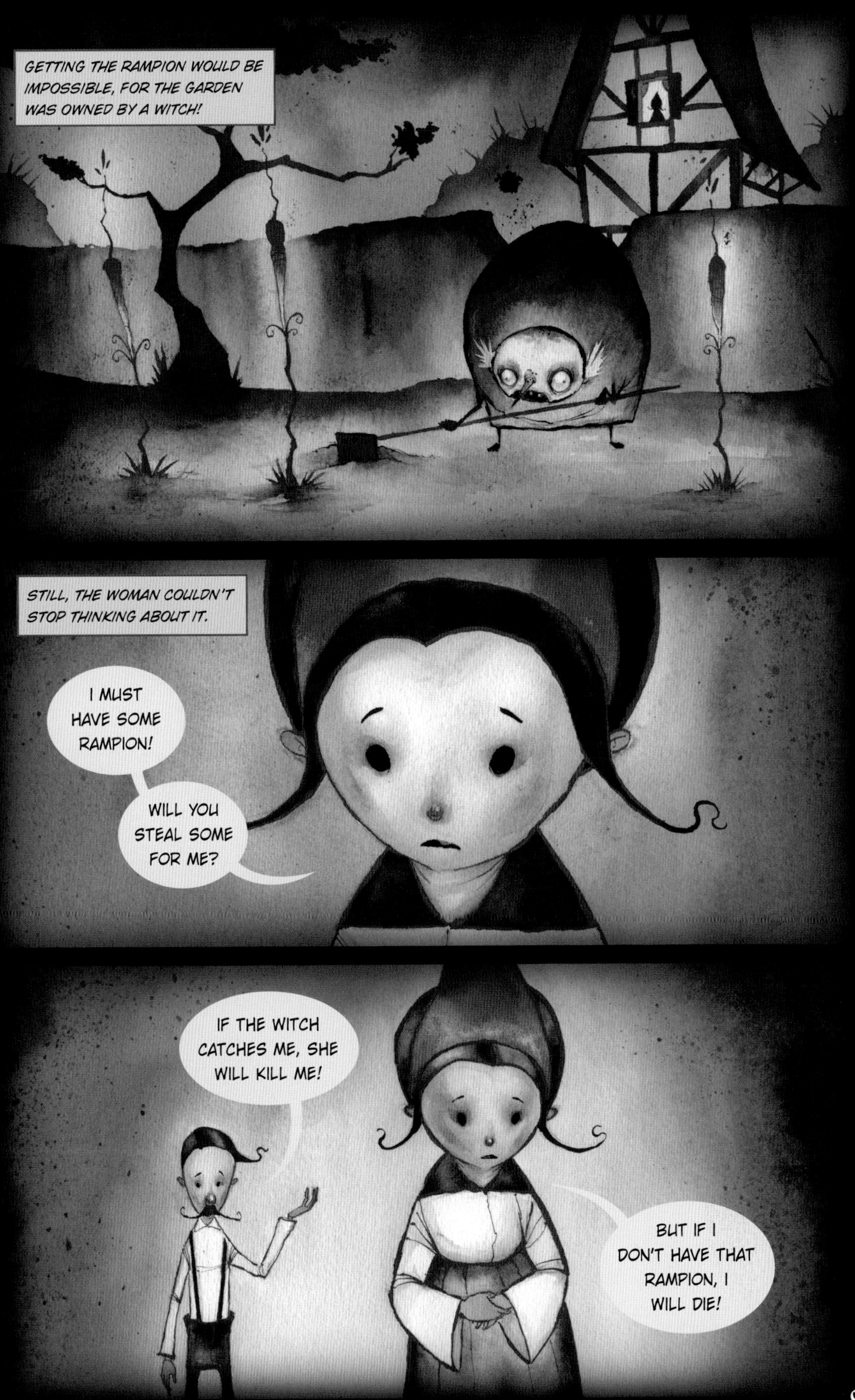
GETTING THE RAMPION WOULD BE IMPOSSIBLE, FOR THE GARDEN WAS OWNED BY A WITCH!
STILL, THE WOMAN COULDN'T STOP THINKING ABOUT IT.
I MUST HAVE SOME RAMPION!
WILL YOU STEAL SOME FOR ME?
IF THE WITCH CATCHES ME, SHE WILL KILL ME!
BUT IF I DON'T HAVE THAT RAMPION, I WILL DIE!

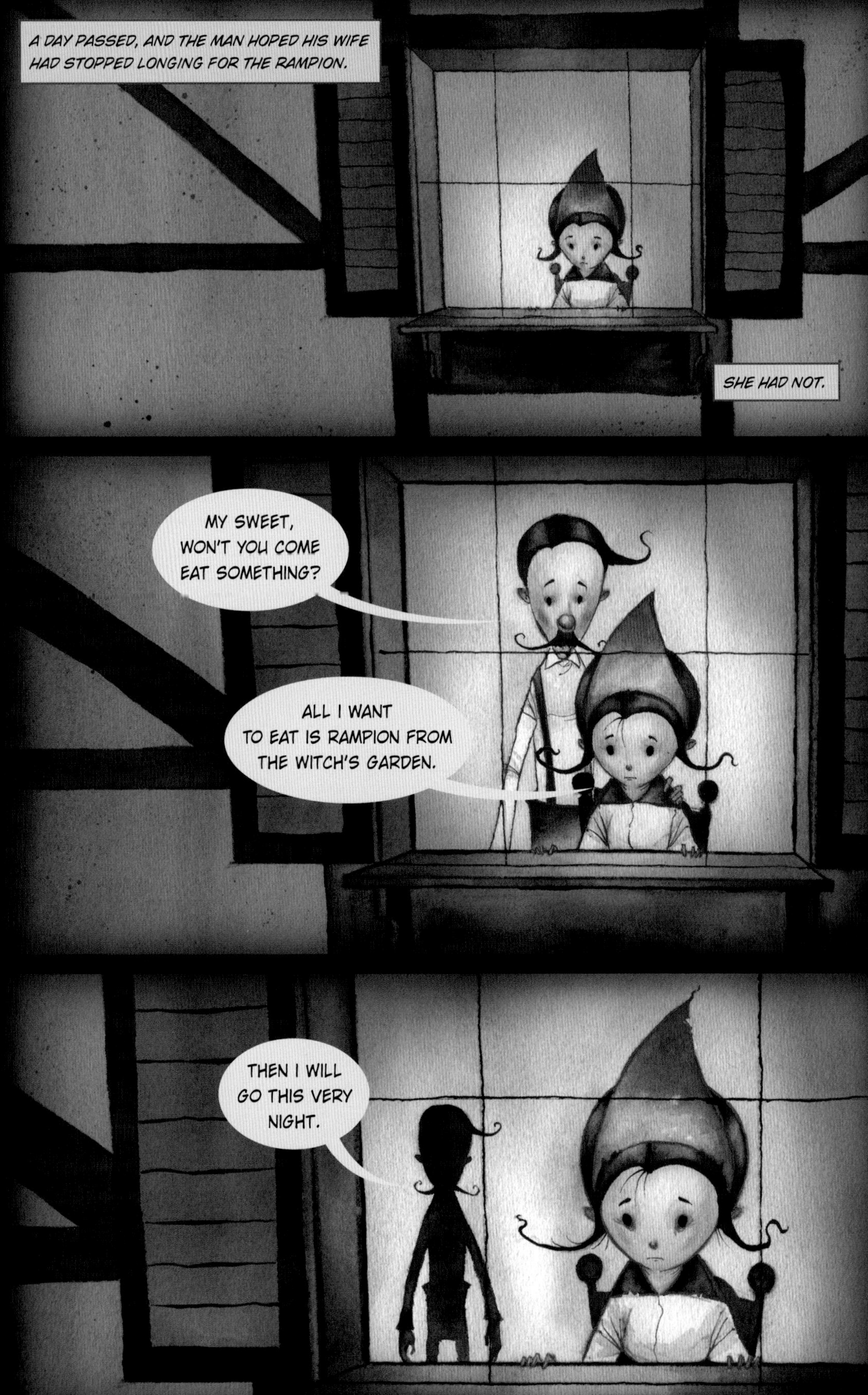

A DAY PASSED, AND THE MAN HOPED HIS WIFE HAD STOPPED LONGING FOR THE RAMPION.
SHE HAD NOT.
MY SWEET, WON'T YOU COME EAT SOMETHING?
ALL I WANT TO EAT IS RAMPION FROM THE WITCH'S GARDEN.
THEN I WILL GO THIS VERY NIGHT.

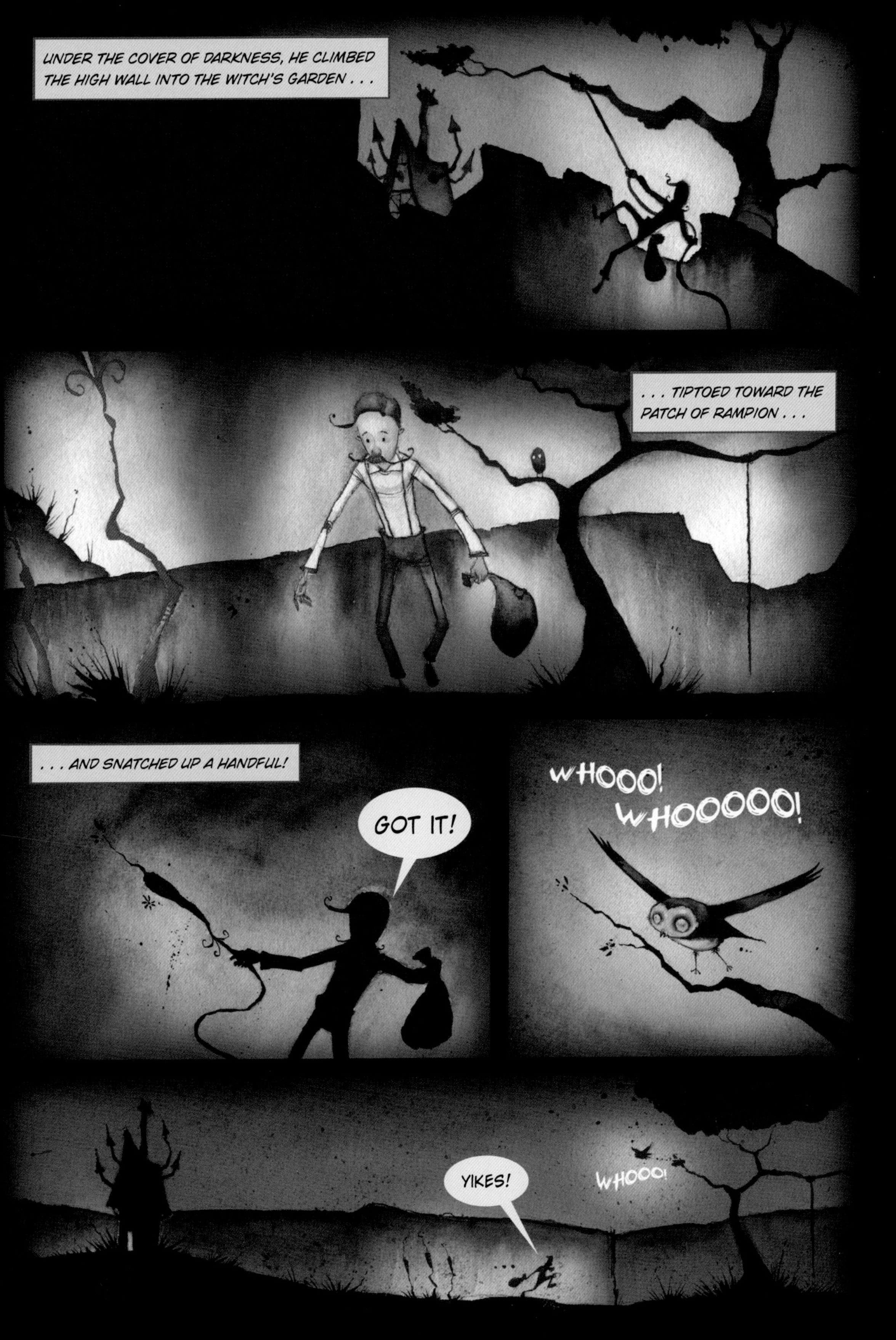
UNDER THE COVER OF DARKNESS, HE CLIMBED THE HIGH WALL INTO THE WITCH'S GARDEN . . .
. . . TIPTOED TOWARD THE PATCH OF RAMPION . . .
. . . AND SNATCHED UP A HANDFUL!
GOT IT!
WHOOO!
WHOOOOOO!
YIKES!
WHOOO!

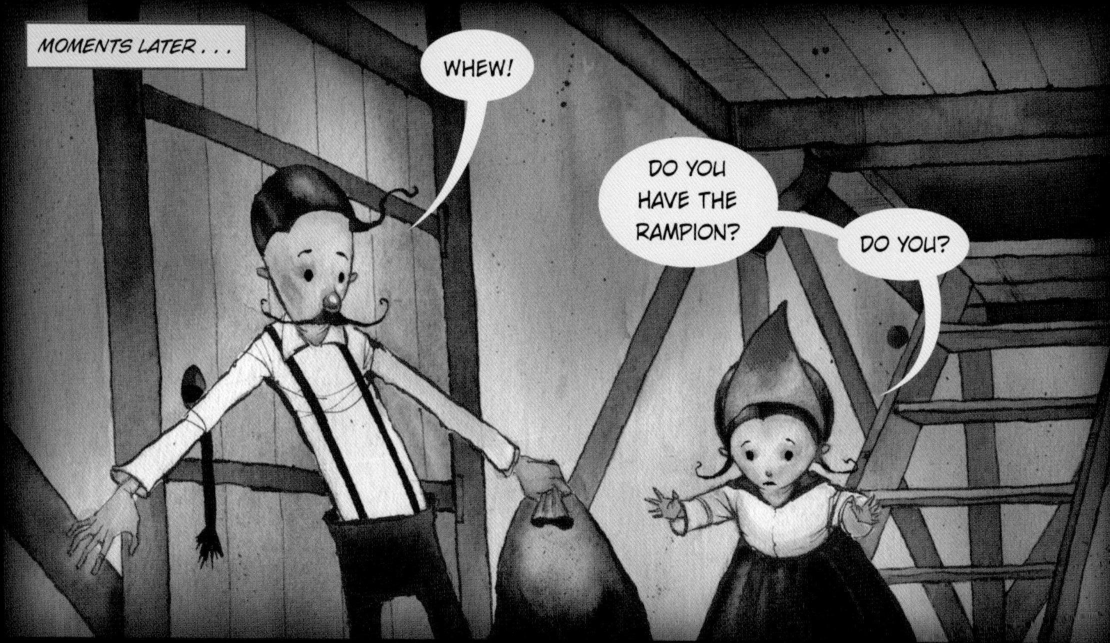
MOMENTS LATER . . .
WHEW!
DO YOU HAVE THE RAMPION?
DO YOU?

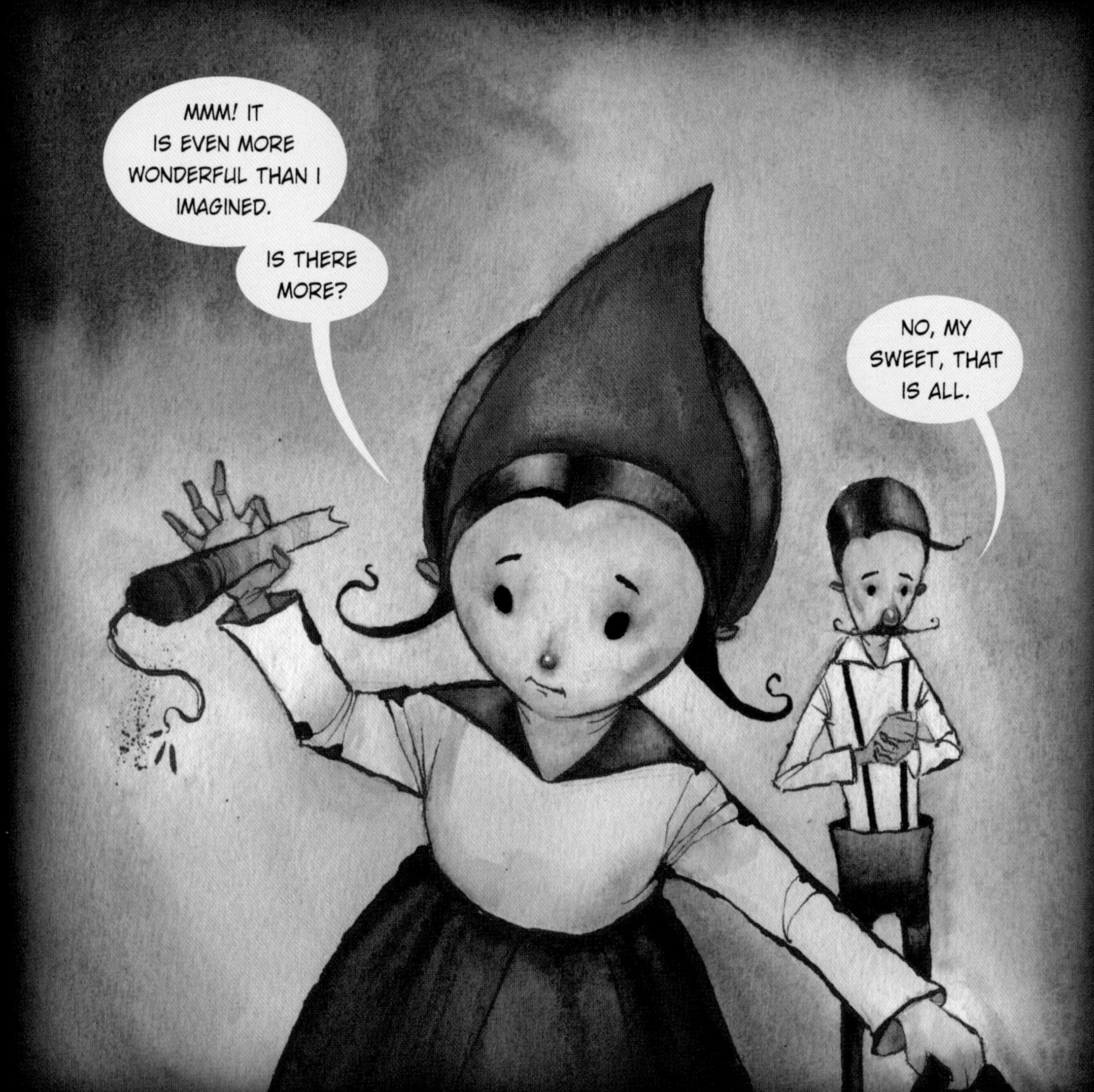
MMM! IT IS EVEN MORE WONDERFUL THAN I IMAGINED.
IS THERE MORE?
NO, MY SWEET, THAT IS ALL.

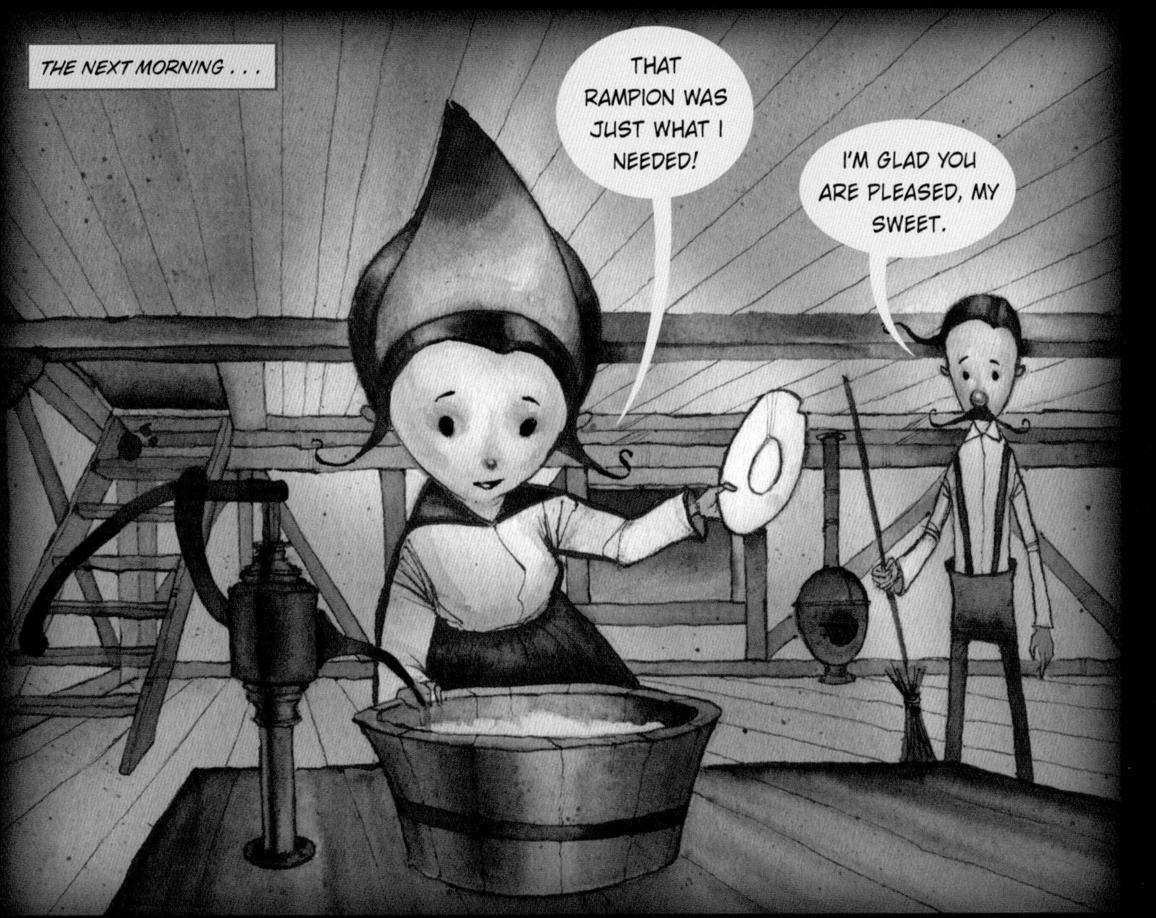
THE NEXT MORNING . . .
THAT RAMPION WAS JUST WHAT I NEEDED!
I'M GLAD YOU ARE PLEASED, MY SWEET.

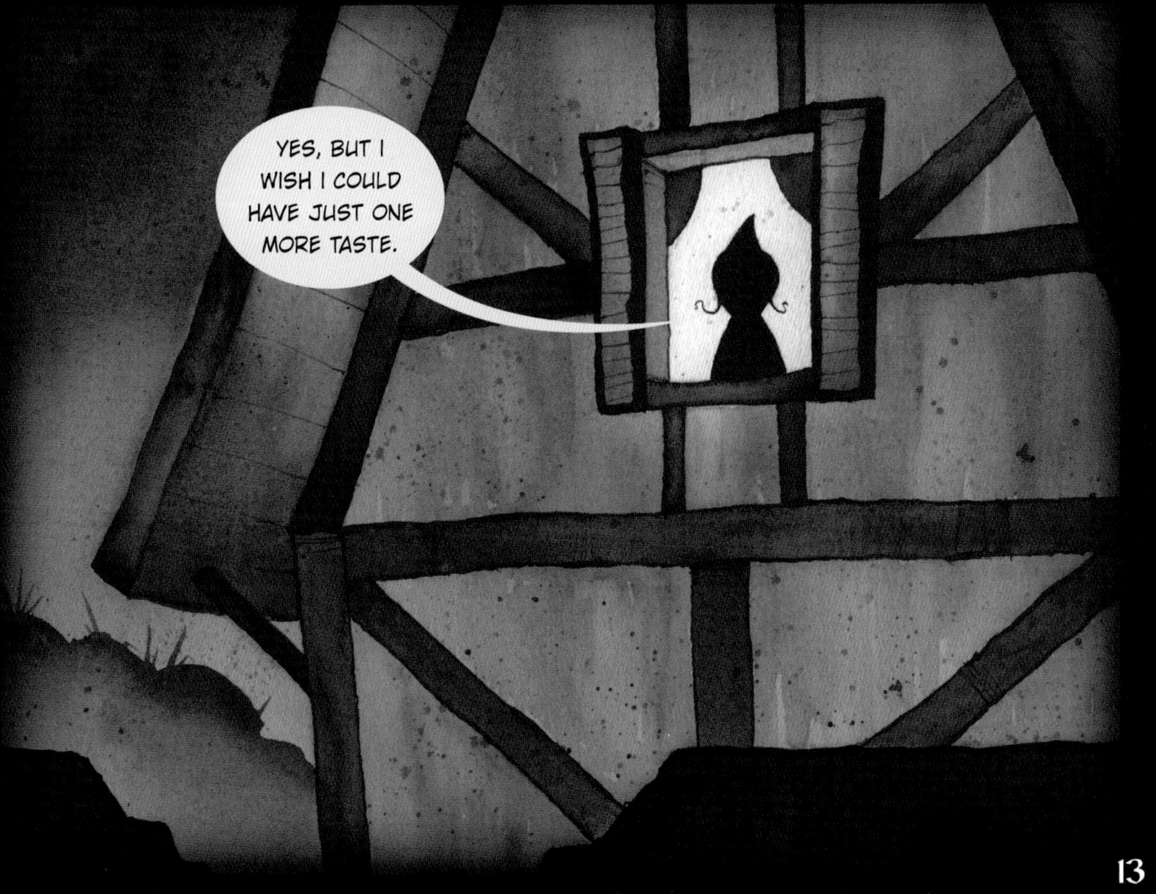
YES, BUT I WISH I COULD HAVE JUST ONE MORE TASTE.

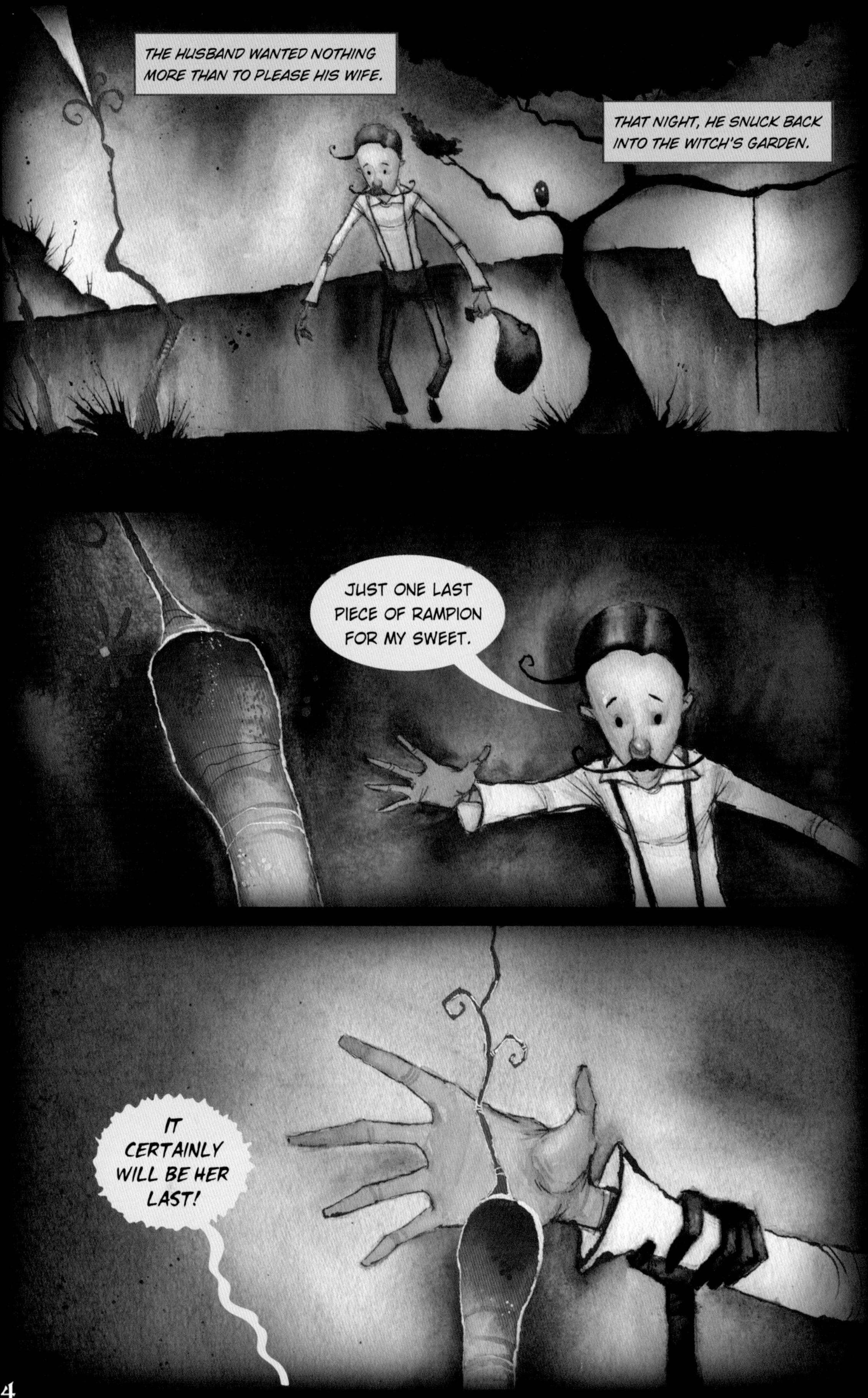
THE HUSBAND WANTED NOTHING MORE THAN TO PLEASE HIS WIFE.
THAT NIGHT, HE SNUCK BACK INTO THE WITCH'S GARDEN.
JUST ONE LAST PIECE OF RAMPION FOR MY SWEET.
IT CERTAINLY WILL BE HER LAST!

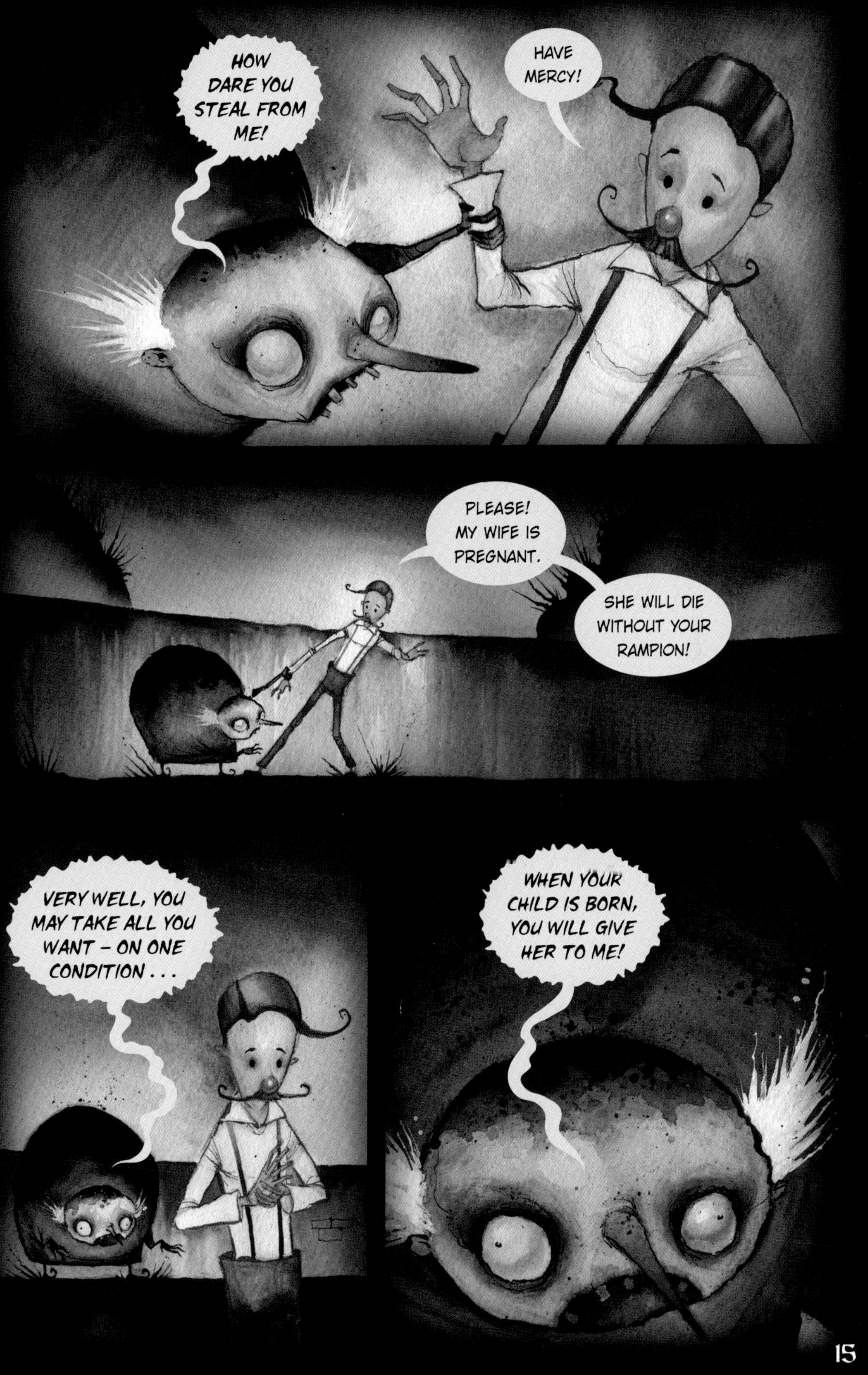
HOW DARE YOU STEAL FROM ME!
HAVE MERCY!
PLEASE! MY WIFE IS PREGNANT.
SHE WILL DIE WITHOUT YOUR RAMPION!
VERY WELL, YOU MAY TAKE ALL YOU WANT – ON ONE CONDITION . . .
WHEN YOUR CHILD IS BORN, YOU WILL GIVE HER TO ME!

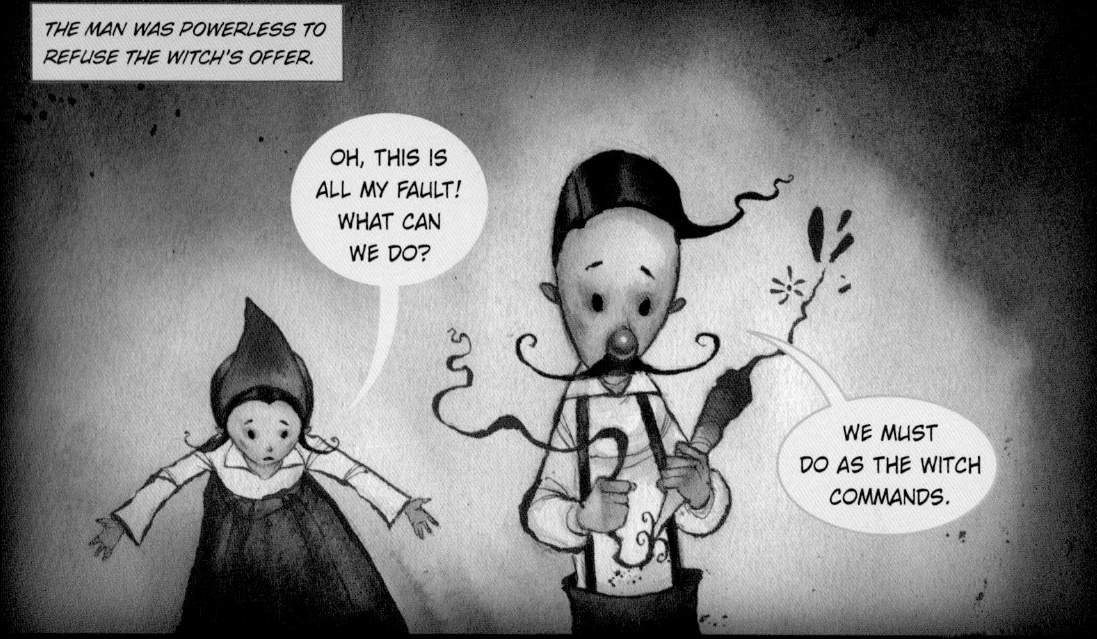
THE MAN WAS POWERLESS TO REFUSE THE WITCH'S OFFER.
OH, THIS IS ALL MY FAULT! WHAT CAN WE DO?
WE MUST DO AS THE WITCH COMMANDS.

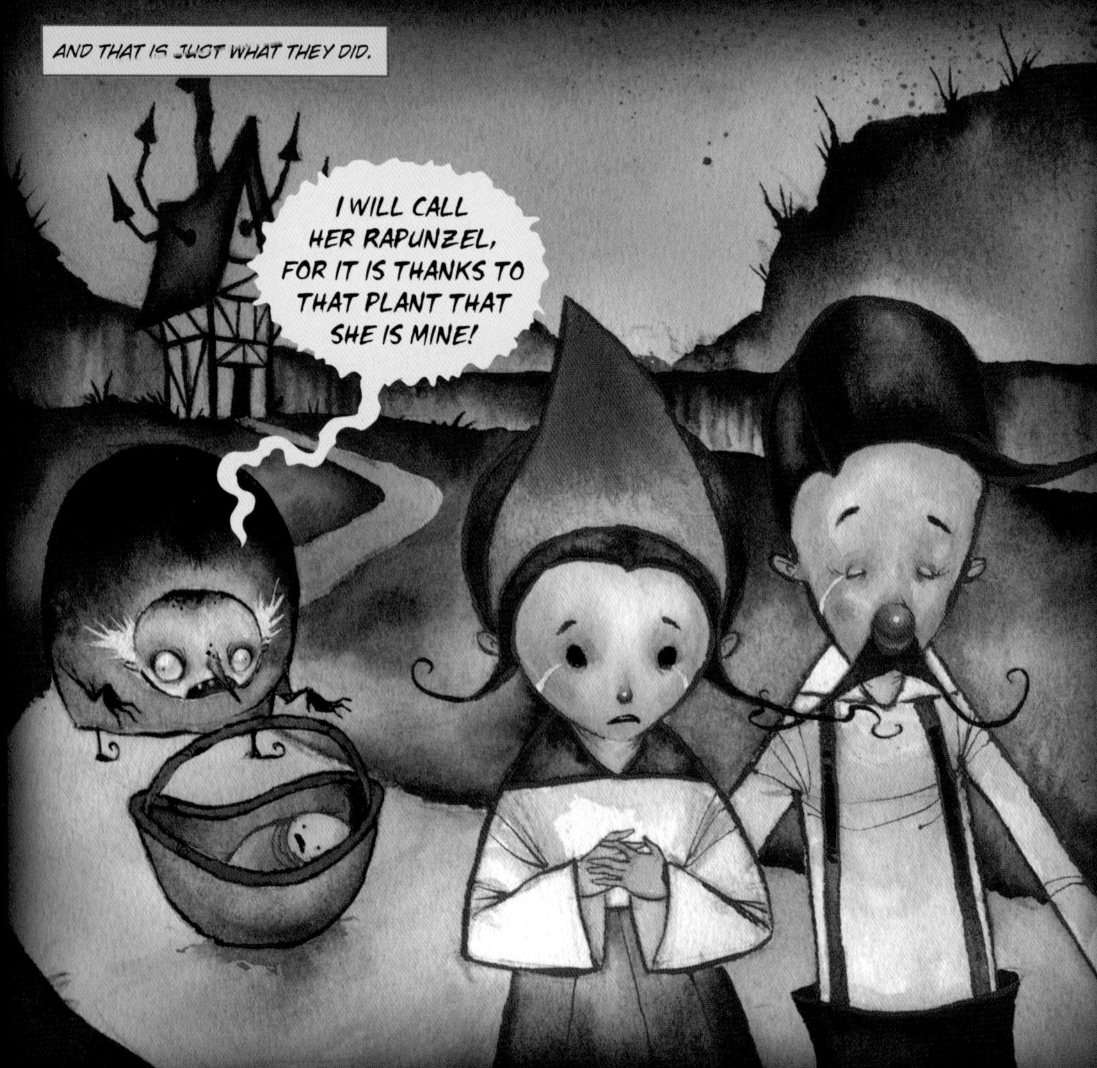
AND THAT IS JUST WHAT THEY DID.
I WILL CALL HER RAPUNZEL, FOR IT IS THANKS TO THAT PLANT THAT SHE IS MINE!

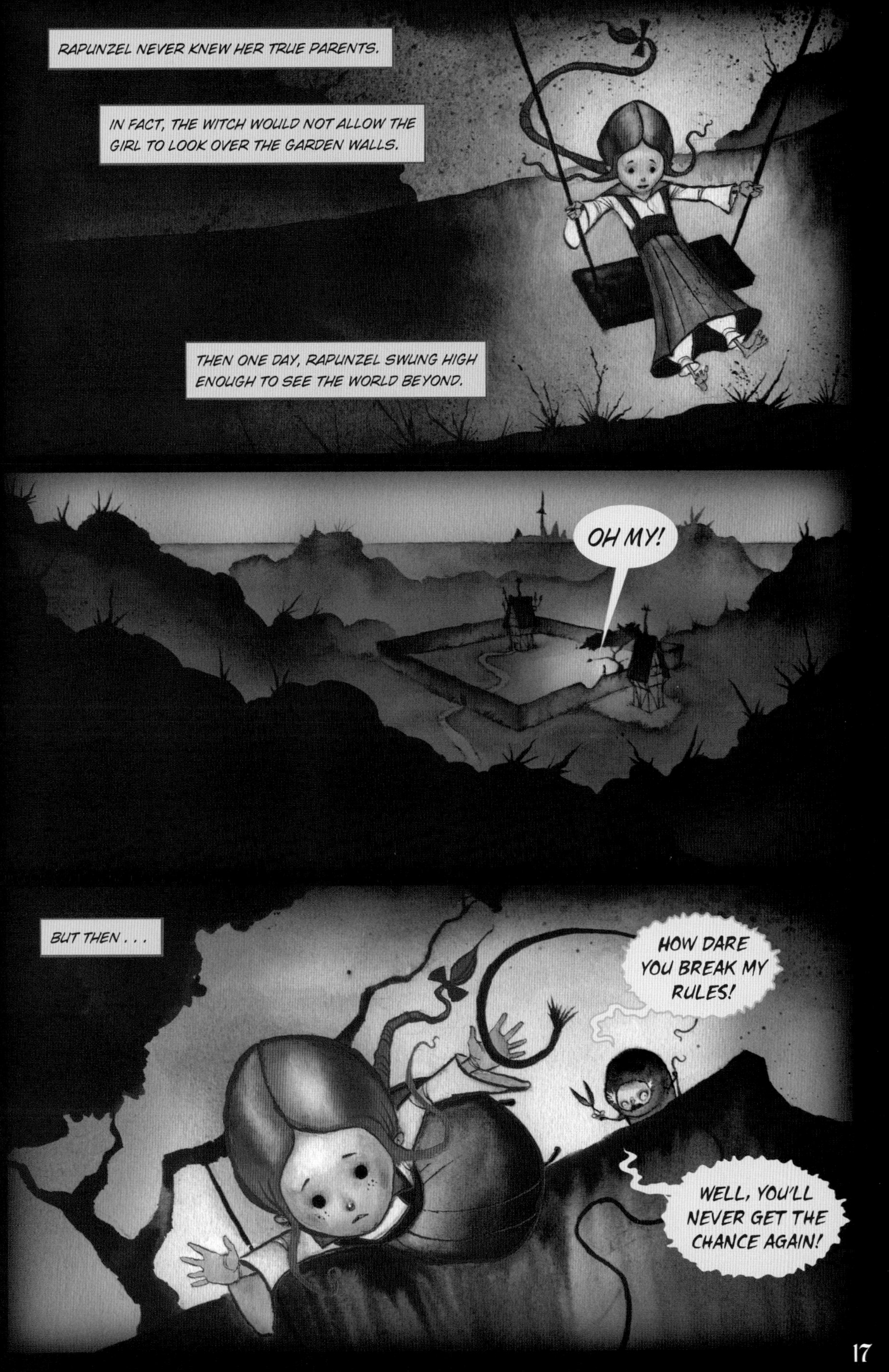

RAPUNZEL NEVER KNEW HER TRUE PARENTS.
IN FACT, THE WITCH WOULD NOT ALLOW THE GIRL TO LOOK OVER THE GARDEN WALLS.
THEN ONE DAY, RAPUNZEL SWUNG HIGH ENOUGH TO SEE THE WORLD BEYOND.
OH MY!
BUT THEN . . .
HOW DARE YOU BREAK MY RULES!
WELL, YOU'LL NEVER GET THE CHANCE AGAIN!

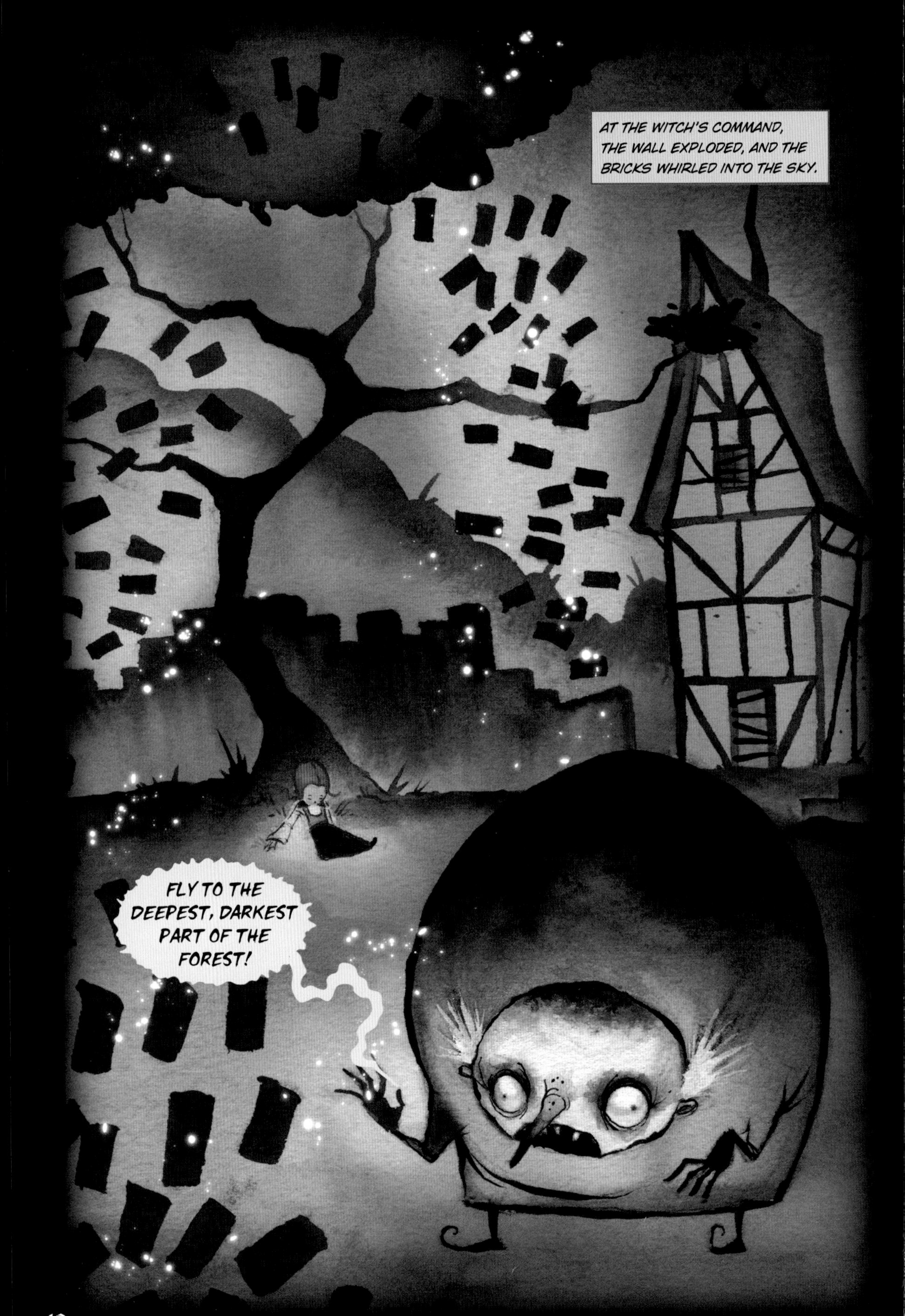
AT THE WITCH'S COMMAND, THE WALL EXPLODED, AND THE BRICKS WHIRLED INTO THE SKY.
FLY TO THE DEEPEST, DARKEST PART OF THE FOREST!

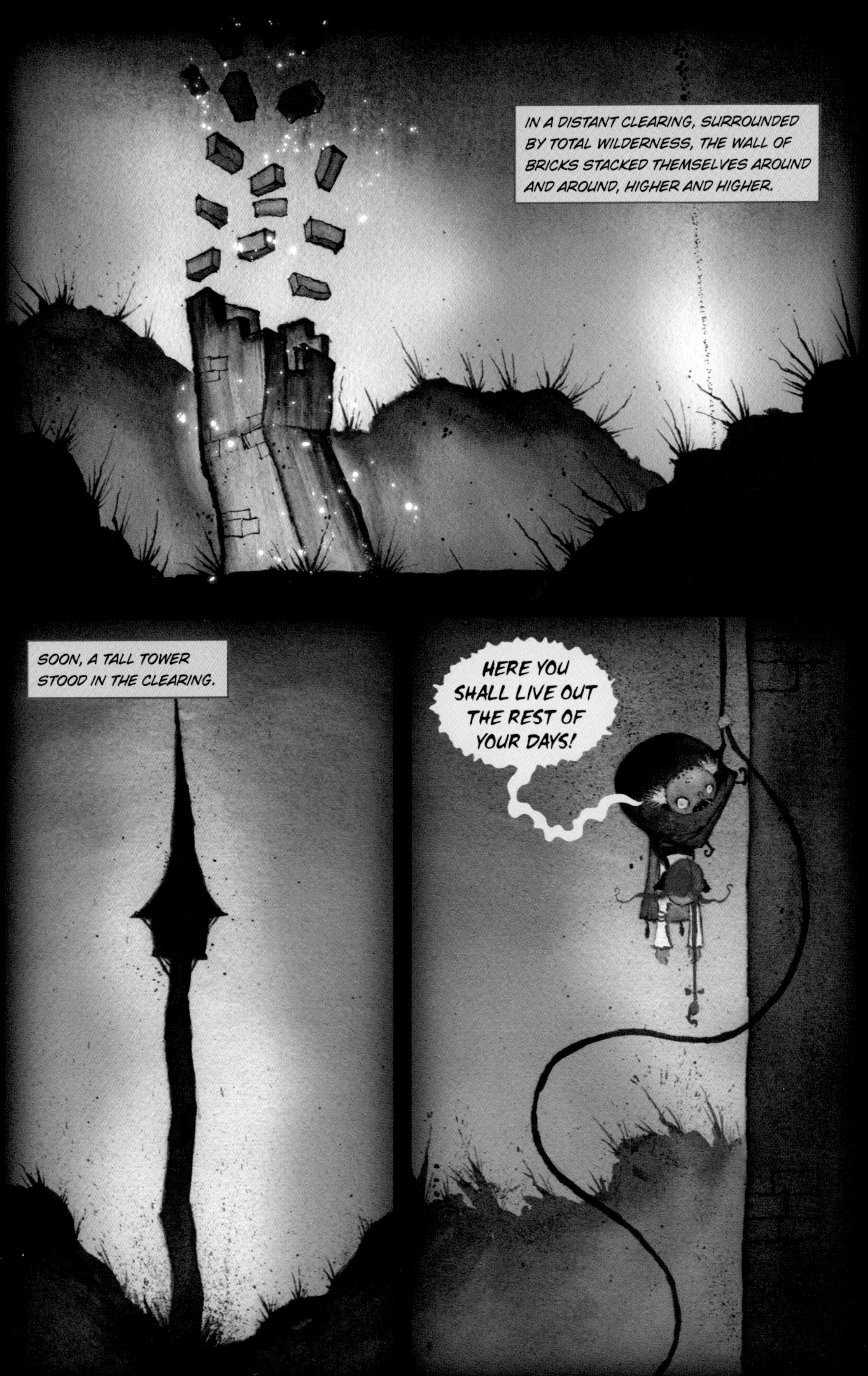
IN A DISTANT CLEARING, SURROUNDED BY TOTAL WILDERNESS, THE WALL OF BRICKS STACKED THEMSELVES AROUND AND AROUND, HIGHER AND HIGHER.
SOON, A TALL TOWER STOOD IN THE CLEARING.
HERE YOU SHALL LIVE OUT THE REST OF YOUR DAYS!

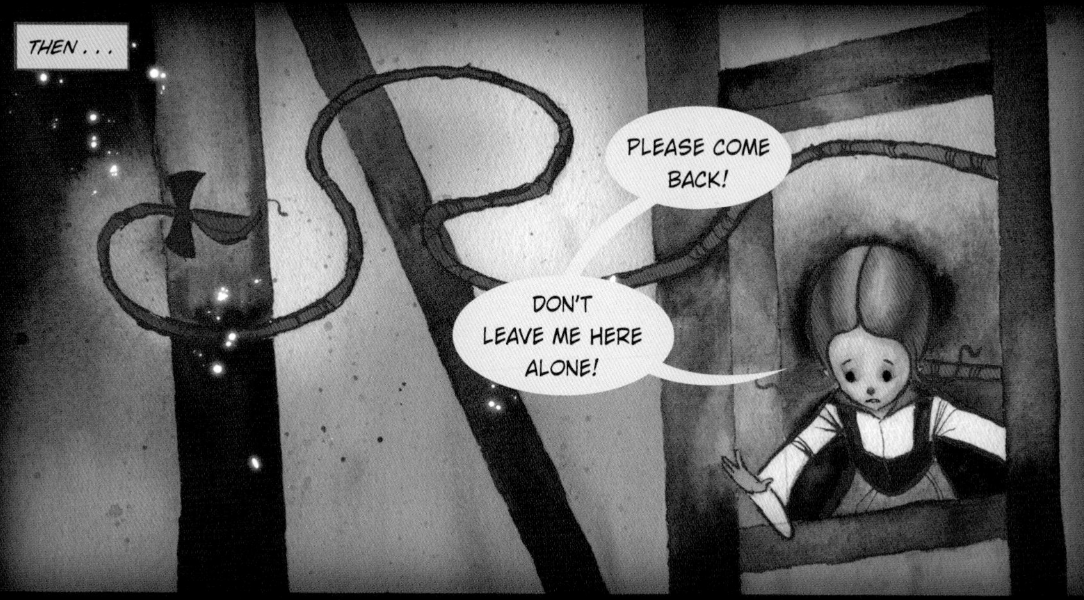
THEN . . .
PLEASE COME BACK!
DON'T LEAVE ME HERE ALONE!

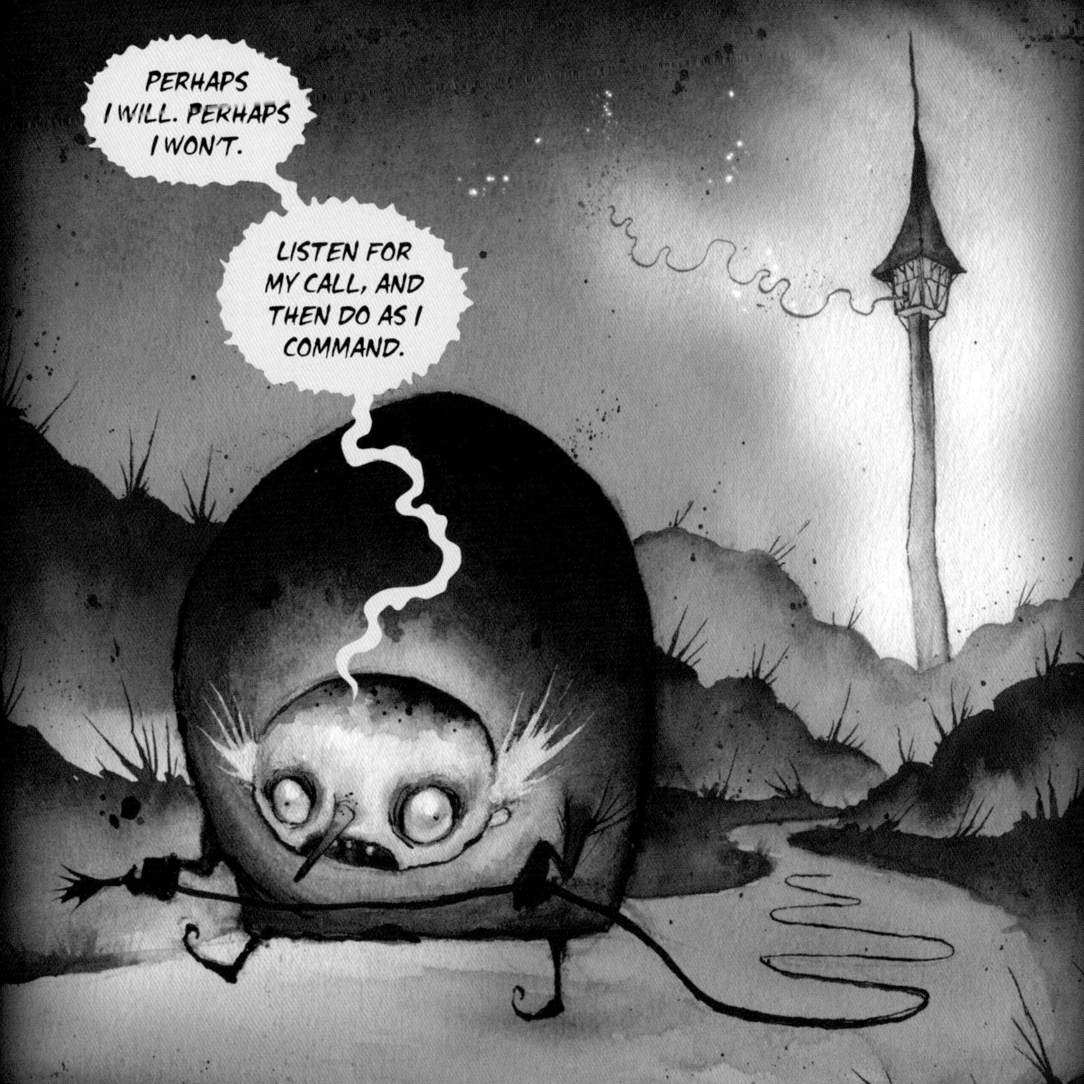
PERHAPS I WILL. PERHAPS I WON'T.
LISTEN FOR MY CALL, AND THEN DO AS I COMMAND.

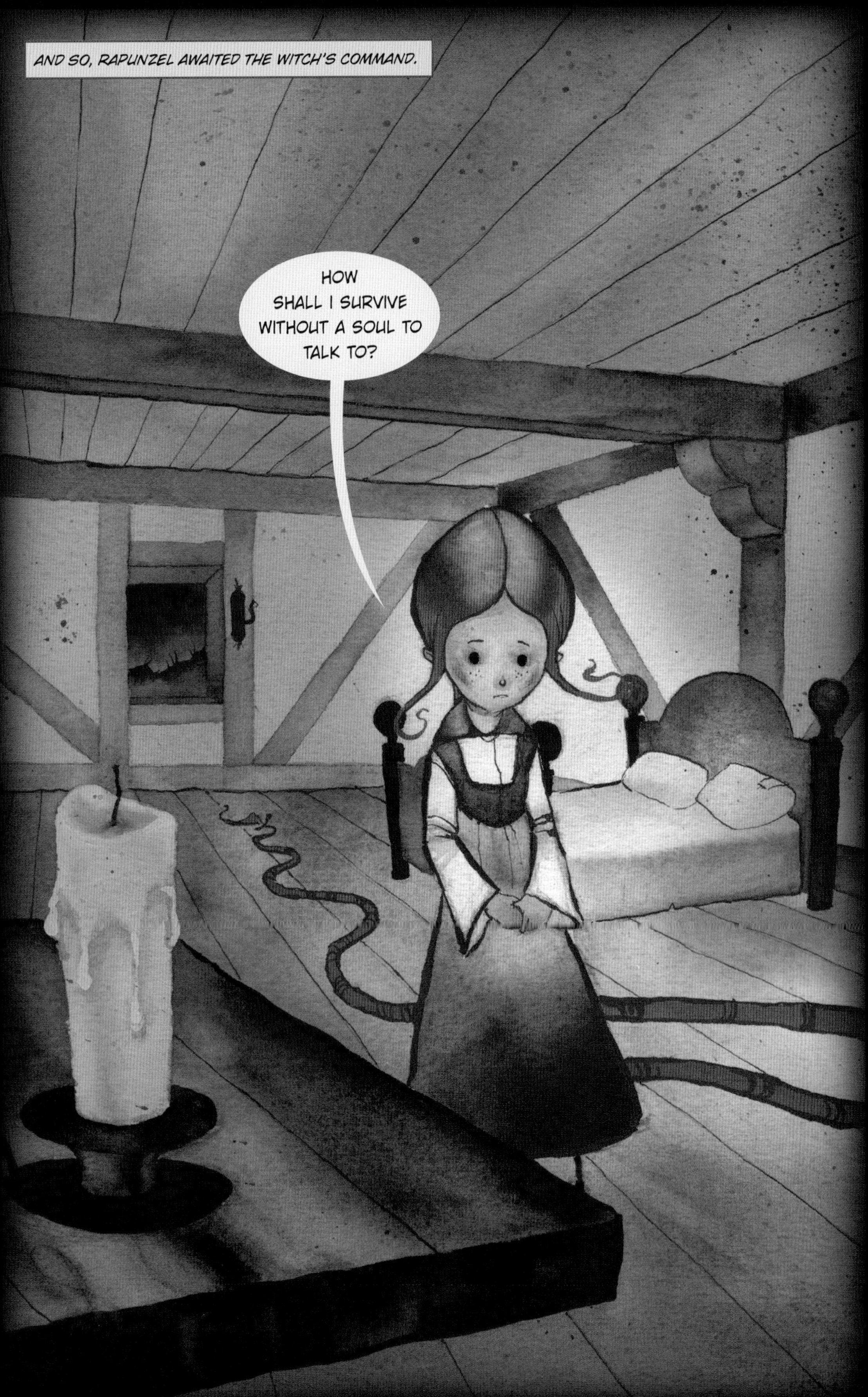
AND SO, RAPUNZEL AWAITED THE WITCH'S COMMAND.
HOW SHALL I SURVIVE WITHOUT A SOUL TO TALK TO?

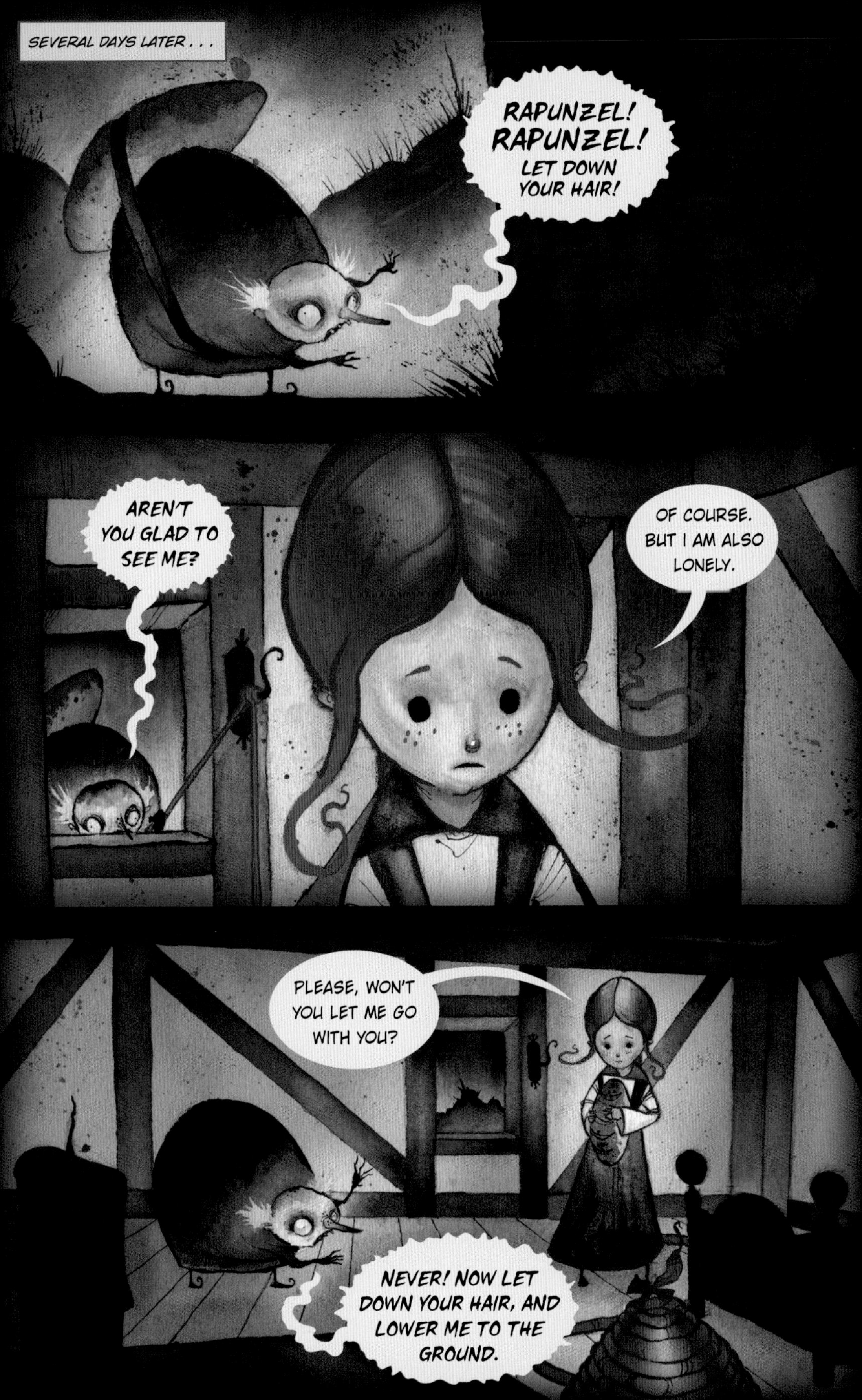
SEVERAL DAYS LATER . . .
RAPUNZEL! RAPUNZEL! LET DOWN YOUR HAIR!
AREN'T YOU GLAD TO SEE ME?
OF COURSE. BUT I AM ALSO LONELY.
PLEASE, WON'T YOU LET ME GO WITH YOU?
NEVER! NOW LET DOWN YOUR HAIR, AND LOWER ME TO THE GROUND.

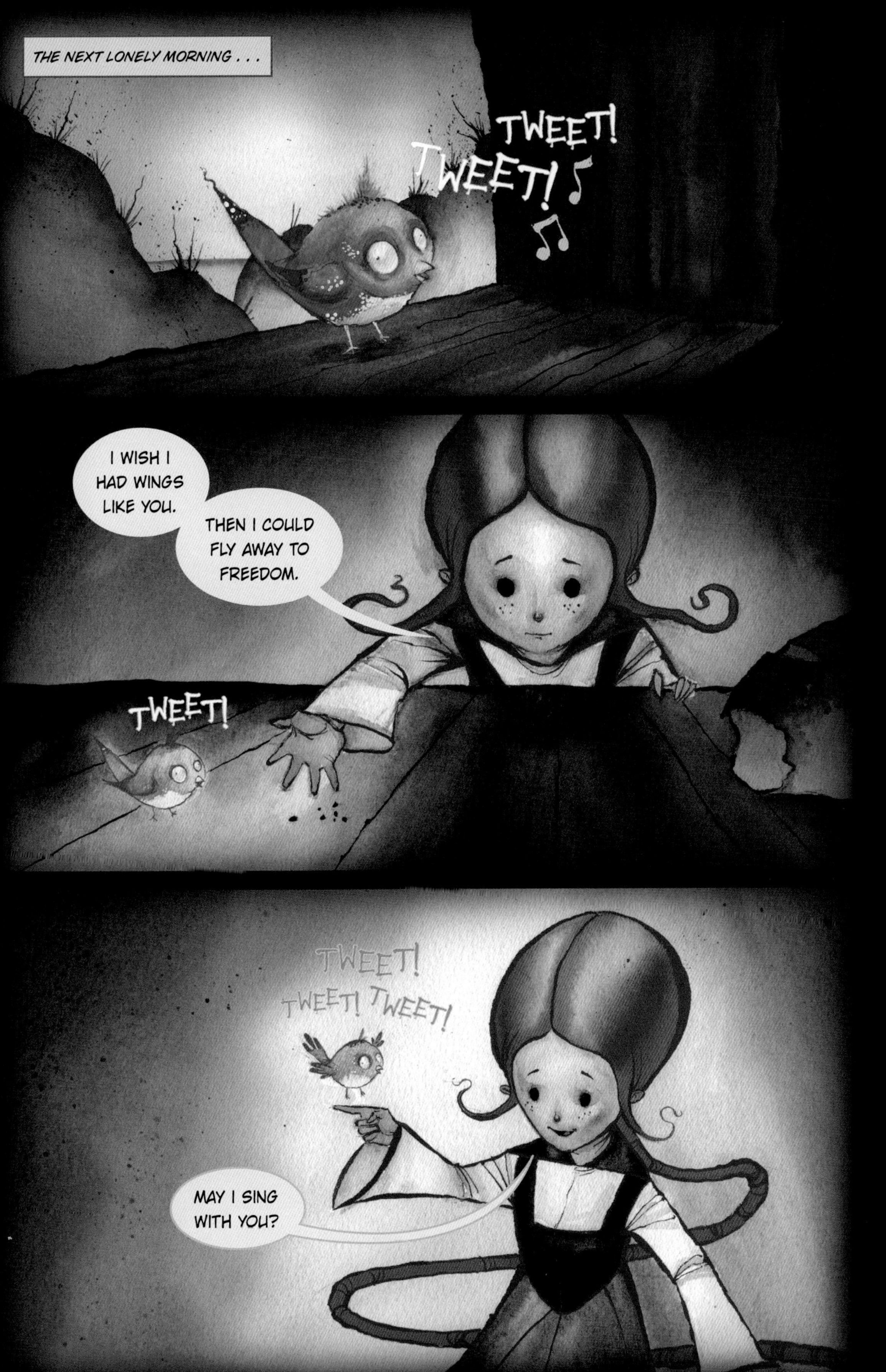
THE NEXT LONELY MORNING . . .
TWEET!
TWEET!
I WISH I HAD WINGS LIKE YOU.
THEN I COULD FLY AWAY TO FREEDOM.
TWEET!
TWEET!
TWEET! TWEET!
MAY I SING WITH YOU?

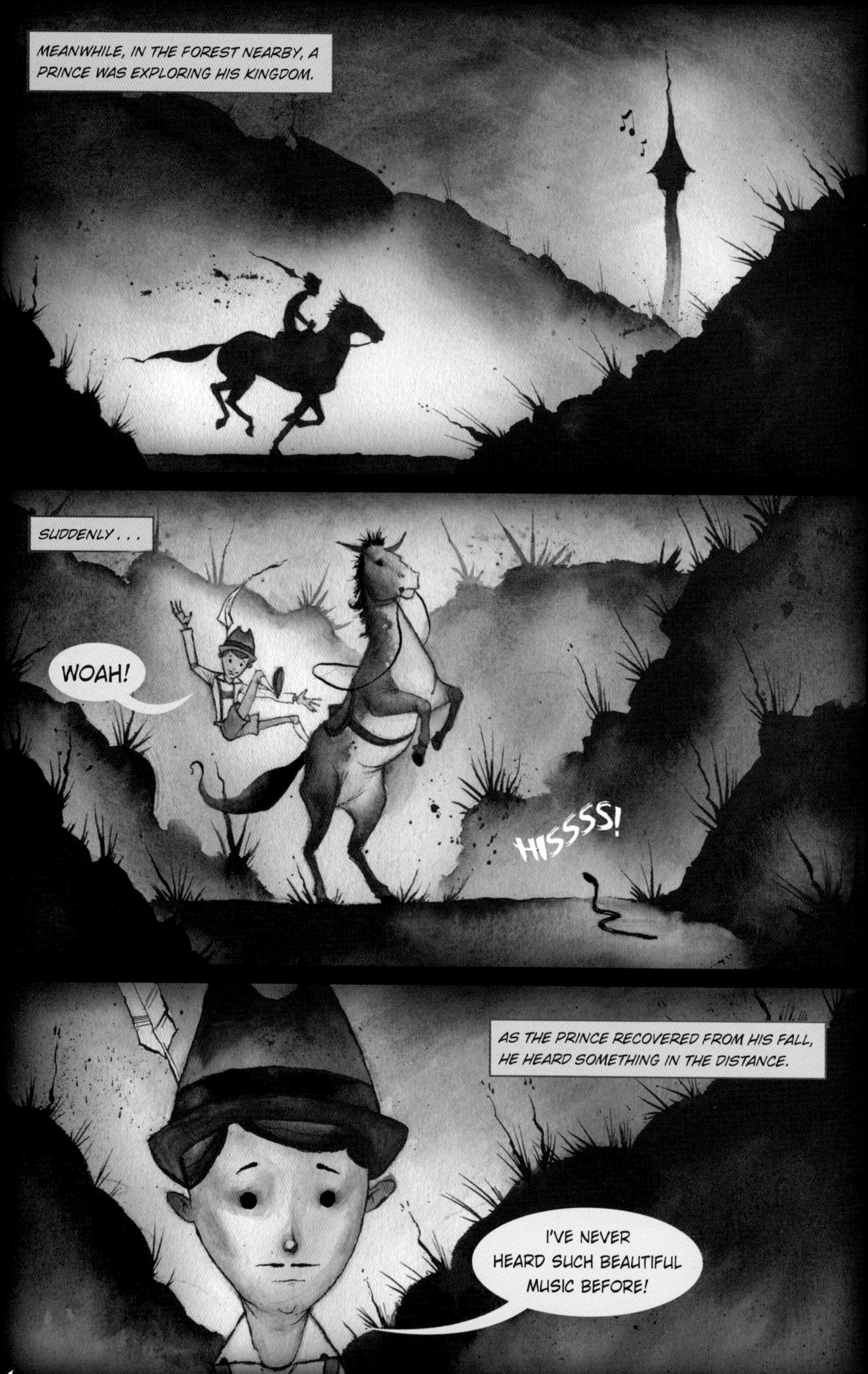
MEANWHILE, IN THE FOREST NEARBY, A PRINCE WAS EXPLORING HIS KINGDOM.
SUDDENLY . . .
WOAH!
HISSSS!
AS THE PRINCE RECOVERED FROM HIS FALL, HE HEARD SOMETHING IN THE DISTANCE.
I'VE NEVER HEARD SUCH BEAUTIFUL MUSIC BEFORE!

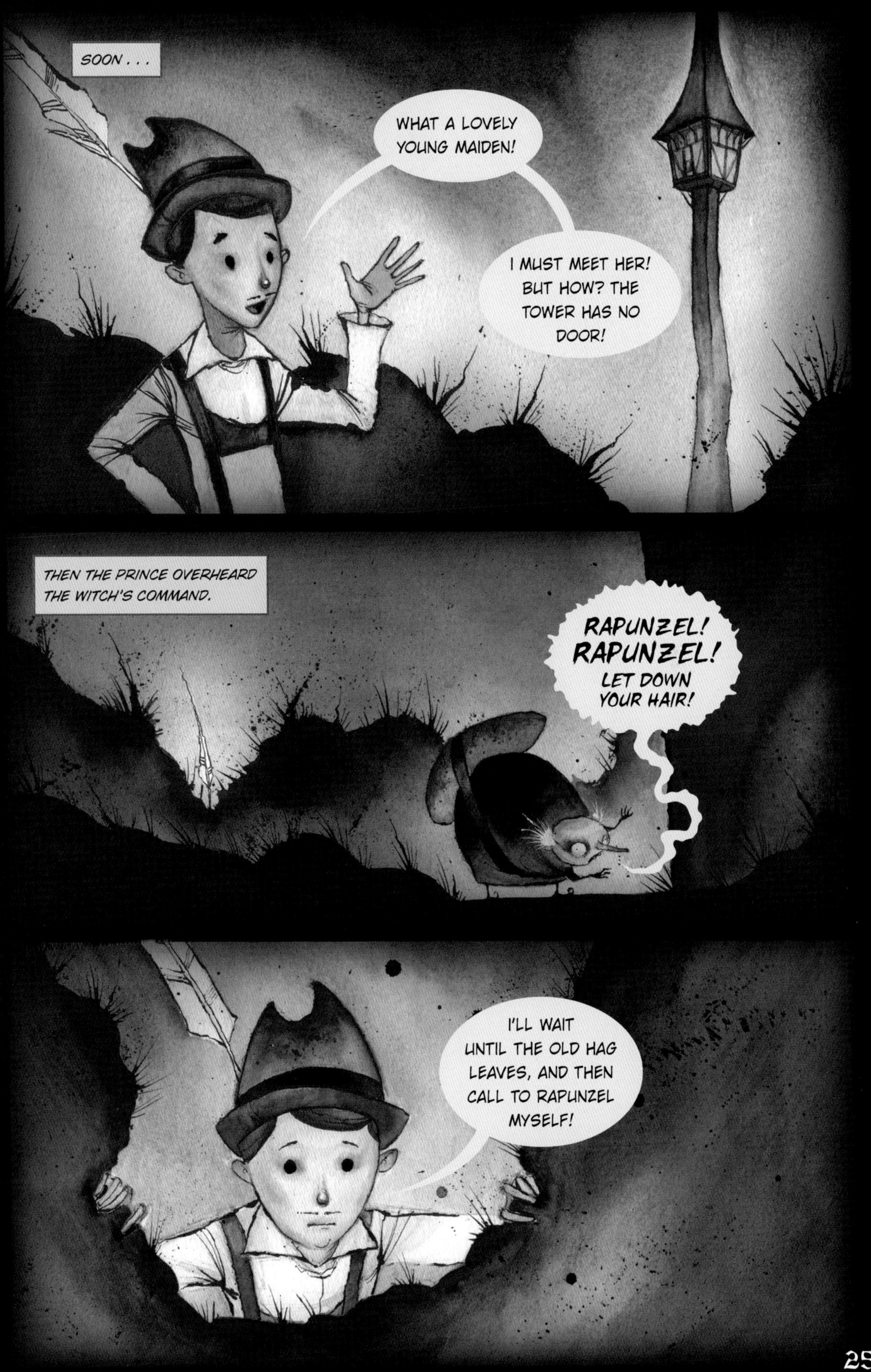
SOON . . .
WHAT A LOVELY YOUNG MAIDEN!
I MUST MEET HER! BUT HOW? THE TOWER HAS NO DOOR!
THEN THE PRINCE OVERHEARD THE WITCH'S COMMAND.
RAPUNZEL! RAPUNZEL! LET DOWN YOUR HAIR!
I'LL WAIT UNTIL THE OLD HAG LEAVES, AND THEN CALL TO RAPUNZEL MYSELF!

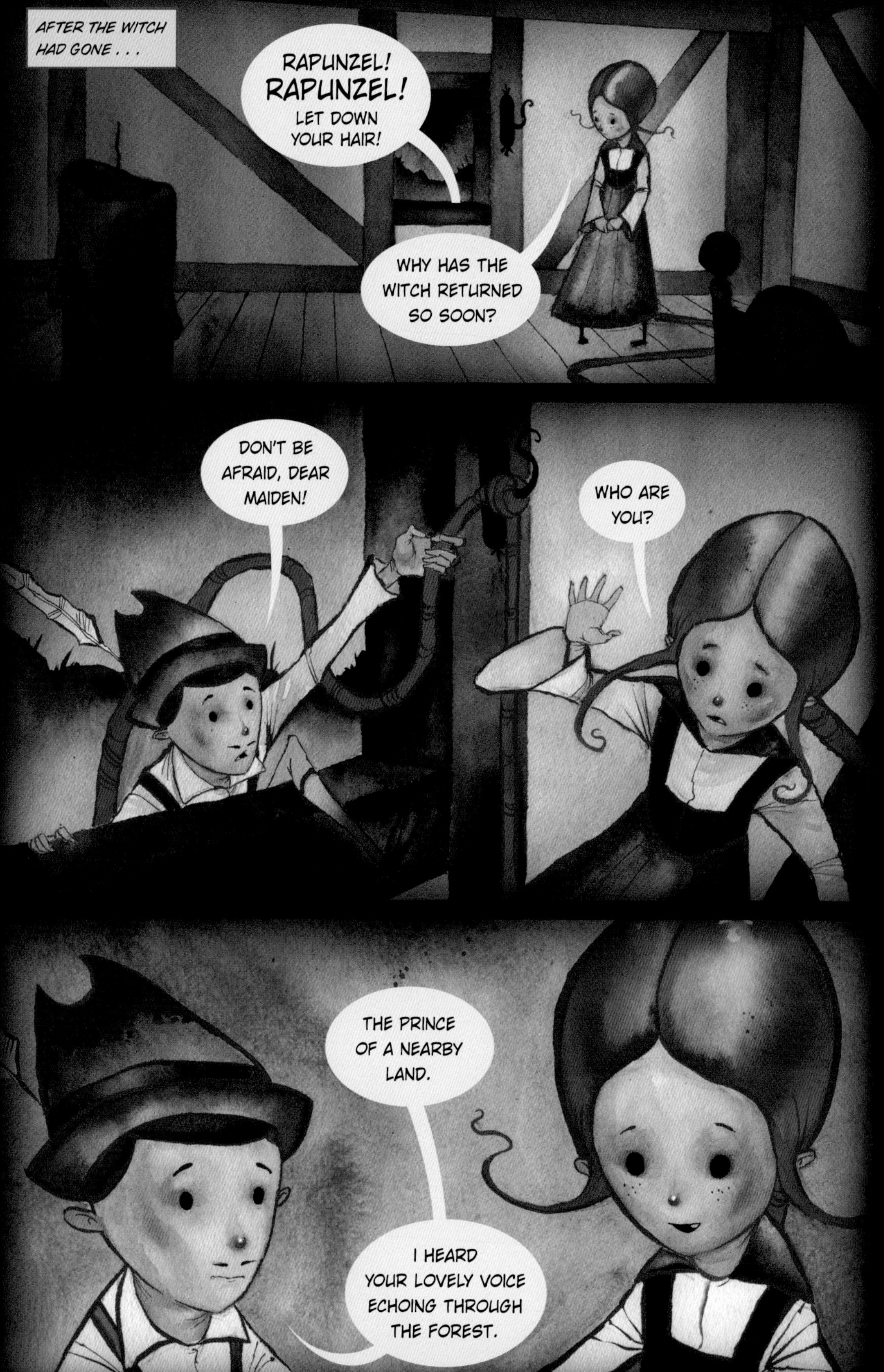
AFTER THE WITCH HAD GONE . . .
RAPUNZEL! RAPUNZEL! LET DOWN YOUR HAIR!
WHY HAS THE WITCH RETURNED SO SOON?
DON'T BE AFRAID, DEAR MAIDEN!
WHO ARE YOU?
THE PRINCE OF A NEARBY LAND.
I HEARD YOUR LOVELY VOICE ECHOING THROUGH THE FOREST.

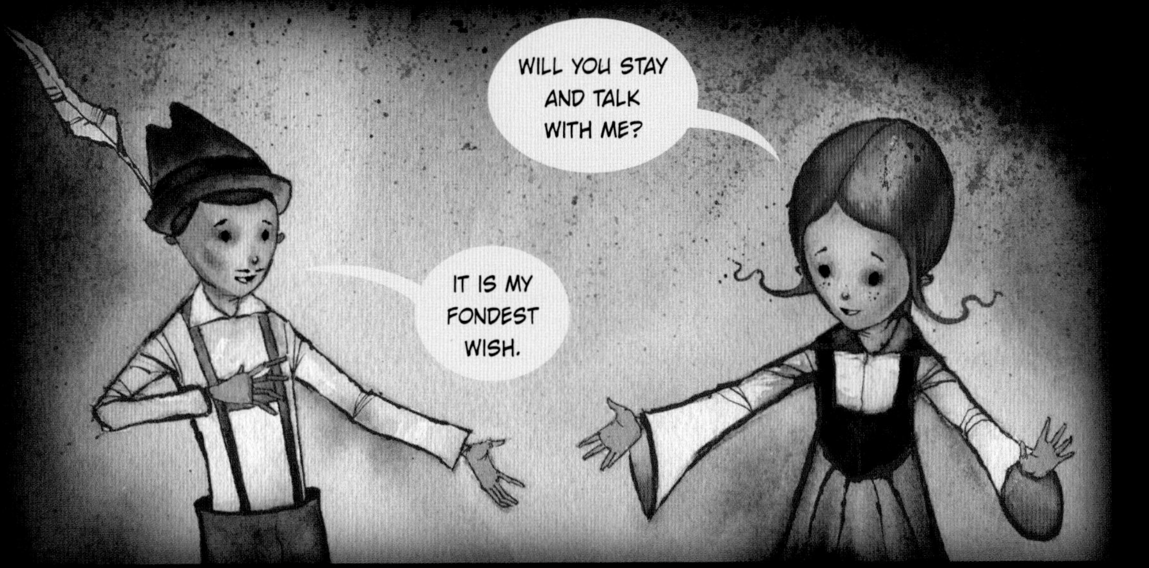
WILL YOU STAY AND TALK WITH ME?
IT IS MY FONDEST WISH.

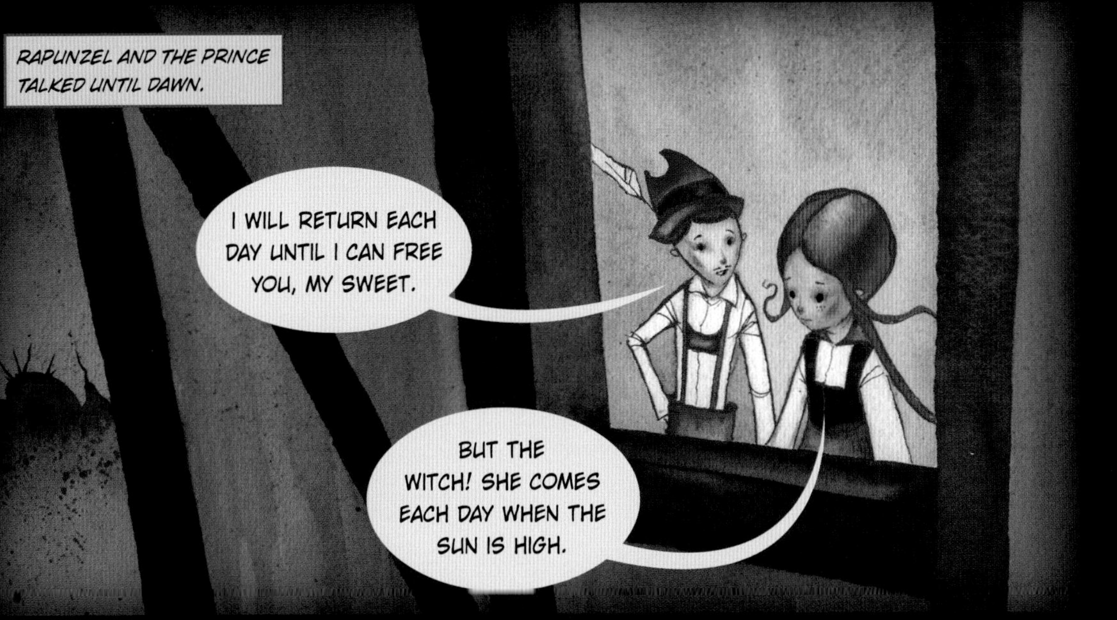
RAPUNZEL AND THE PRINCE TALKED UNTIL DAWN.
I WILL RETURN EACH DAY UNTIL I CAN FREE YOU, MY SWEET.
BUT THE WITCH! SHE COMES EACH DAY WHEN THE SUN IS HIGH.

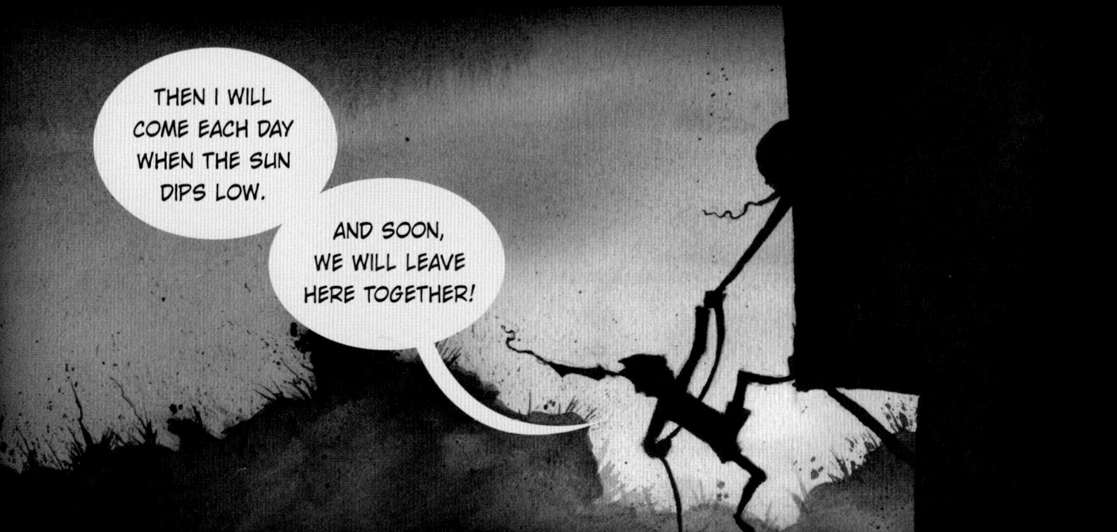
THEN I WILL COME EACH DAY WHEN THE SUN DIPS LOW.
AND SOON, WE WILL LEAVE HERE TOGETHER!

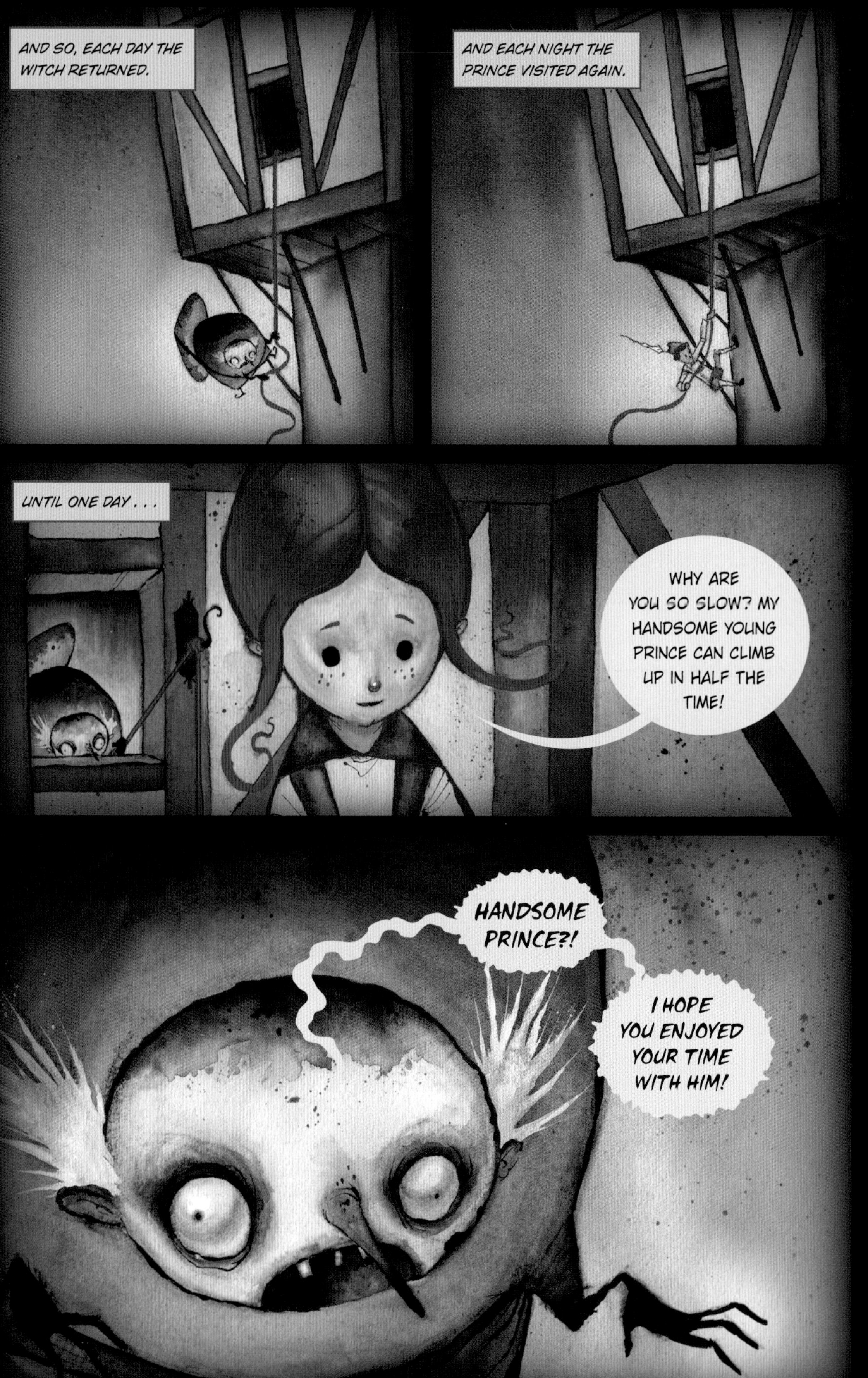
AND SO, EACH DAY THE WITCH RETURNED.
AND EACH NIGHT THE PRINCE VISITED AGAIN.
UNTIL ONE DAY . . .
WHY ARE YOU SO SLOW? MY HANDSOME YOUNG PRINCE CAN CLIMB UP IN HALF THE TIME!
HANDSOME PRINCE?!
I HOPE YOU ENJOYED YOUR TIME WITH HIM!

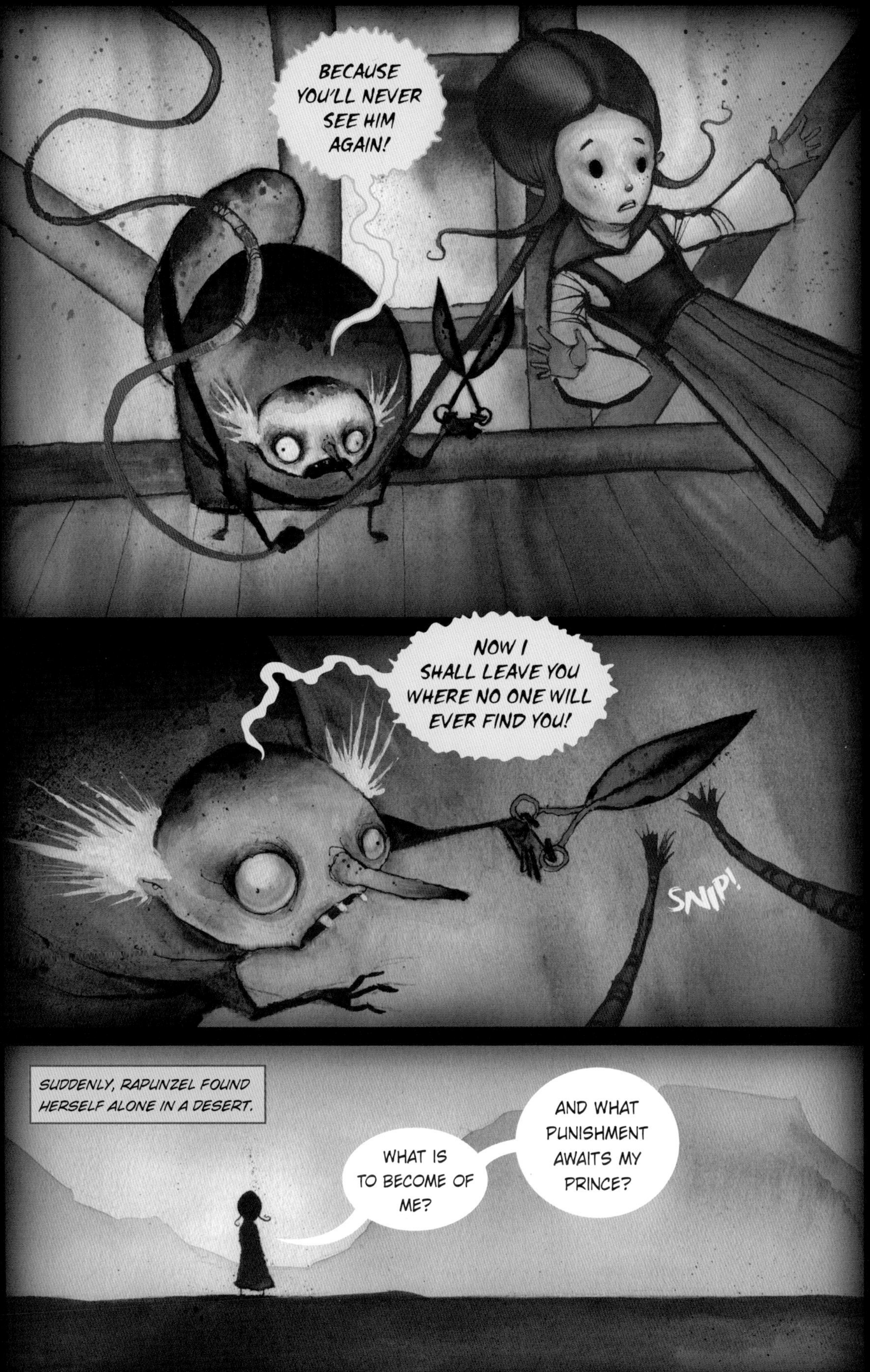
BECAUSE YOU'LL NEVER SEE HIM AGAIN!
NOW I SHALL LEAVE YOU WHERE NO ONE WILL EVER FIND YOU!
SNIP!
SUDDENLY, RAPUNZEL FOUND HERSELF ALONE IN A DESERT.
WHAT IS TO BECOME OF ME?
AND WHAT PUNISHMENT AWAITS MY PRINCE?

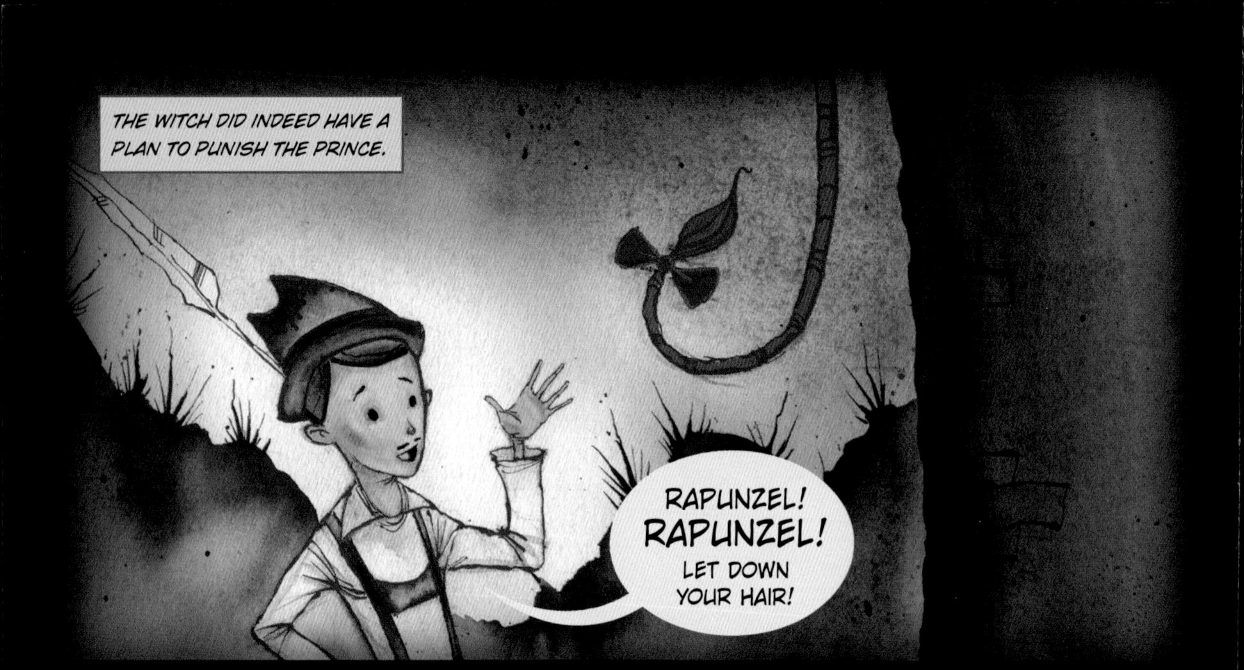
THE WITCH DID INDEED HAVE A PLAN TO PUNISH THE PRINCE.
RAPUNZEL! RAPUNZEL! LET DOWN YOUR HAIR!

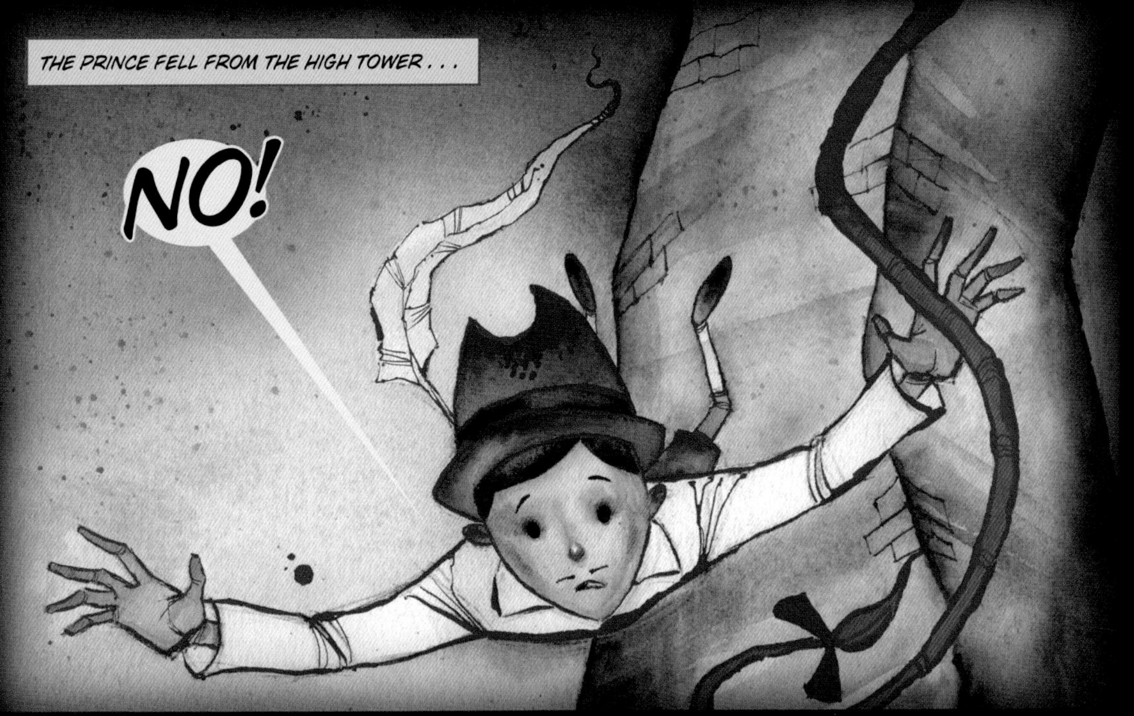
THE PRINCE FELL FROM THE HIGH TOWER . . .
NO!

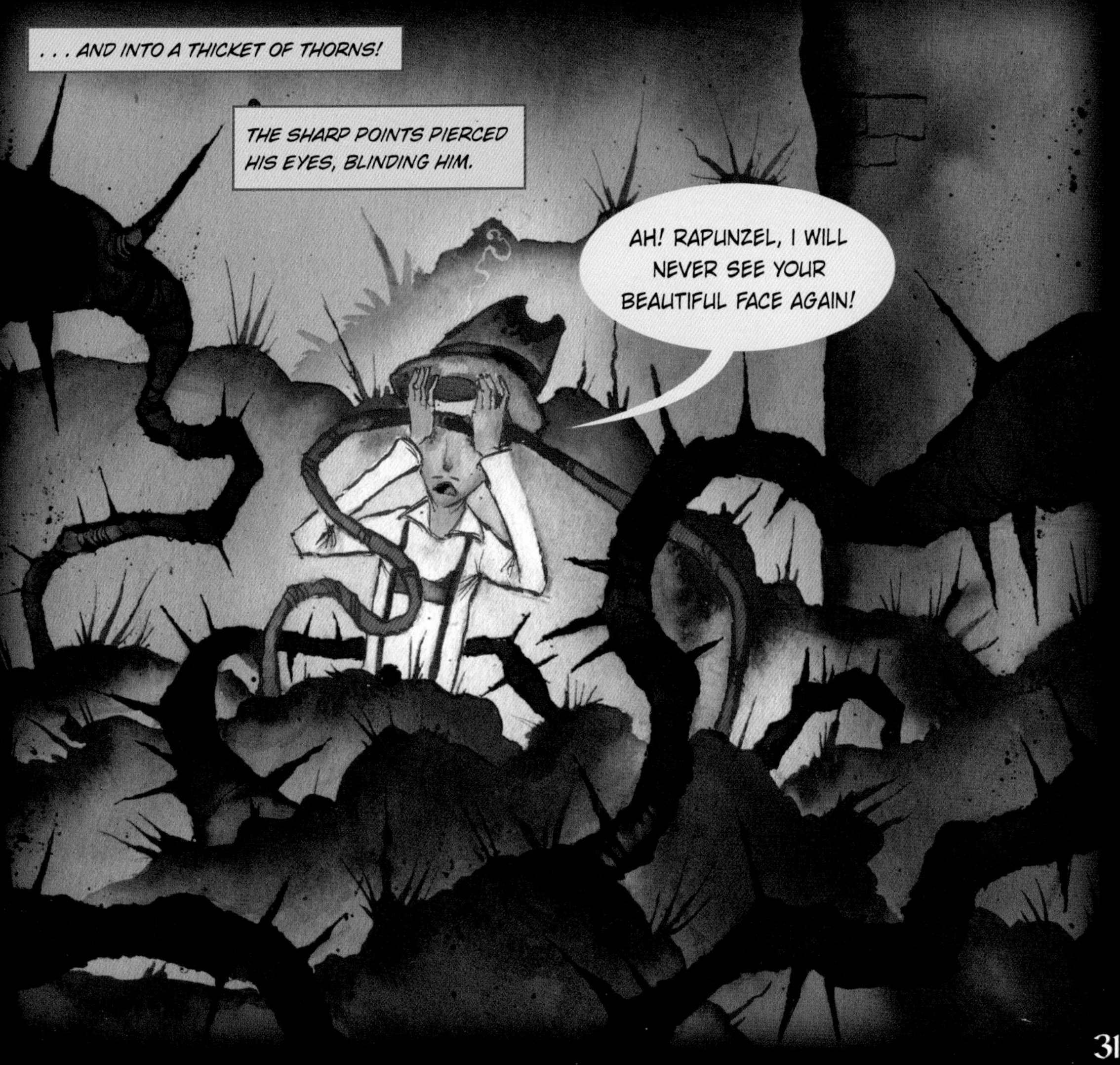
. . . AND INTO A THICKET OF THORNS!
THE SHARP POINTS PIERCED HIS EYES, BLINDING HIM.
AH! RAPUNZEL, I WILL NEVER SEE YOUR BEAUTIFUL FACE AGAIN!

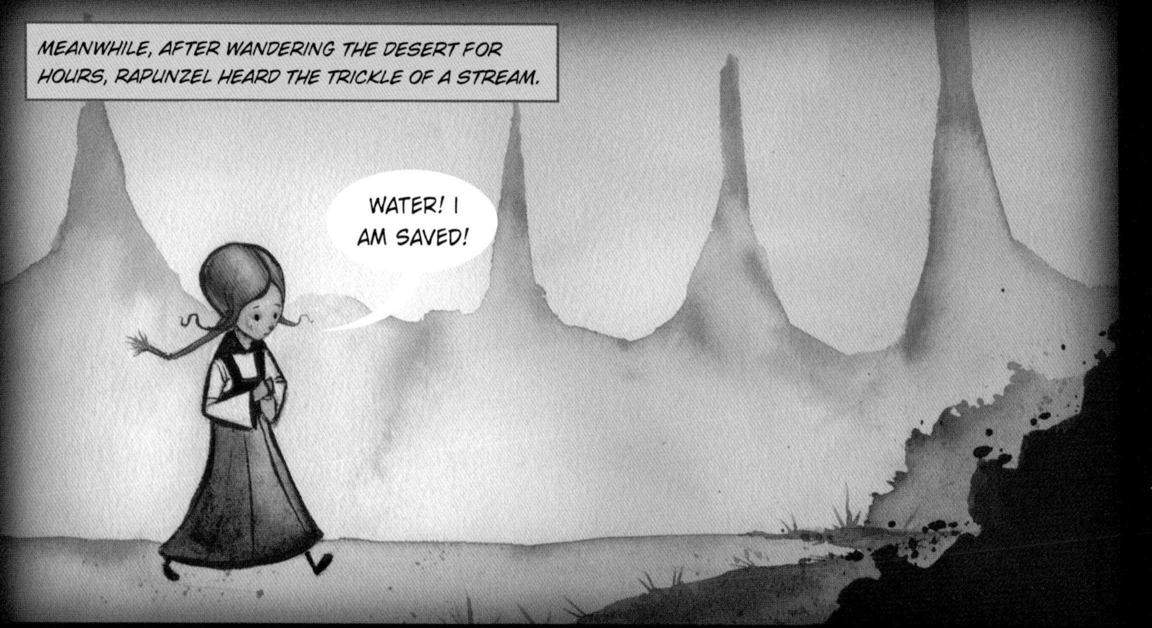
MEANWHILE, AFTER WANDERING THE DESERT FOR HOURS, RAPUNZEL HEARD THE TRICKLE OF A STREAM.
WATER! I AM SAVED!

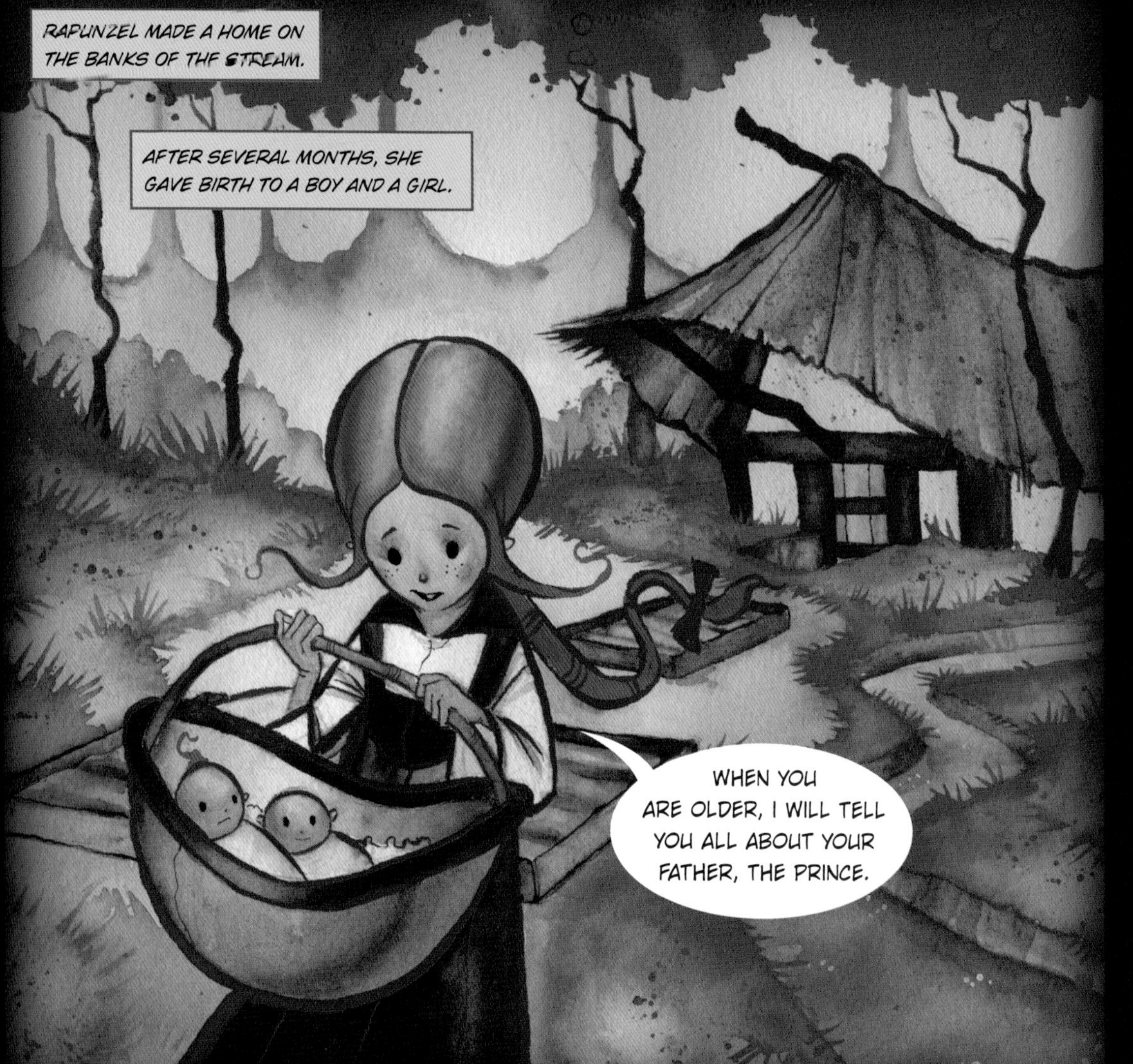
RAPUNZEL MADE A HOME ON THE BANKS OF THE STREAM.
AFTER SEVERAL MONTHS, SHE GAVE BIRTH TO A BOY AND A GIRL.
WHEN YOU ARE OLDER, I WILL TELL YOU ALL ABOUT YOUR FATHER, THE PRINCE.

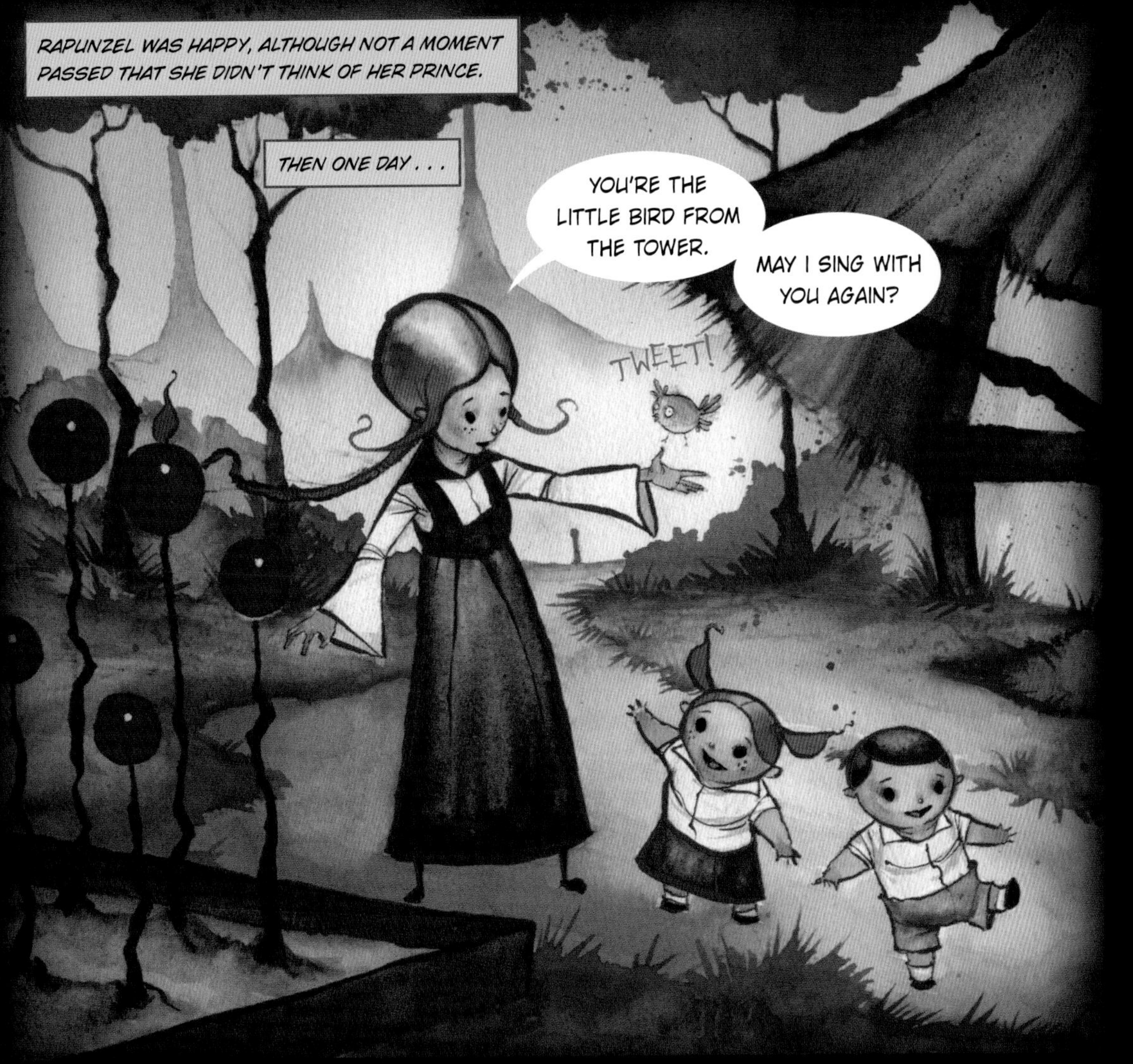
RAPUNZEL WAS HAPPY, ALTHOUGH NOT A MOMENT PASSED THAT SHE DIDN'T THINK OF HER PRINCE.
THEN ONE DAY . . .
YOU'RE THE LITTLE BIRD FROM THE TOWER.
MAY I SING WITH YOU AGAIN?
TWEET!

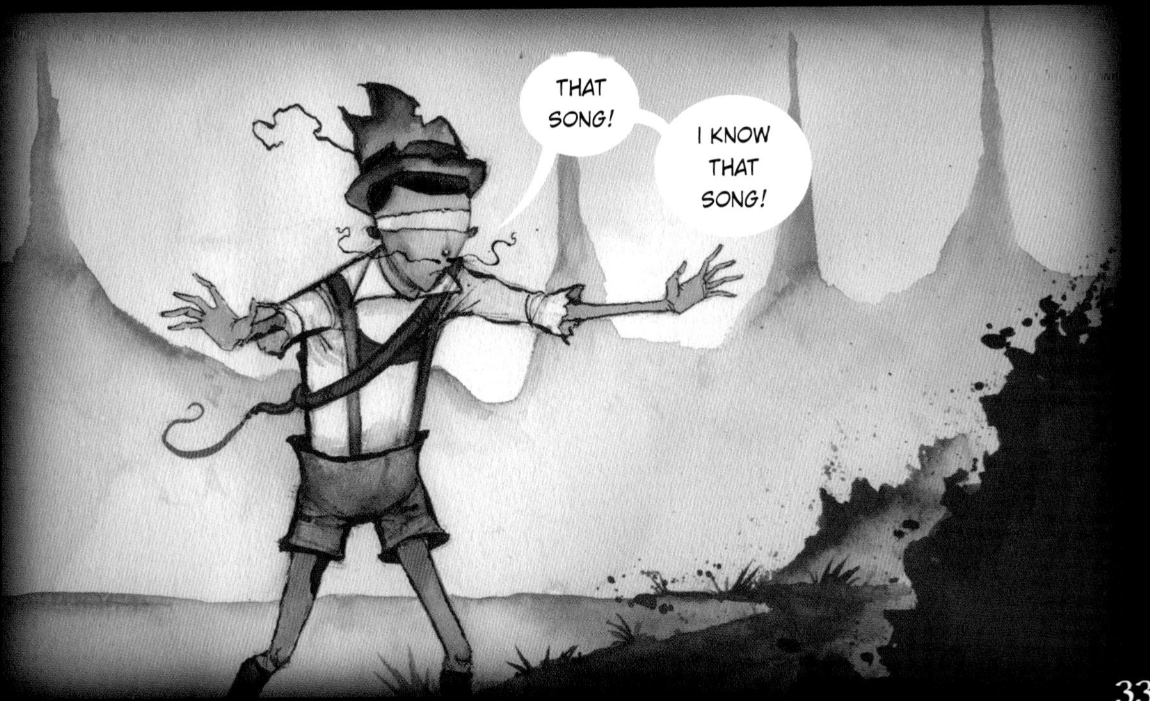
THAT SONG!
I KNOW THAT SONG!

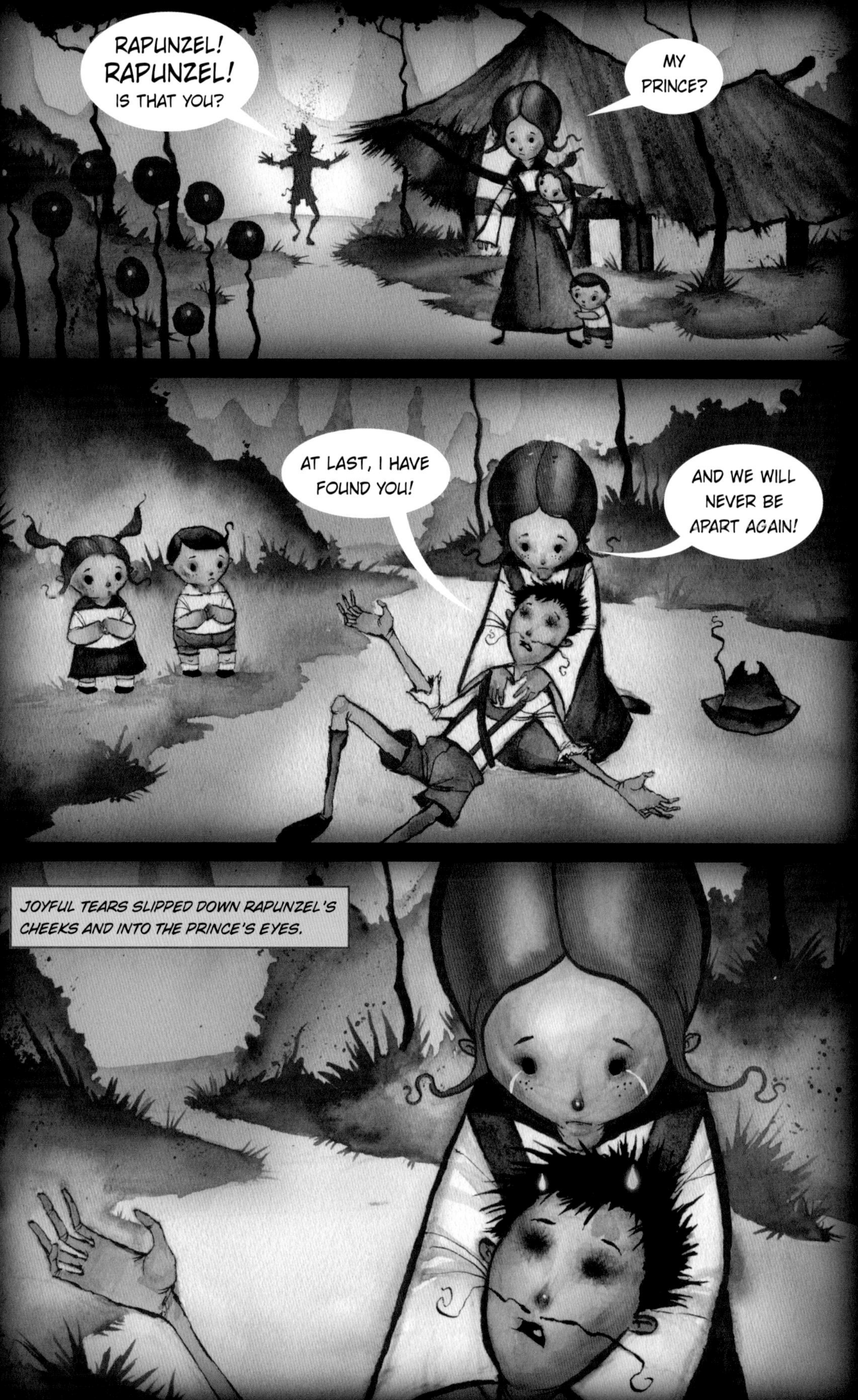
RAPUNZEL! RAPUNZEL! IS THAT YOU?
MY PRINCE?
AT LAST, I HAVE FOUND YOU!
AND WE WILL NEVER BE APART AGAIN!
JOYFUL TEARS SLIPPED DOWN RAPUNZEL'S CHEEKS AND INTO THE PRINCE'S EYES.

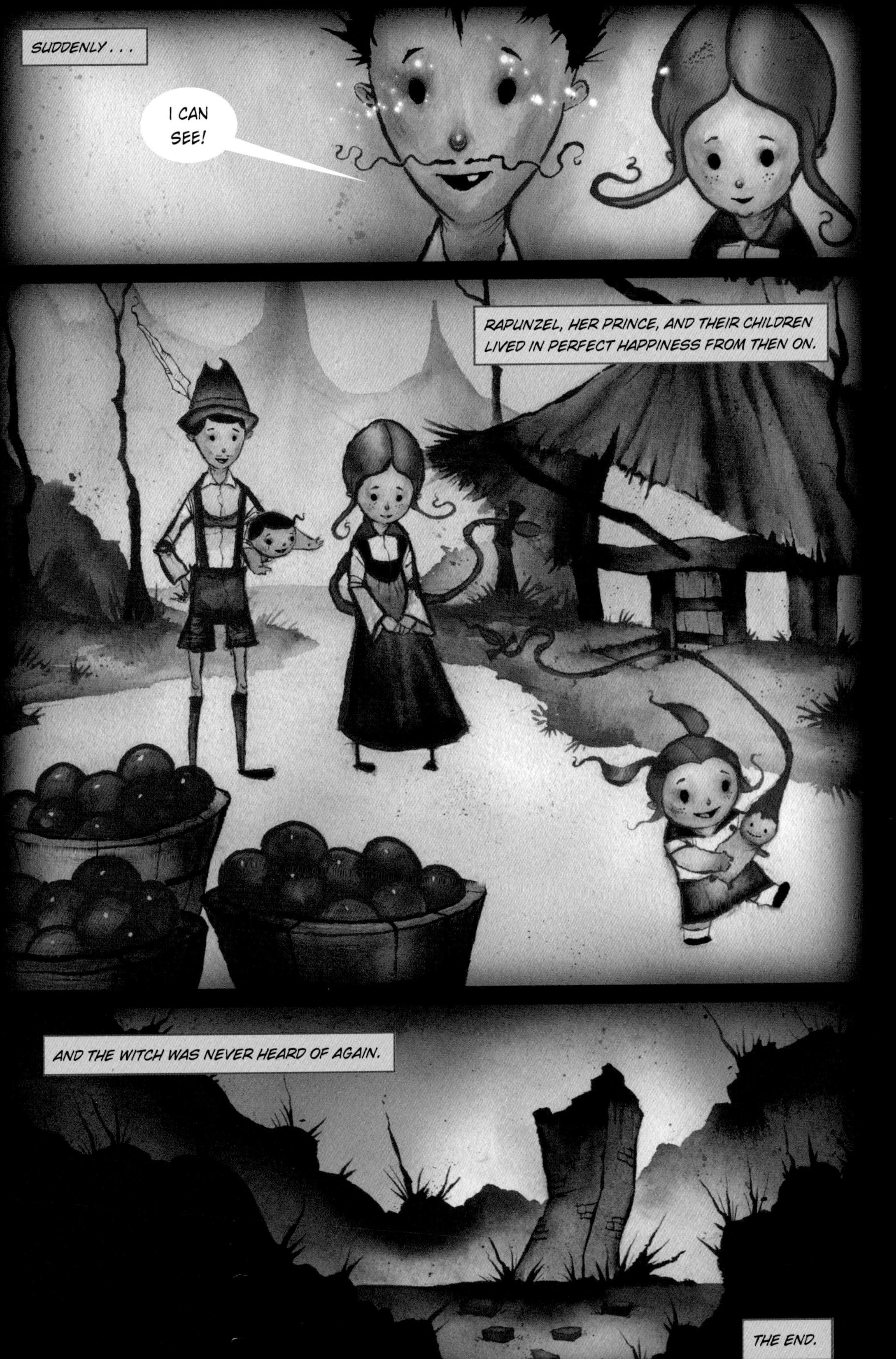
SUDDENLY . . .
I CAN SEE!
RAPUNZEL, HER PRINCE, AND THEIR CHILDREN LIVED IN PERFECT HAPPINESS FROM THEN ON.
AND THE WITCH WAS NEVER HEARD OF AGAIN.
THE END.

The History of
Rapunzel

Rapunzel and her beautiful hair have been around for centuries. Italian Giambattista Basile wrote down a similar tale called "Petrosinella" in 1637. In this version, the mother-to-be craves petrosine, the Italian word for parsley. The witch doesn't separate Petrosinella and her prince. Instead, they run away and marry in secret.

Sixty years later, a French woman, Charlotte Rose de Caumont de la Force, published a collection of fairy tales. A Rapunzel-like story was named "Persinette." Persille is the French word for parsley.

Unlike in Basile's version, the couple in the French story do not quickly find a happy ending. The witch continues to make them suffer in the wilderness, even after they have found one another. Finally, though, she realizes she has been wrong. She delivers them to the prince's castle, where Persinette and her family live happily ever after.

"Persinette" was translated into German several times. In one of the German versions the vegetable of choice became rapunzel. Eventually, Jacob and Wilhelm Grimm wrote down the tale. These well-known German brothers recorded many of Europe's folktales and fairy tales. "Rapunzel" is among the most famous of the more than 200 stories the Grimm brothers recorded. And their tale is the most common version told today.

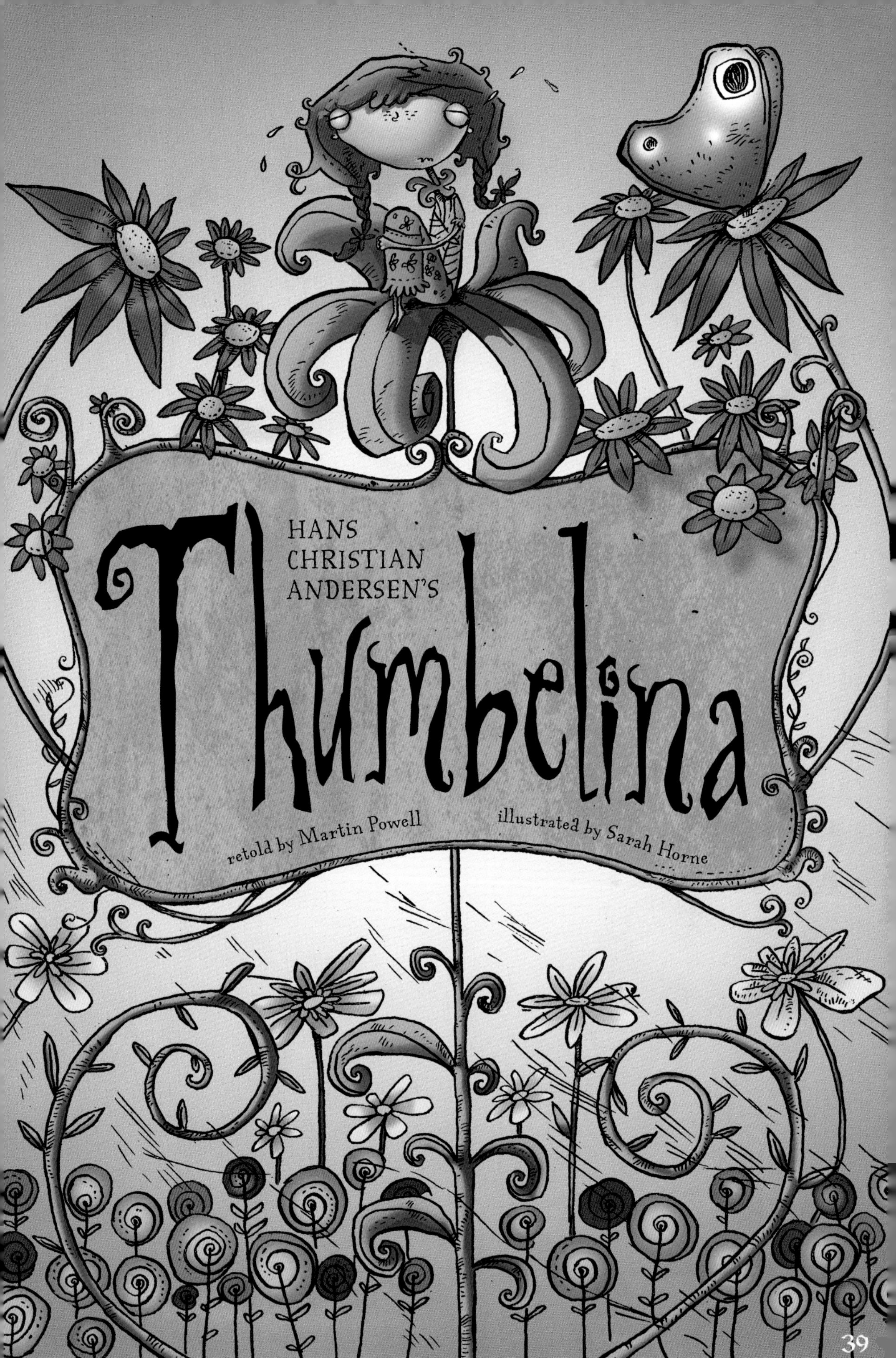
HANS CHRISTIAN ANDERSEN'S
Thumbelina
retold by Martin Powell
illustrated by Sarah Horne

CAST OF CHARACTERS

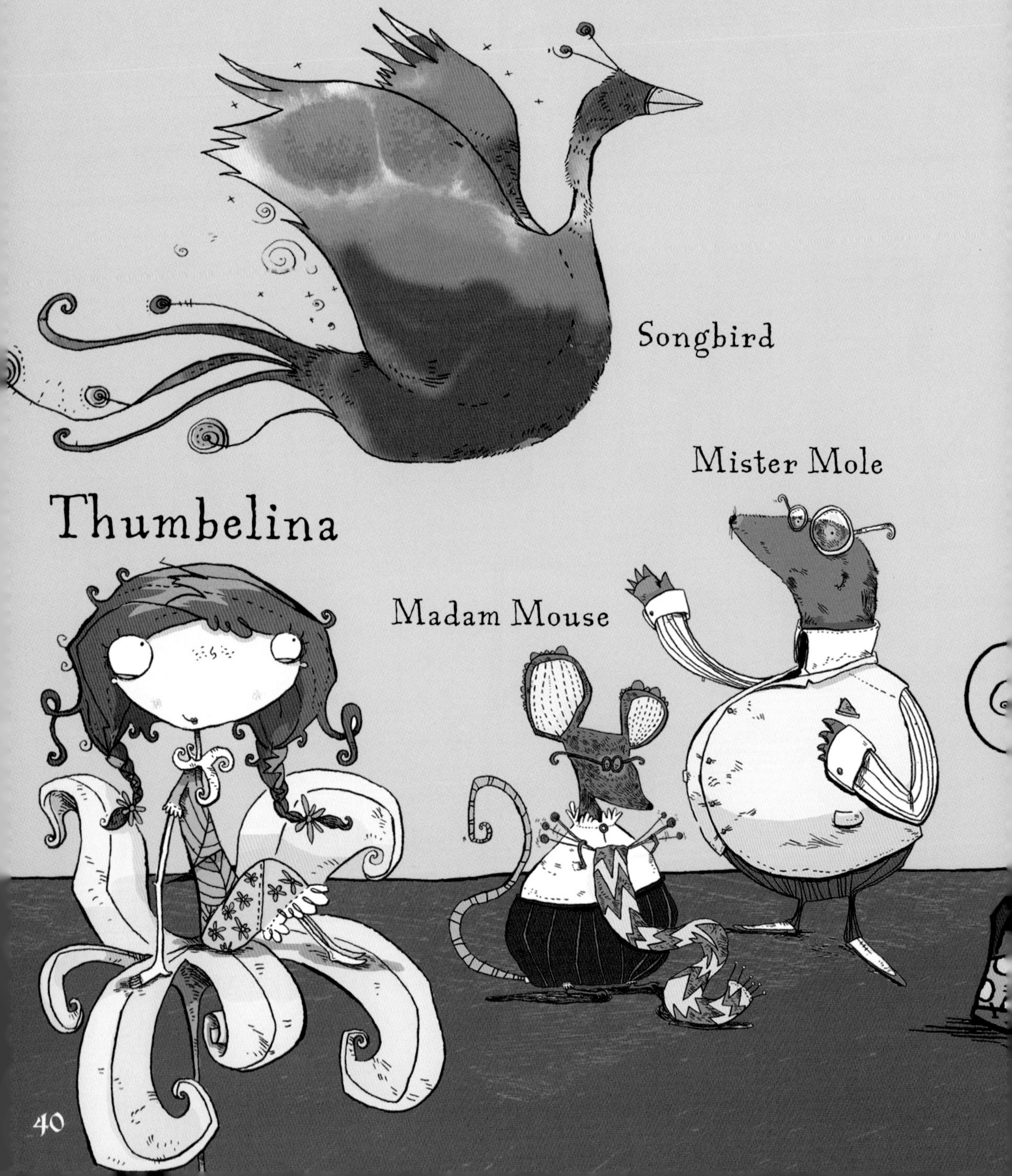
Songbird
Mister Mole
Thumbelina
Madam Mouse

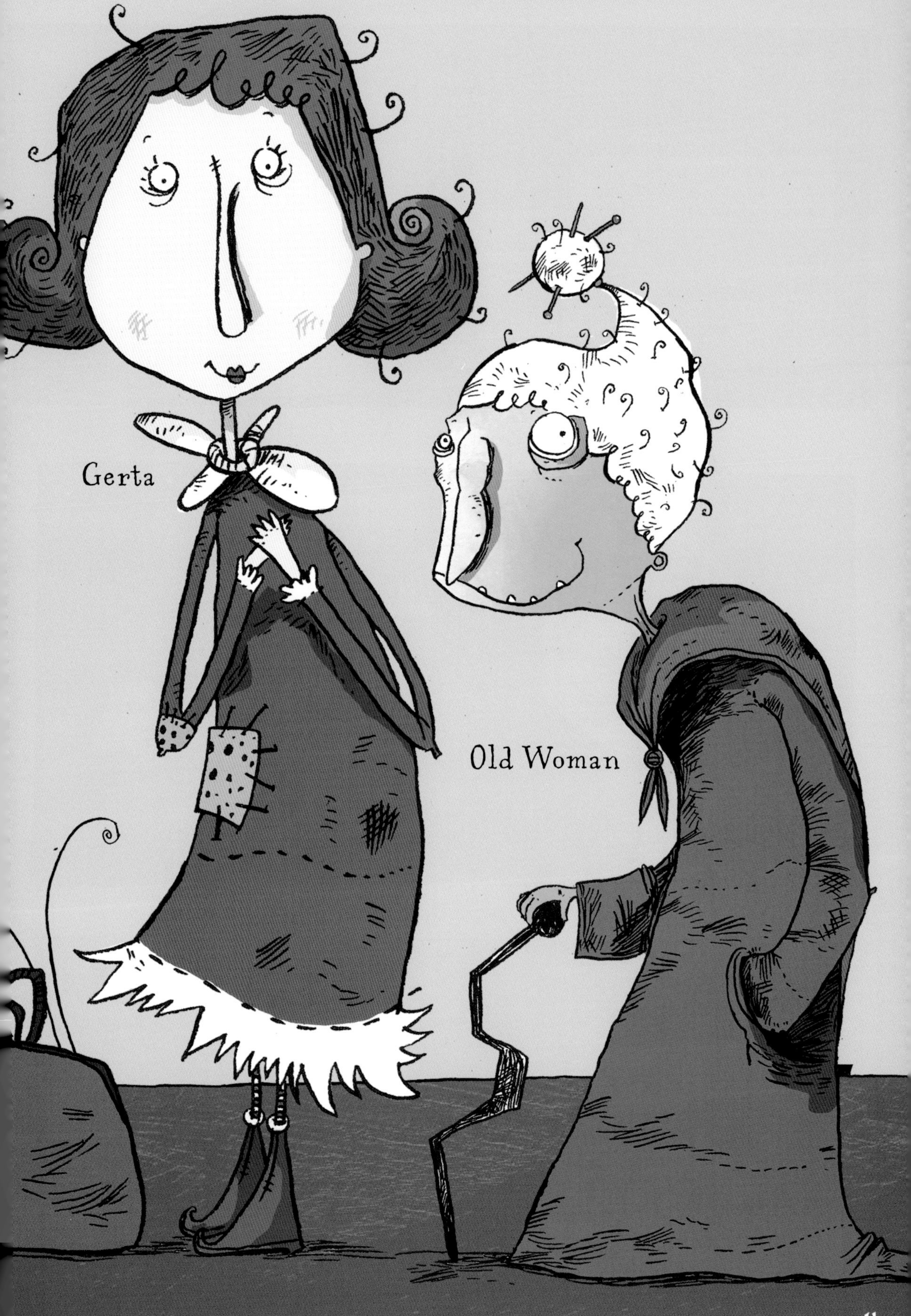
Gerta
Old Woman

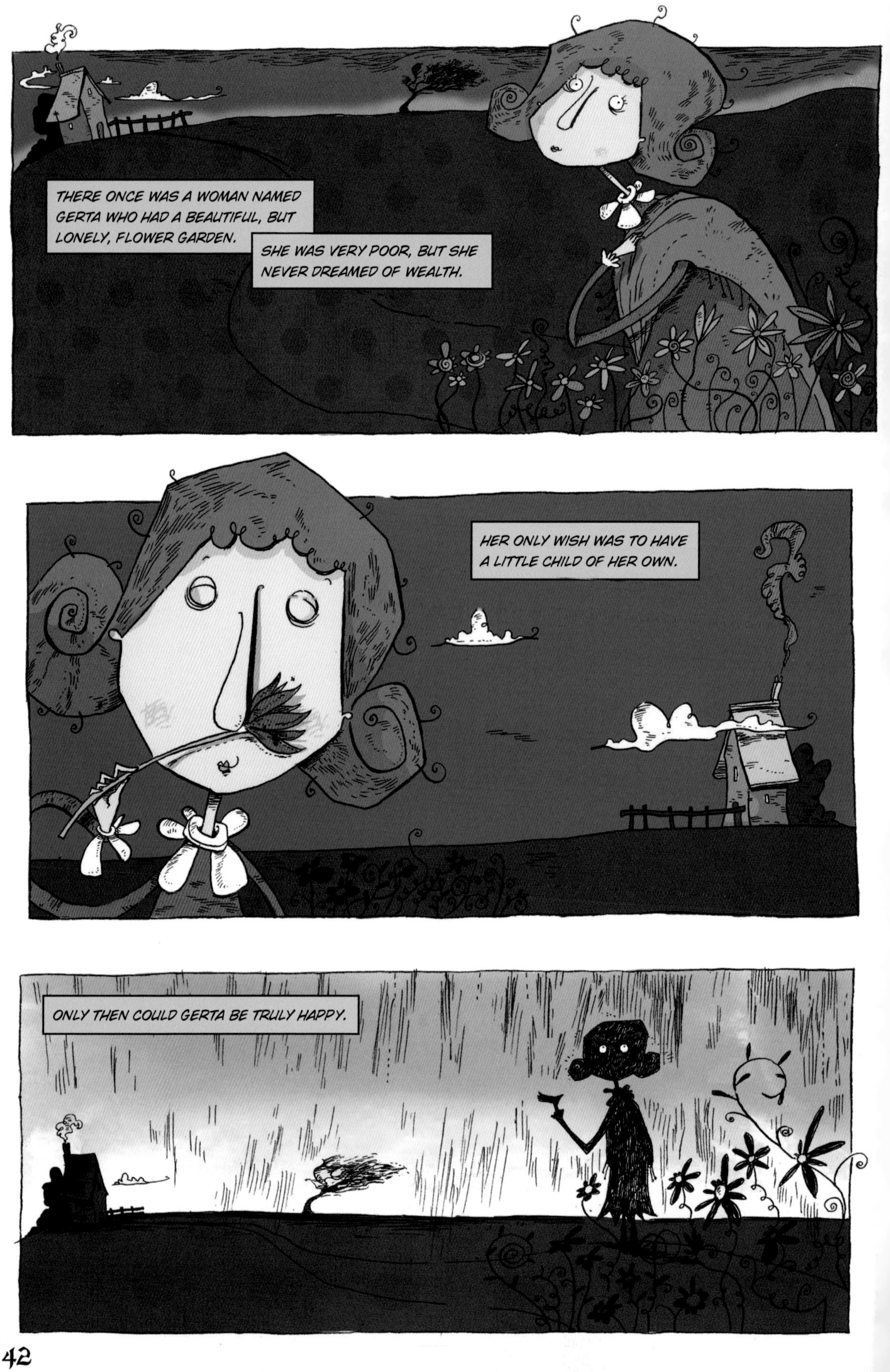
THERE ONCE WAS A WOMAN NAMED GERTA WHO HAD A BEAUTIFUL, BUT LONELY, FLOWER GARDEN.
SHE WAS VERY POOR, BUT SHE NEVER DREAMED OF WEALTH.
HER ONLY WISH WAS TO HAVE A LITTLE CHILD OF HER OWN.
ONLY THEN COULD GERTA BE TRULY HAPPY.

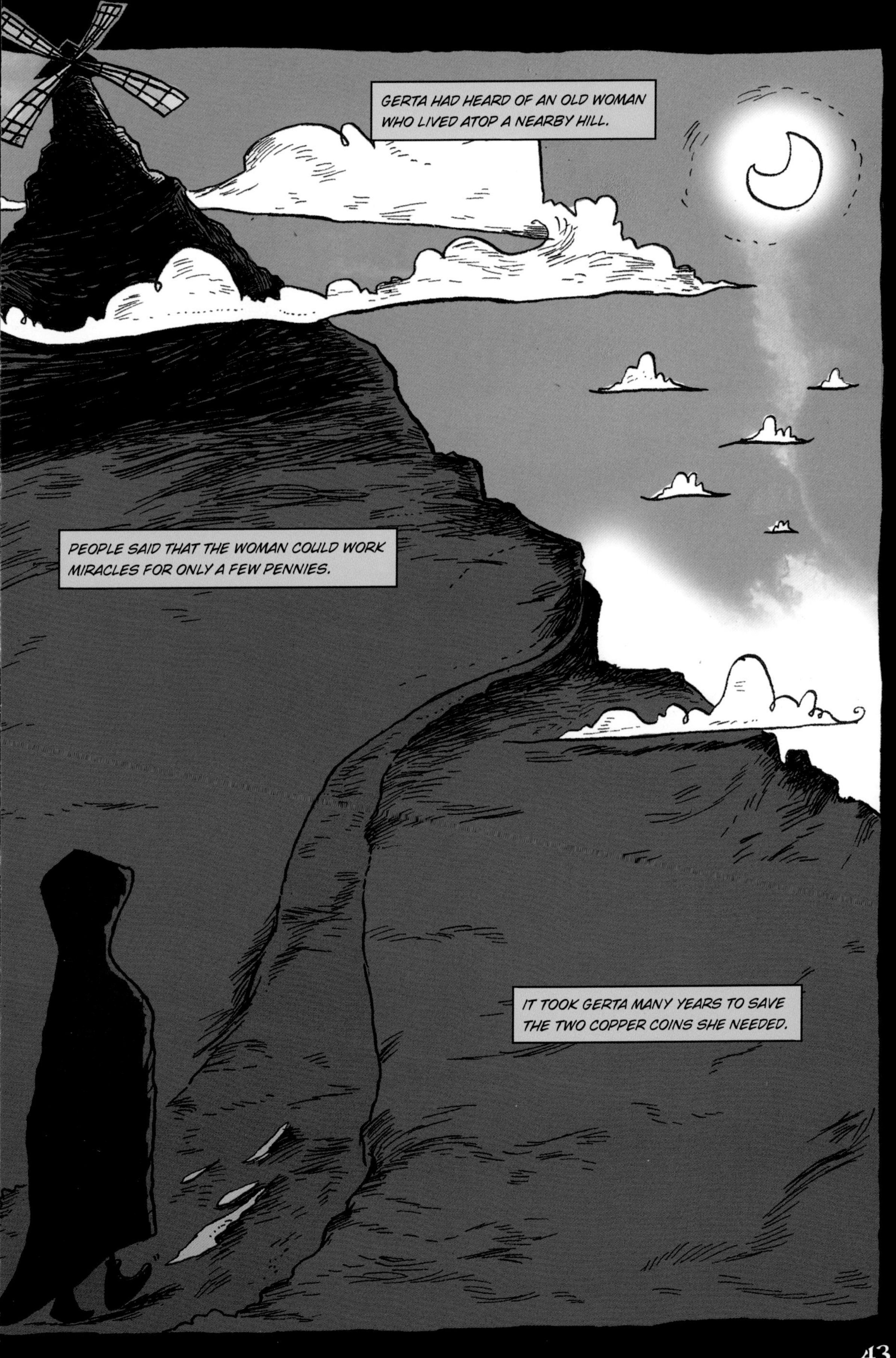
GERTA HAD HEARD OF AN OLD WOMAN WHO LIVED ATOP A NEARBY HILL.
PEOPLE SAID THAT THE WOMAN COULD WORK MIRACLES FOR ONLY A FEW PENNIES.
IT TOOK GERTA MANY YEARS TO SAVE THE TWO COPPER COINS SHE NEEDED.

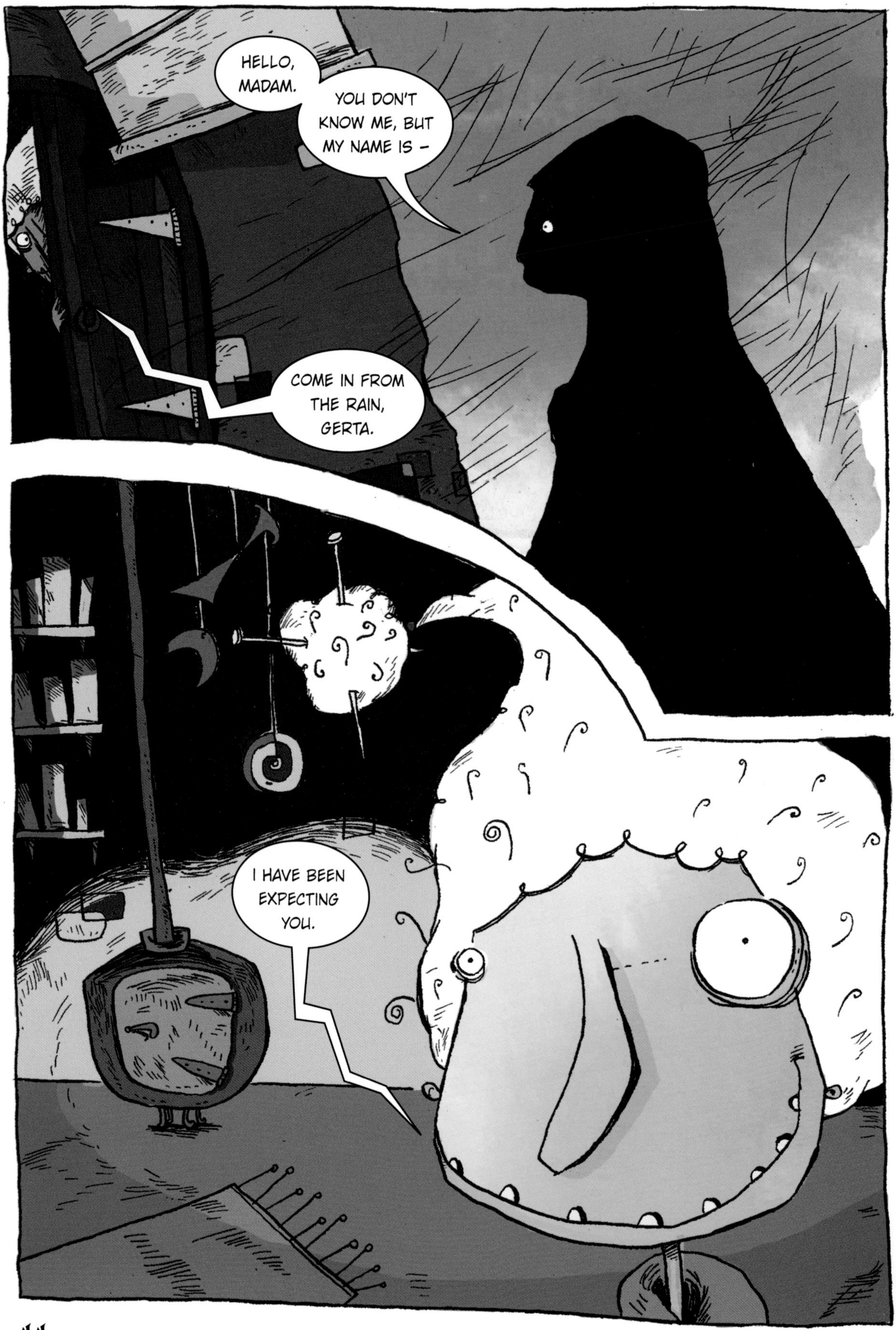
HELLO, MADAM.
YOU DON'T KNOW ME, BUT MY NAME IS –
COME IN FROM THE RAIN, GERTA.
I HAVE BEEN EXPECTING YOU.

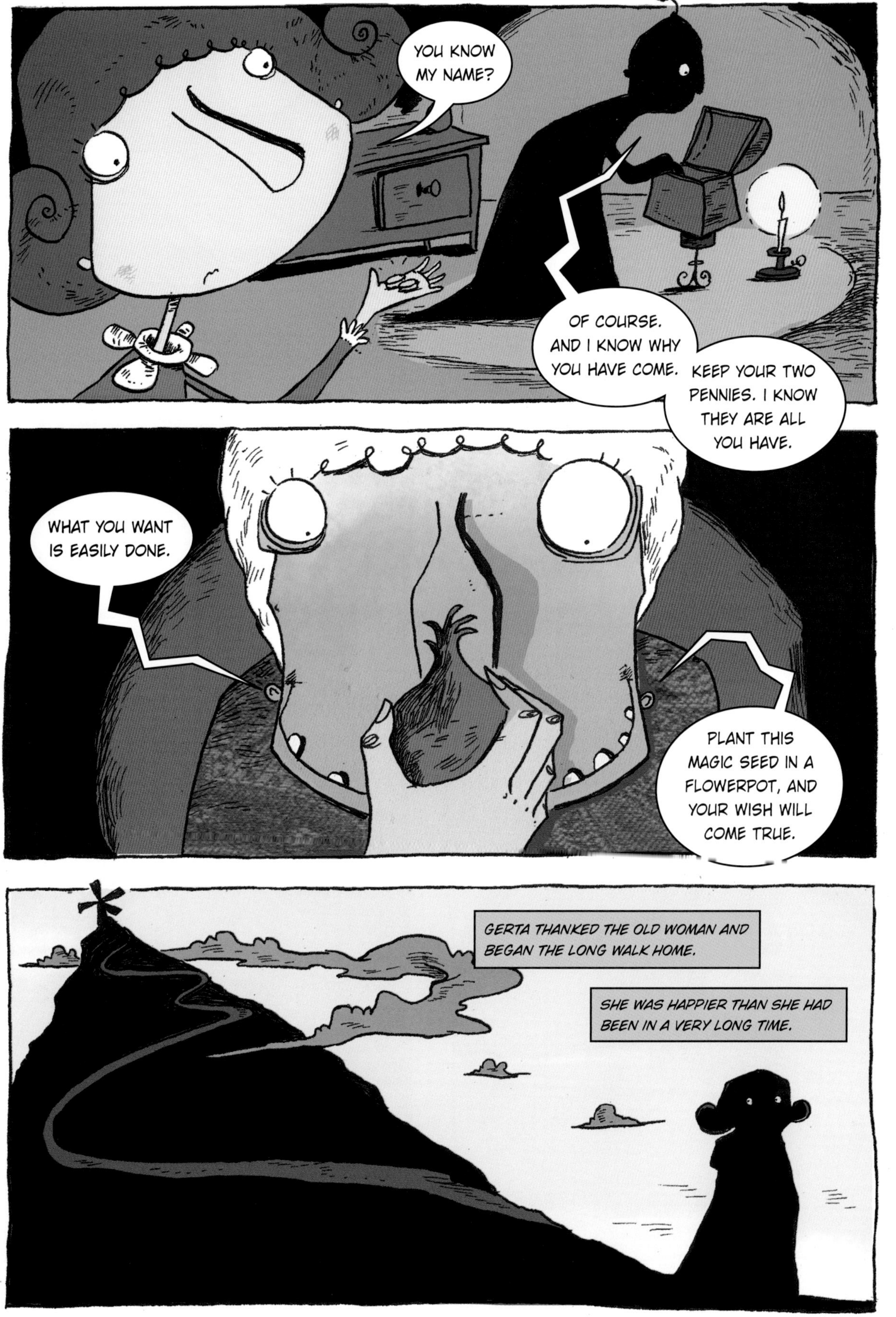
YOU KNOW MY NAME?
OF COURSE. AND I KNOW WHY YOU HAVE COME.
KEEP YOUR TWO PENNIES. I KNOW THEY ARE ALL YOU HAVE.
WHAT YOU WANT IS EASILY DONE.
PLANT THIS MAGIC SEED IN A FLOWERPOT, AND YOUR WISH WILL COME TRUE.
GERTA THANKED THE OLD WOMAN AND BEGAN THE LONG WALK HOME.
SHE WAS HAPPIER THAN SHE HAD BEEN IN A VERY LONG TIME.

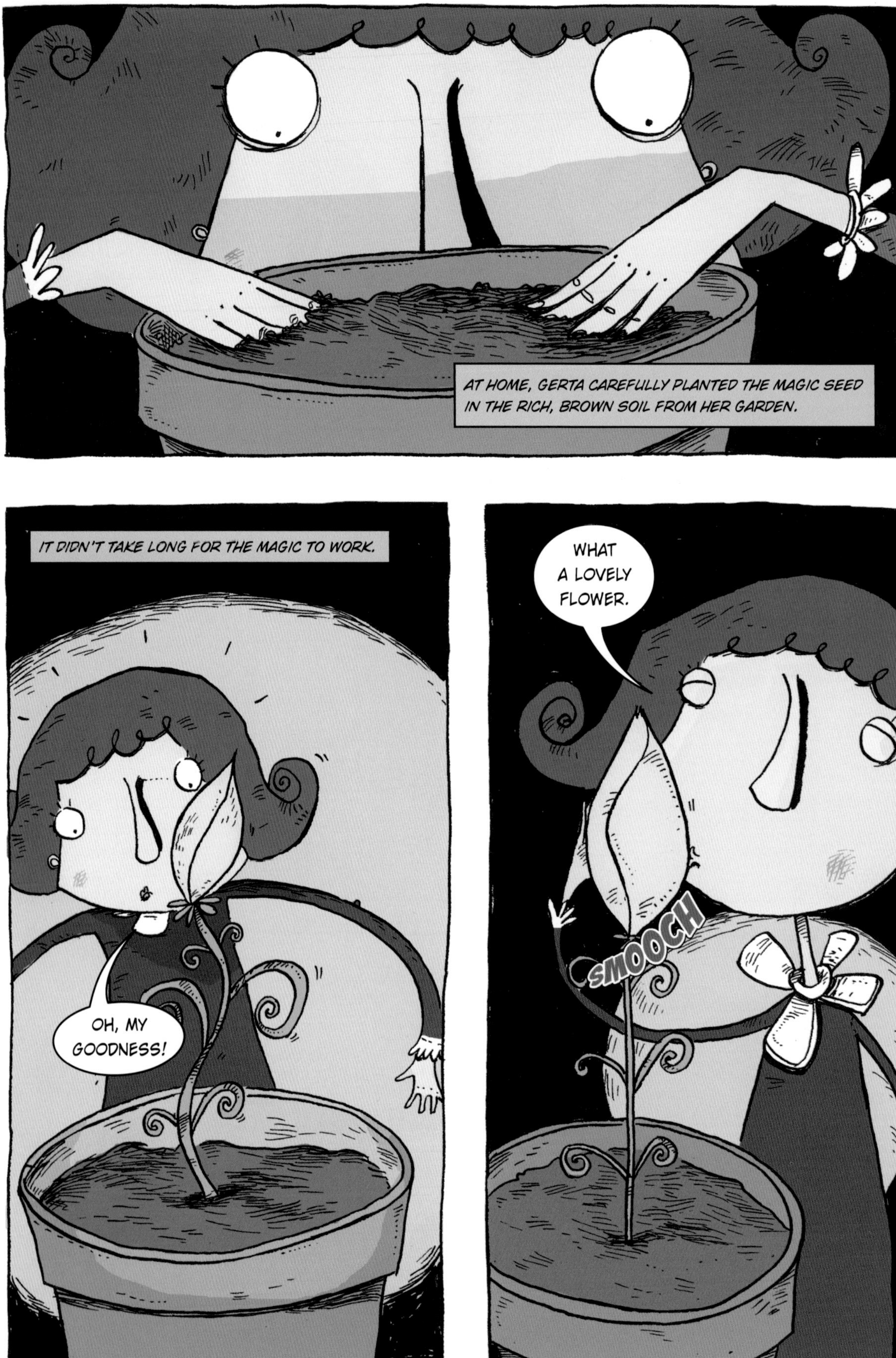
AT HOME, GERTA CAREFULLY PLANTED THE MAGIC SEED IN THE RICH, BROWN SOIL FROM HER GARDEN.
IT DIDN'T TAKE LONG FOR THE MAGIC TO WORK.
OH, MY GOODNESS!
WHAT A LOVELY FLOWER.
SMOOCH

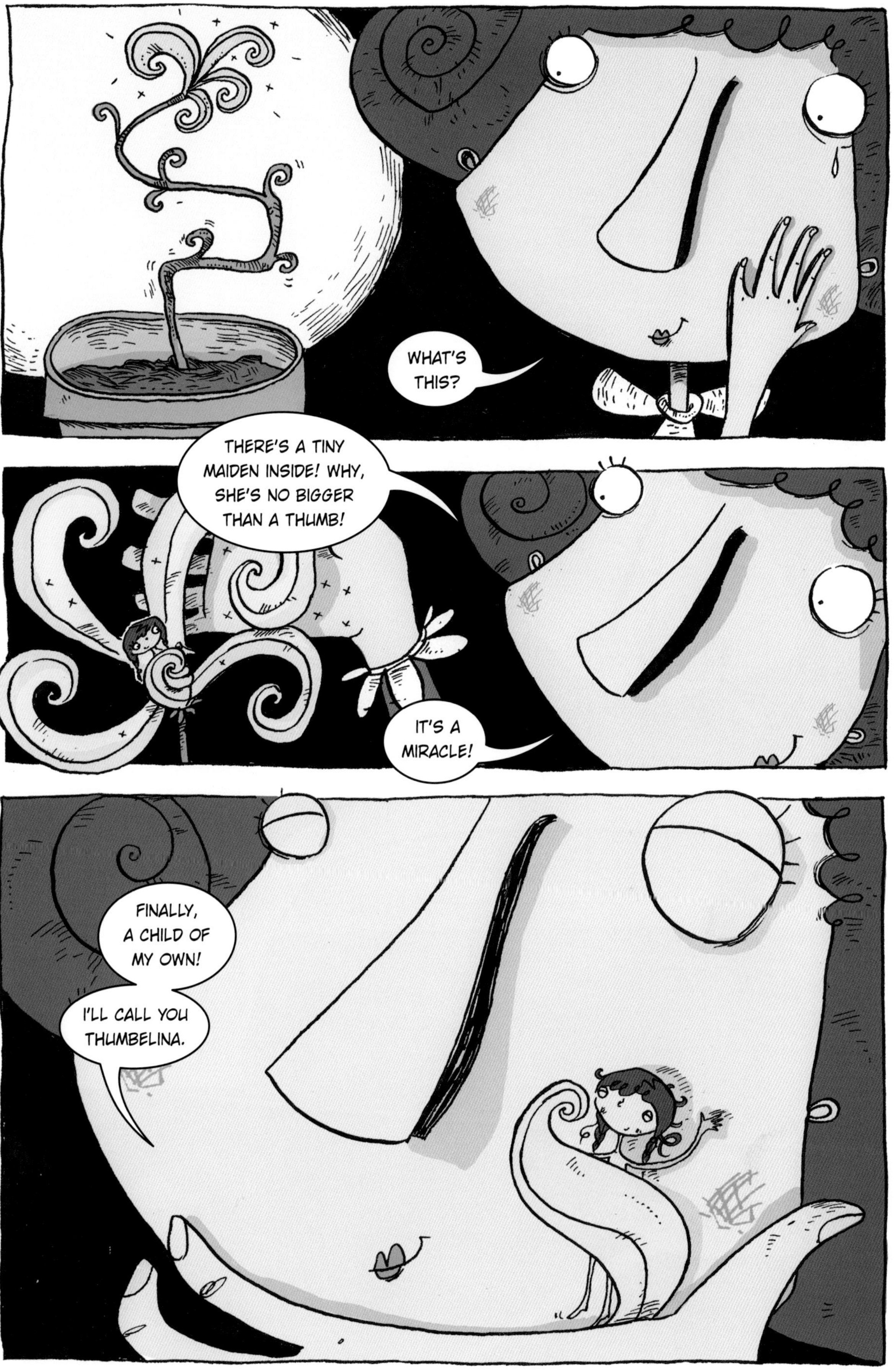
WHAT'S THIS?
THERE'S A TINY MAIDEN INSIDE! WHY, SHE'S NO BIGGER THAN A THUMB!
IT'S A MIRACLE!
FINALLY, A CHILD OF MY OWN!
I'LL CALL YOU THUMBELINA.

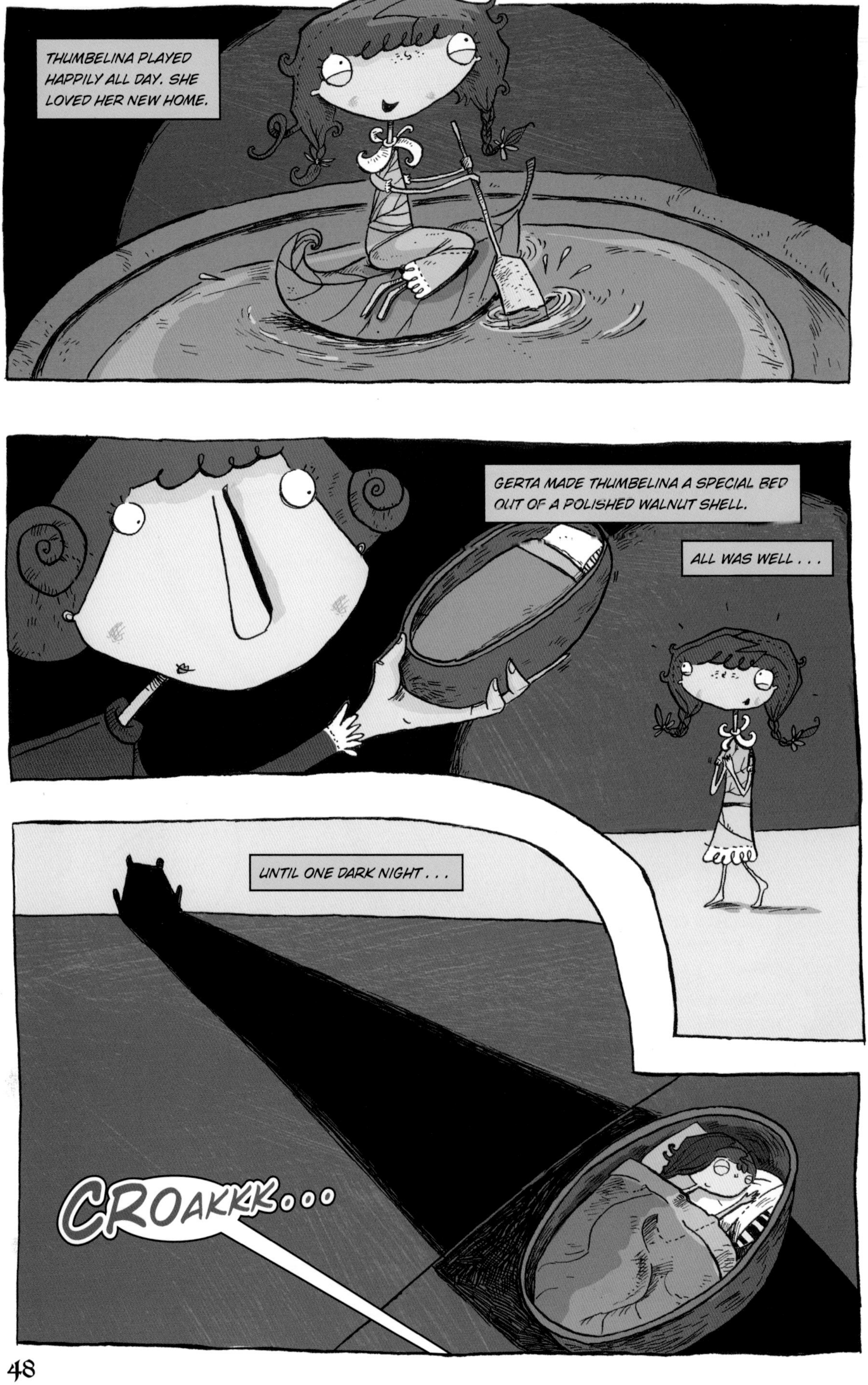
THUMBELINA PLAYED HAPPILY ALL DAY. SHE LOVED HER NEW HOME.
GERTA MADE THUMBELINA A SPECIAL BED OUT OF A POLISHED WALNUT SHELL.
ALL WAS WELL . . .
UNTIL ONE DARK NIGHT . . .
CROAKKK...

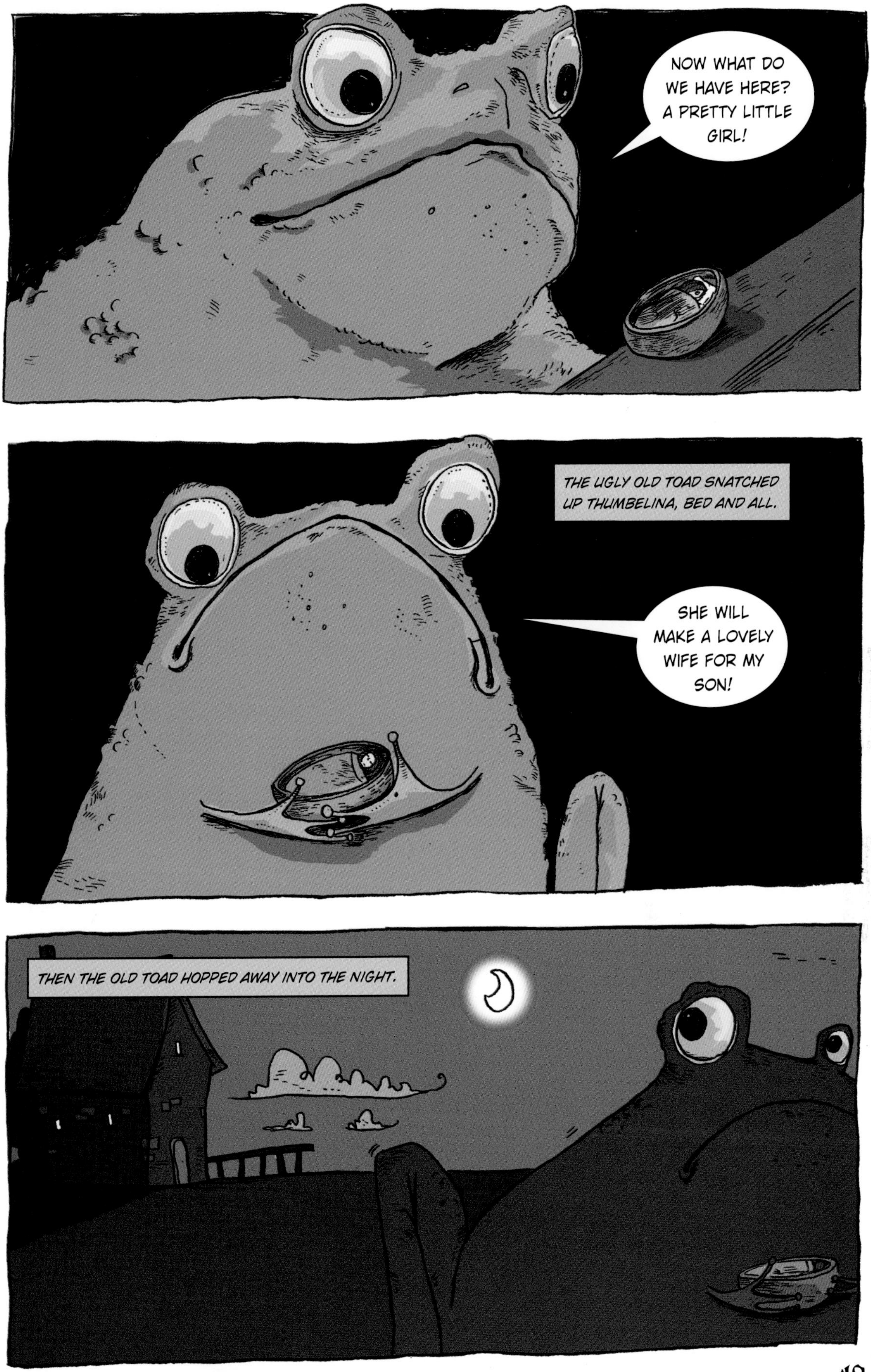
NOW WHAT DO WE HAVE HERE? A PRETTY LITTLE GIRL!
THE UGLY OLD TOAD SNATCHED UP THUMBELINA, BED AND ALL.
SHE WILL MAKE A LOVELY WIFE FOR MY SON!
THEN THE OLD TOAD HOPPED AWAY INTO THE NIGHT.

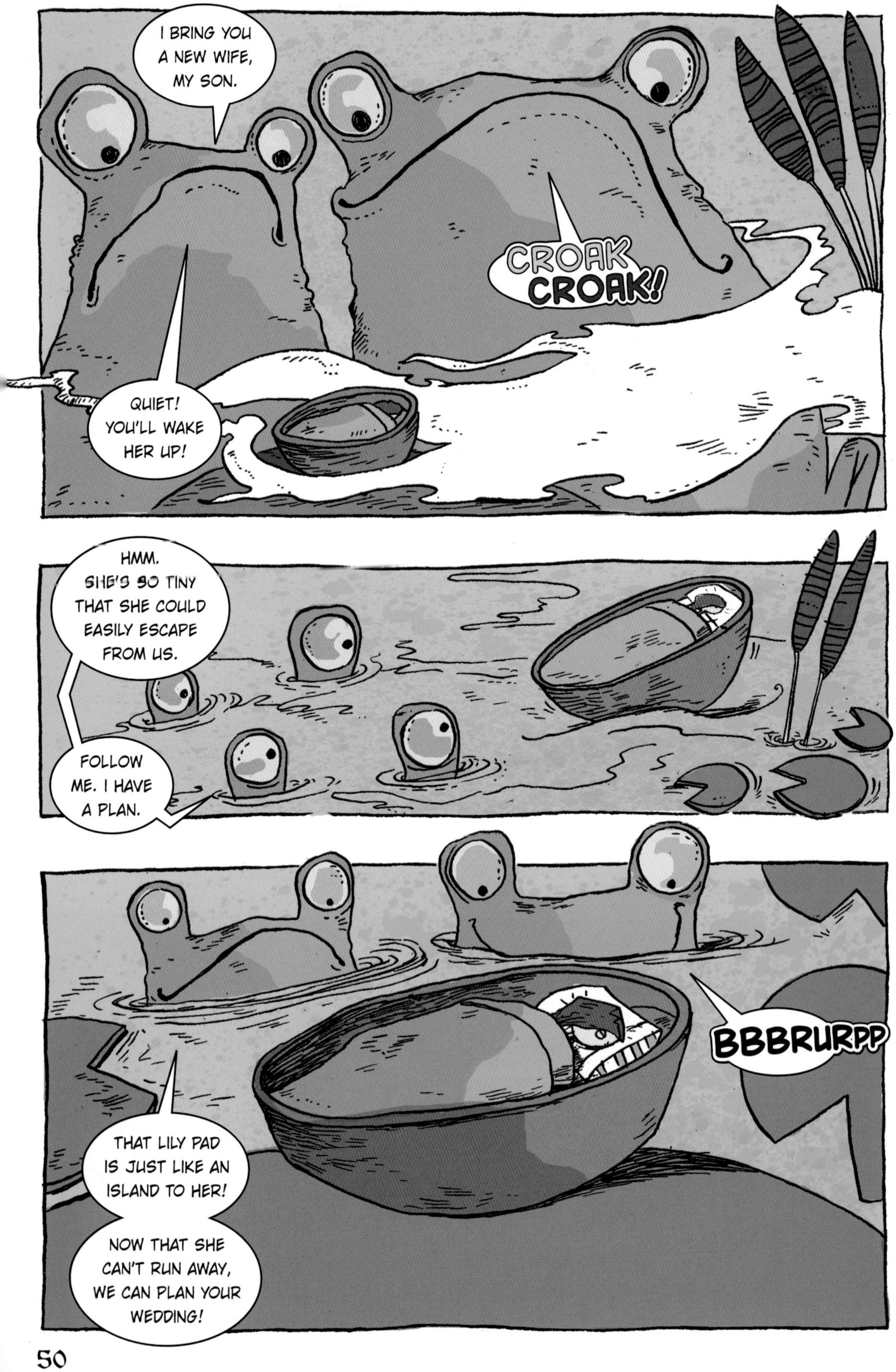
I BRING YOU A NEW WIFE, MY SON.
QUIET! YOU'LL WAKE HER UP!
CROAK CROAK!
HMM. SHE'S SO TINY THAT SHE COULD EASILY ESCAPE FROM US.
FOLLOW ME. I HAVE A PLAN.
BBBRURPP
THAT LILY PAD IS JUST LIKE AN ISLAND TO HER!
NOW THAT SHE CAN'T RUN AWAY, WE CAN PLAN YOUR WEDDING!

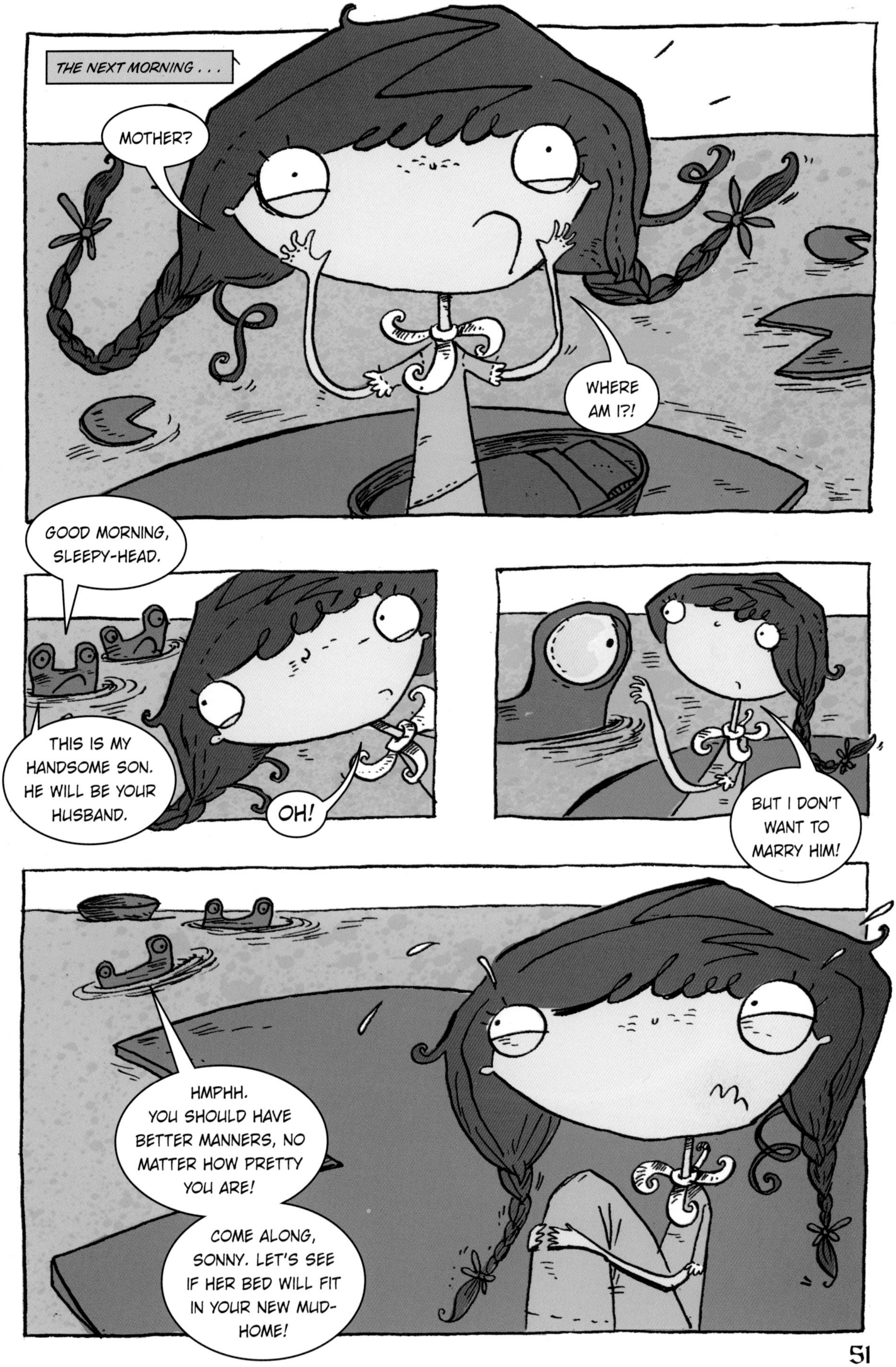
THE NEXT MORNING . . .
MOTHER?
WHERE AM I?!
GOOD MORNING, SLEEPY-HEAD.
THIS IS MY HANDSOME SON. HE WILL BE YOUR HUSBAND.
OH!
BUT I DON'T WANT TO MARRY HIM!
HMPHH. YOU SHOULD HAVE BETTER MANNERS, NO MATTER HOW PRETTY YOU ARE!
COME ALONG, SONNY. LET'S SEE IF HER BED WILL FIT IN YOUR NEW MUD-HOME!

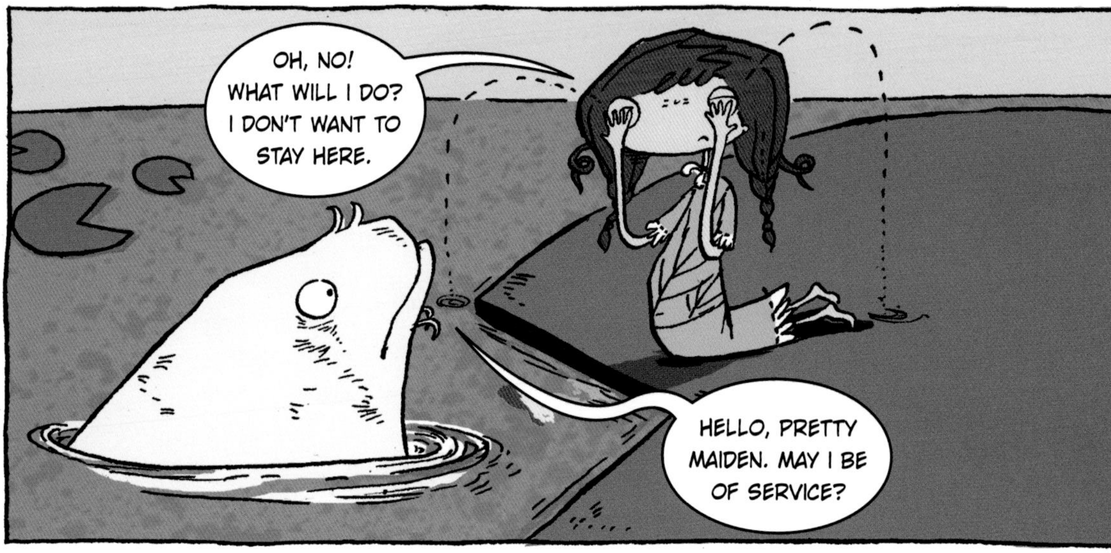
OH, NO! WHAT WILL I DO? I DON'T WANT TO STAY HERE.
HELLO, PRETTY MAIDEN. MAY I BE OF SERVICE?

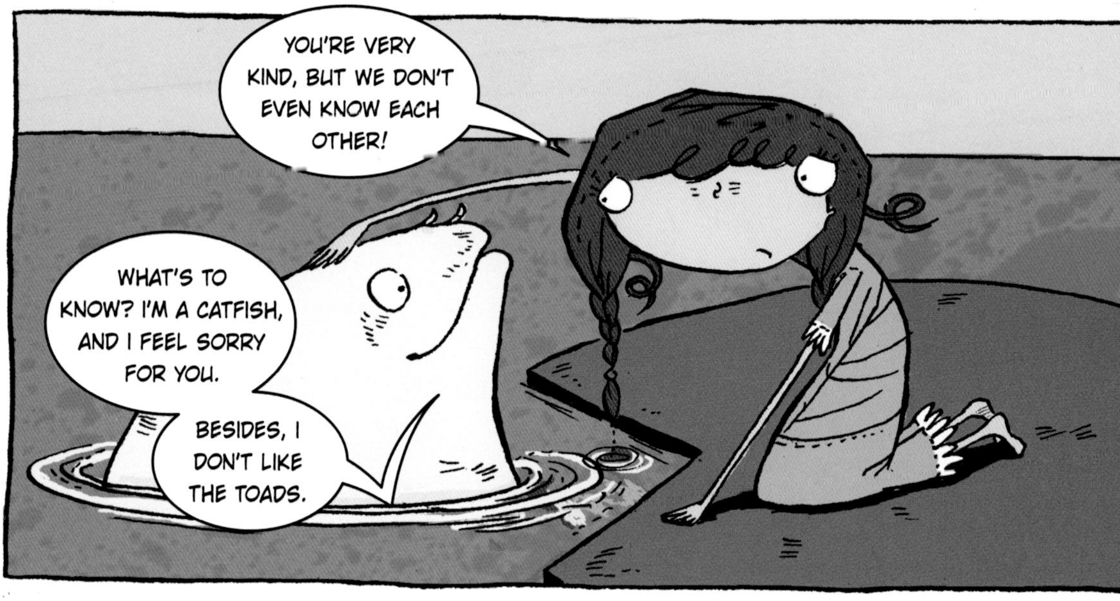
YOU'RE VERY KIND, BUT WE DON'T EVEN KNOW EACH OTHER!
WHAT'S TO KNOW? I'M A CATFISH, AND I FEEL SORRY FOR YOU.
BESIDES, I DON'T LIKE THE TOADS.

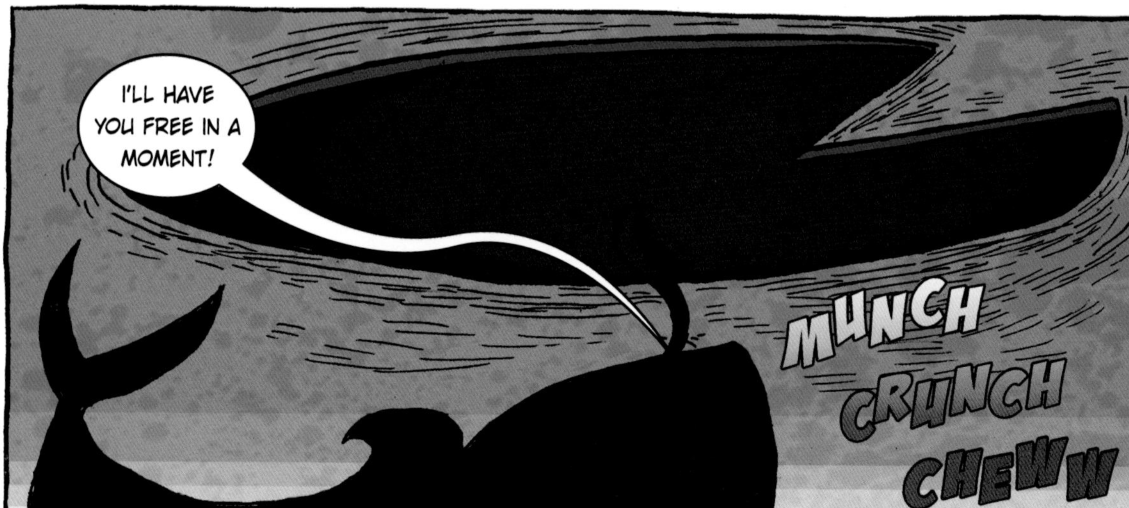
I'LL HAVE YOU FREE IN A MOMENT!
MUNCH
CRUNCH
CHEWW

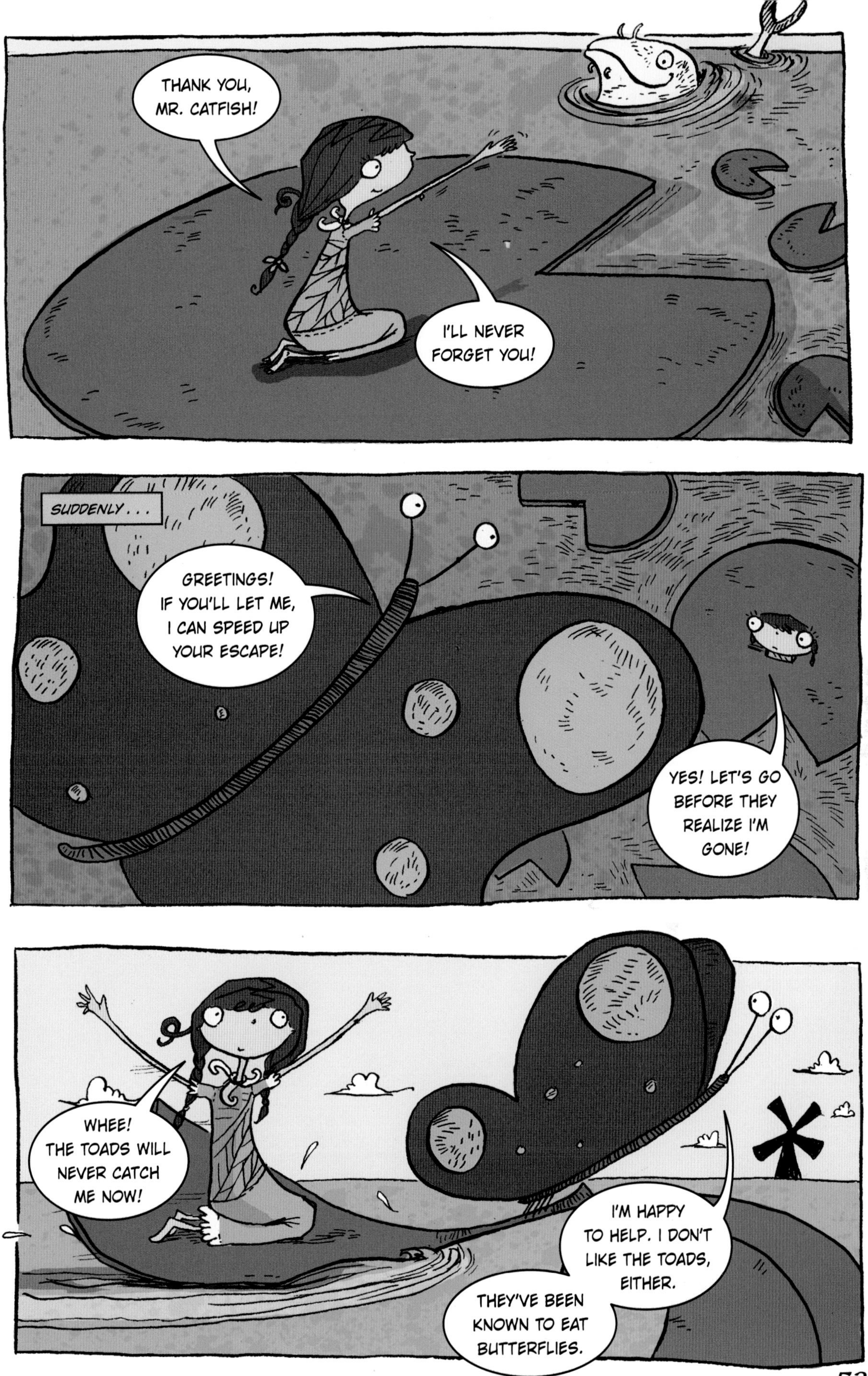
THANK YOU, MR. CATFISH!
I'LL NEVER FORGET YOU!
SUDDENLY . . .
GREETINGS! IF YOU'LL LET ME, I CAN SPEED UP YOUR ESCAPE!
YES! LET'S GO BEFORE THEY REALIZE I'M GONE!
WHEE! THE TOADS WILL NEVER CATCH ME NOW!
I'M HAPPY TO HELP. I DON'T LIKE THE TOADS, EITHER.
THEY'VE BEEN KNOWN TO EAT BUTTERFLIES.

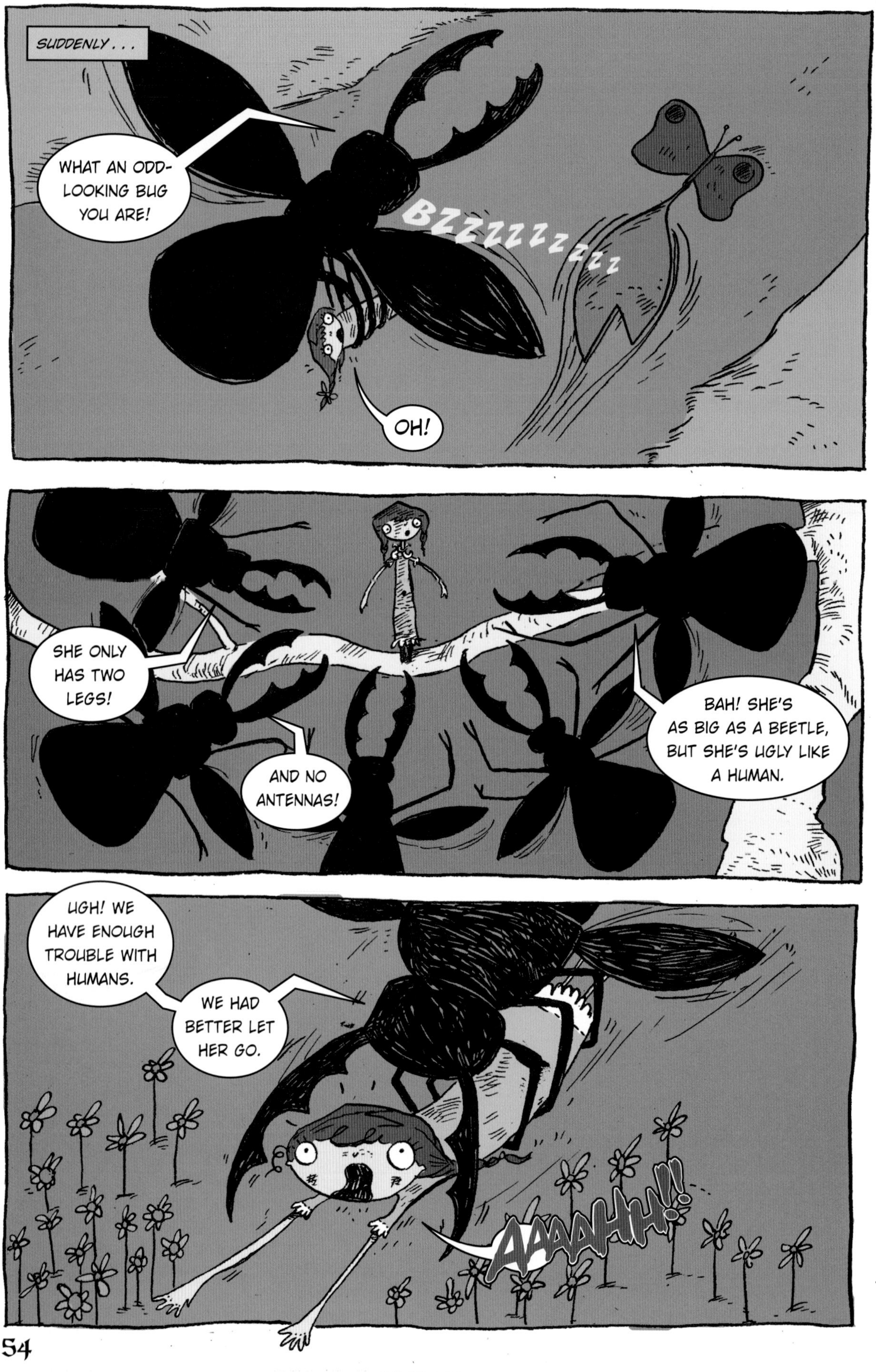
SUDDENLY . . .
WHAT AN ODD-LOOKING BUG YOU ARE!
BZZZZZZZZZ
OH!
SHE ONLY HAS TWO LEGS!
AND NO ANTENNAS!
BAH! SHE'S AS BIG AS A BEETLE, BUT SHE'S UGLY LIKE A HUMAN.
UGH! WE HAVE ENOUGH TROUBLE WITH HUMANS.
WE HAD BETTER LET HER GO.
AAAAHHH!!

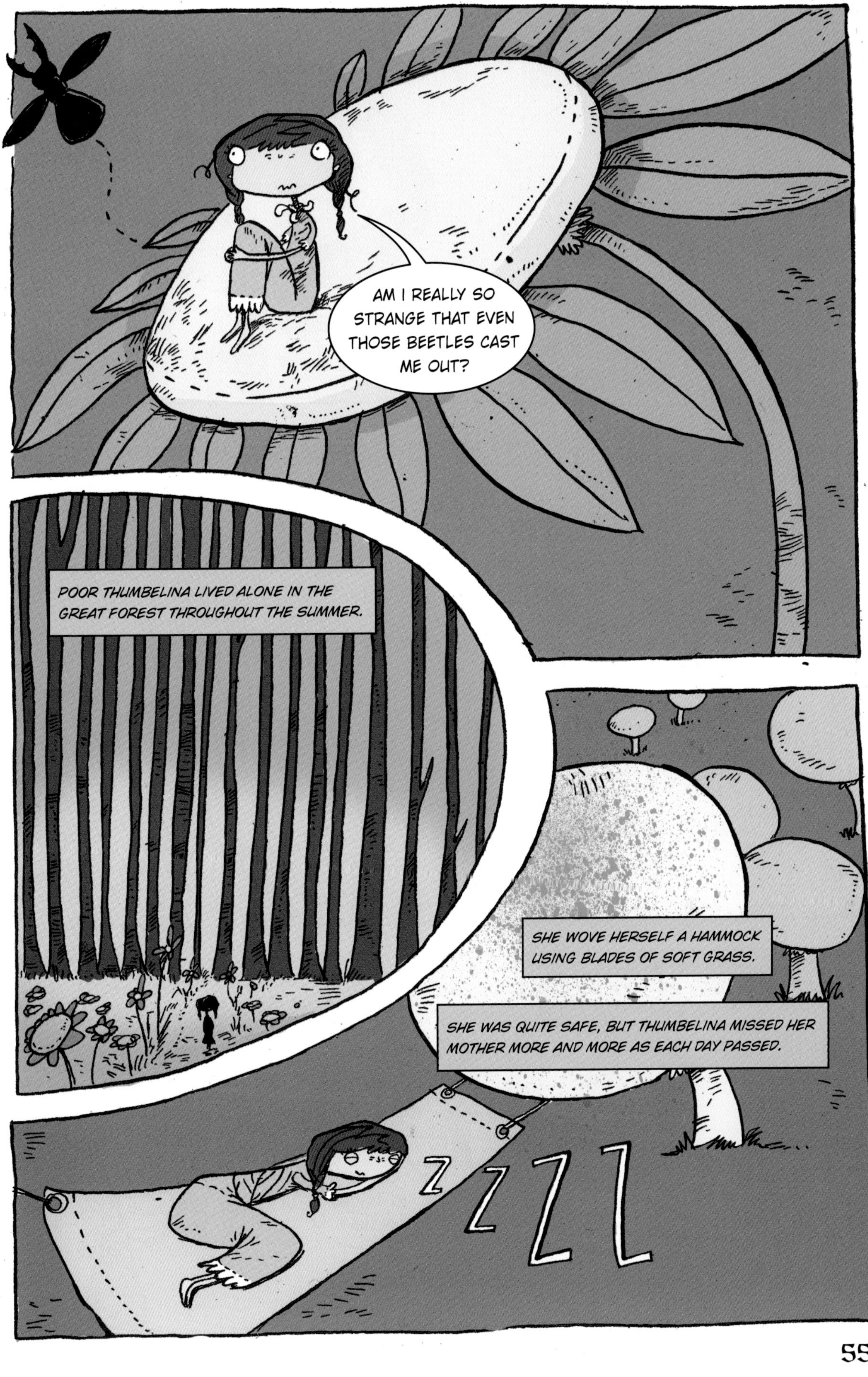
AM I REALLY SO STRANGE THAT EVEN THOSE BEETLES CAST ME OUT?
POOR THUMBELINA LIVED ALONE IN THE GREAT FOREST THROUGHOUT THE SUMMER.
SHE WOVE HERSELF A HAMMOCK USING BLADES OF SOFT GRASS.
SHE WAS QUITE SAFE, BUT THUMBELINA MISSED HER MOTHER MORE AND MORE AS EACH DAY PASSED.
ZZZZ

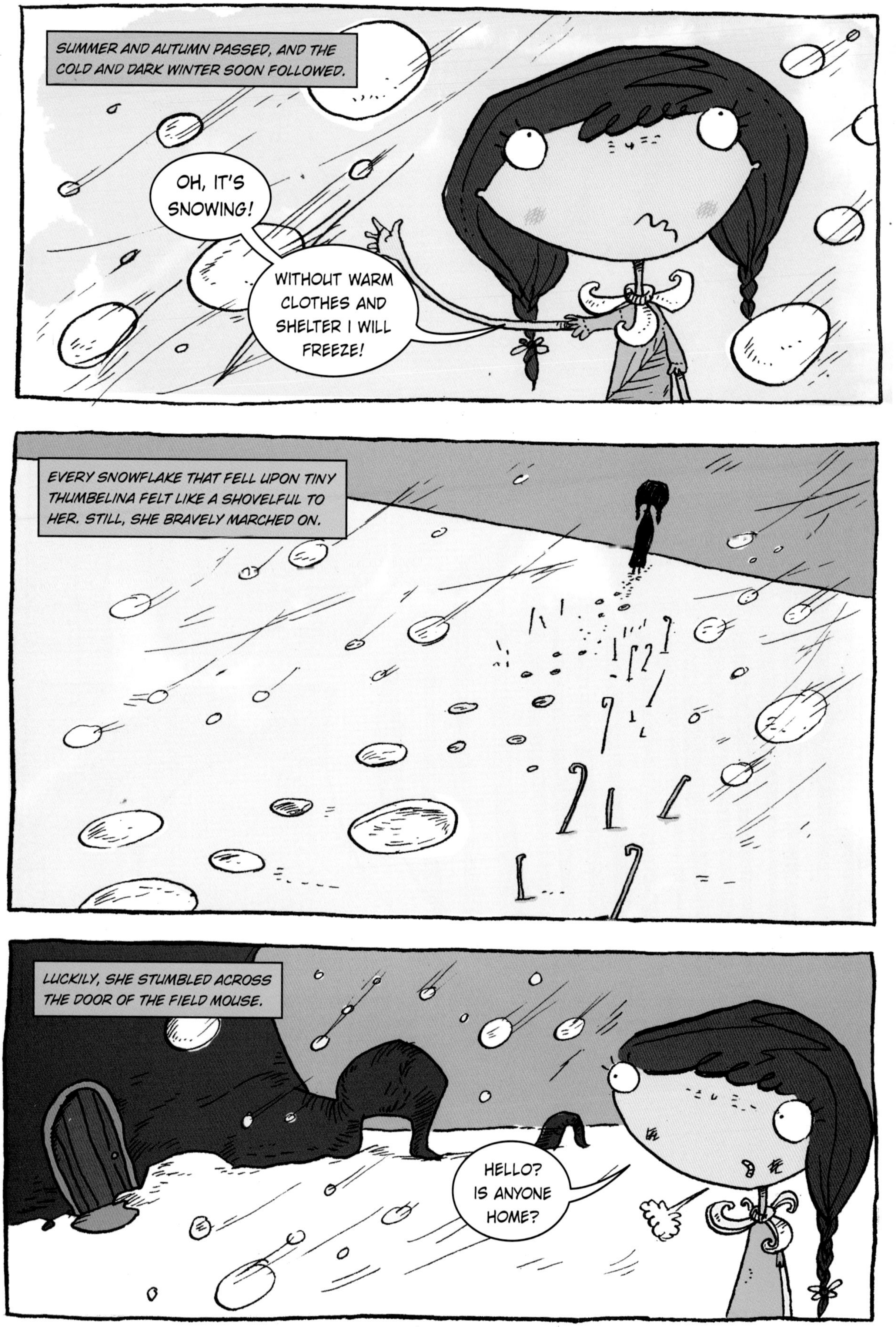
SUMMER AND AUTUMN PASSED, AND THE COLD AND DARK WINTER SOON FOLLOWED.
OH, IT'S SNOWING!
WITHOUT WARM CLOTHES AND SHELTER I WILL FREEZE!
EVERY SNOWFLAKE THAT FELL UPON TINY THUMBELINA FELT LIKE A SHOVELFUL TO HER. STILL, SHE BRAVELY MARCHED ON.
LUCKILY, SHE STUMBLED ACROSS THE DOOR OF THE FIELD MOUSE.
HELLO? IS ANYONE HOME?

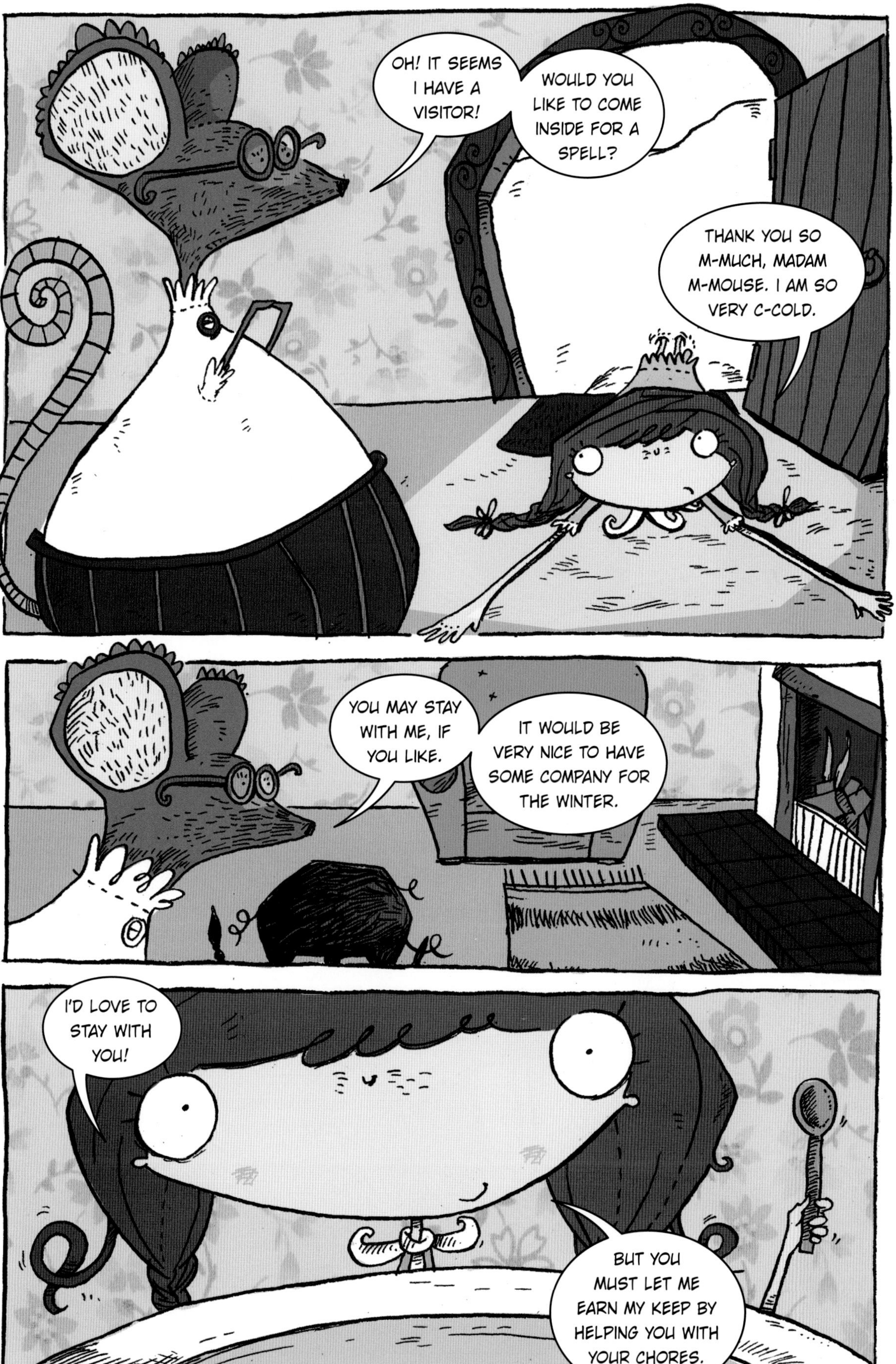
OH! IT SEEMS I HAVE A VISITOR!
WOULD YOU LIKE TO COME INSIDE FOR A SPELL?
THANK YOU SO M-MUCH, MADAM M-MOUSE. I AM SO VERY C-COLD.
YOU MAY STAY WITH ME, IF YOU LIKE.
IT WOULD BE VERY NICE TO HAVE SOME COMPANY FOR THE WINTER.
I'D LOVE TO STAY WITH YOU!
BUT YOU MUST LET ME EARN MY KEEP BY HELPING YOU WITH YOUR CHORES.

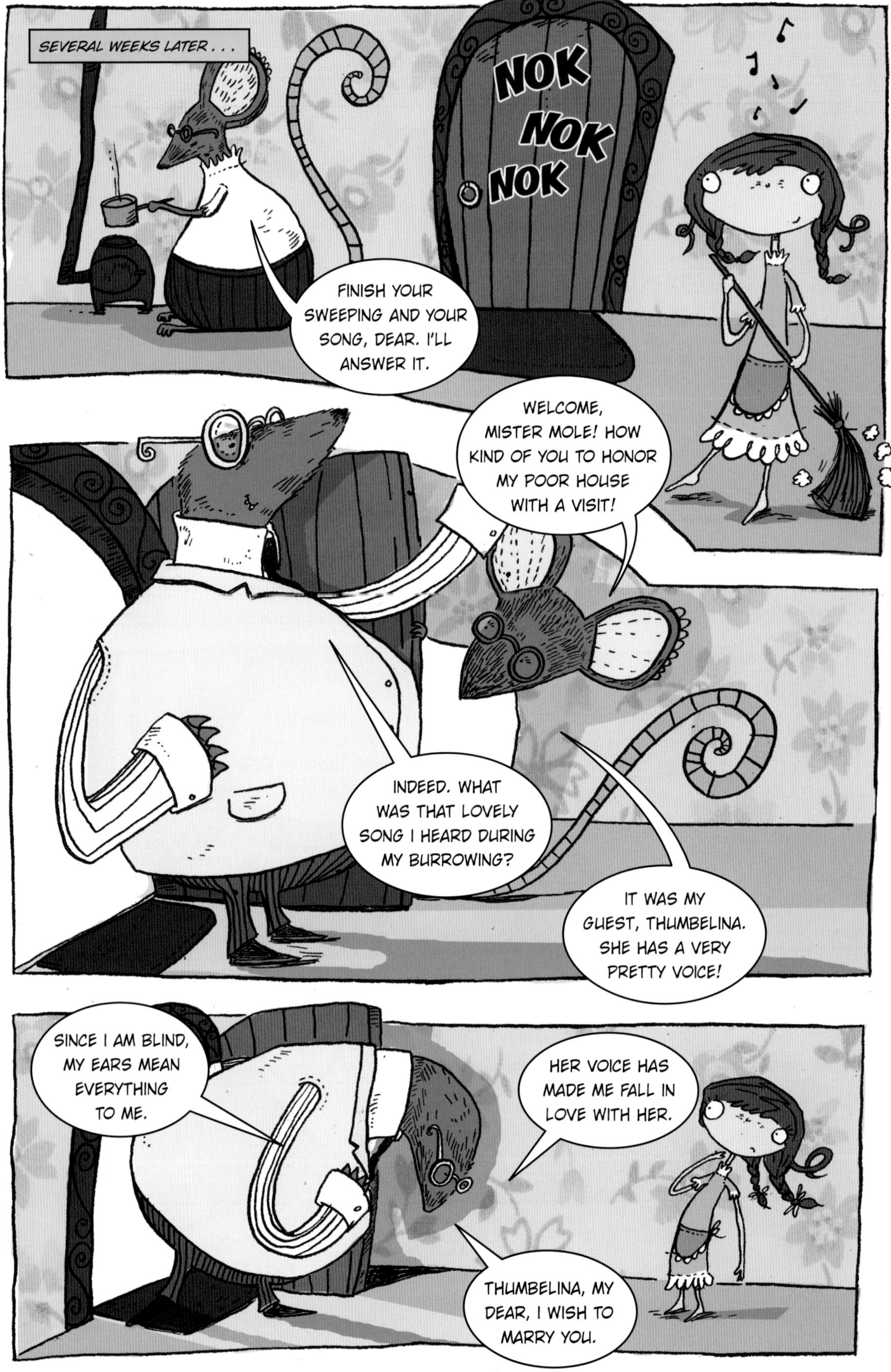
SEVERAL WEEKS LATER . . .
NOK NOK NOK
FINISH YOUR SWEEPING AND YOUR SONG, DEAR. I'LL ANSWER IT.
WELCOME, MISTER MOLE! HOW KIND OF YOU TO HONOR MY POOR HOUSE WITH A VISIT!
INDEED. WHAT WAS THAT LOVELY SONG I HEARD DURING MY BURROWING?
IT WAS MY GUEST, THUMBELINA. SHE HAS A VERY PRETTY VOICE!
SINCE I AM BLIND, MY EARS MEAN EVERYTHING TO ME.
HER VOICE HAS MADE ME FALL IN LOVE WITH HER.
THUMBELINA, MY DEAR, I WISH TO MARRY YOU.

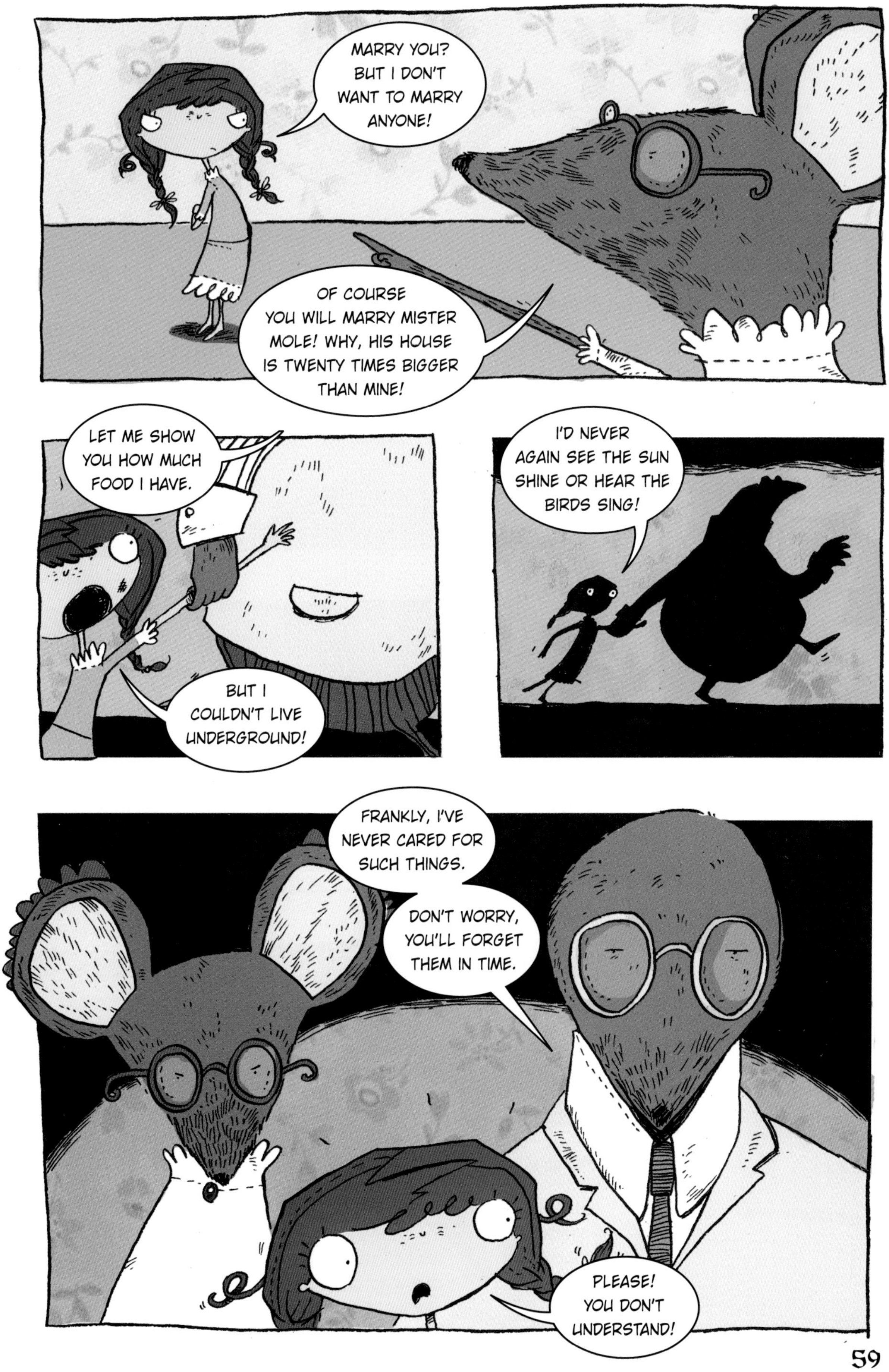
MARRY YOU? BUT I DON'T WANT TO MARRY ANYONE!
OF COURSE YOU WILL MARRY MISTER MOLE! WHY, HIS HOUSE IS TWENTY TIMES BIGGER THAN MINE!
LET ME SHOW YOU HOW MUCH FOOD I HAVE.
BUT I COULDN'T LIVE UNDERGROUND!
I'D NEVER AGAIN SEE THE SUN SHINE OR HEAR THE BIRDS SING!
FRANKLY, I'VE NEVER CARED FOR SUCH THINGS.
DON'T WORRY, YOU'LL FORGET THEM IN TIME.
PLEASE! YOU DON'T UNDERSTAND!

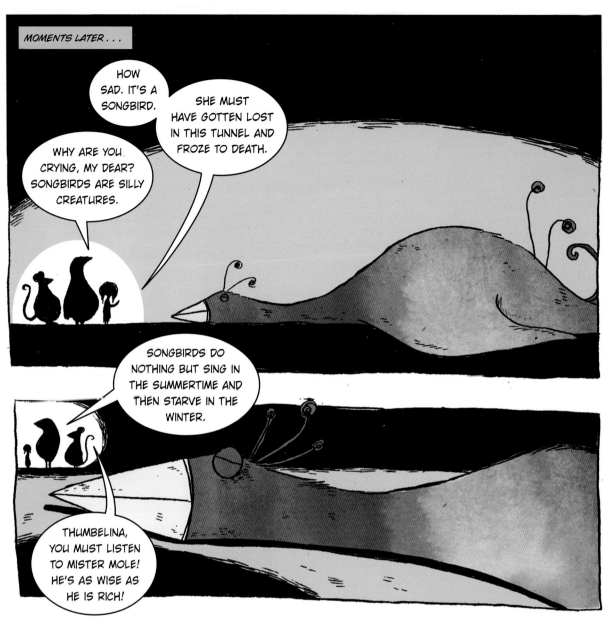

HOW SAD. IT'S A SONGBIRD.

SHE MUST HAVE GOTTEN LOST IN THIS TUNNEL AND FROZE TO DEATH.

WHY ARE YOU CRYING, MY DEAR? SONGBIRDS ARE SILLY CREATURES.

SONGBIRDS DO NOTHING BUT SING IN THE SUMMERTIME AND THEN STARVE IN THE WINTER.

THUMBELINA, YOU MUST LISTEN TO MISTER MOLE! HE'S AS WISE AS HE IS RICH!

LATER THAT NIGHT, THUMBELINA CREPT BACK INTO THE DARK TUNNEL.

I CAN'T STOP THINKING ABOUT THIS POOR SONGBIRD.

PERHAPS YOU'RE THE SAME ONE WHO SANG TO ME ALL SUMMER.

I CAN'T BURY HER IN THIS FROZEN GROUND. I'LL COVER HER WITH THIS BLANKET UNTIL SPRING.
MMMM . . . THAT FEELS MUCH BETTER.
THANK YOU FOR HELPING ME, LITTLE GIRL!
YOU'RE ALIVE!
AND MUCH WARMER NOW, TOO!
I HURT MY WING LAST AUTUMN, AND CRAWLED INTO THIS HOLE BEFORE THE SNOW FELL.
I FEEL A LOT BETTER NOW, AND I THINK I CAN FLY AGAIN!

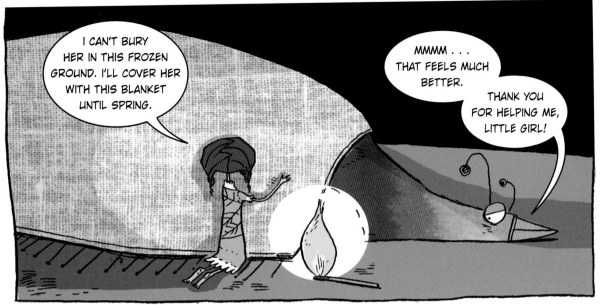

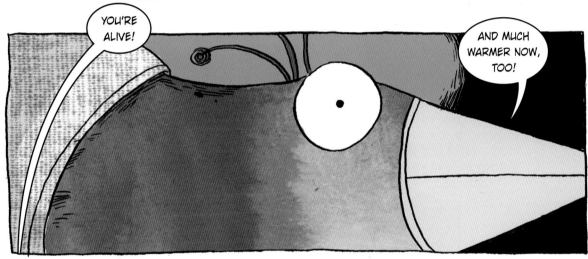

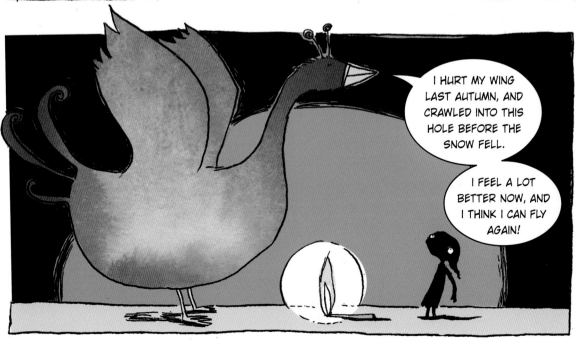

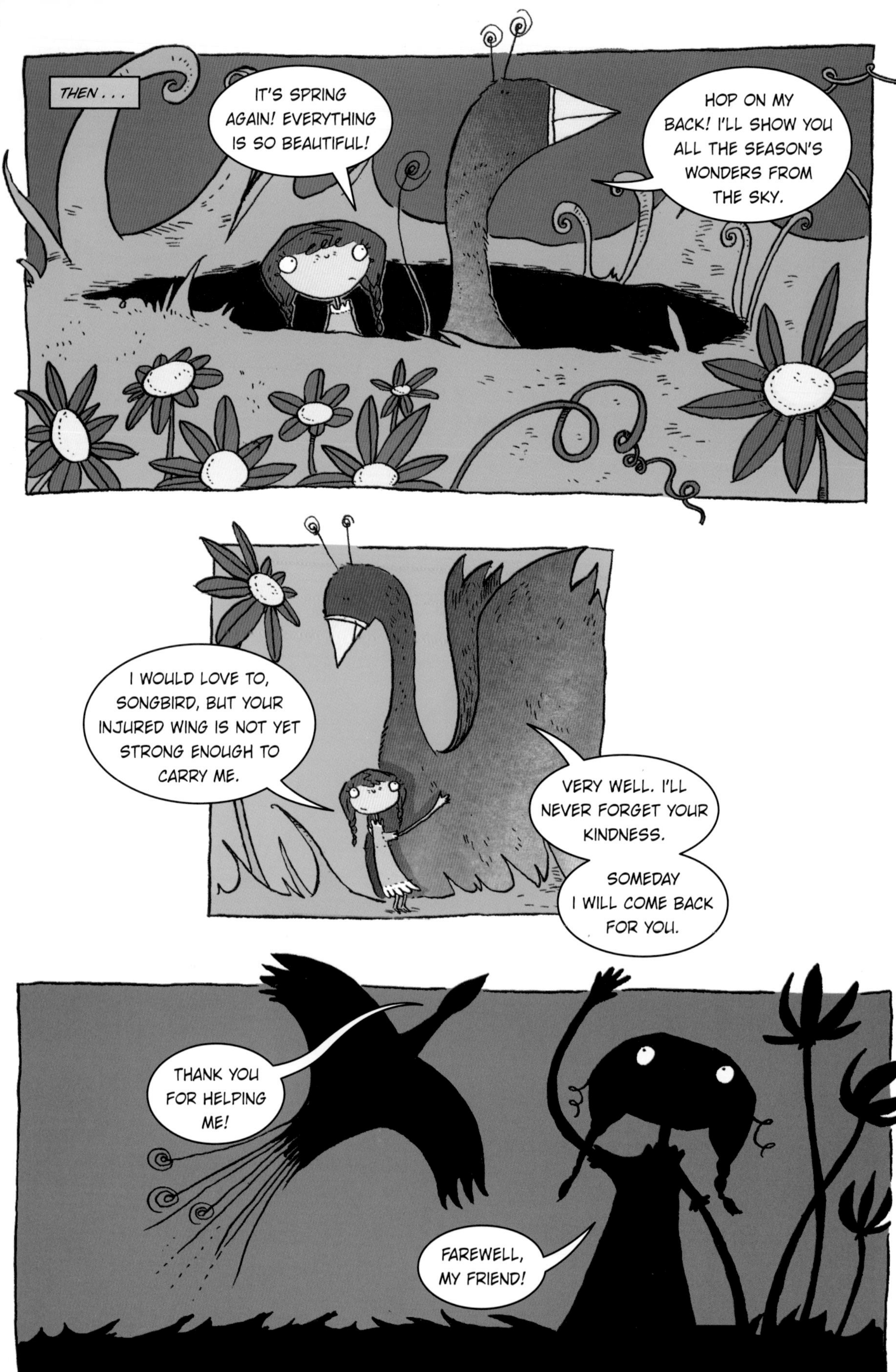
THEN . . .
IT'S SPRING AGAIN! EVERYTHING IS SO BEAUTIFUL!
HOP ON MY BACK! I'LL SHOW YOU ALL THE SEASON'S WONDERS FROM THE SKY.
I WOULD LOVE TO, SONGBIRD, BUT YOUR INJURED WING IS NOT YET STRONG ENOUGH TO CARRY ME.
VERY WELL. I'LL NEVER FORGET YOUR KINDNESS.
SOMEDAY I WILL COME BACK FOR YOU.
THANK YOU FOR HELPING ME!
FAREWELL, MY FRIEND!

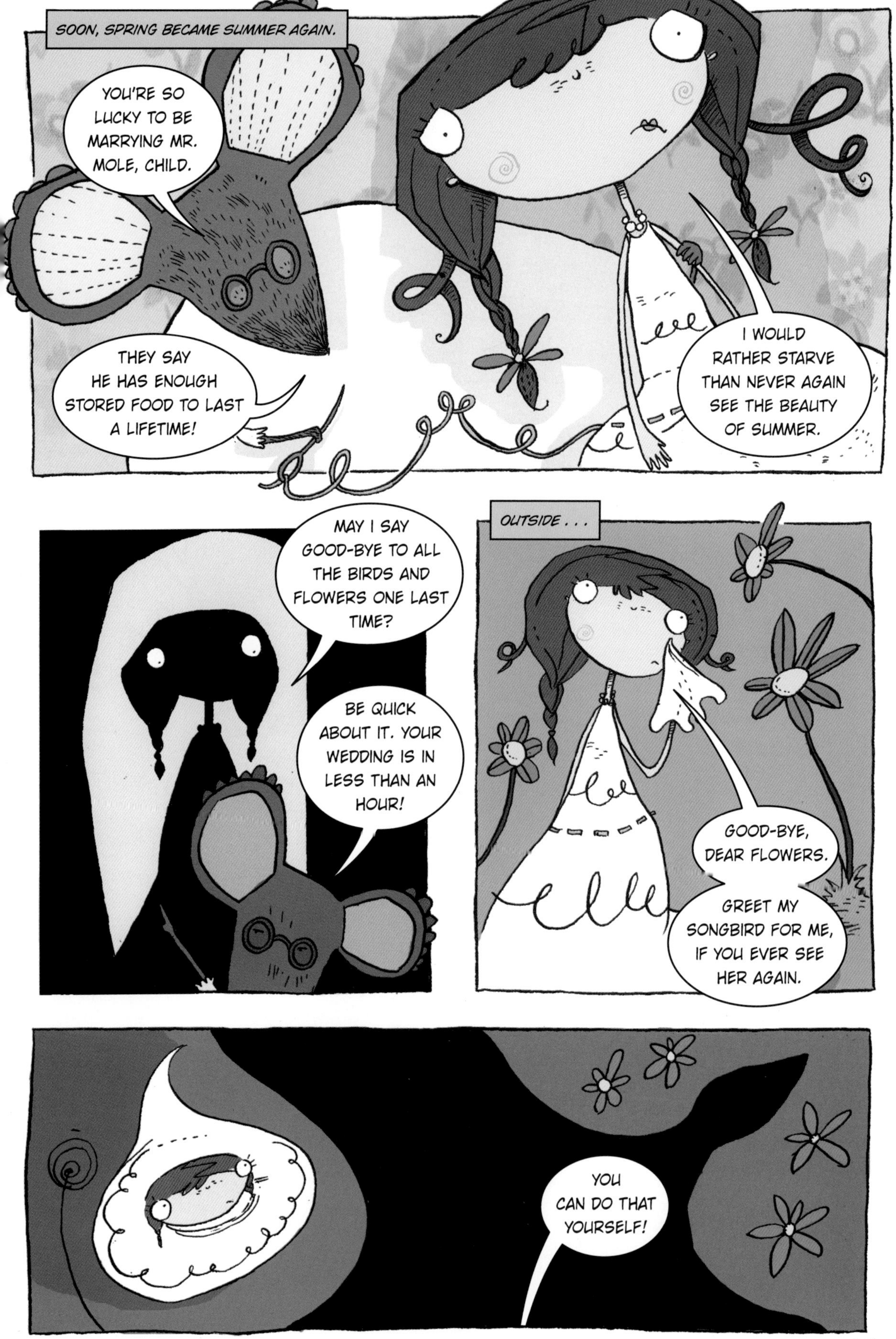
SOON, SPRING BECAME SUMMER AGAIN.
YOU'RE SO LUCKY TO BE MARRYING MR. MOLE, CHILD.
THEY SAY HE HAS ENOUGH STORED FOOD TO LAST A LIFETIME!
I WOULD RATHER STARVE THAN NEVER AGAIN SEE THE BEAUTY OF SUMMER.
MAY I SAY GOOD-BYE TO ALL THE BIRDS AND FLOWERS ONE LAST TIME?
BE QUICK ABOUT IT. YOUR WEDDING IS IN LESS THAN AN HOUR!
OUTSIDE . . .
GOOD-BYE, DEAR FLOWERS.
GREET MY SONGBIRD FOR ME, IF YOU EVER SEE HER AGAIN.
YOU CAN DO THAT YOURSELF!

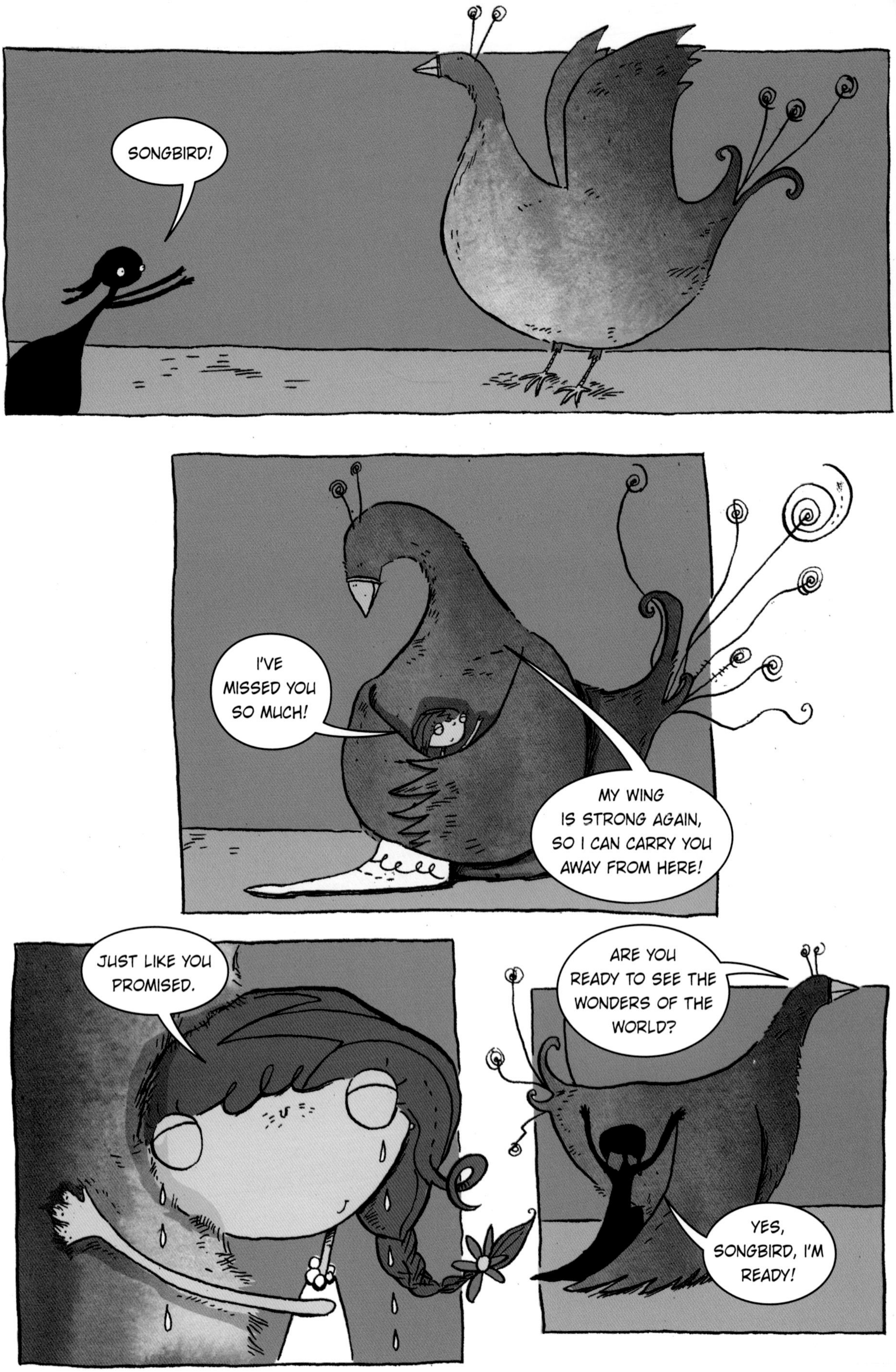
SONGBIRD!
I'VE MISSED YOU SO MUCH!
MY WING IS STRONG AGAIN, SO I CAN CARRY YOU AWAY FROM HERE!
JUST LIKE YOU PROMISED.
ARE YOU READY TO SEE THE WONDERS OF THE WORLD?
YES, SONGBIRD, I'M READY!

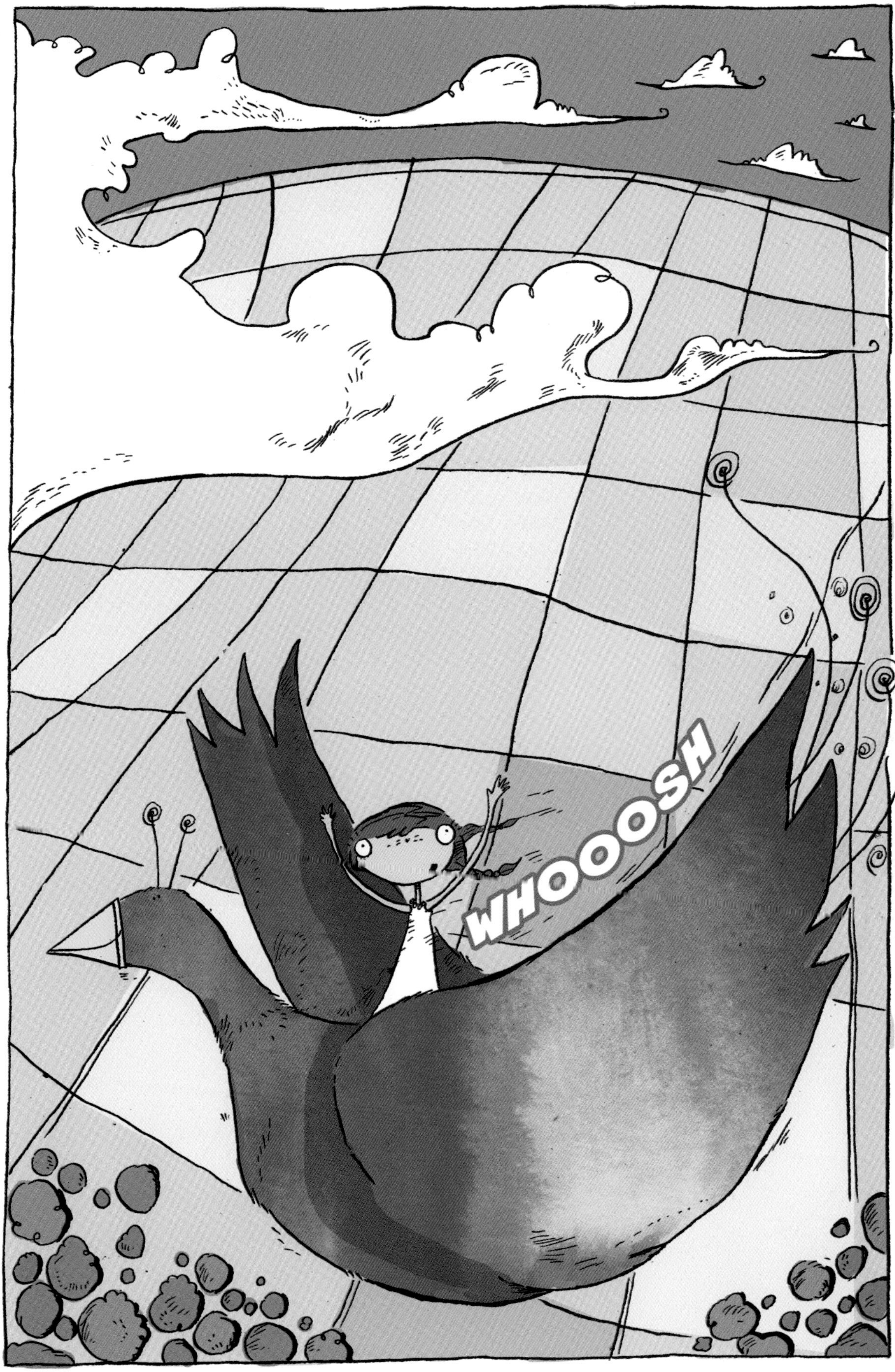
WHOOOSH

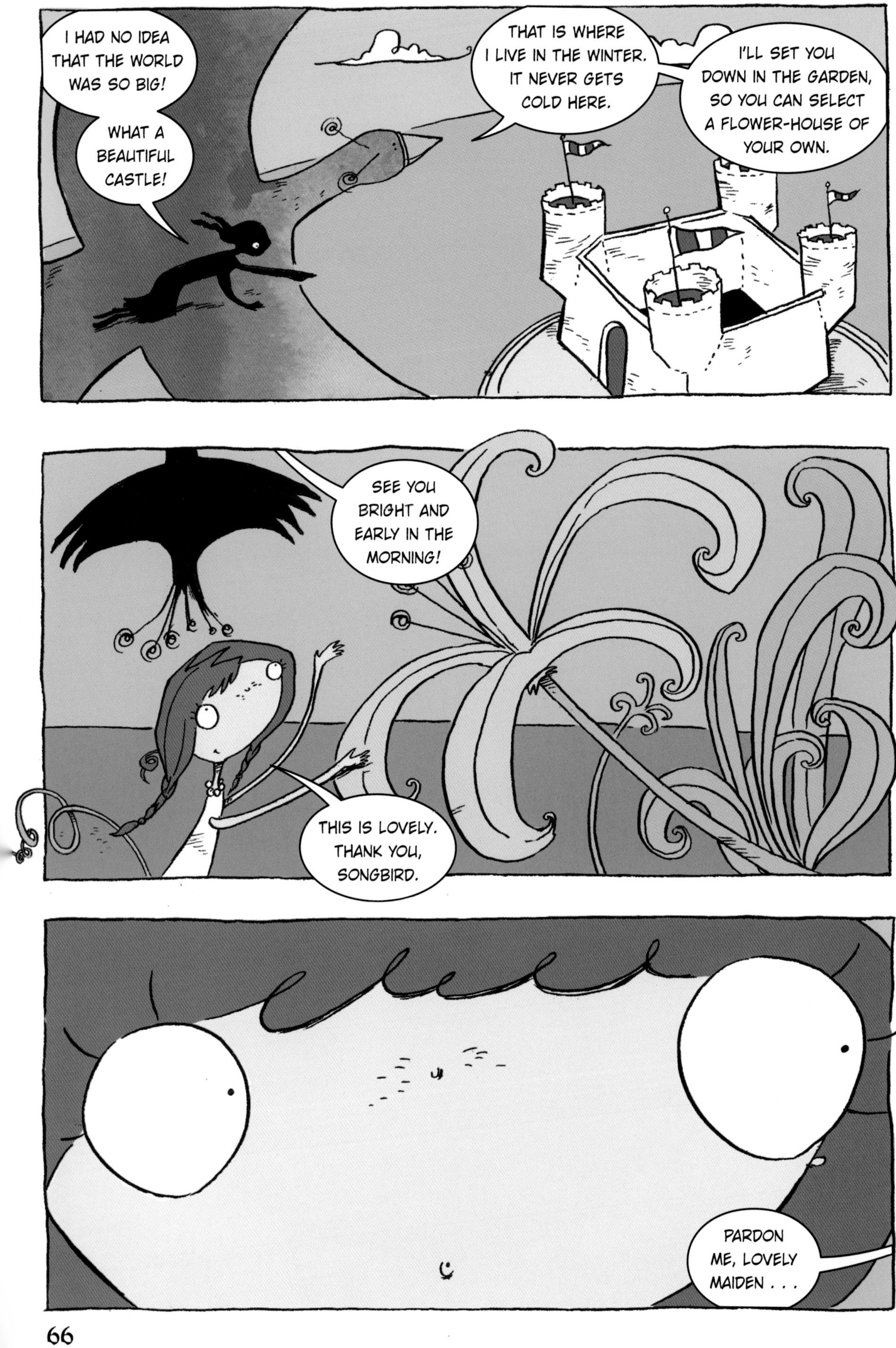
I HAD NO IDEA THAT THE WORLD WAS SO BIG!
WHAT A BEAUTIFUL CASTLE!
THAT IS WHERE I LIVE IN THE WINTER. IT NEVER GETS COLD HERE.
I'LL SET YOU DOWN IN THE GARDEN, SO YOU CAN SELECT A FLOWER-HOUSE OF YOUR OWN.
SEE YOU BRIGHT AND EARLY IN THE MORNING!
THIS IS LOVELY. THANK YOU, SONGBIRD.
PARDON ME, LOVELY MAIDEN . . .

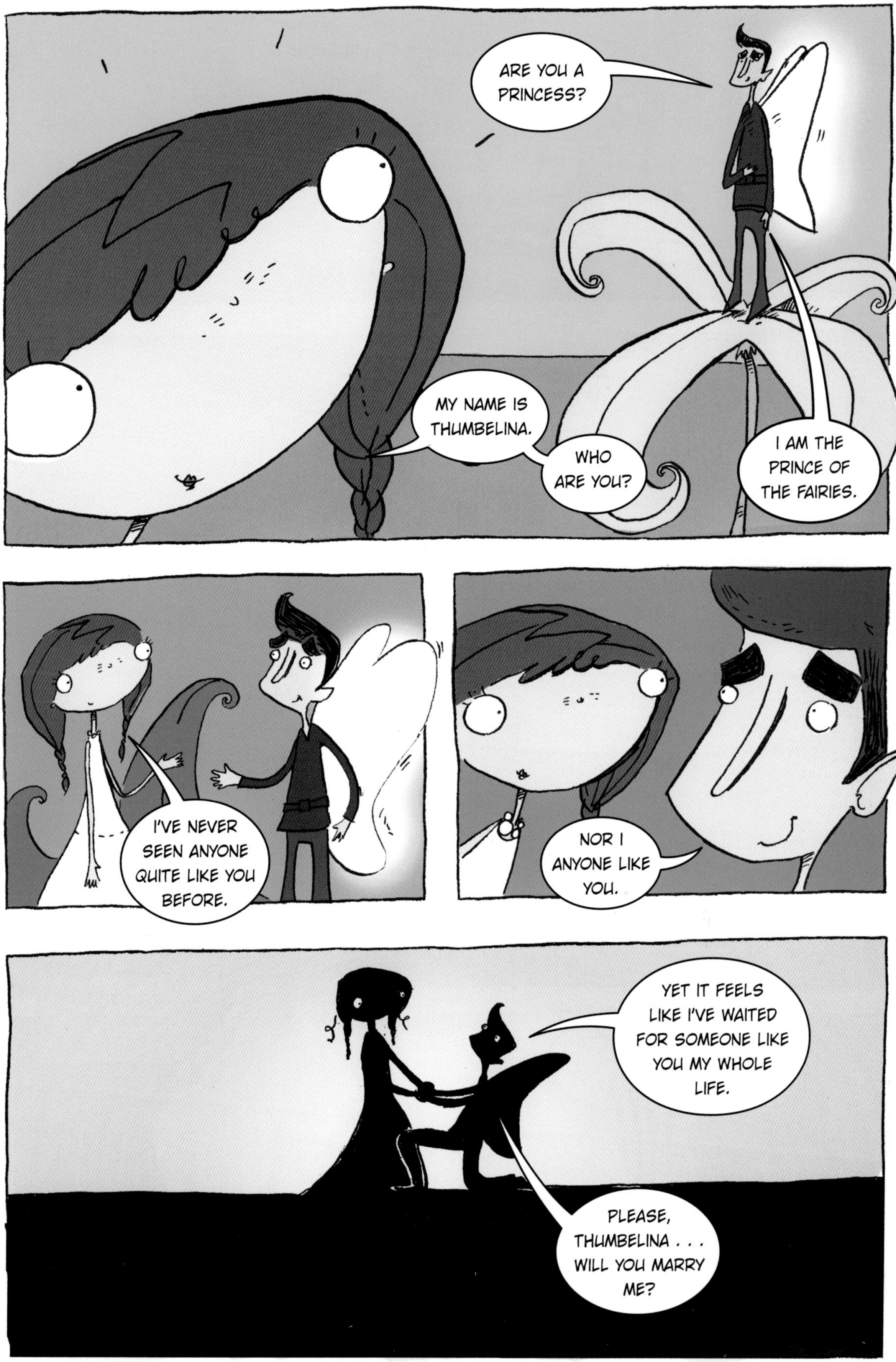
ARE YOU A PRINCESS?
MY NAME IS THUMBELINA.
WHO ARE YOU?
I AM THE PRINCE OF THE FAIRIES.
I'VE NEVER SEEN ANYONE QUITE LIKE YOU BEFORE.
NOR I ANYONE LIKE YOU.
YET IT FEELS LIKE I'VE WAITED FOR SOMEONE LIKE YOU MY WHOLE LIFE.
PLEASE, THUMBELINA . . . WILL YOU MARRY ME?

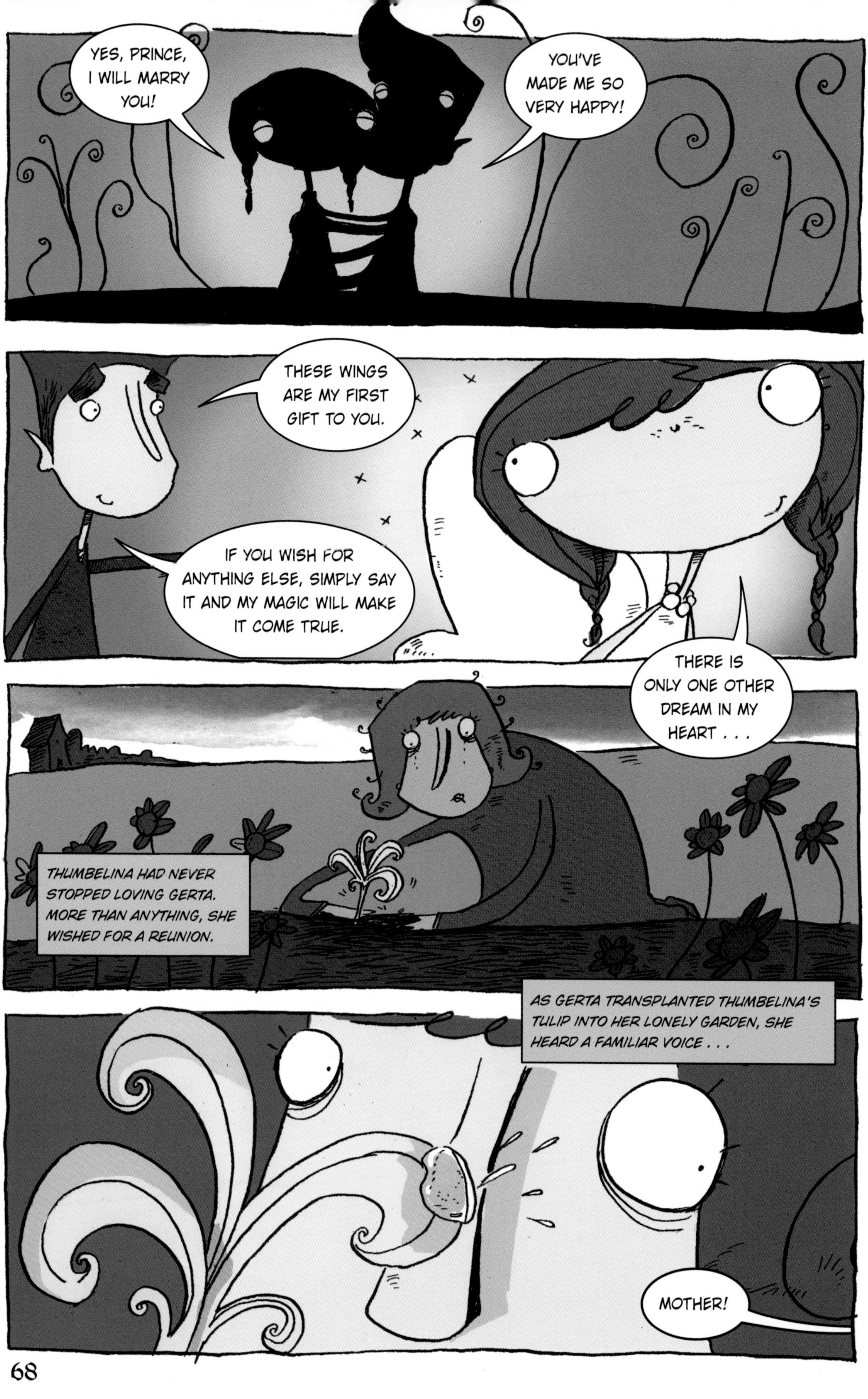
YES, PRINCE, I WILL MARRY YOU!
YOU'VE MADE ME SO VERY HAPPY!
THESE WINGS ARE MY FIRST GIFT TO YOU.
IF YOU WISH FOR ANYTHING ELSE, SIMPLY SAY IT AND MY MAGIC WILL MAKE IT COME TRUE.
THERE IS ONLY ONE OTHER DREAM IN MY HEART . . .
THUMBELINA HAD NEVER STOPPED LOVING GERTA. MORE THAN ANYTHING, SHE WISHED FOR A REUNION.
AS GERTA TRANSPLANTED THUMBELINA'S TULIP INTO HER LONELY GARDEN, SHE HEARD A FAMILIAR VOICE . . .
MOTHER!

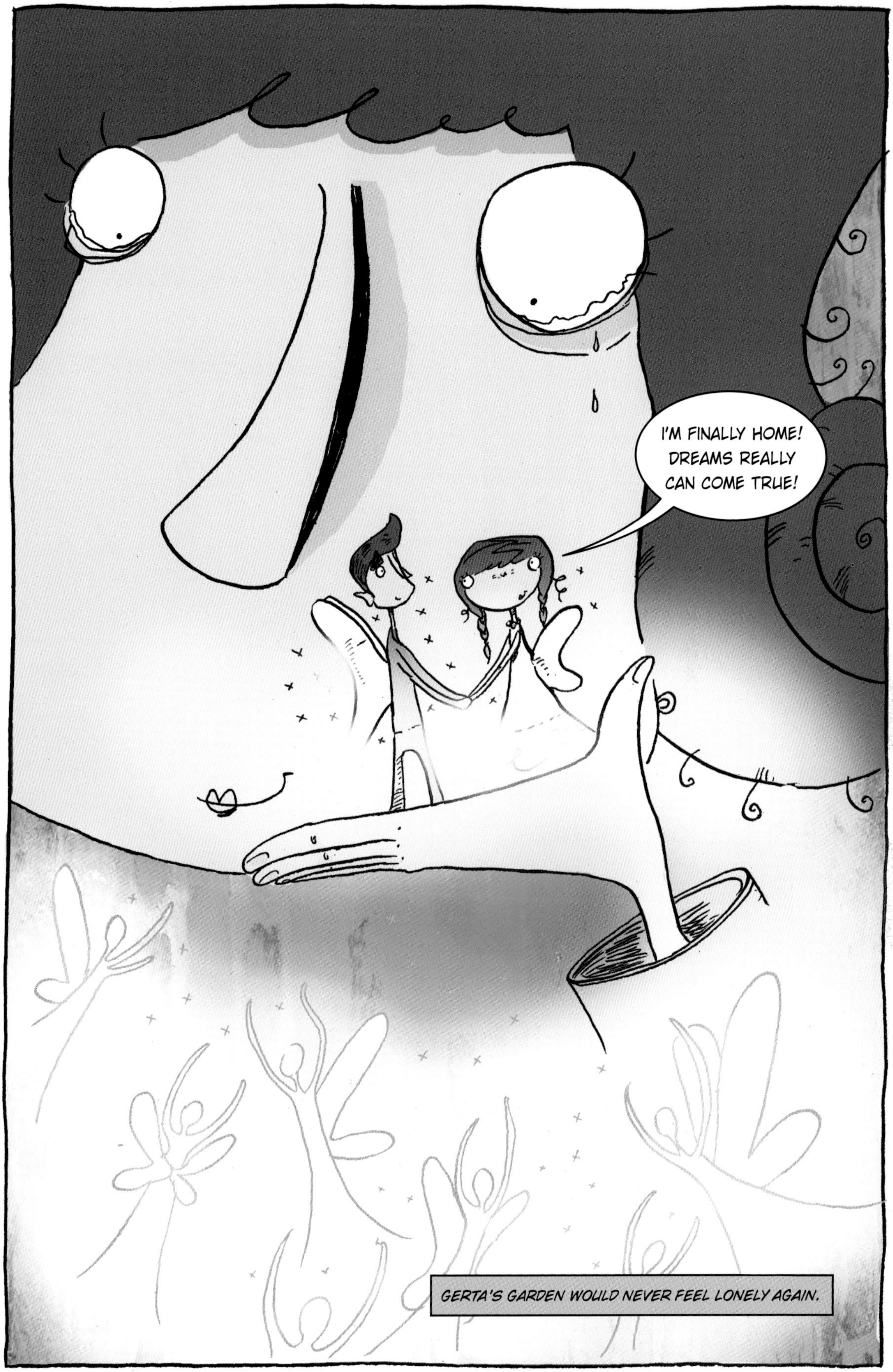
I'M FINALLY HOME! DREAMS REALLY CAN COME TRUE!
GERTA'S GARDEN WOULD NEVER FEEL LONELY AGAIN.

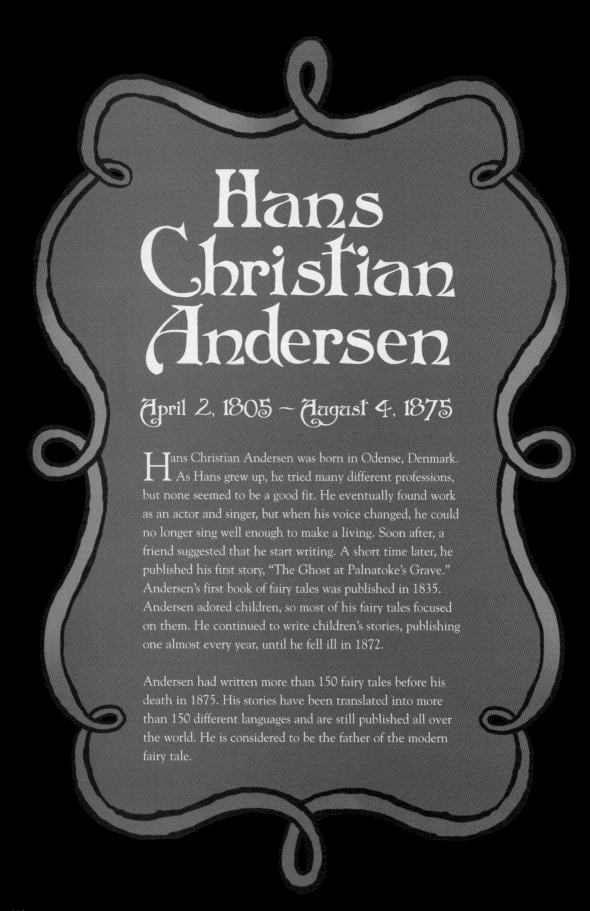

Hans Christian Andersen

April 2, 1805 ~ August 4, 1875

Hans Christian Andersen was born in Odense, Denmark. As Hans grew up, he tried many different professions, but none seemed to be a good fit. He eventually found work as an actor and singer, but when his voice changed, he could no longer sing well enough to make a living. Soon after, a friend suggested that he start writing. A short time later, he published his first story, "The Ghost at Palnatoke's Grave." Andersen's first book of fairy tales was published in 1835. Andersen adored children, so most of his fairy tales focused on them. He continued to write children's stories, publishing one almost every year, until he fell ill in 1872.

Andersen had written more than 150 fairy tales before his death in 1875. His stories have been translated into more than 150 different languages and are still published all over the world. He is considered to be the father of the modern fairy tale.

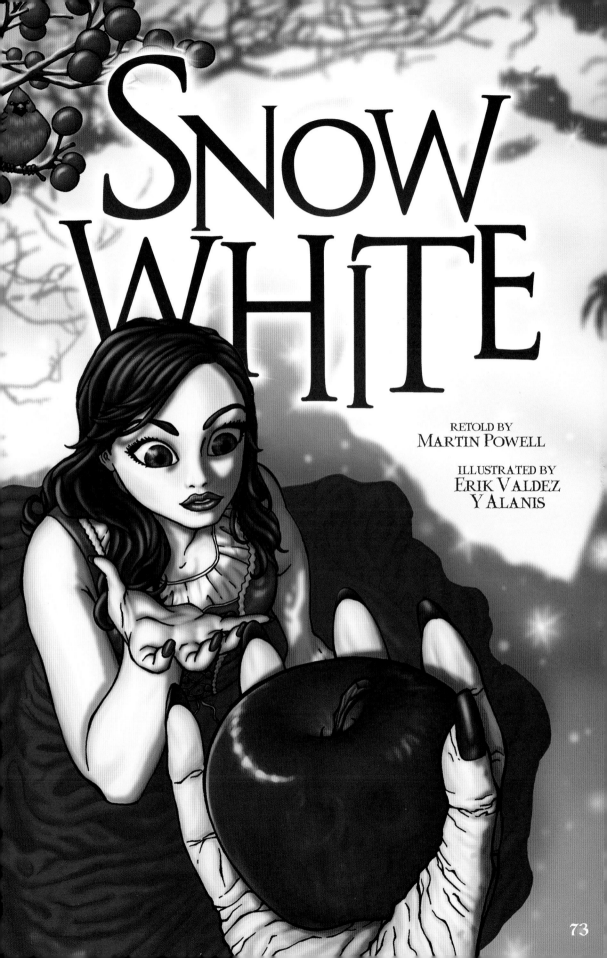

SNOW WHITE

RETOLD BY
MARTIN POWELL

ILLUSTRATED BY
ERIK VALDEZ
Y ALANIS

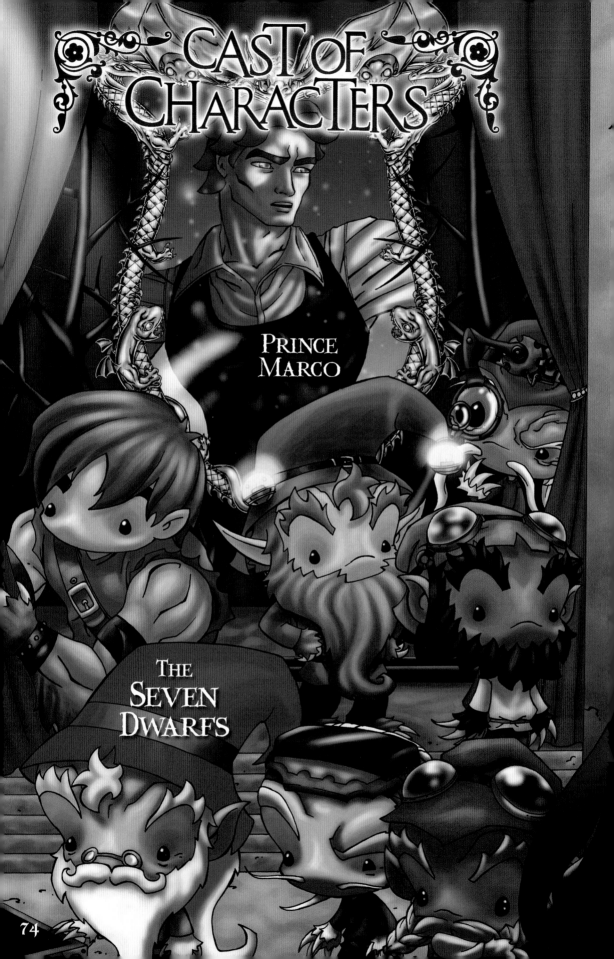

CAST OF CHARACTERS

PRINCE
MARCO

THE
SEVEN
DWARFS

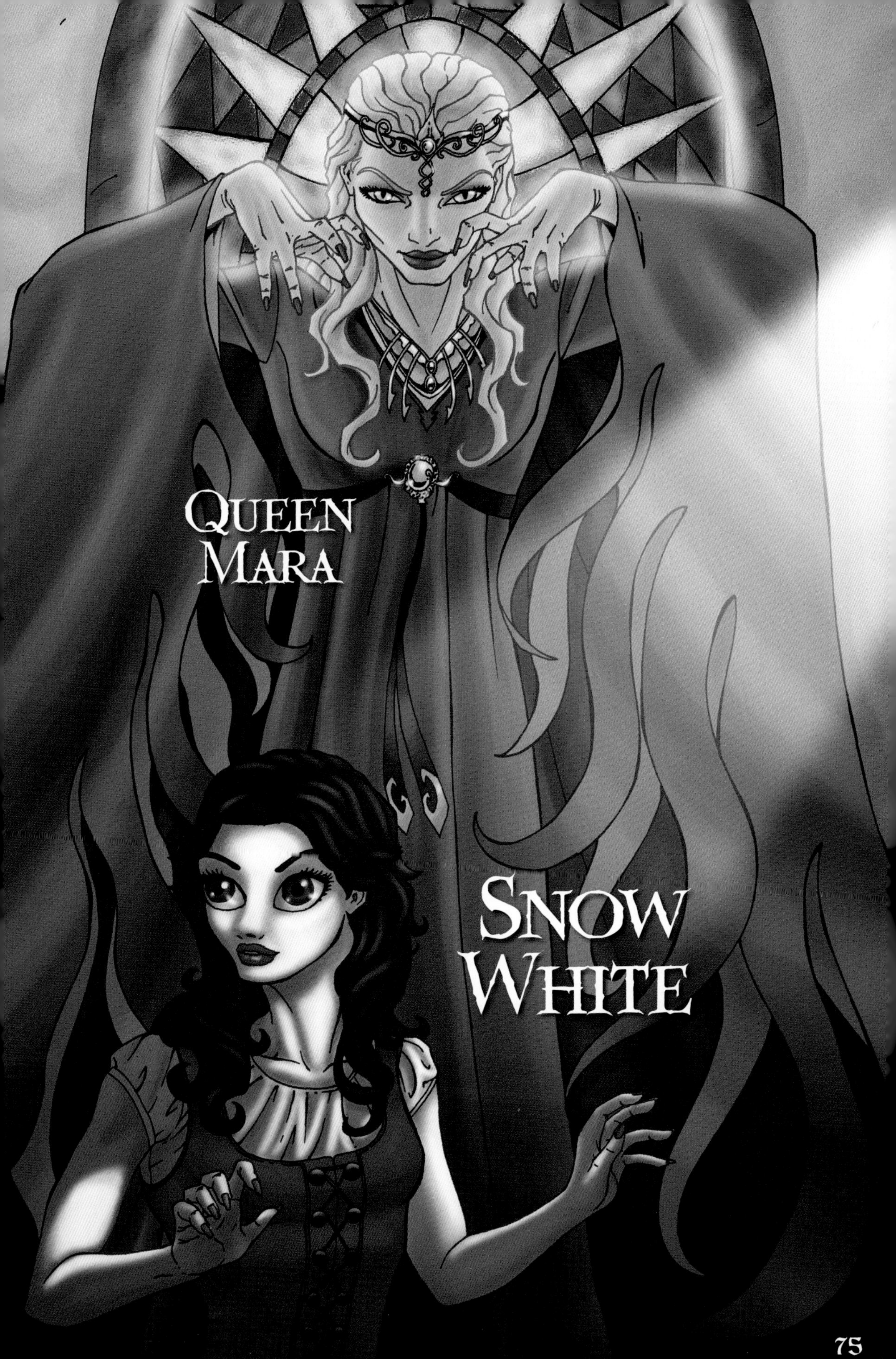
QUEEN MARA
SNOW WHITE

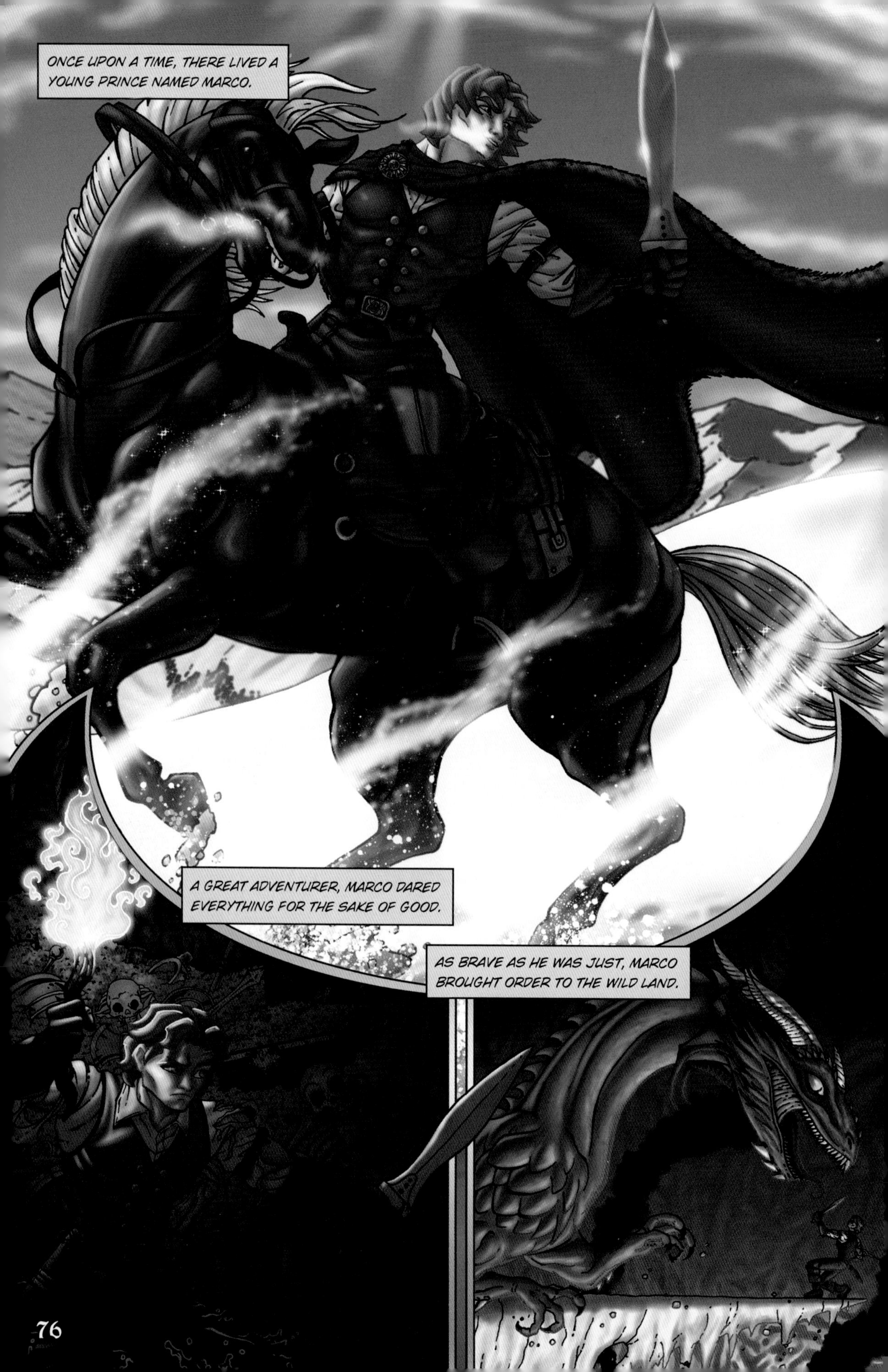
ONCE UPON A TIME, THERE LIVED A YOUNG PRINCE NAMED MARCO.
A GREAT ADVENTURER, MARCO DARED EVERYTHING FOR THE SAKE OF GOOD.
AS BRAVE AS HE WAS JUST, MARCO BROUGHT ORDER TO THE WILD LAND.

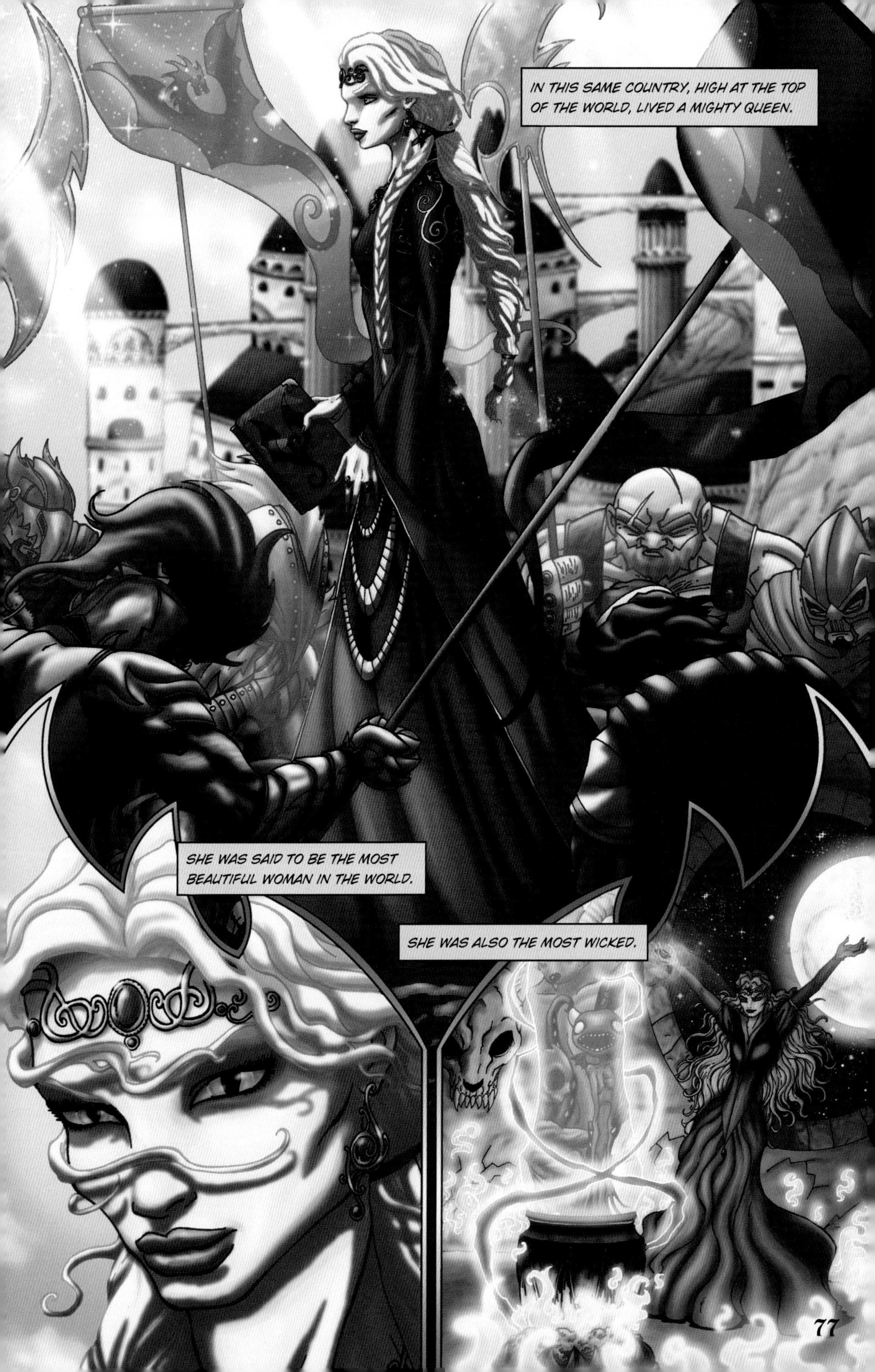
IN THIS SAME COUNTRY, HIGH AT THE TOP OF THE WORLD, LIVED A MIGHTY QUEEN.
SHE WAS SAID TO BE THE MOST BEAUTIFUL WOMAN IN THE WORLD.
SHE WAS ALSO THE MOST WICKED.

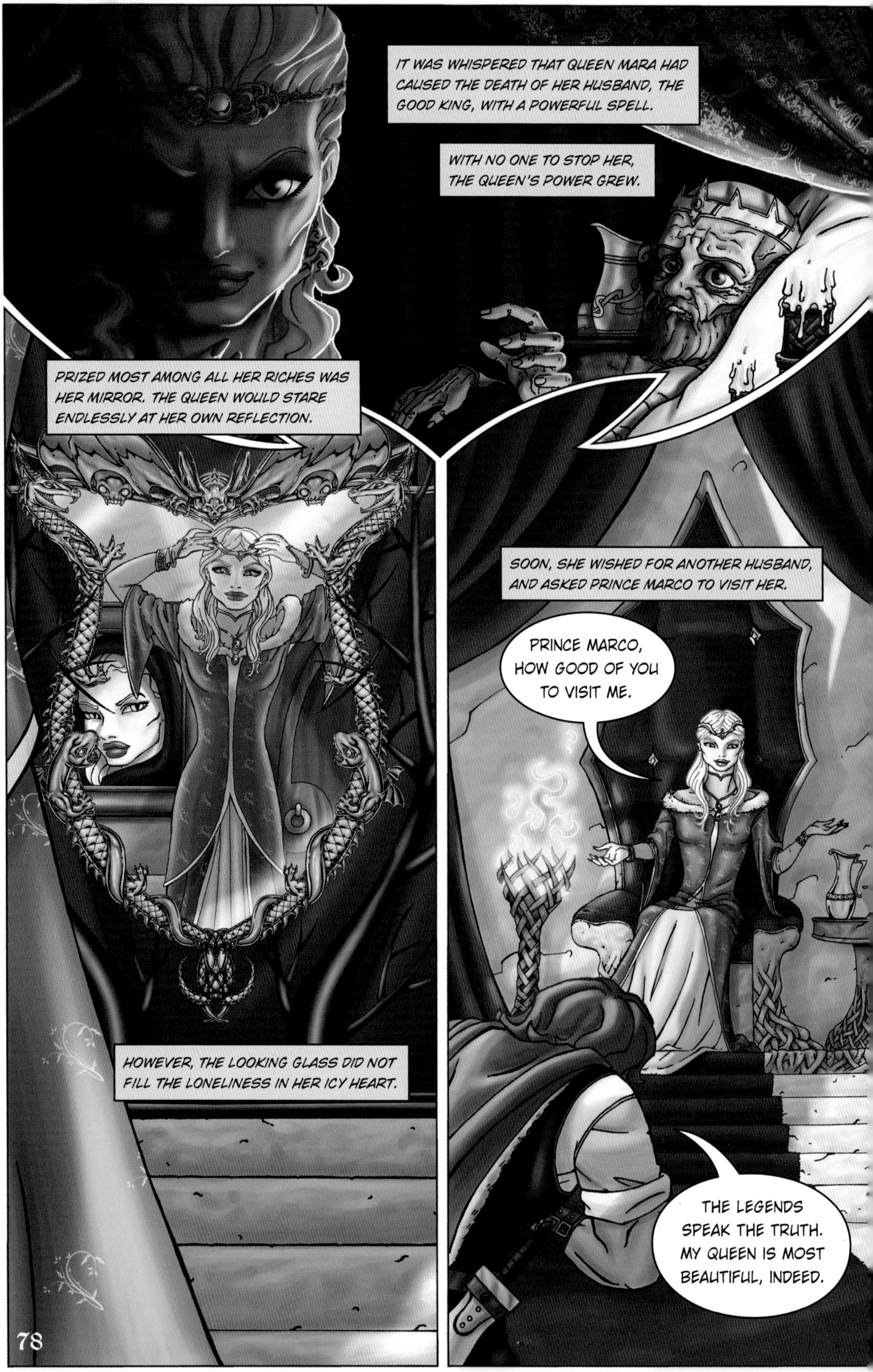
IT WAS WHISPERED THAT QUEEN MARA HAD CAUSED THE DEATH OF HER HUSBAND, THE GOOD KING, WITH A POWERFUL SPELL.
WITH NO ONE TO STOP HER, THE QUEEN'S POWER GREW.
PRIZED MOST AMONG ALL HER RICHES WAS HER MIRROR. THE QUEEN WOULD STARE ENDLESSLY AT HER OWN REFLECTION.
HOWEVER, THE LOOKING GLASS DID NOT FILL THE LONELINESS IN HER ICY HEART.
SOON, SHE WISHED FOR ANOTHER HUSBAND, AND ASKED PRINCE MARCO TO VISIT HER.
PRINCE MARCO, HOW GOOD OF YOU TO VISIT ME.
THE LEGENDS SPEAK THE TRUTH. MY QUEEN IS MOST BEAUTIFUL, INDEED.

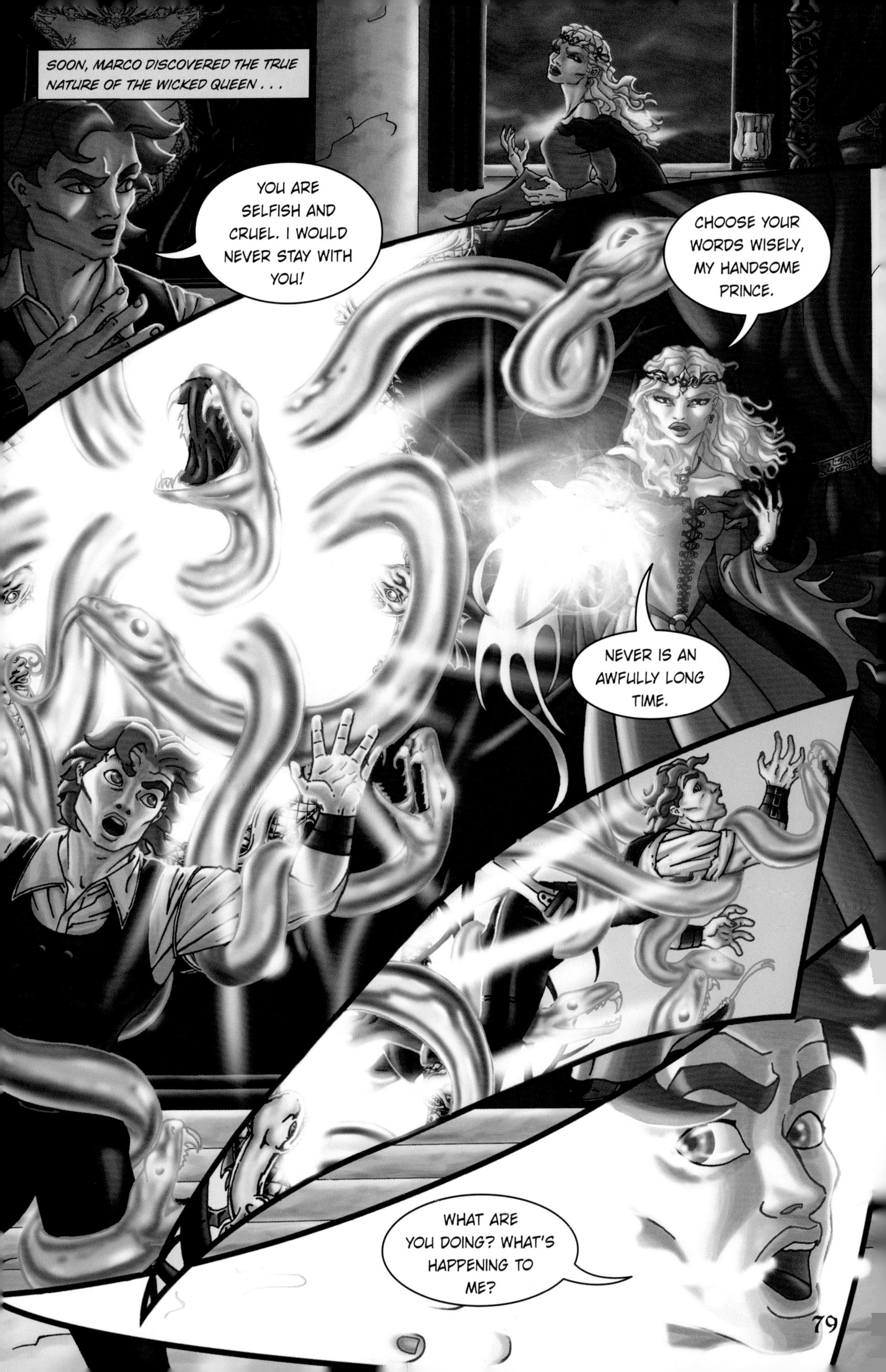
SOON, MARCO DISCOVERED THE TRUE NATURE OF THE WICKED QUEEN . . .
YOU ARE SELFISH AND CRUEL. I WOULD NEVER STAY WITH YOU!
CHOOSE YOUR WORDS WISELY, MY HANDSOME PRINCE.
NEVER IS AN AWFULLY LONG TIME.
WHAT ARE YOU DOING? WHAT'S HAPPENING TO ME?

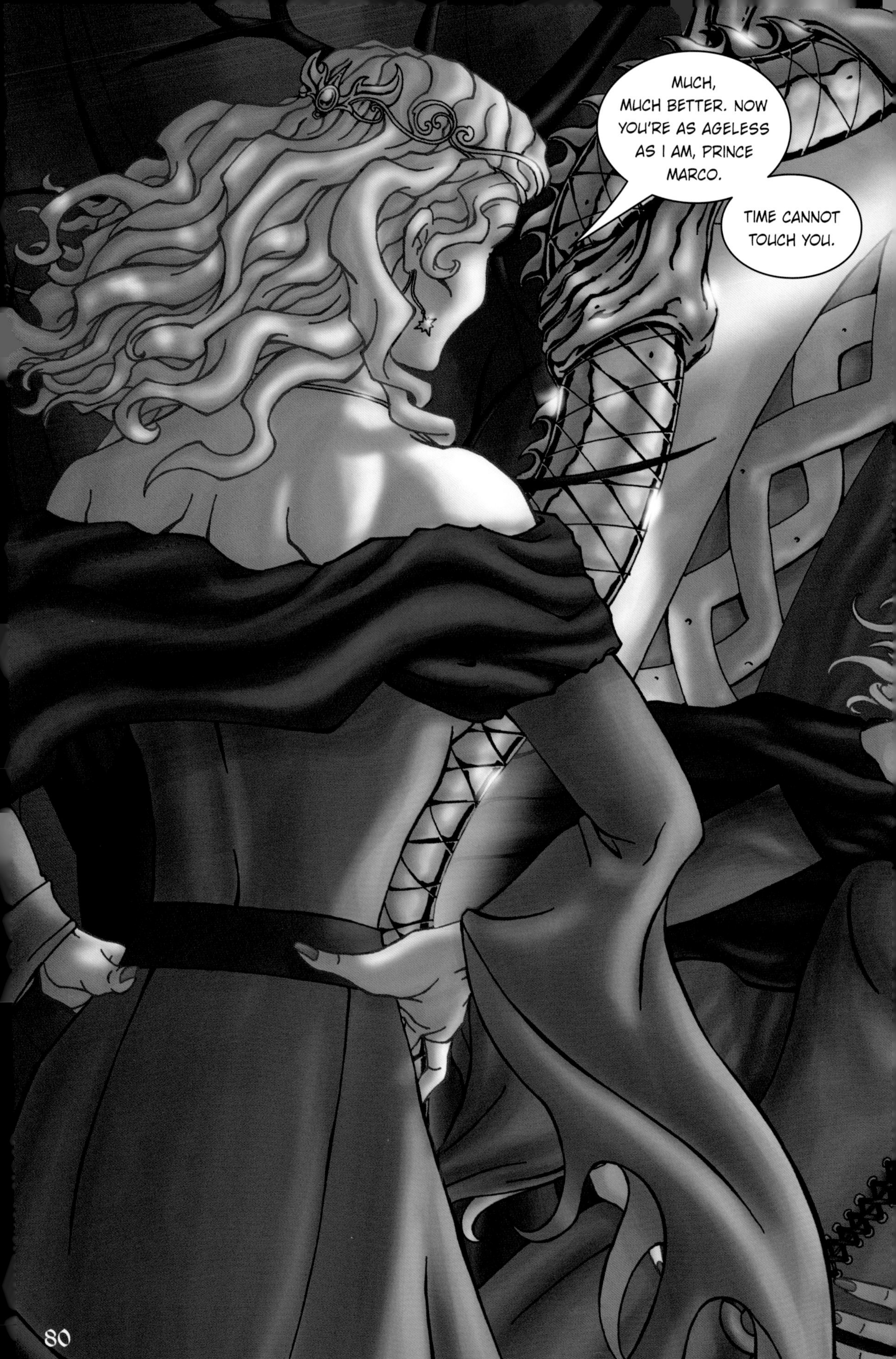
MUCH, MUCH BETTER. NOW YOU'RE AS AGELESS AS I AM, PRINCE MARCO.
TIME CANNOT TOUCH YOU.

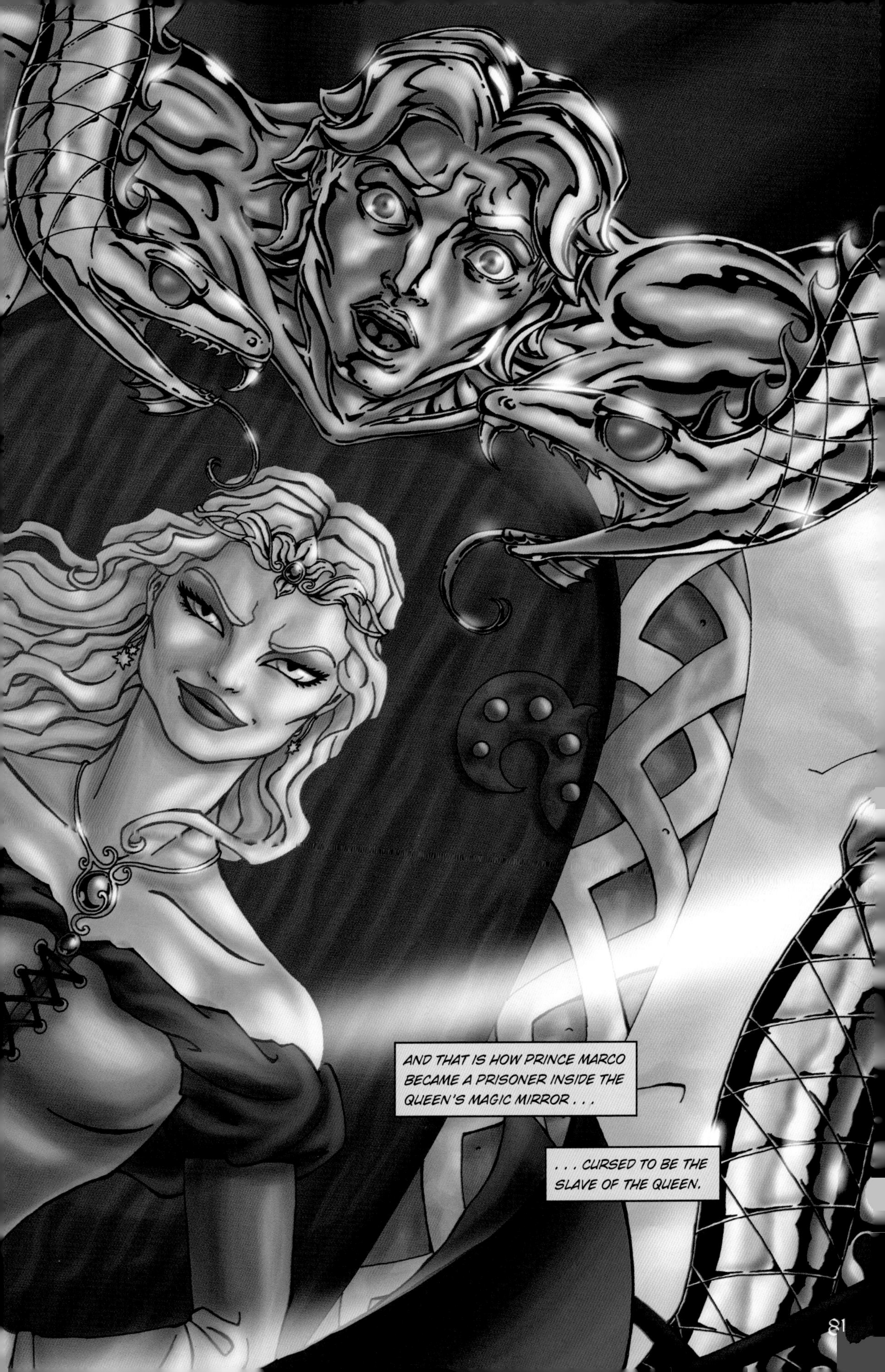
AND THAT IS HOW PRINCE MARCO BECAME A PRISONER INSIDE THE QUEEN'S MAGIC MIRROR . . .
. . . CURSED TO BE THE SLAVE OF THE QUEEN.

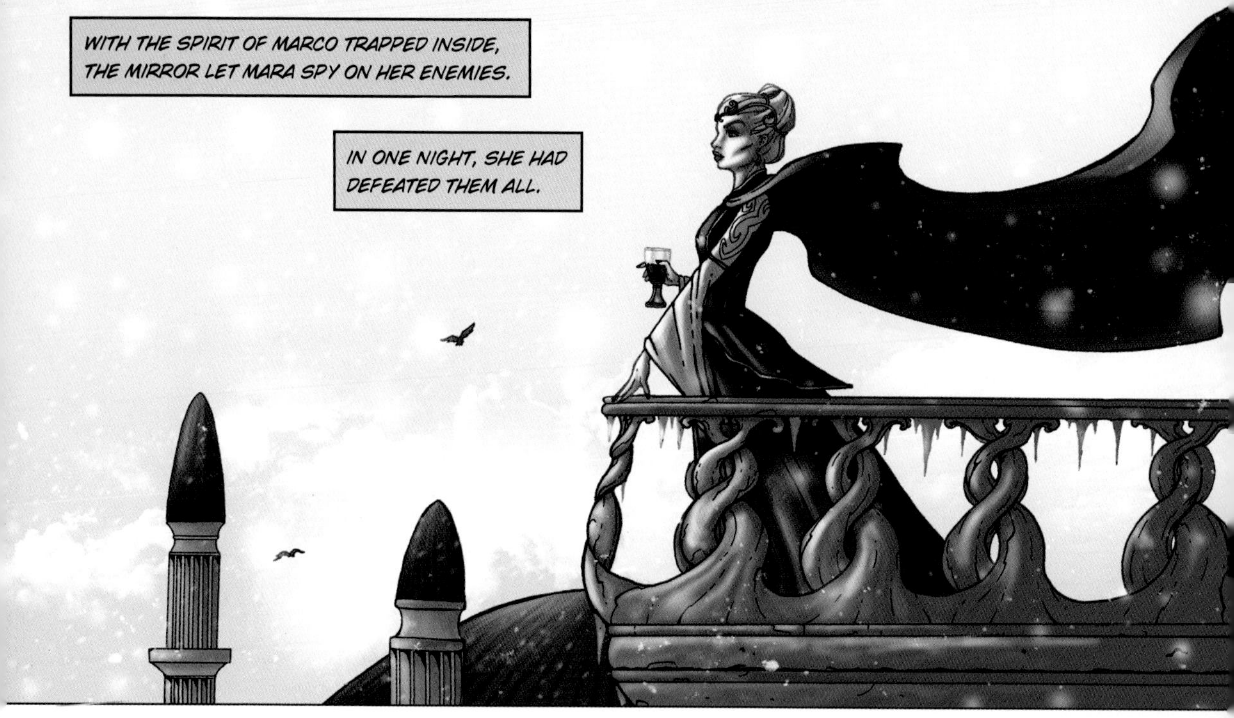
WITH THE SPIRIT OF MARCO TRAPPED INSIDE, THE MIRROR LET MARA SPY ON HER ENEMIES.
IN ONE NIGHT, SHE HAD DEFEATED THEM ALL.

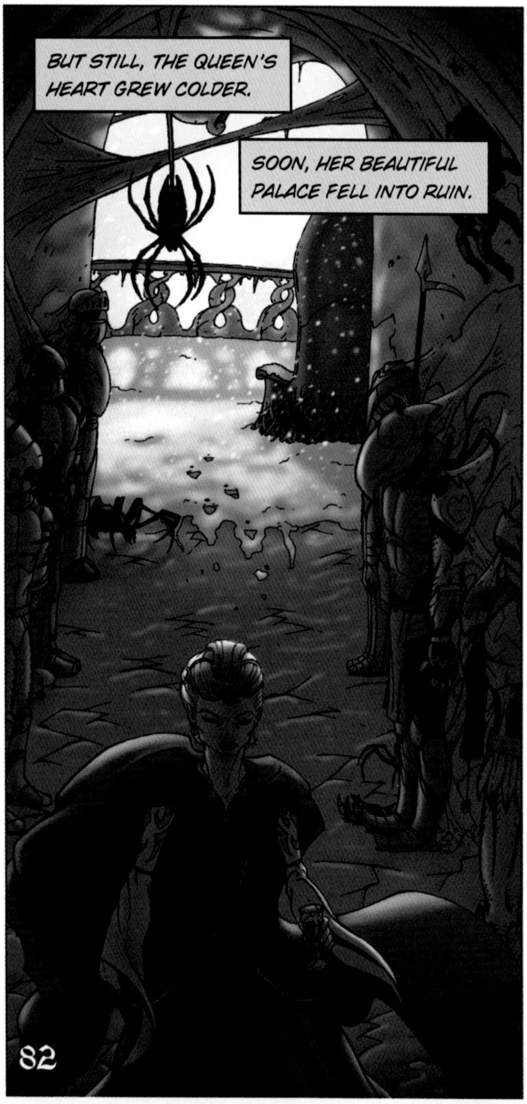
BUT STILL, THE QUEEN'S HEART GREW COLDER.
SOON, HER BEAUTIFUL PALACE FELL INTO RUIN.

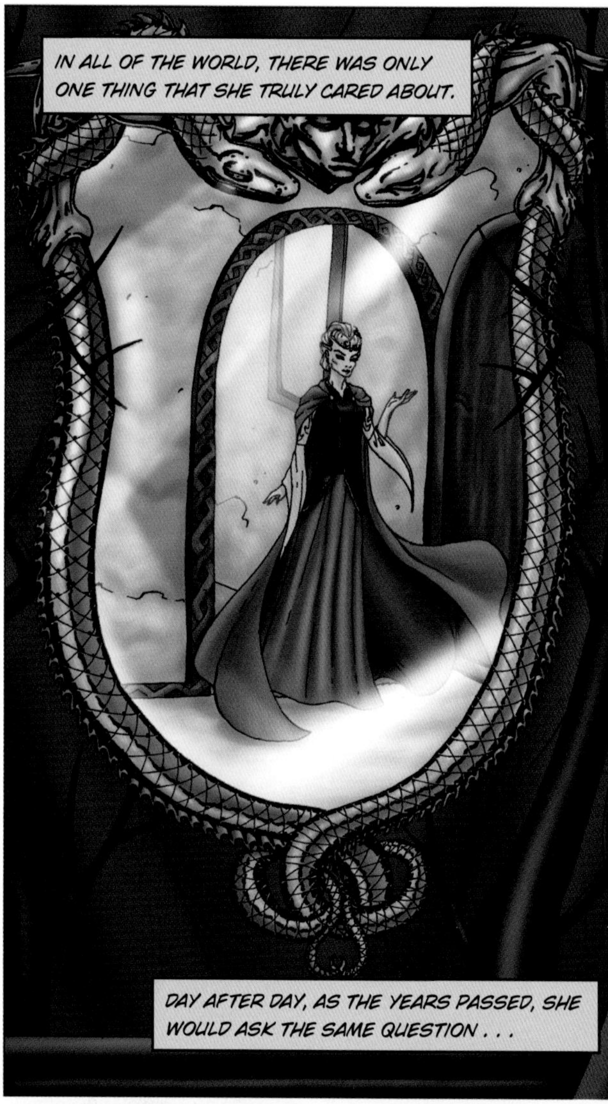
IN ALL OF THE WORLD, THERE WAS ONLY ONE THING THAT SHE TRULY CARED ABOUT.
DAY AFTER DAY, AS THE YEARS PASSED, SHE WOULD ASK THE SAME QUESTION . . .

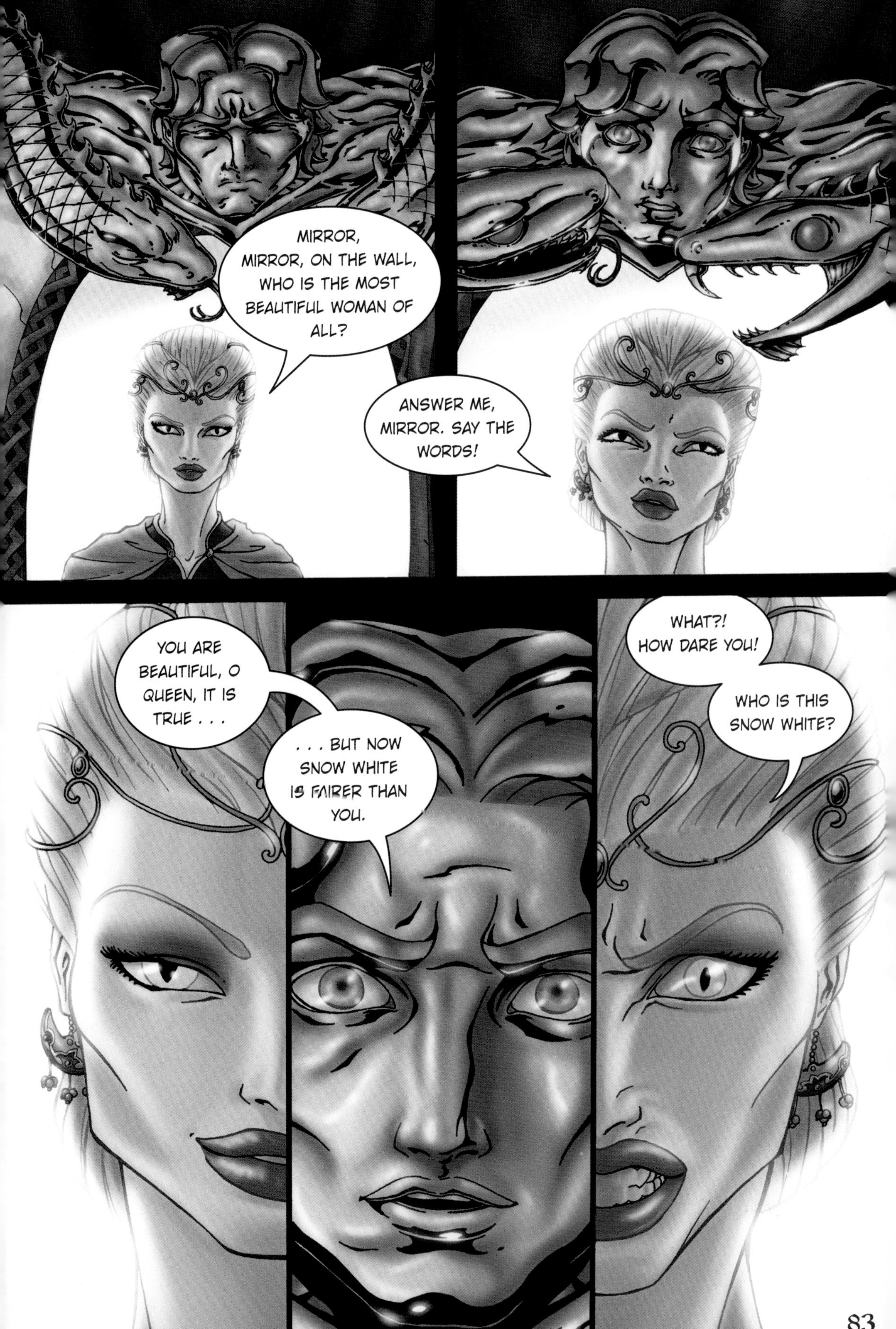
MIRROR, MIRROR, ON THE WALL, WHO IS THE MOST BEAUTIFUL WOMAN OF ALL?
ANSWER ME, MIRROR. SAY THE WORDS!
YOU ARE BEAUTIFUL, O QUEEN, IT IS TRUE . . .
. . . BUT NOW SNOW WHITE IS FAIRER THAN YOU.
WHAT?! HOW DARE YOU!
WHO IS THIS SNOW WHITE?

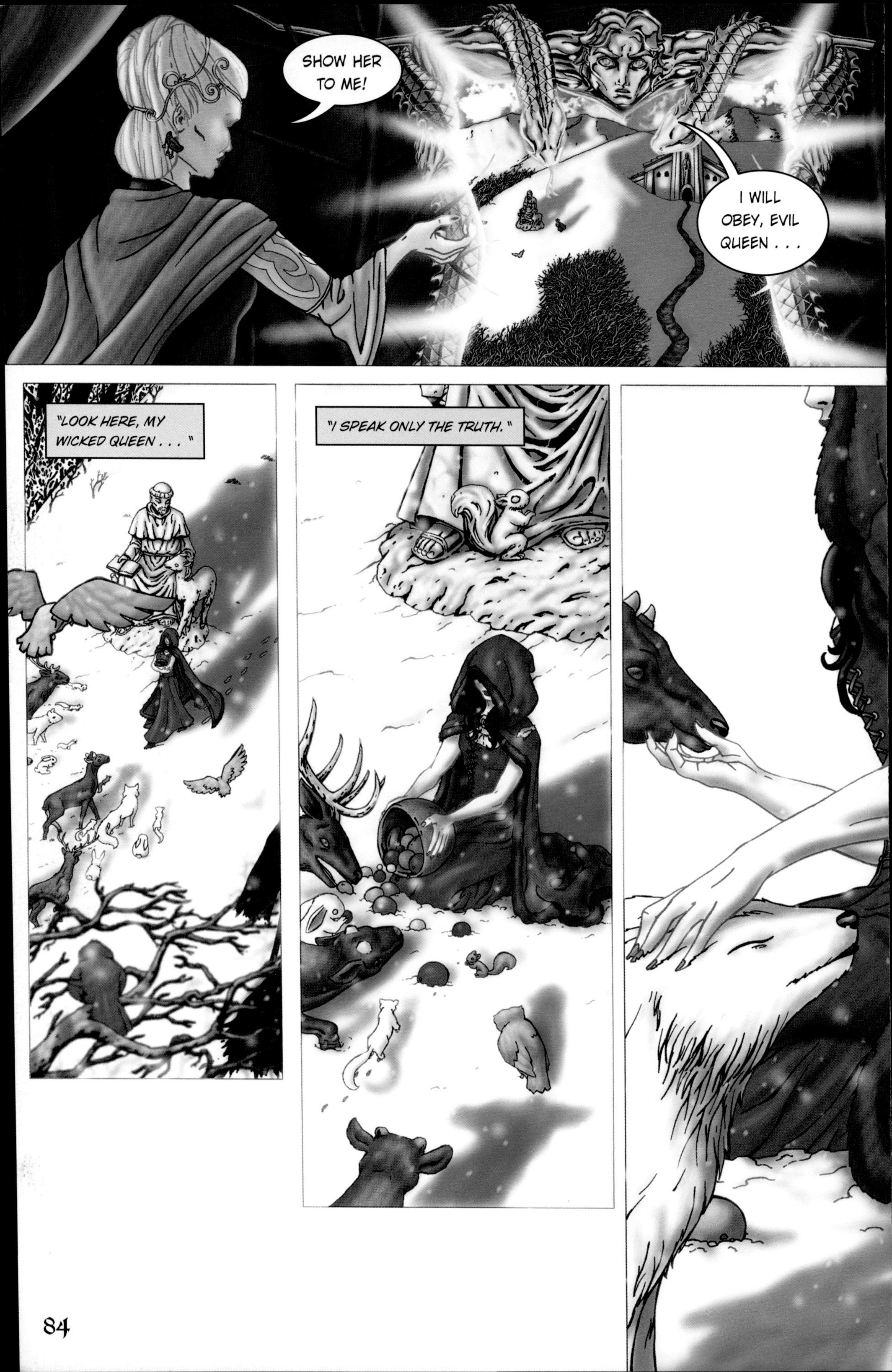
SHOW HER TO ME!
I WILL OBEY, EVIL QUEEN . . .
"LOOK HERE, MY WICKED QUEEN . . . "
"I SPEAK ONLY THE TRUTH."

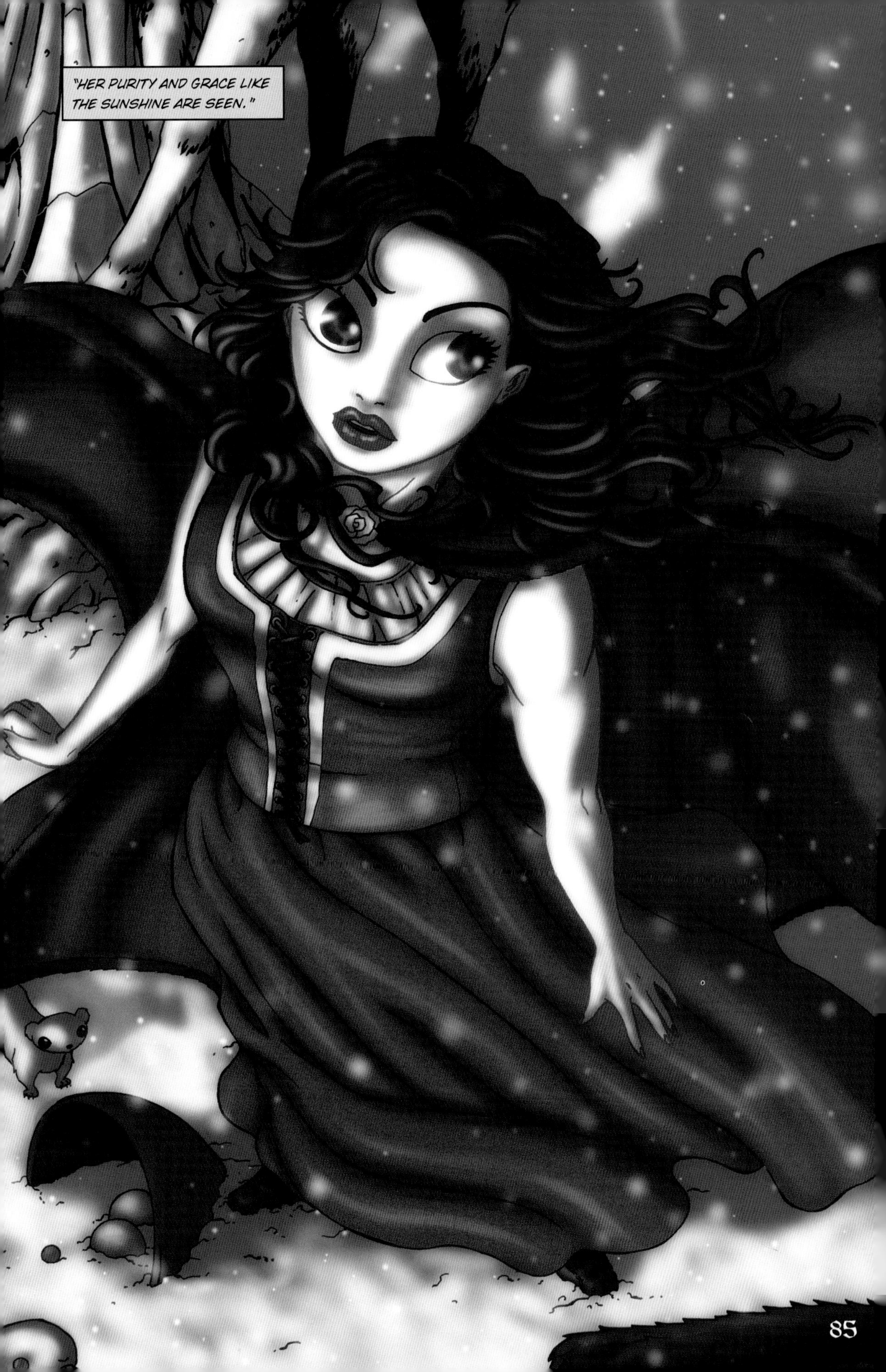
"HER PURITY AND GRACE LIKE THE SUNSHINE ARE SEEN."

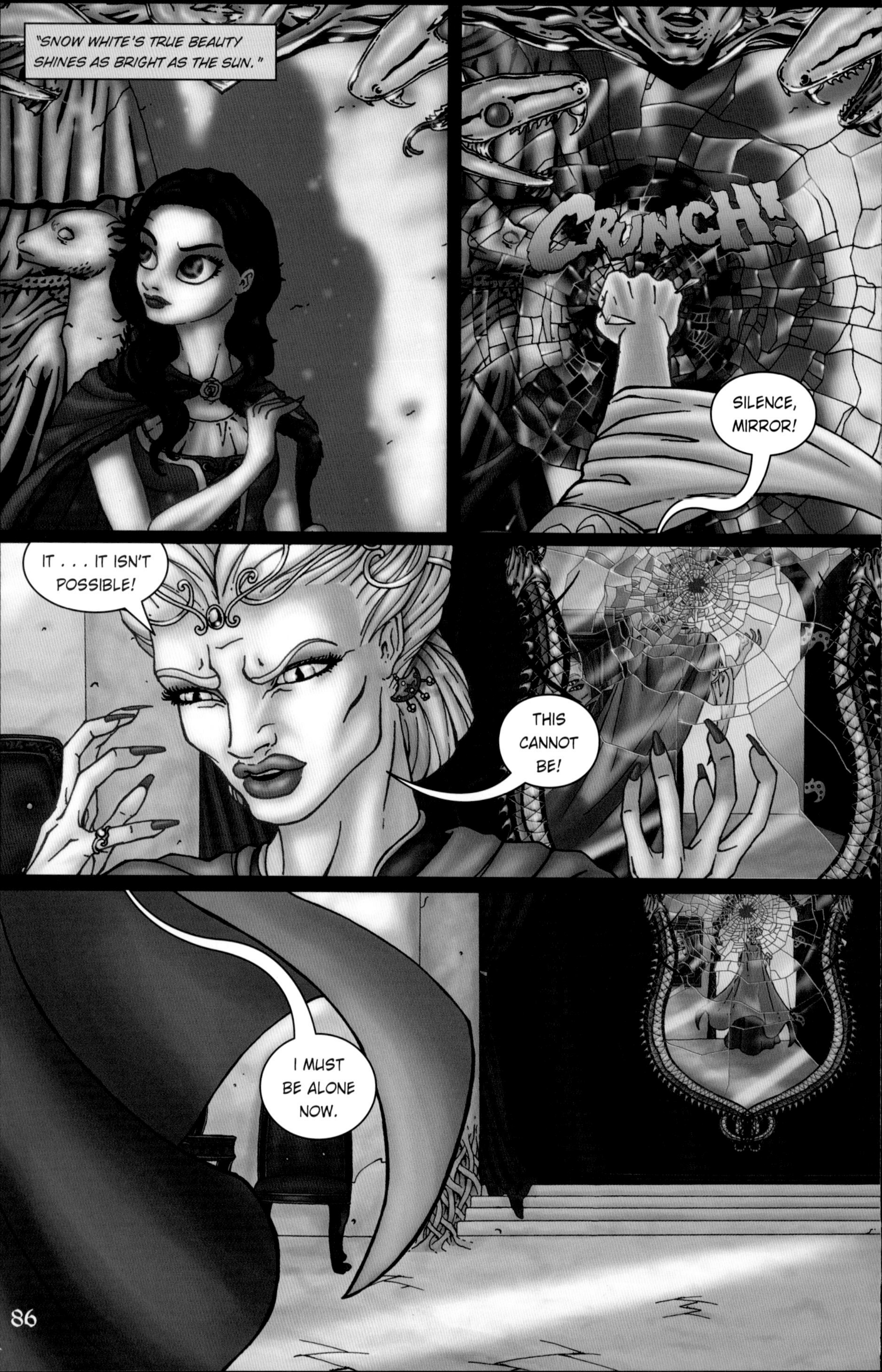
"SNOW WHITE'S TRUE BEAUTY SHINES AS BRIGHT AS THE SUN."
CRUNCH!
SILENCE, MIRROR!
IT . . . IT ISN'T POSSIBLE!
THIS CANNOT BE!
I MUST BE ALONE NOW.

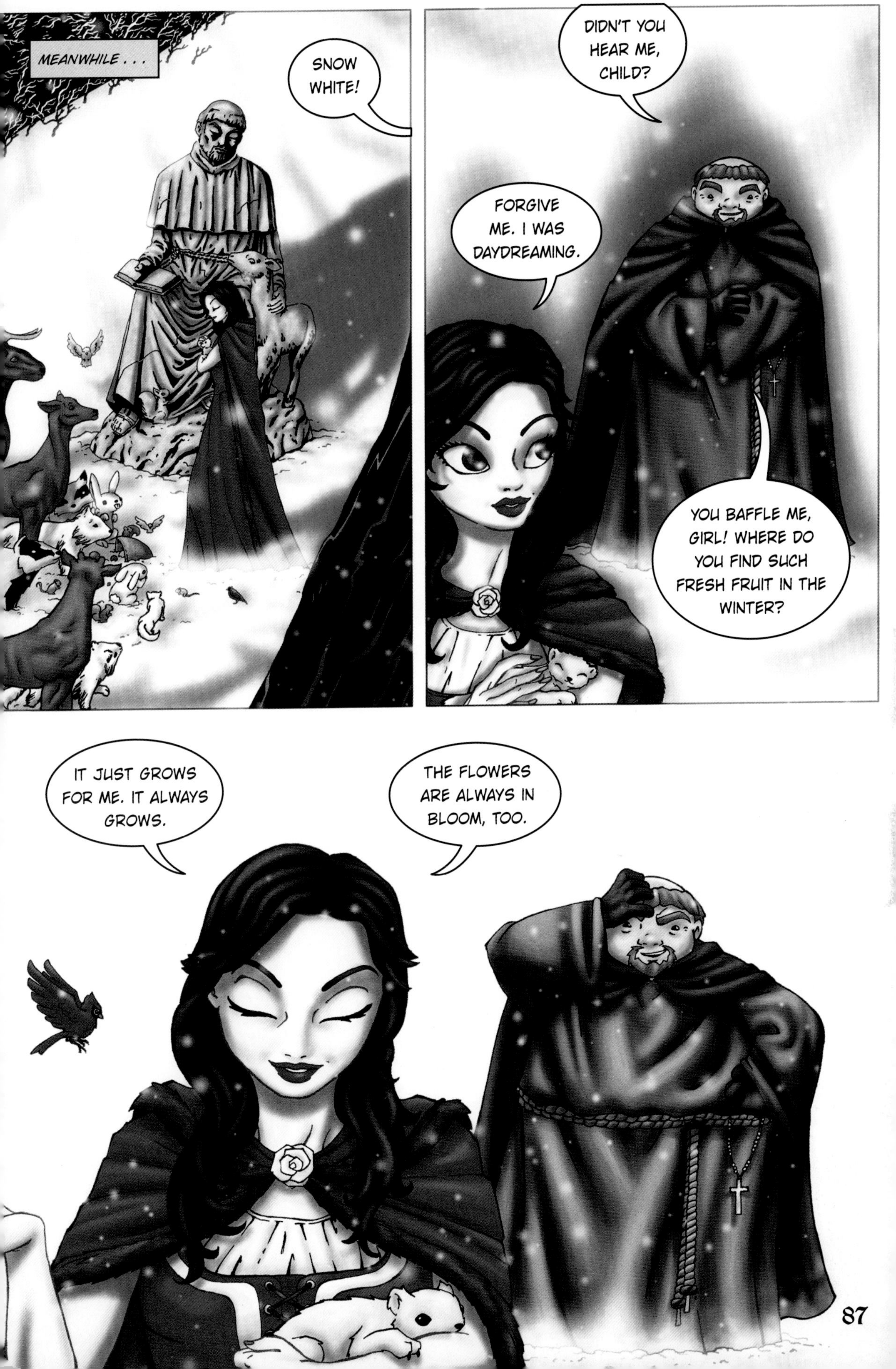
MEANWHILE . . .
SNOW WHITE!
DIDN'T YOU HEAR ME, CHILD?
FORGIVE ME. I WAS DAYDREAMING.
YOU BAFFLE ME, GIRL! WHERE DO YOU FIND SUCH FRESH FRUIT IN THE WINTER?
IT JUST GROWS FOR ME. IT ALWAYS GROWS.
THE FLOWERS ARE ALWAYS IN BLOOM, TOO.

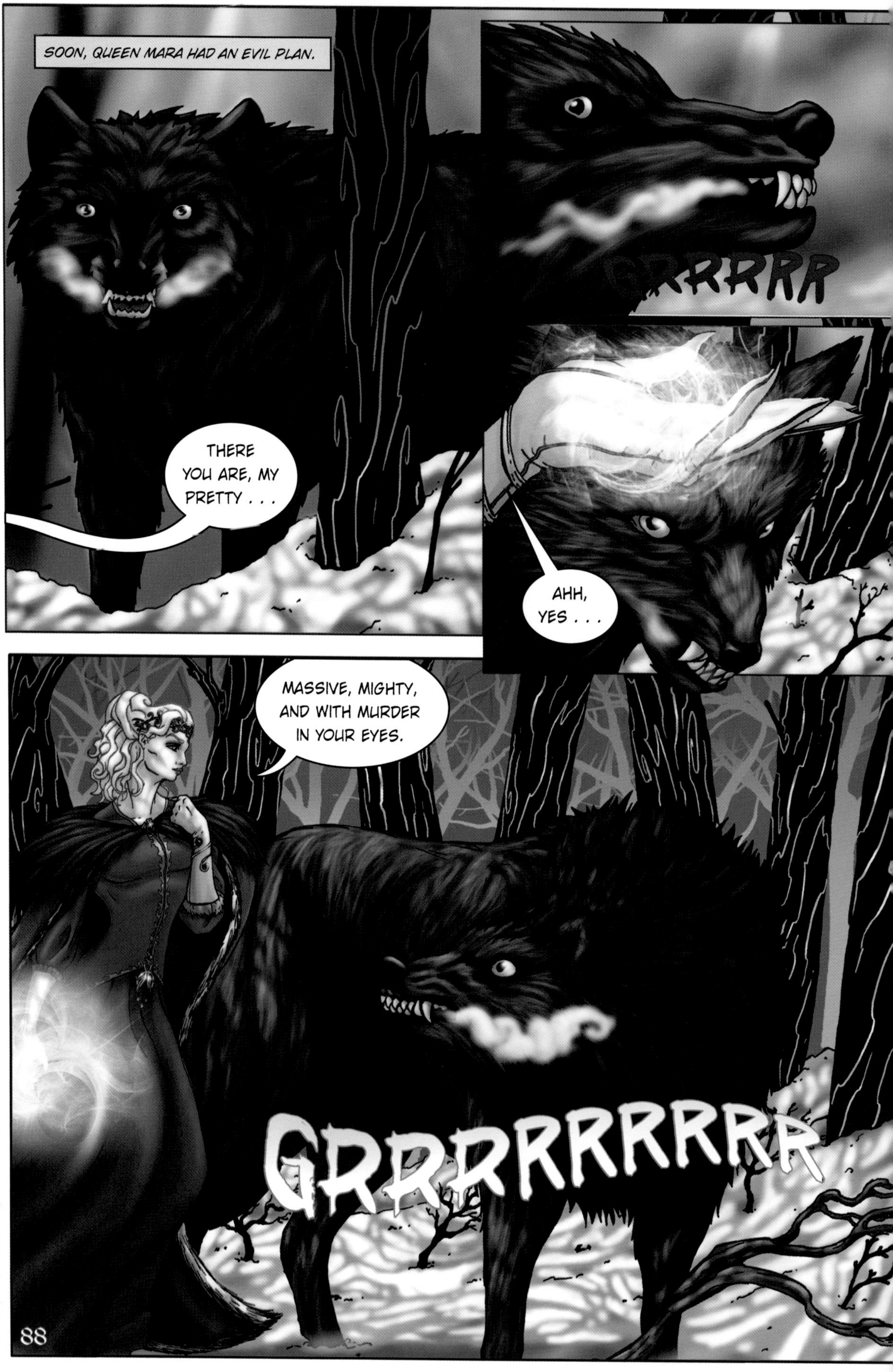
SOON, QUEEN MARA HAD AN EVIL PLAN.
GRRRRRR
THERE YOU ARE, MY PRETTY . . .
AHH, YES . . .
MASSIVE, MIGHTY, AND WITH MURDER IN YOUR EYES.
GRRRRRRRRR

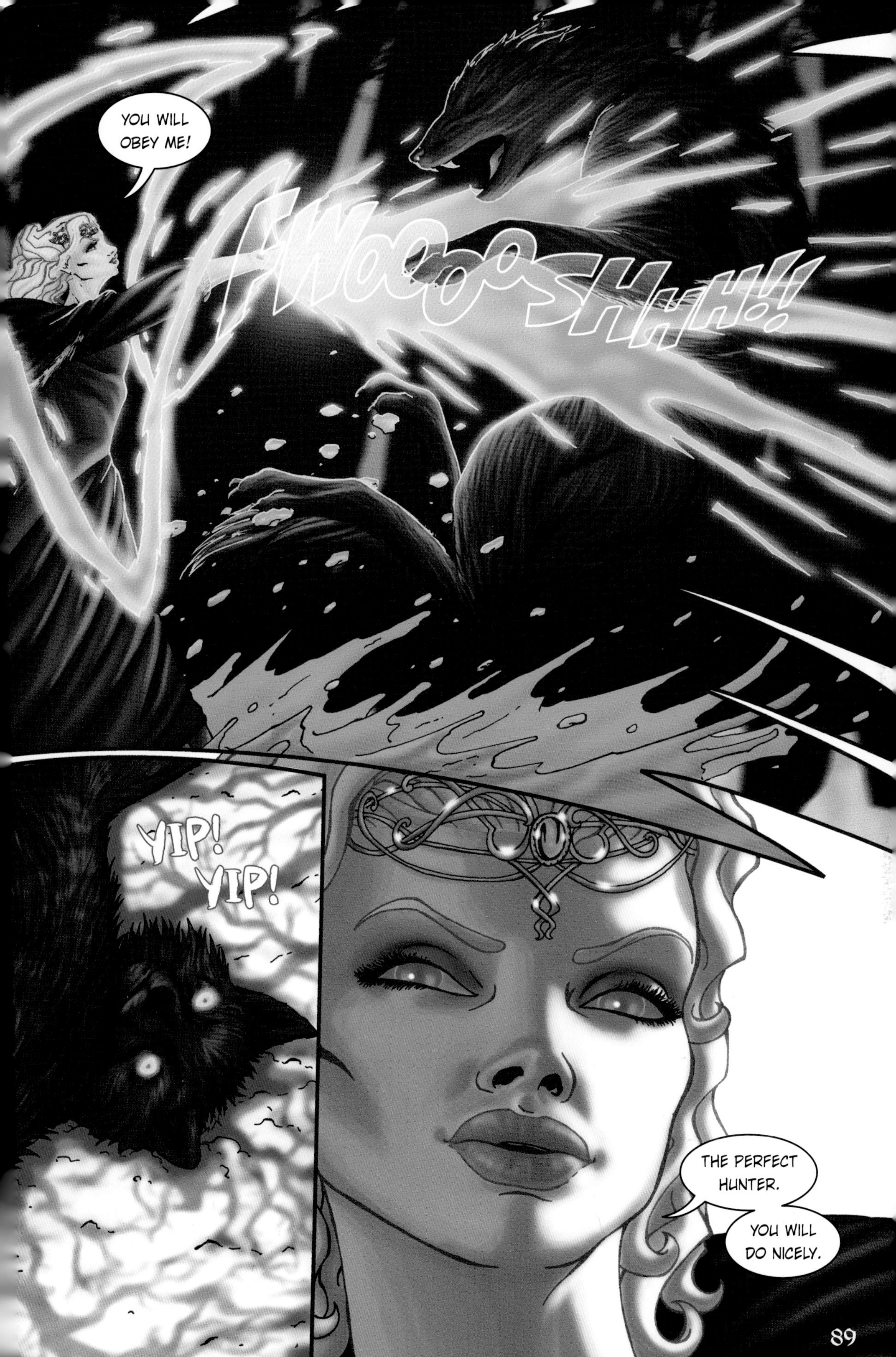
YOU WILL OBEY ME!
FWOOOOSHHH!!
YIP! YIP!
THE PERFECT HUNTER.
YOU WILL DO NICELY.

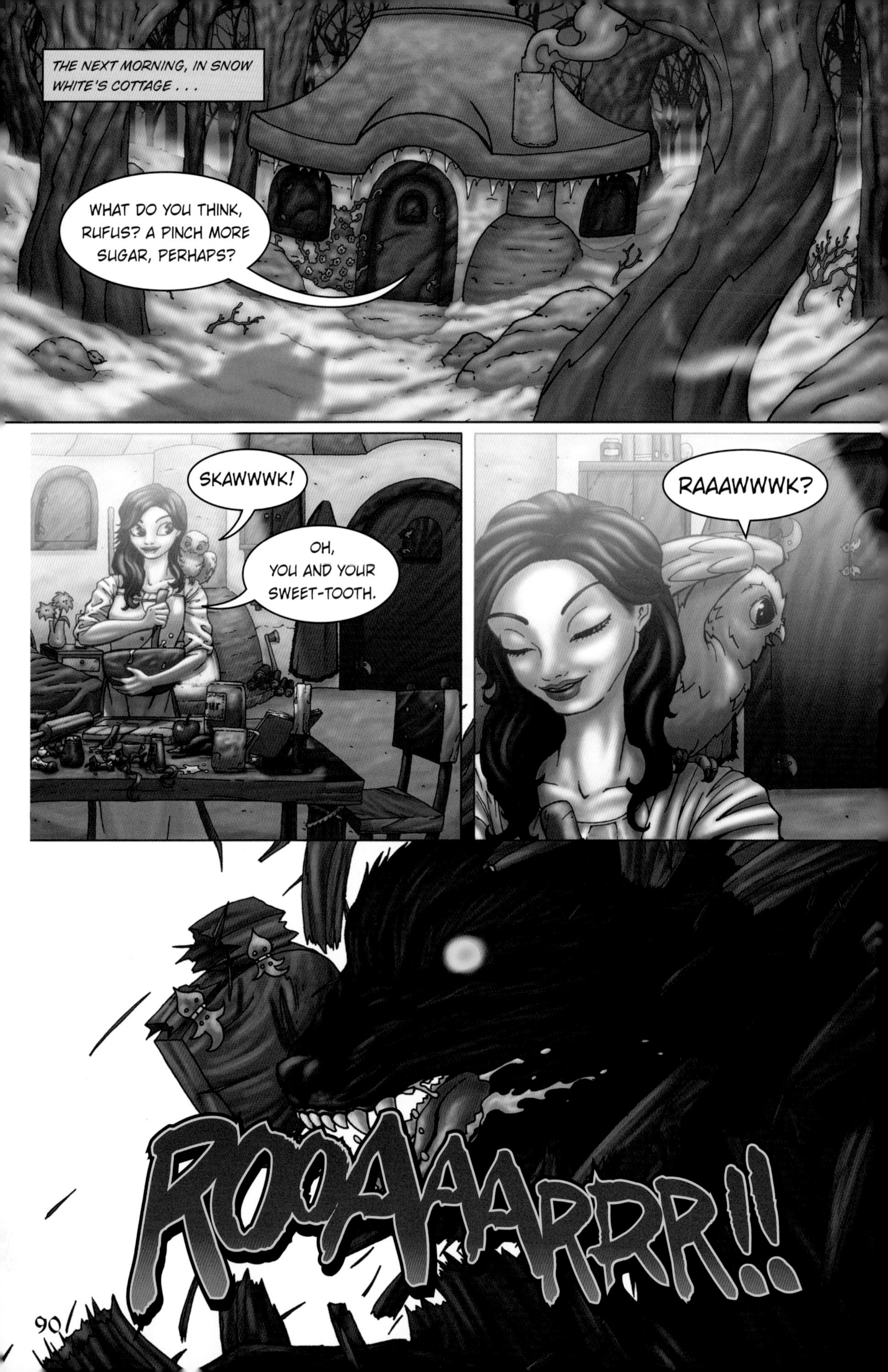
THE NEXT MORNING, IN SNOW WHITE'S COTTAGE . . .
WHAT DO YOU THINK, RUFUS? A PINCH MORE SUGAR, PERHAPS?
SKAWWWK!
OH, YOU AND YOUR SWEET-TOOTH.
RAAAWWWK?
ROOAAARRR!!

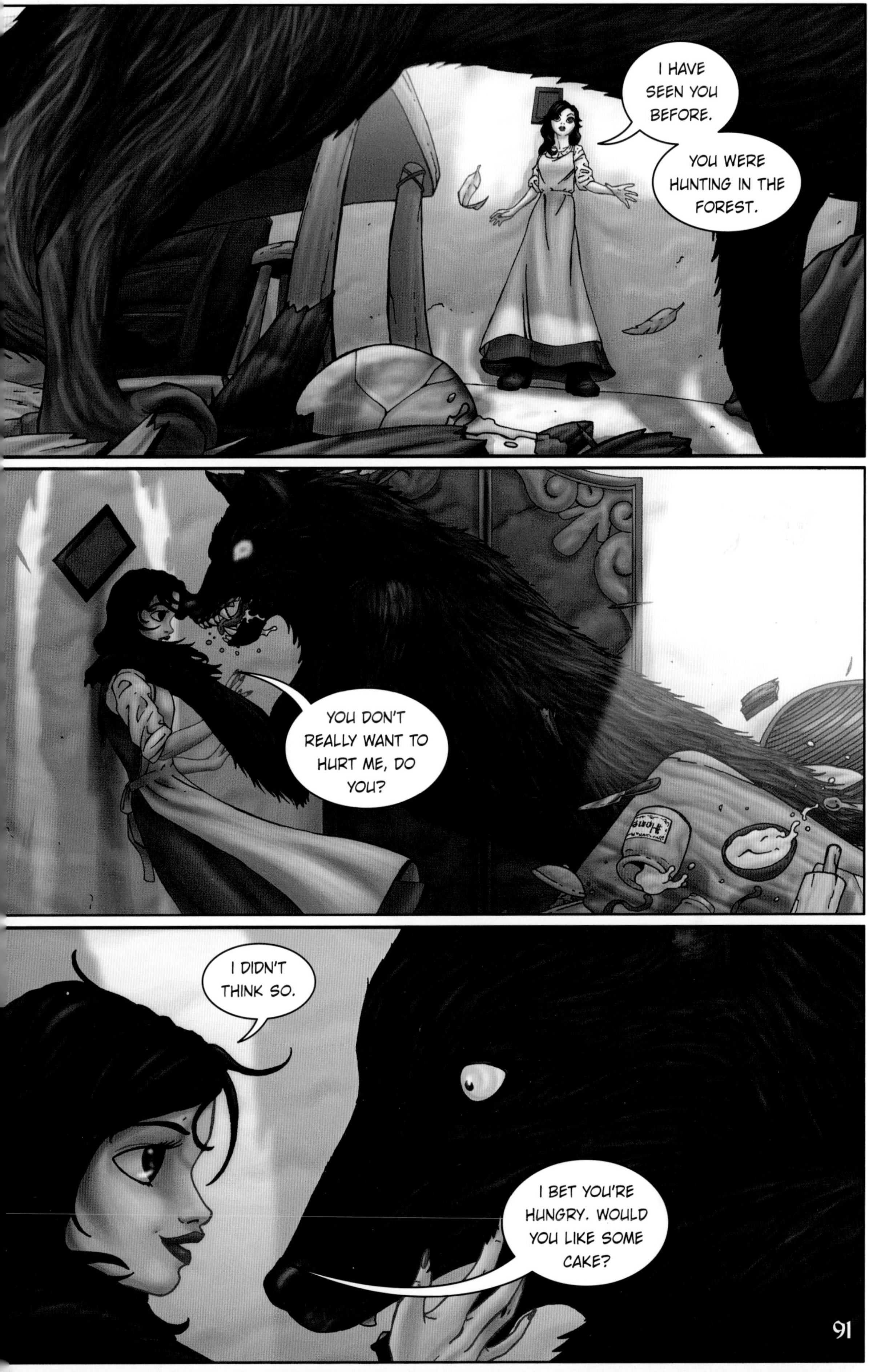
I HAVE SEEN YOU BEFORE.
YOU WERE HUNTING IN THE FOREST.
YOU DON'T REALLY WANT TO HURT ME, DO YOU?
I DIDN'T THINK SO.
I BET YOU'RE HUNGRY. WOULD YOU LIKE SOME CAKE?

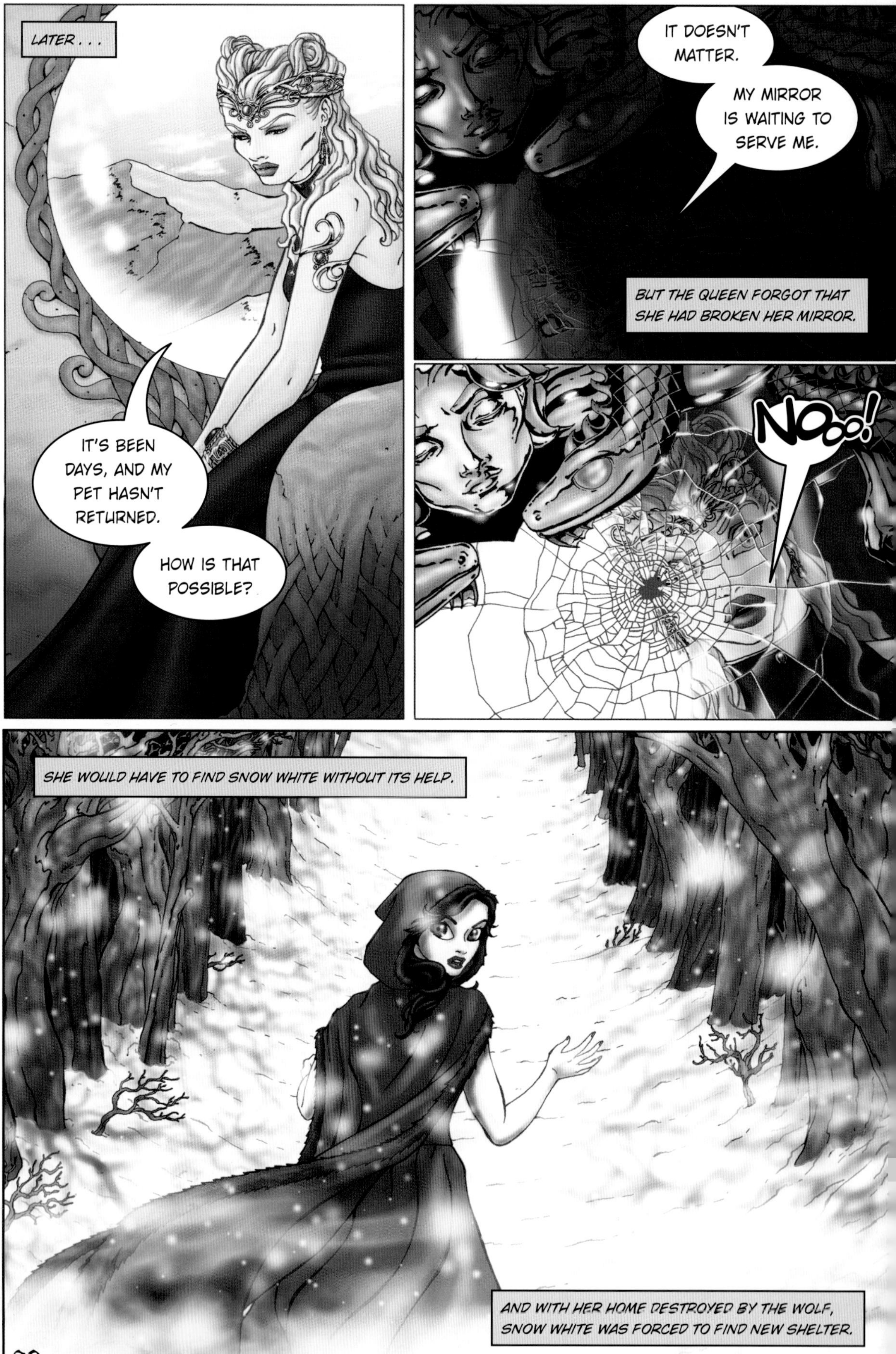
LATER . . .
IT'S BEEN DAYS, AND MY PET HASN'T RETURNED.
HOW IS THAT POSSIBLE?
IT DOESN'T MATTER.
MY MIRROR IS WAITING TO SERVE ME.
BUT THE QUEEN FORGOT THAT SHE HAD BROKEN HER MIRROR.
NOooo!
SHE WOULD HAVE TO FIND SNOW WHITE WITHOUT ITS HELP.
AND WITH HER HOME DESTROYED BY THE WOLF, SNOW WHITE WAS FORCED TO FIND NEW SHELTER.

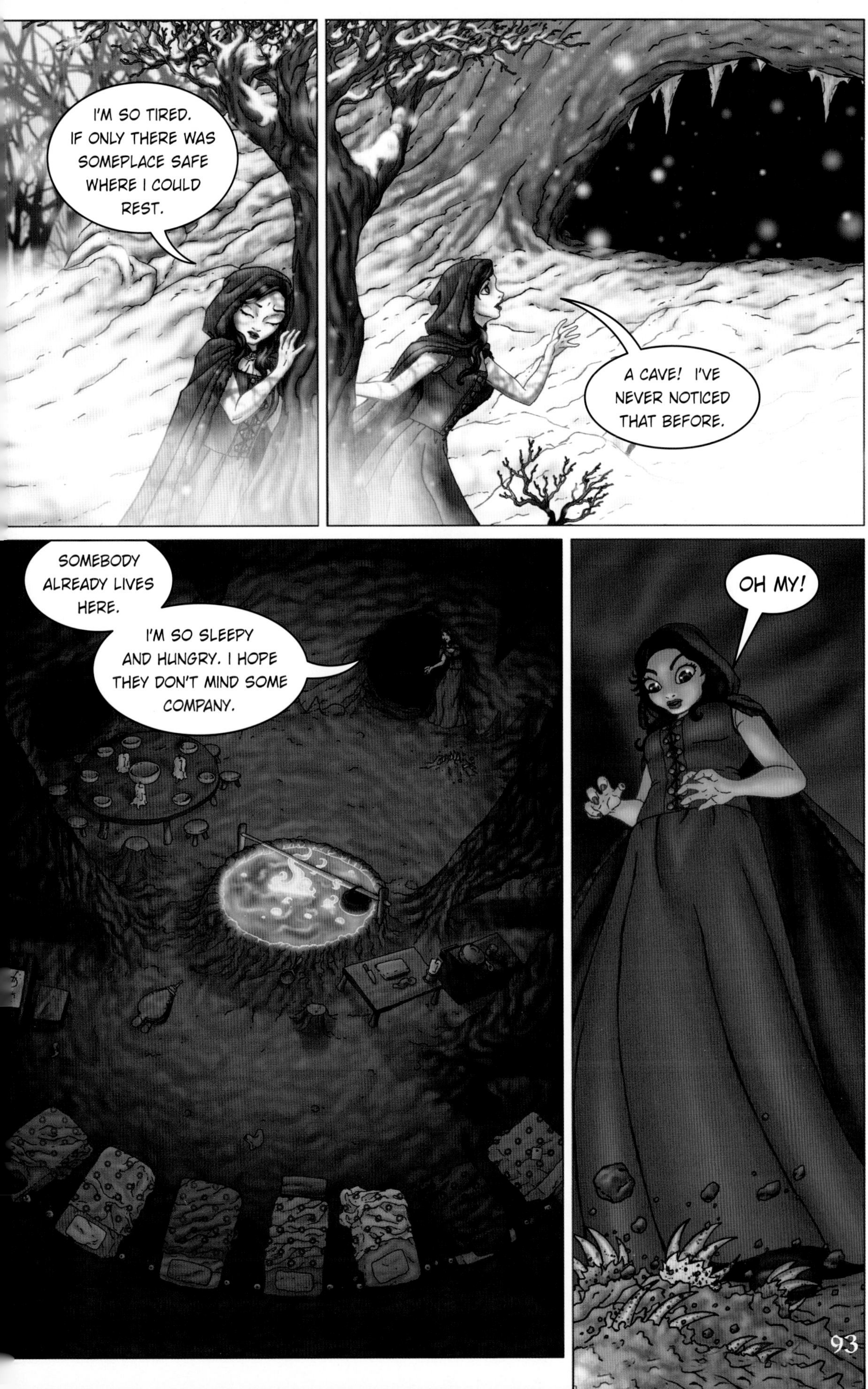
I'M SO TIRED. IF ONLY THERE WAS SOMEPLACE SAFE WHERE I COULD REST.
A CAVE! I'VE NEVER NOTICED THAT BEFORE.
SOMEBODY ALREADY LIVES HERE.
I'M SO SLEEPY AND HUNGRY. I HOPE THEY DON'T MIND SOME COMPANY.
OH MY!

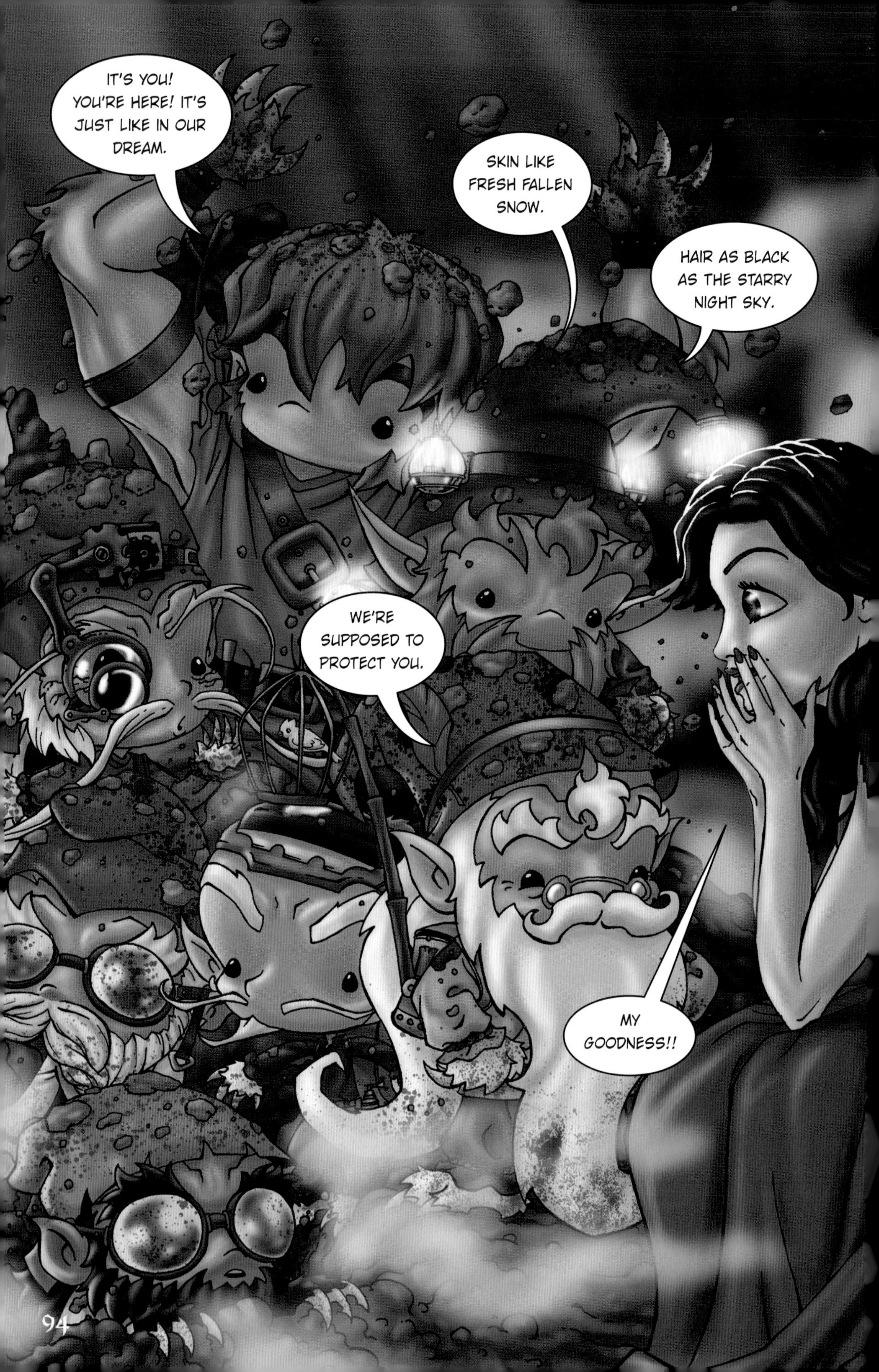
IT'S YOU! YOU'RE HERE! IT'S JUST LIKE IN OUR DREAM.
SKIN LIKE FRESH FALLEN SNOW.
HAIR AS BLACK AS THE STARRY NIGHT SKY.
WE'RE SUPPOSED TO PROTECT YOU.
MY GOODNESS!!

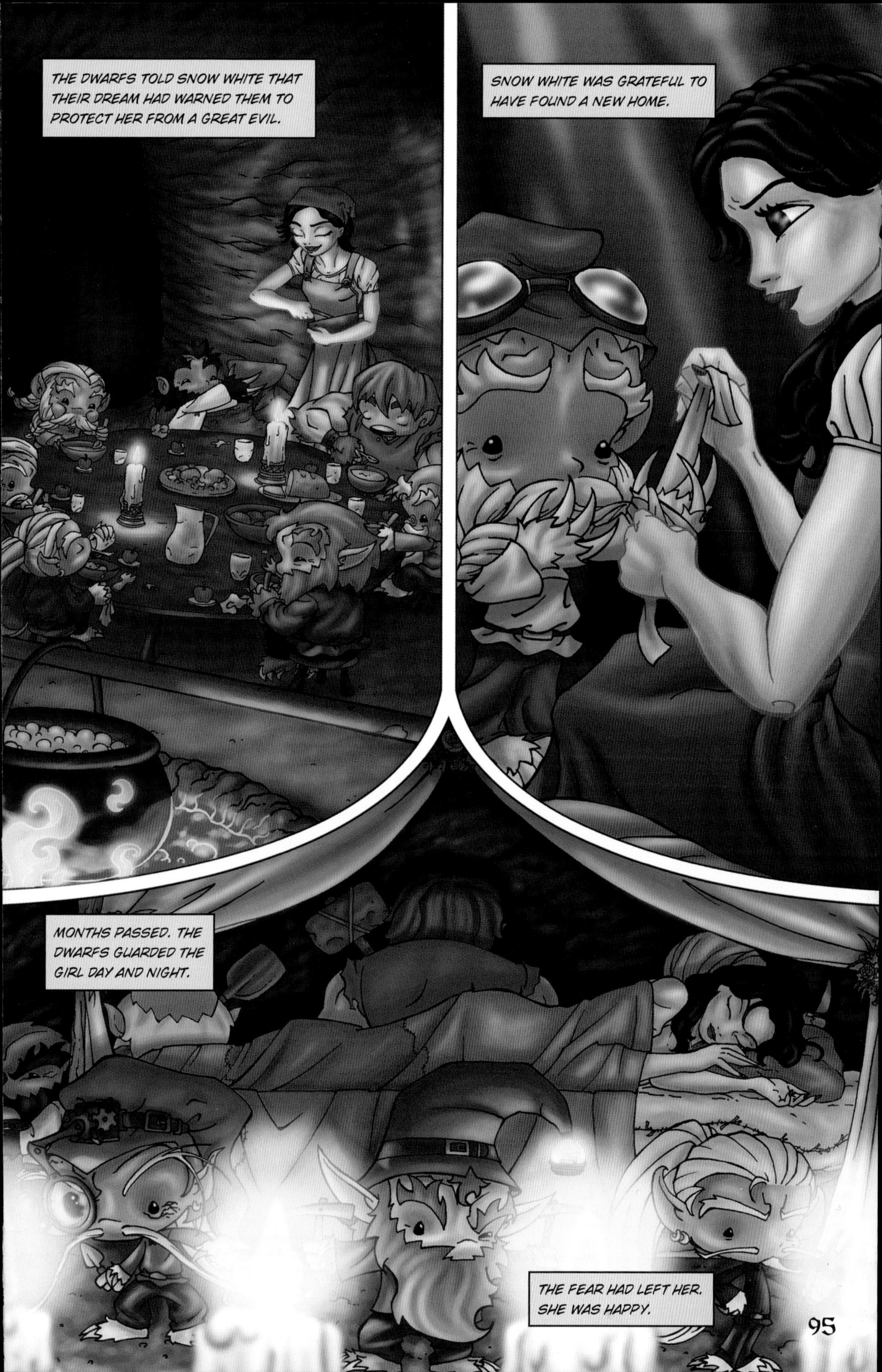
THE DWARFS TOLD SNOW WHITE THAT THEIR DREAM HAD WARNED THEM TO PROTECT HER FROM A GREAT EVIL.
SNOW WHITE WAS GRATEFUL TO HAVE FOUND A NEW HOME.
MONTHS PASSED. THE DWARFS GUARDED THE GIRL DAY AND NIGHT.
THE FEAR HAD LEFT HER. SHE WAS HAPPY.

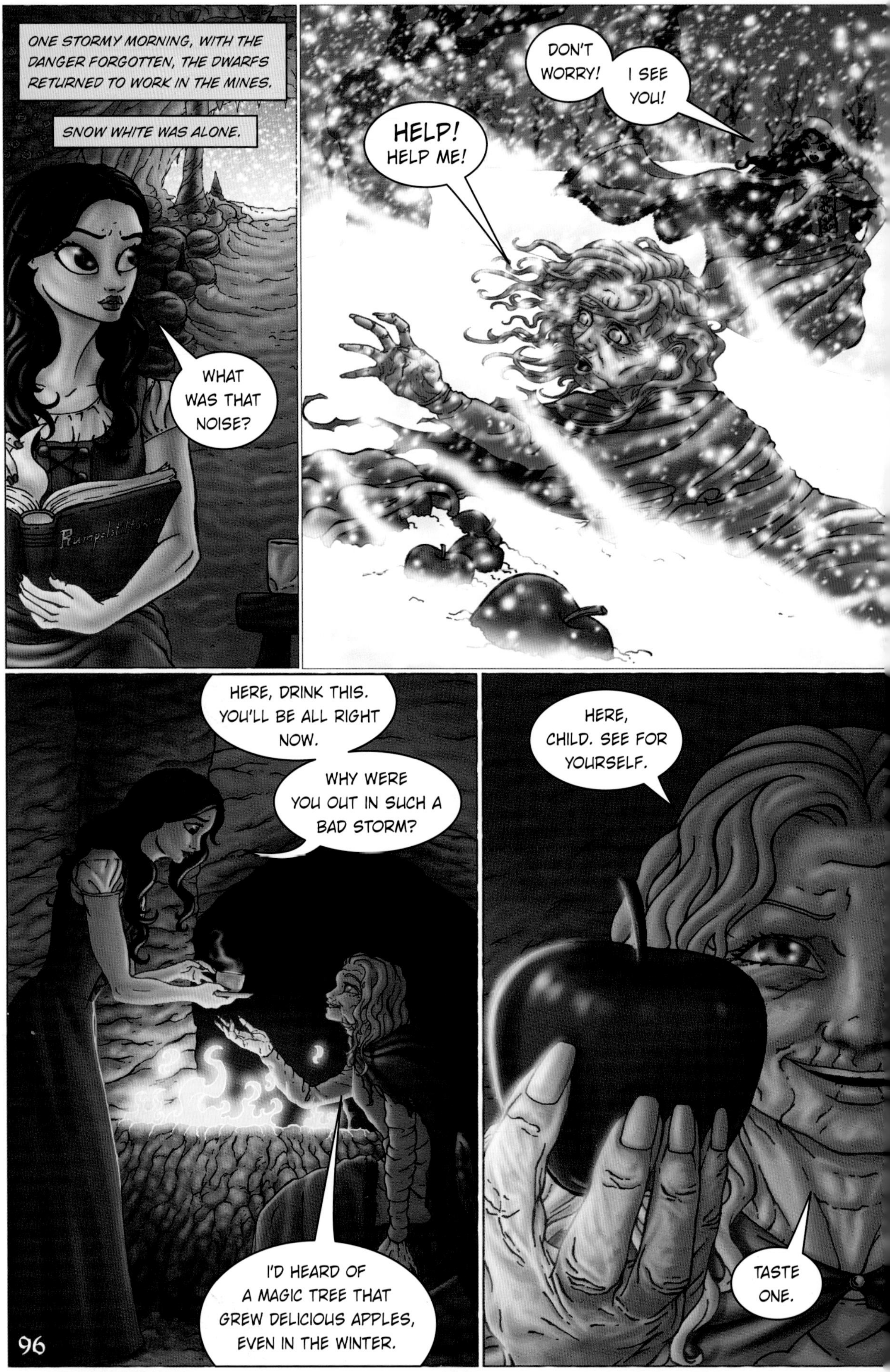
ONE STORMY MORNING, WITH THE DANGER FORGOTTEN, THE DWARFS RETURNED TO WORK IN THE MINES.
SNOW WHITE WAS ALONE.
WHAT WAS THAT NOISE?
HELP! HELP ME!
DON'T WORRY!
I SEE YOU!
HERE, DRINK THIS. YOU'LL BE ALL RIGHT NOW.
WHY WERE YOU OUT IN SUCH A BAD STORM?
I'D HEARD OF A MAGIC TREE THAT GREW DELICIOUS APPLES, EVEN IN THE WINTER.
HERE, CHILD. SEE FOR YOURSELF.
TASTE ONE.

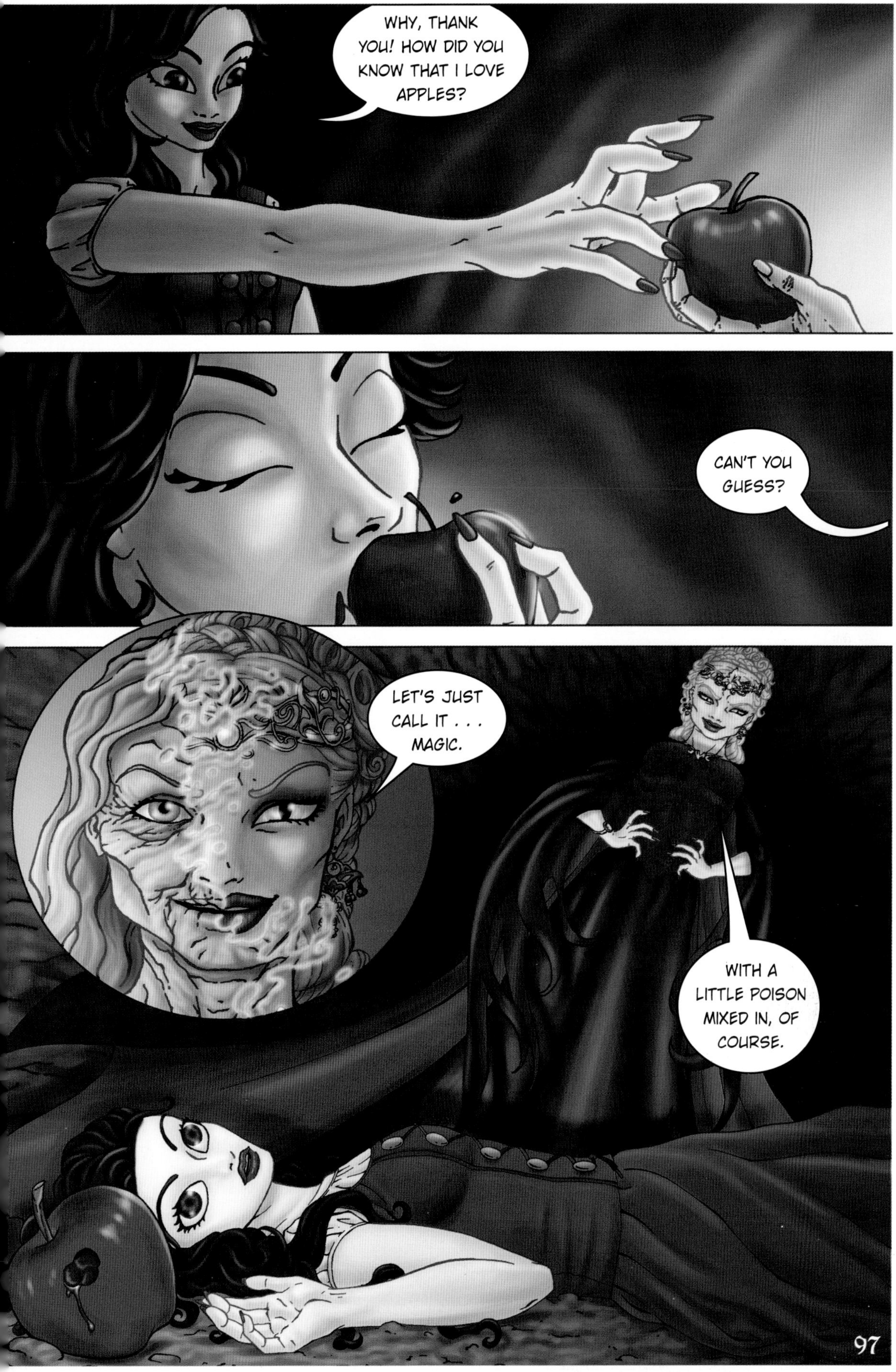
WHY, THANK YOU! HOW DID YOU KNOW THAT I LOVE APPLES?
CAN'T YOU GUESS?
LET'S JUST CALL IT . . . MAGIC.
WITH A LITTLE POISON MIXED IN, OF COURSE.

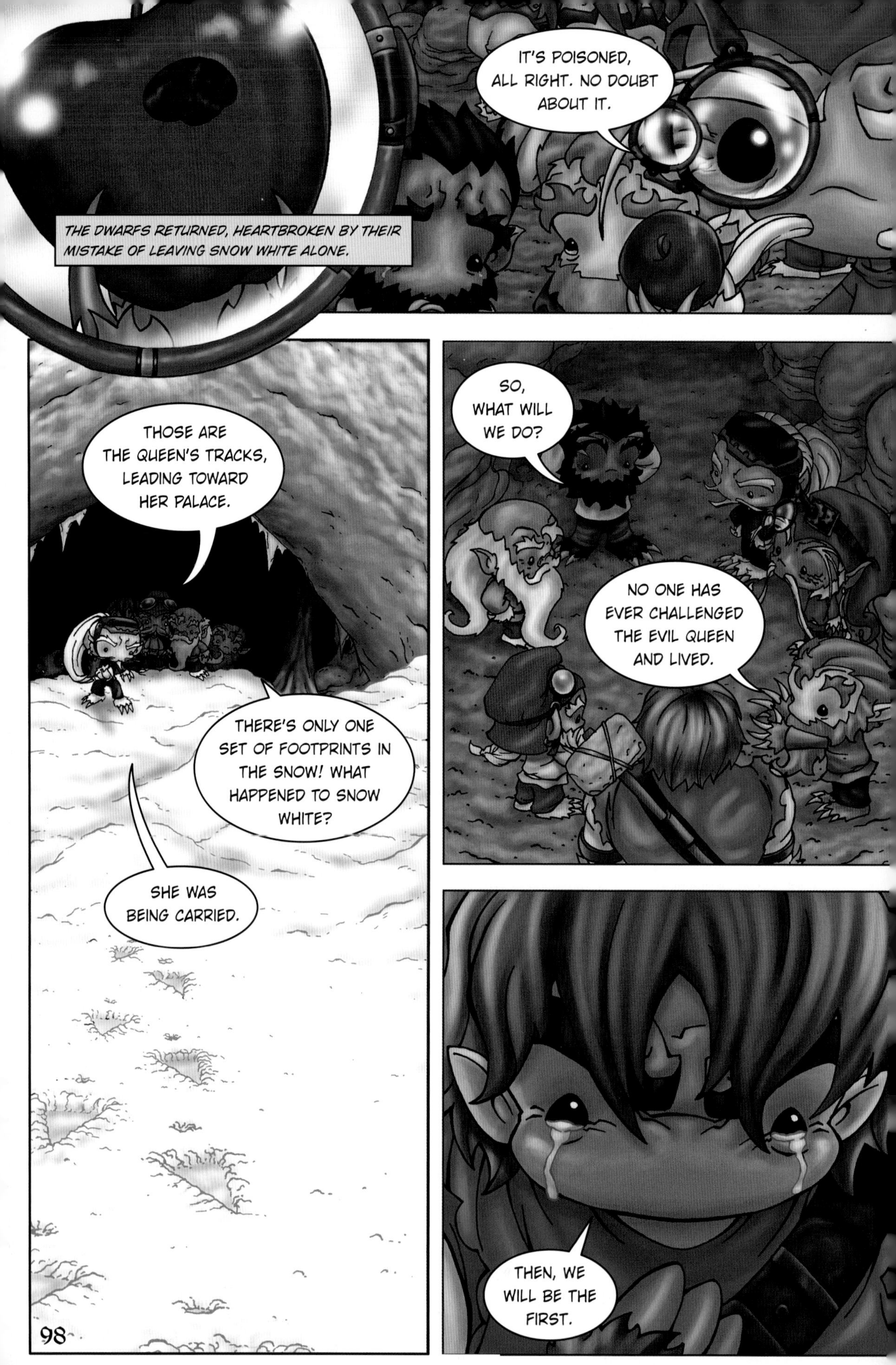
IT'S POISONED, ALL RIGHT. NO DOUBT ABOUT IT.
THE DWARFS RETURNED, HEARTBROKEN BY THEIR MISTAKE OF LEAVING SNOW WHITE ALONE.
THOSE ARE THE QUEEN'S TRACKS, LEADING TOWARD HER PALACE.
THERE'S ONLY ONE SET OF FOOTPRINTS IN THE SNOW! WHAT HAPPENED TO SNOW WHITE?
SHE WAS BEING CARRIED.
SO, WHAT WILL WE DO?
NO ONE HAS EVER CHALLENGED THE EVIL QUEEN AND LIVED.
THEN, WE WILL BE THE FIRST.

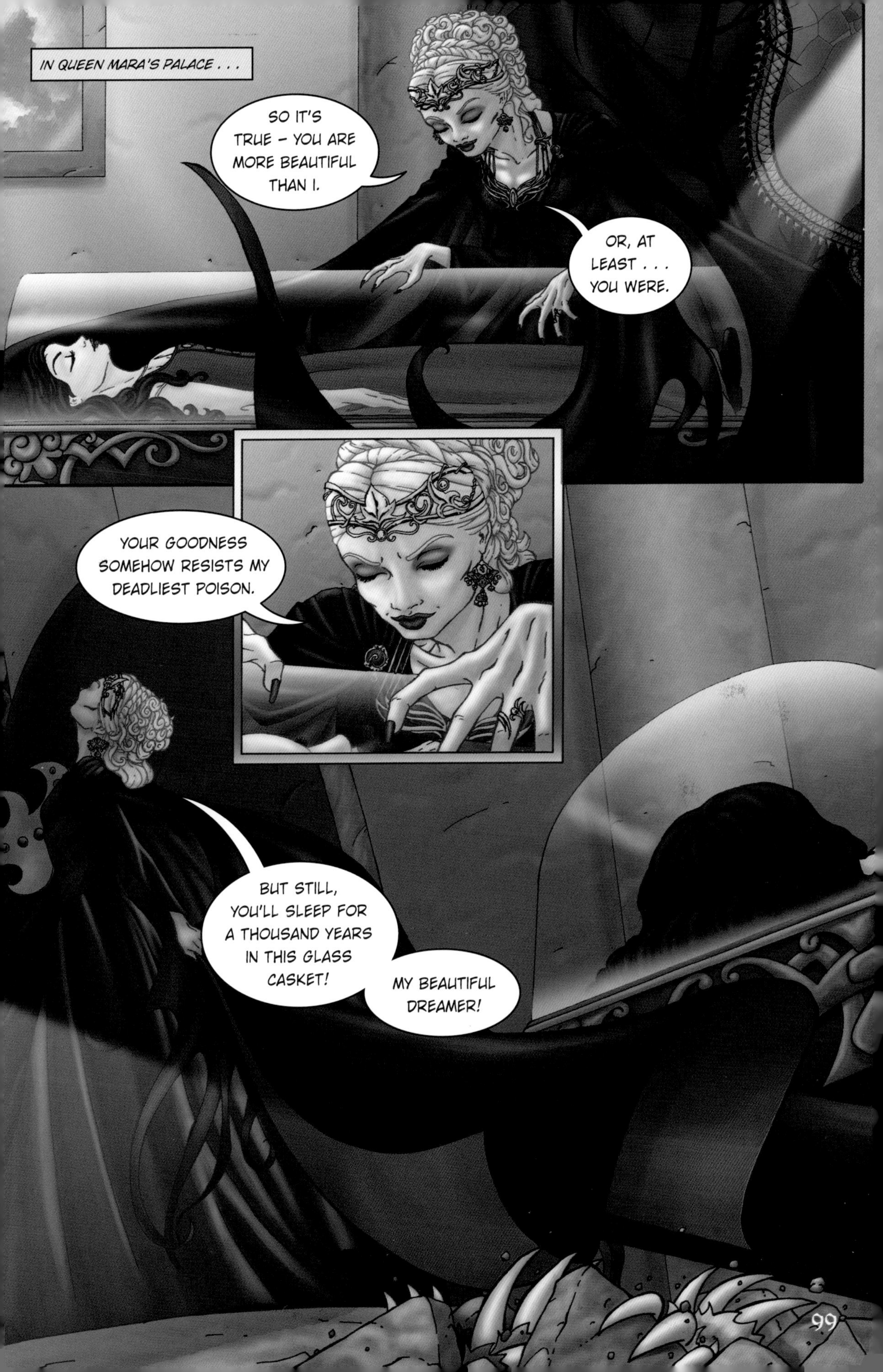
IN QUEEN MARA'S PALACE . . .
SO IT'S TRUE – YOU ARE MORE BEAUTIFUL THAN I.
OR, AT LEAST . . . YOU WERE.
YOUR GOODNESS SOMEHOW RESISTS MY DEADLIEST POISON.
BUT STILL, YOU'LL SLEEP FOR A THOUSAND YEARS IN THIS GLASS CASKET!
MY BEAUTIFUL DREAMER!

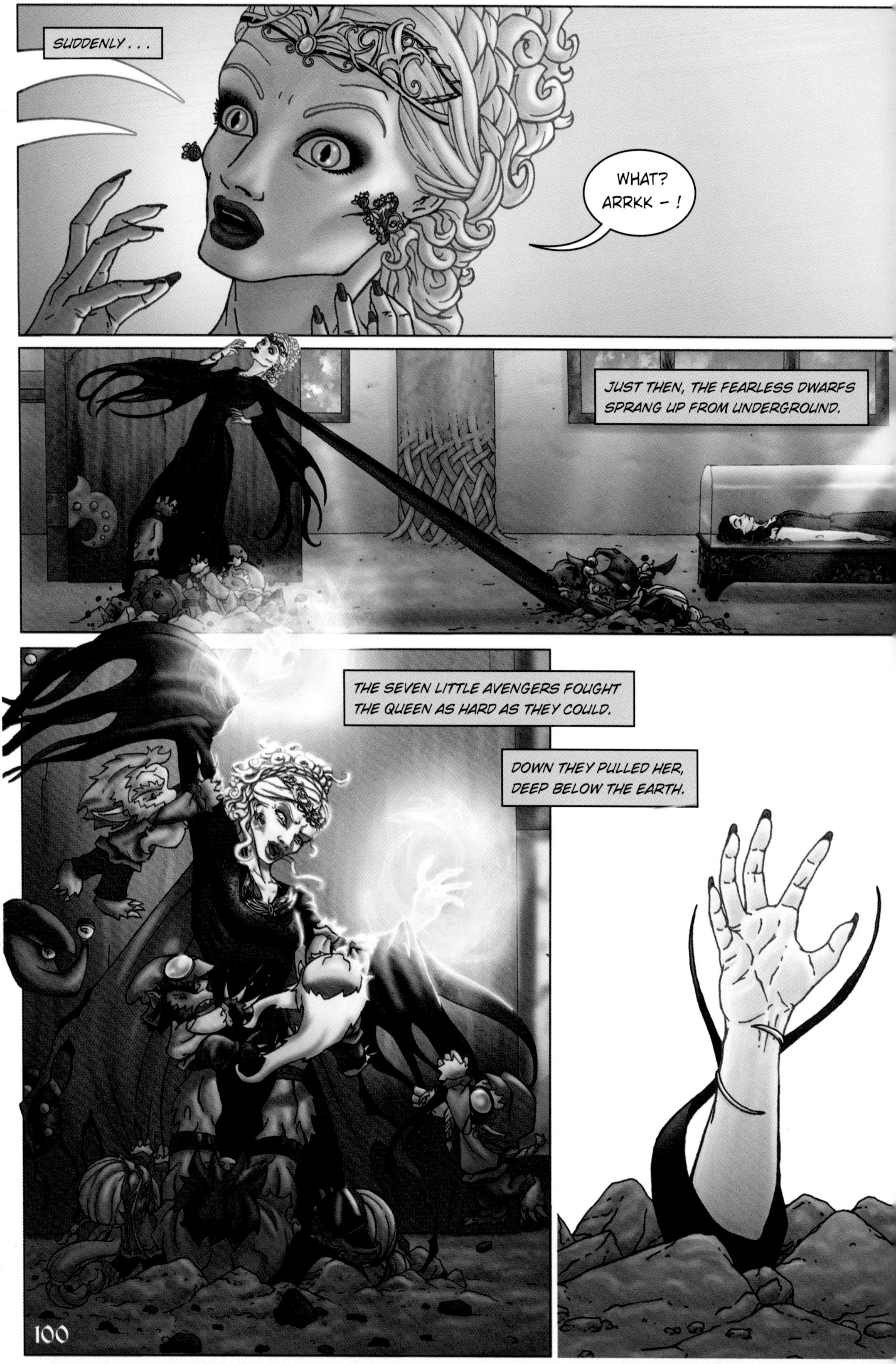
SUDDENLY . . .
WHAT? ARRKK – !
JUST THEN, THE FEARLESS DWARFS SPRANG UP FROM UNDERGROUND.
THE SEVEN LITTLE AVENGERS FOUGHT THE QUEEN AS HARD AS THEY COULD.
DOWN THEY PULLED HER, DEEP BELOW THE EARTH.

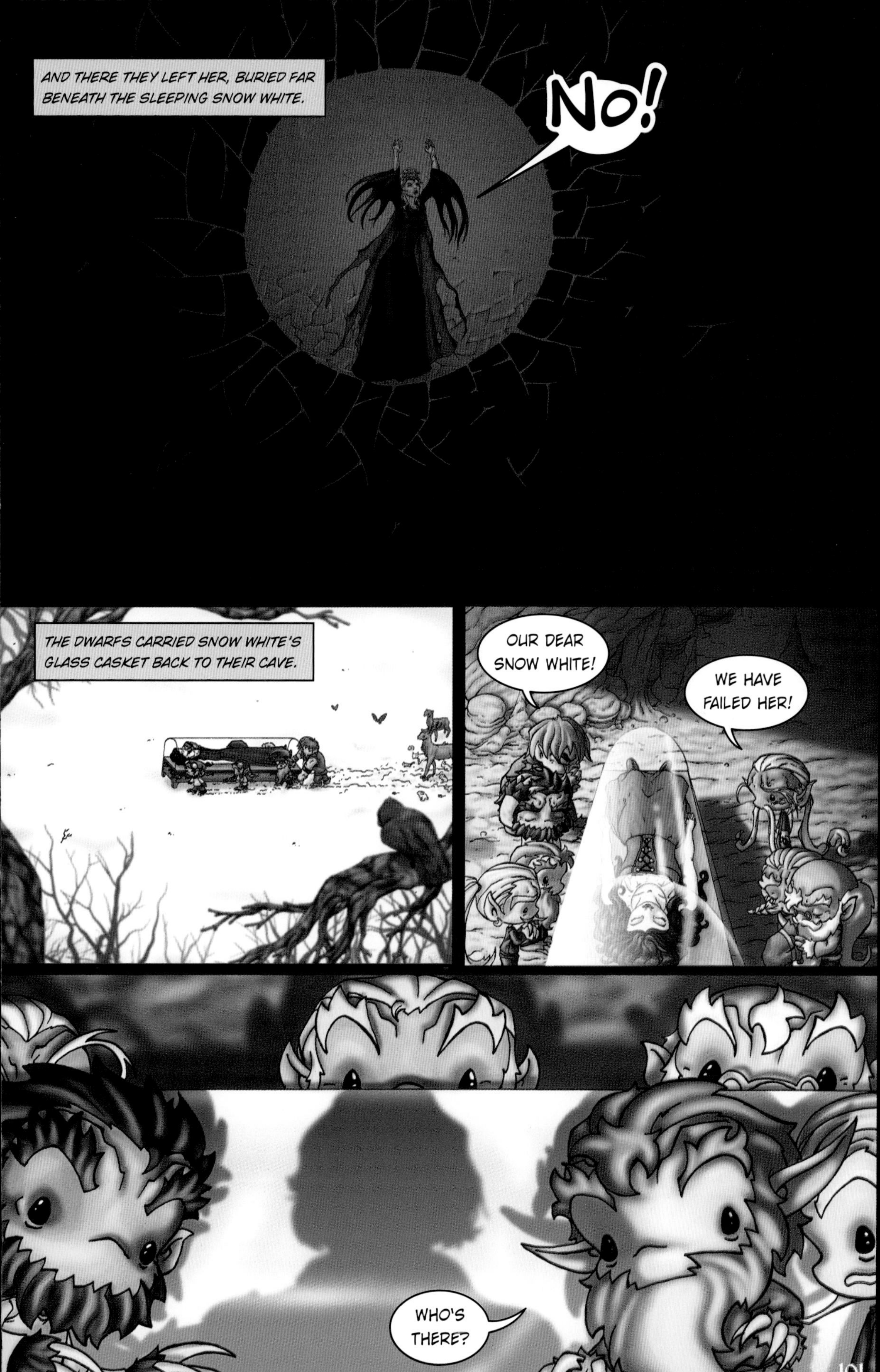
AND THERE THEY LEFT HER, BURIED FAR BENEATH THE SLEEPING SNOW WHITE.
No!
THE DWARFS CARRIED SNOW WHITE'S GLASS CASKET BACK TO THEIR CAVE.
OUR DEAR SNOW WHITE!
WE HAVE FAILED HER!
WHO'S THERE?

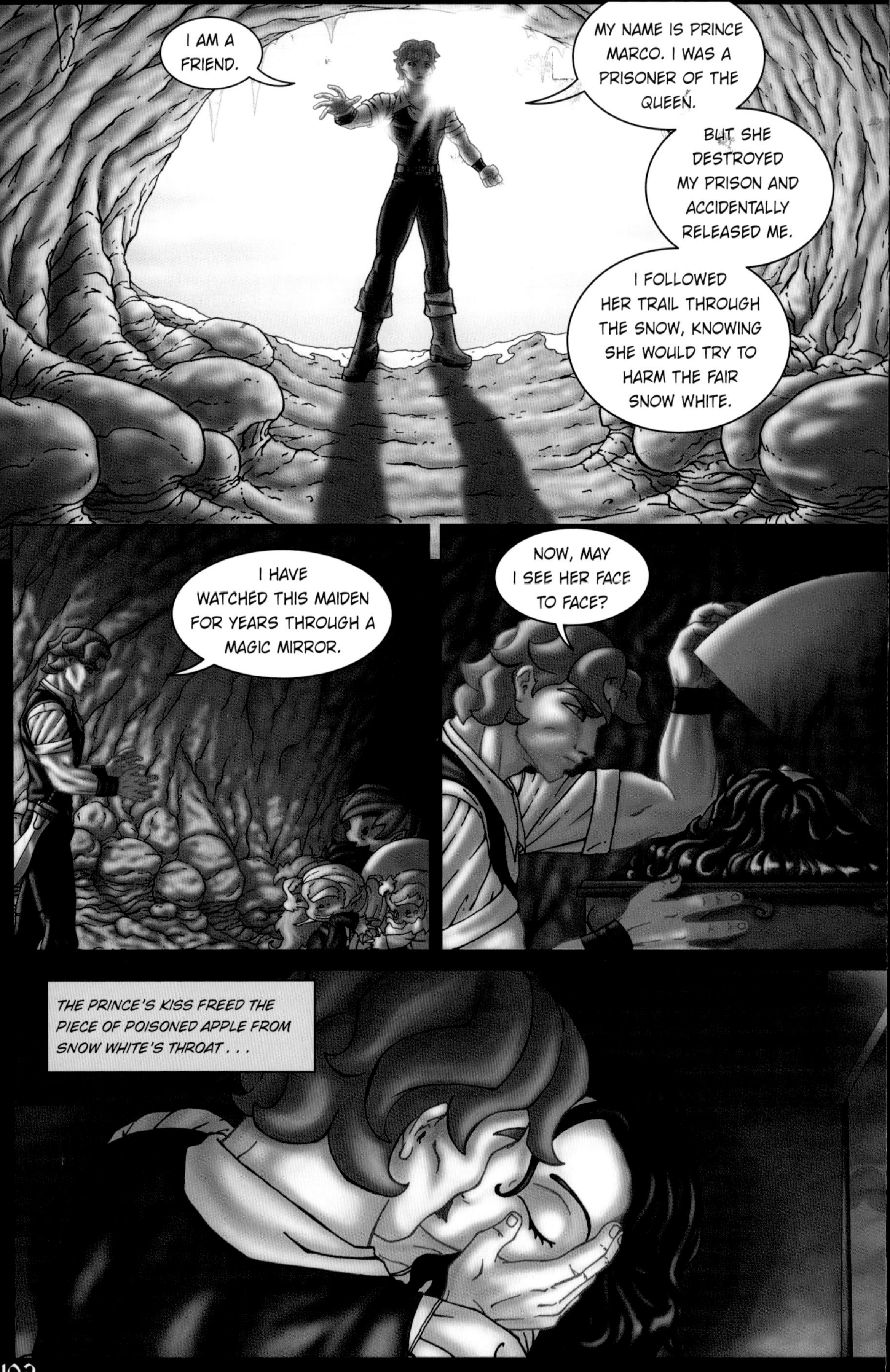
I AM A FRIEND.
MY NAME IS PRINCE MARCO. I WAS A PRISONER OF THE QUEEN.
BUT SHE DESTROYED MY PRISON AND ACCIDENTALLY RELEASED ME.
I FOLLOWED HER TRAIL THROUGH THE SNOW, KNOWING SHE WOULD TRY TO HARM THE FAIR SNOW WHITE.
I HAVE WATCHED THIS MAIDEN FOR YEARS THROUGH A MAGIC MIRROR.
NOW, MAY I SEE HER FACE TO FACE?
THE PRINCE'S KISS FREED THE PIECE OF POISONED APPLE FROM SNOW WHITE'S THROAT . . .

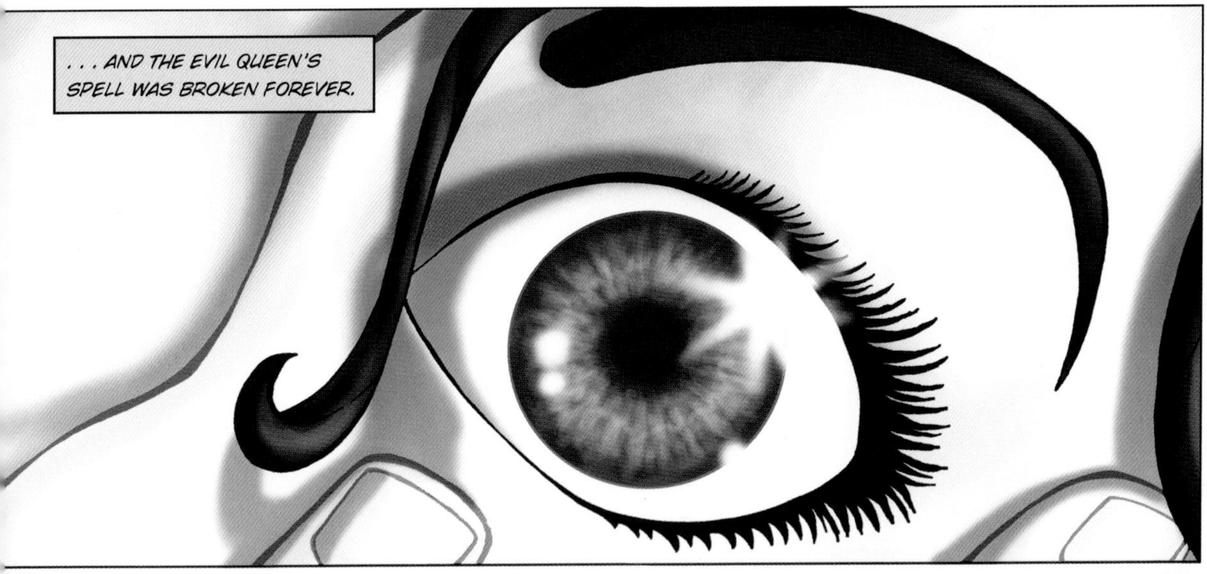
. . . AND THE EVIL QUEEN'S SPELL WAS BROKEN FOREVER.

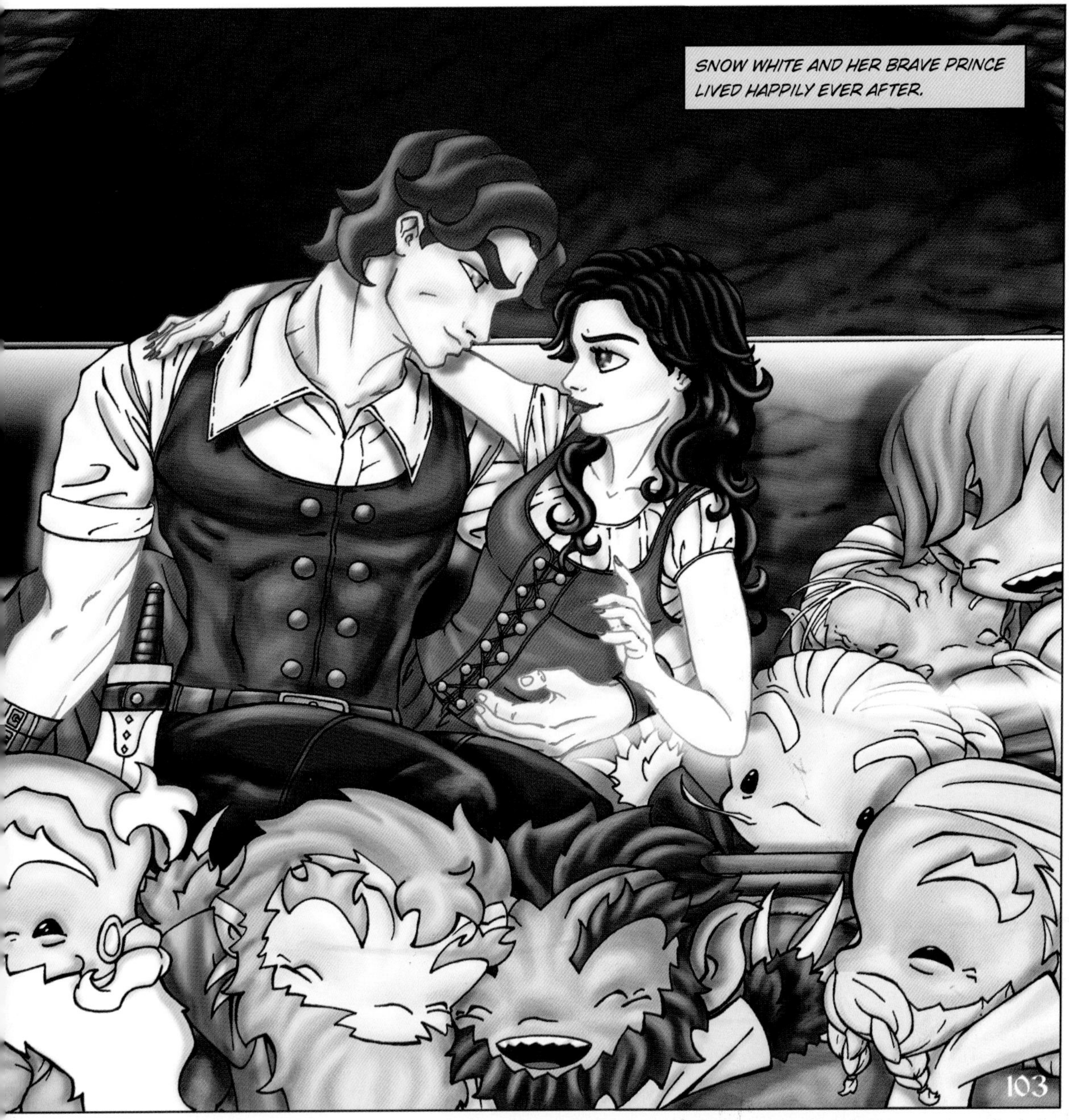
SNOW WHITE AND HER BRAVE PRINCE LIVED HAPPILY EVER AFTER.

The History of
Snow White

Stories similar to "Snow White" are found in cultures throughout the world. Some details of the centuries-old tale vary, according to location. A Scottish version, for example, has a talking fish in a well rather than a magic mirror.

Like many fairy tales, the most well-known version comes from the Brothers Grimm. Jacob and Wilhelm Grimm were German brothers who published collections of oral fairy tales in the 1800s. Family friends Jeannette and Amalie Hassenpflug told the Grimm brothers the story. Many of the details of the sisters' story were similar to Italian versions. The dwarfs, however, must have been a German addition. German folk tales often include stocky little men who work underground.

The Grimm version of "Snow White" was used as the basis for the 1937 Walt Disney movie, *Snow White and the Seven Dwarfs*. It was the first American full-length animated movie. The movie is credited with naming the dwarfs and giving them personalities. The seven names were picked from a list of 50 possibilities, including Awful, Dirty, and Hoppy.

Some historians think that Snow White's character was based on a real person. Margaret von Waldeck lived in Germany in the 1500s, 200 years before the Grimm brothers were born. She lived in a mining town, was loved by a handsome prince, Phillip II of Spain, and was poisoned at the early age of 21. The villain was never found.

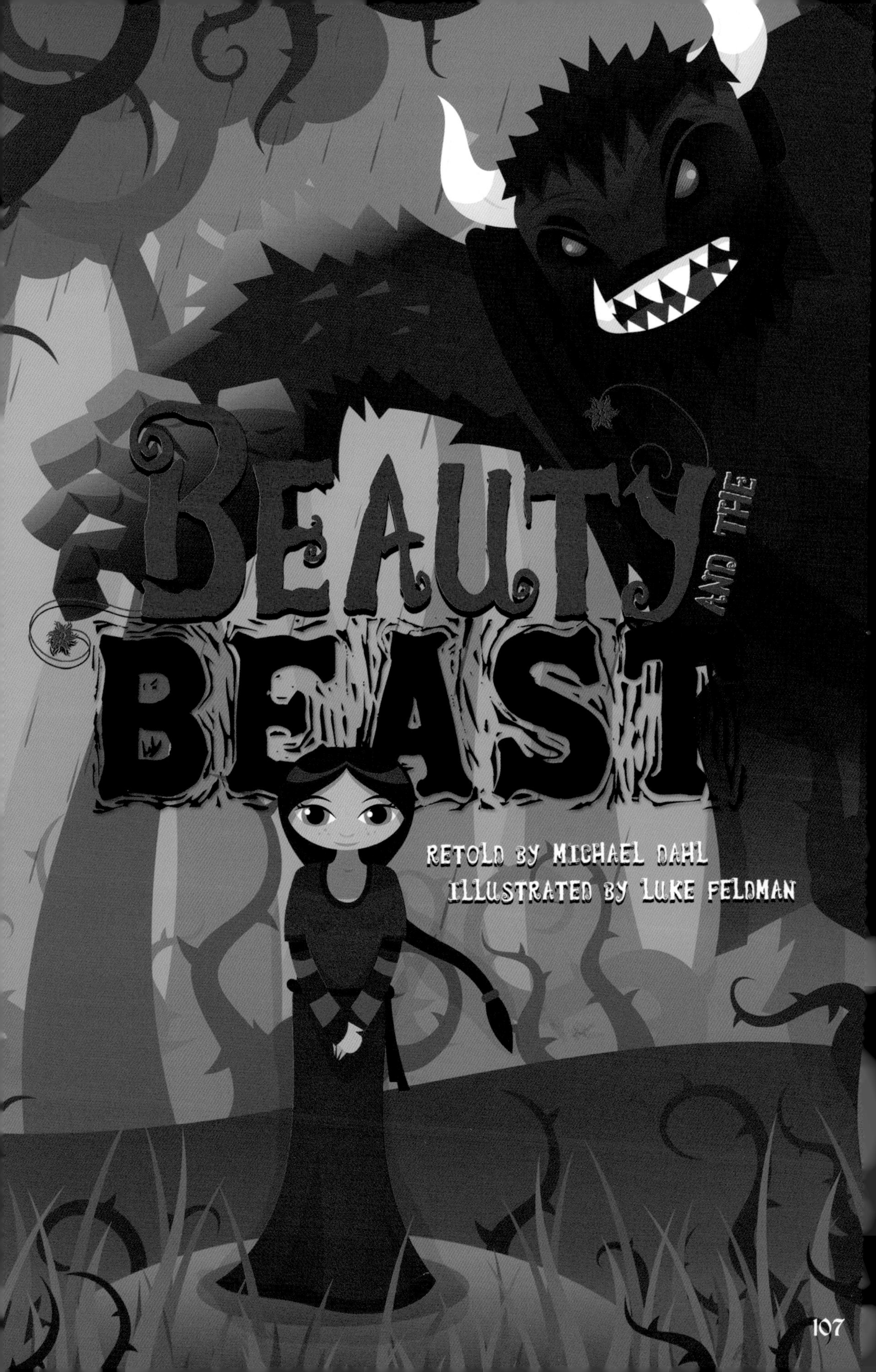
BEAUTY AND THE BEAST
RETOLD BY MICHAEL DAHL
ILLUSTRATED BY LUKE FELDMAN

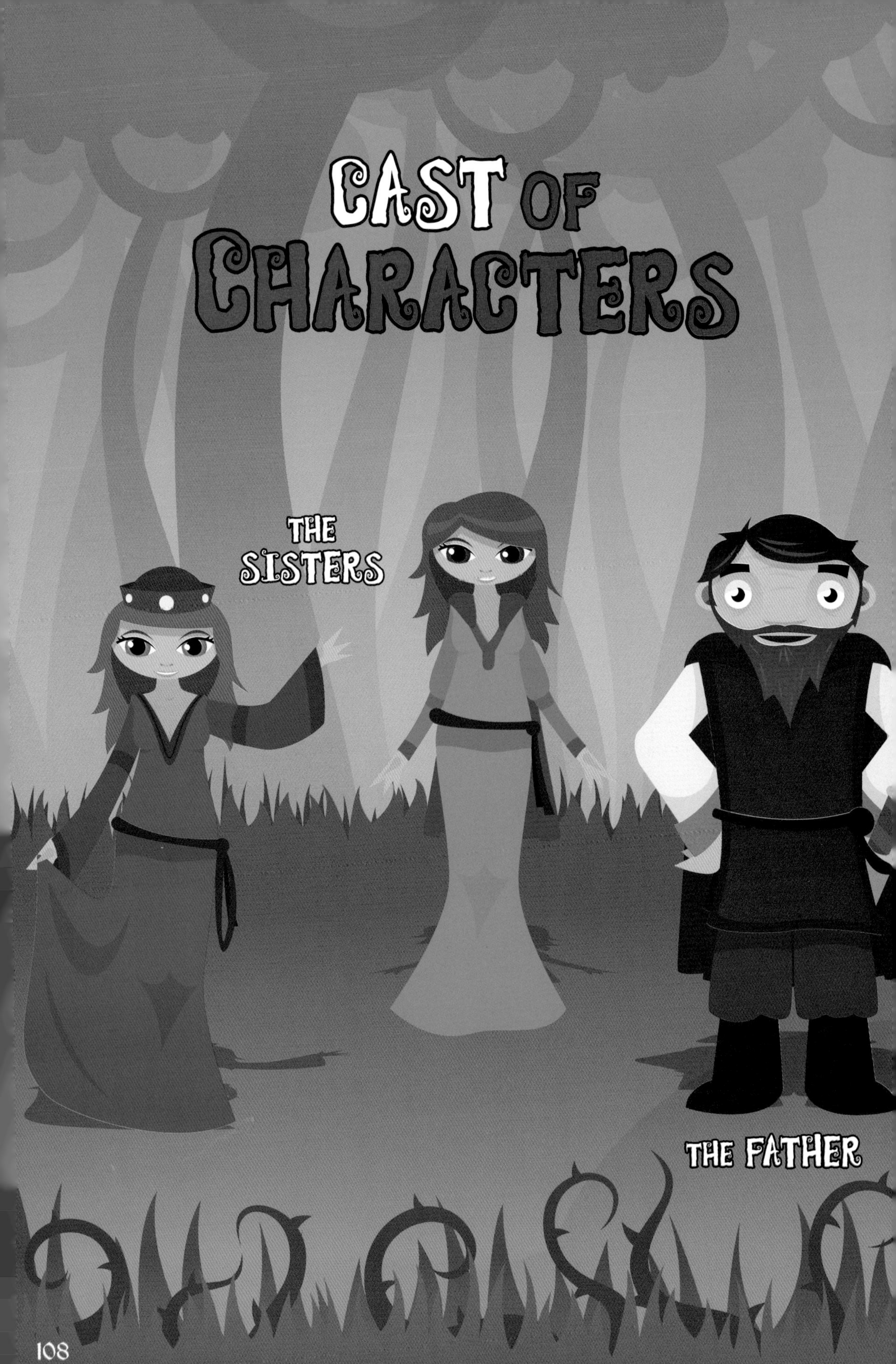
CAST OF CHARACTERS
THE SISTERS
THE FATHER

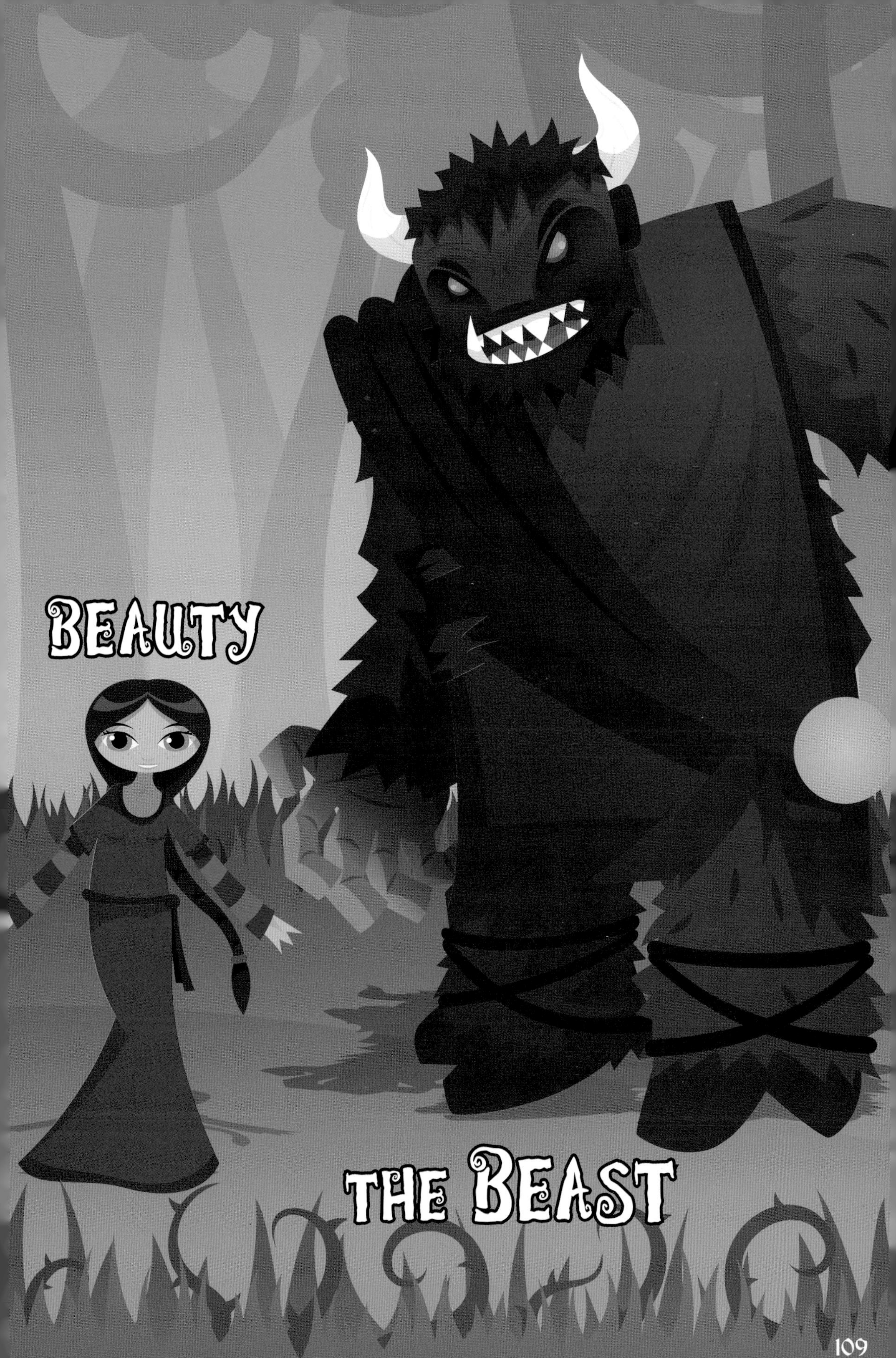
BEAUTY
THE BEAST

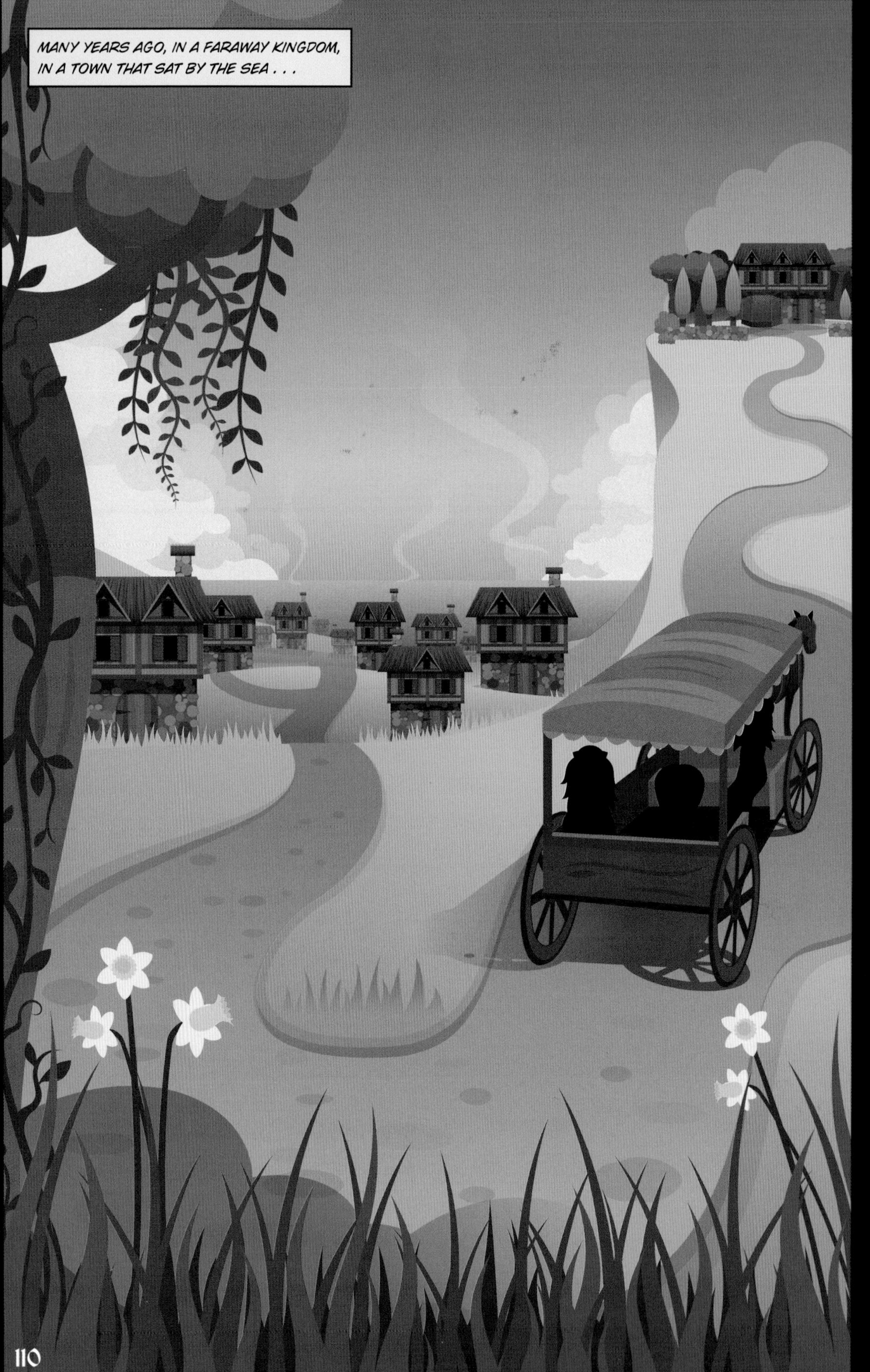
MANY YEARS AGO, IN A FARAWAY KINGDOM, IN A TOWN THAT SAT BY THE SEA . . .

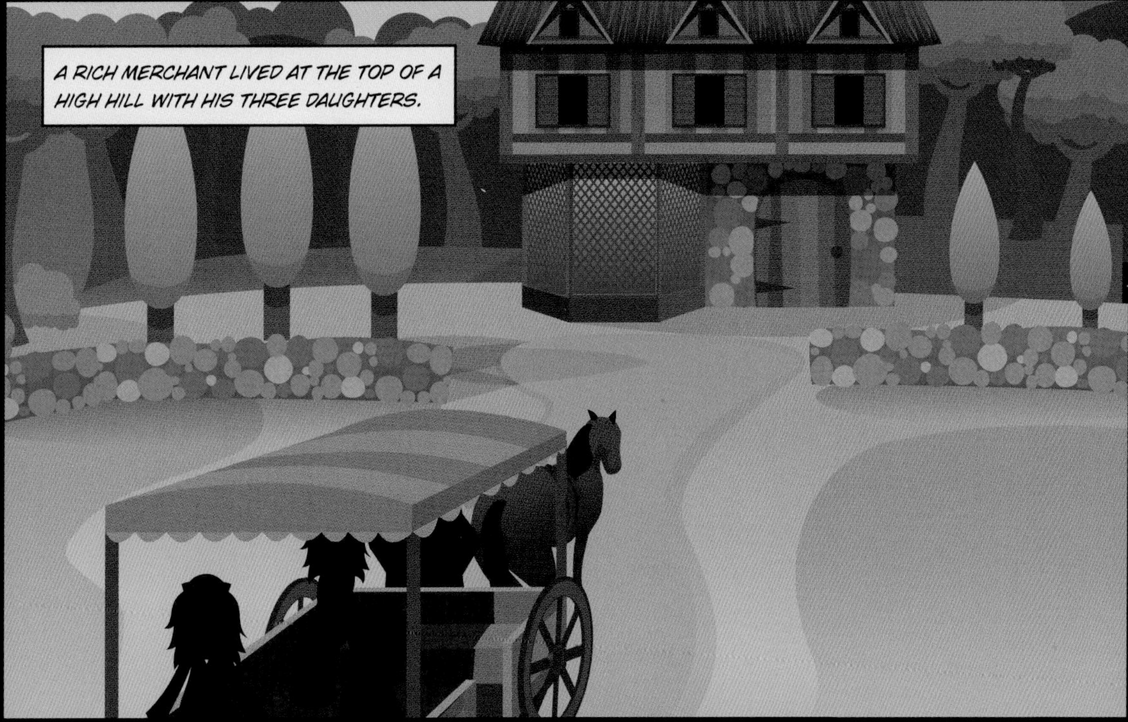
A RICH MERCHANT LIVED AT THE TOP OF A HIGH HILL WITH HIS THREE DAUGHTERS.

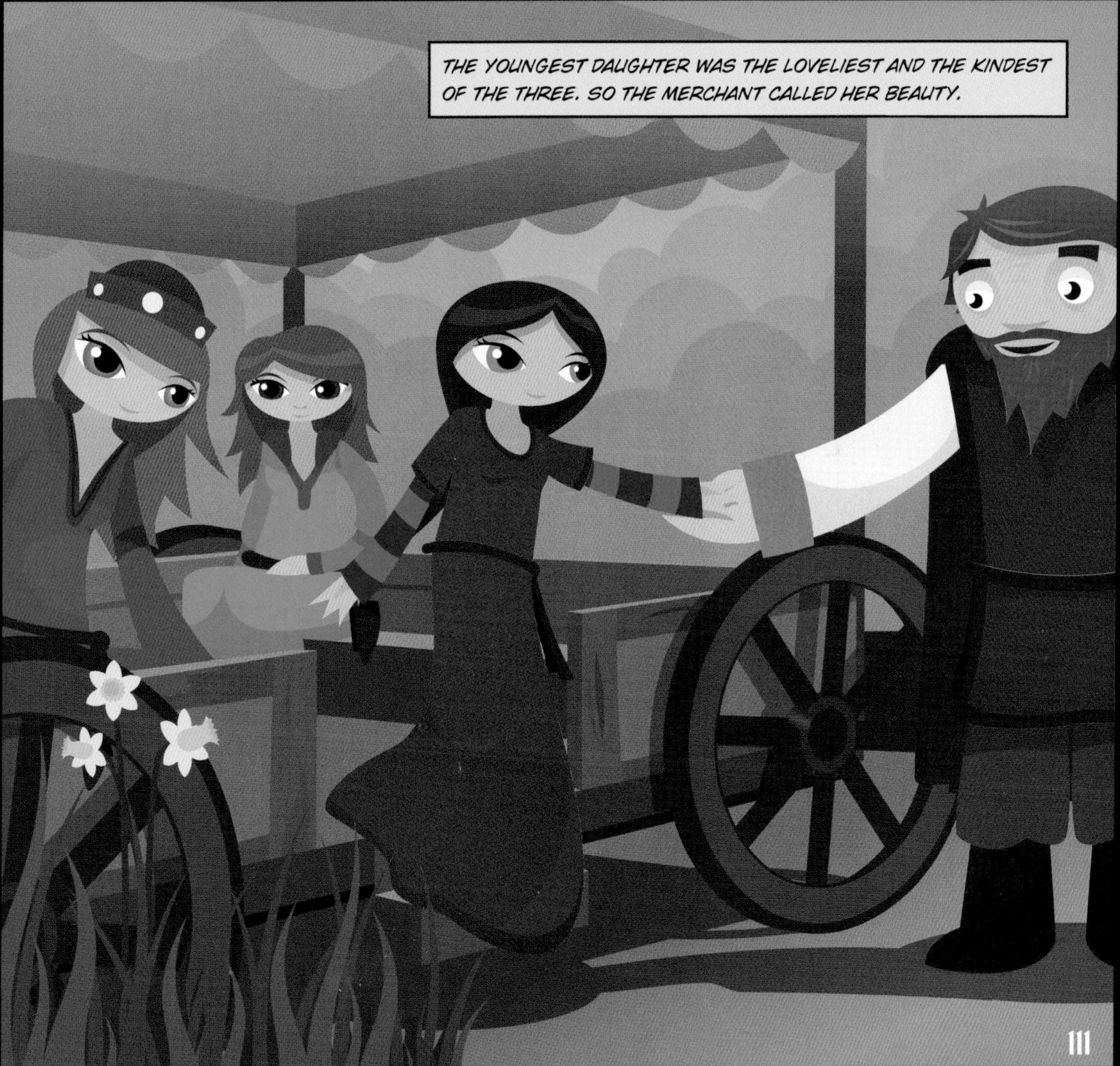
THE YOUNGEST DAUGHTER WAS THE LOVELIEST AND THE KINDEST OF THE THREE. SO THE MERCHANT CALLED HER BEAUTY.

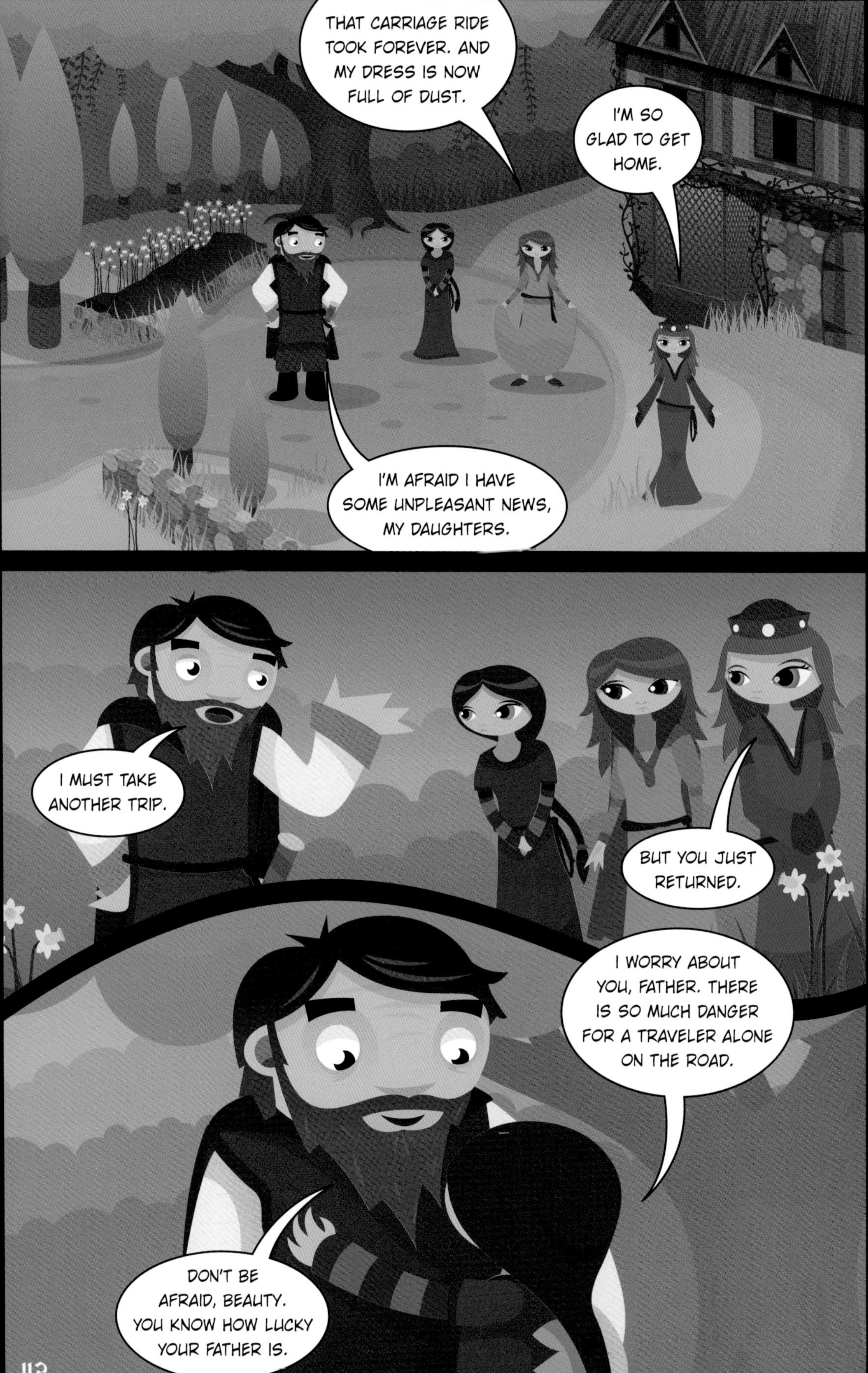

THAT CARRIAGE RIDE TOOK FOREVER. AND MY DRESS IS NOW FULL OF DUST.
I'M SO GLAD TO GET HOME.
I'M AFRAID I HAVE SOME UNPLEASANT NEWS, MY DAUGHTERS.
I MUST TAKE ANOTHER TRIP.
BUT YOU JUST RETURNED.
I WORRY ABOUT YOU, FATHER. THERE IS SO MUCH DANGER FOR A TRAVELER ALONE ON THE ROAD.
DON'T BE AFRAID, BEAUTY. YOU KNOW HOW LUCKY YOUR FATHER IS.

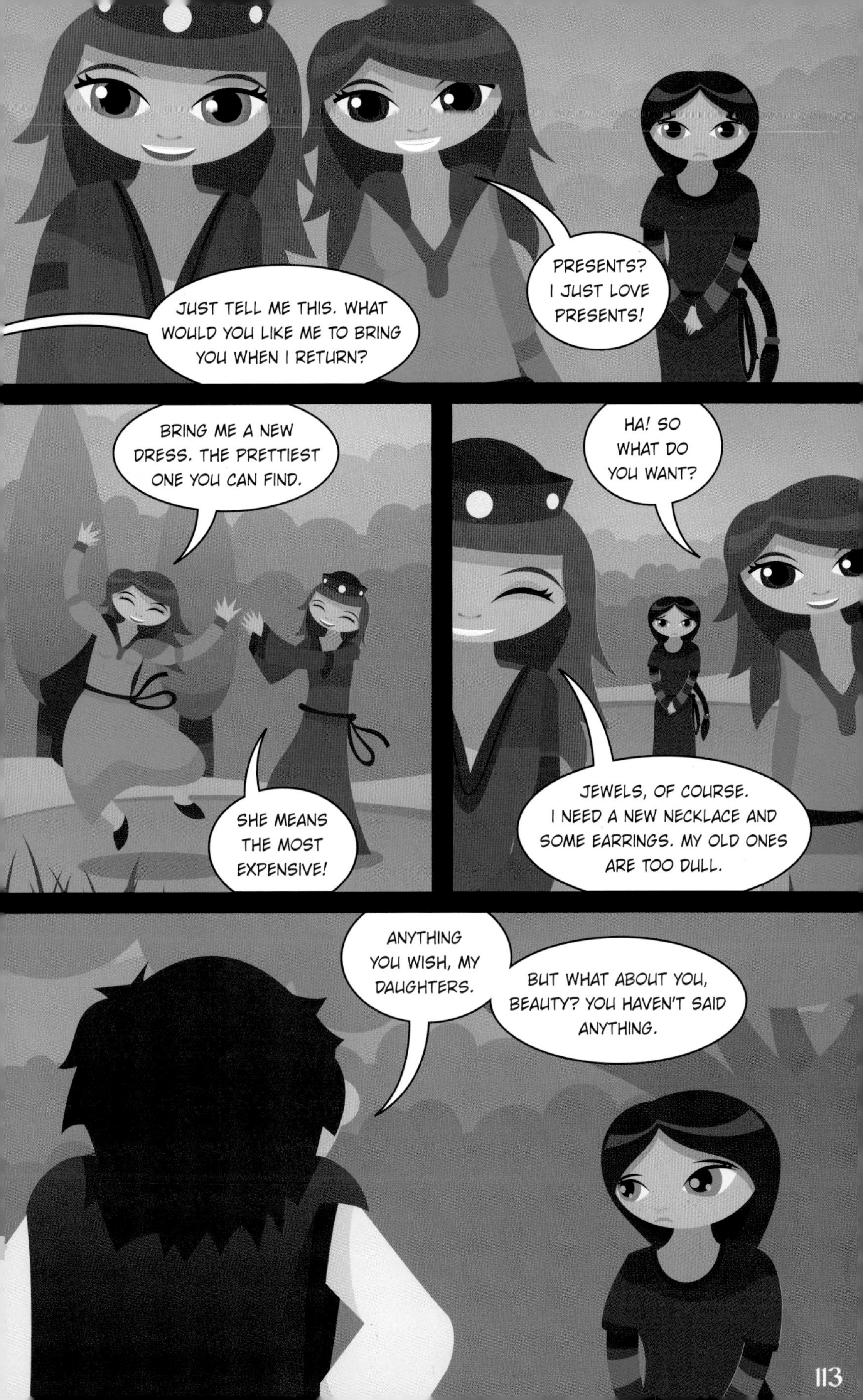
JUST TELL ME THIS. WHAT WOULD YOU LIKE ME TO BRING YOU WHEN I RETURN?
PRESENTS? I JUST LOVE PRESENTS!
BRING ME A NEW DRESS. THE PRETTIEST ONE YOU CAN FIND.
SHE MEANS THE MOST EXPENSIVE!
HA! SO WHAT DO YOU WANT?
JEWELS, OF COURSE. I NEED A NEW NECKLACE AND SOME EARRINGS. MY OLD ONES ARE TOO DULL.
ANYTHING YOU WISH, MY DAUGHTERS.
BUT WHAT ABOUT YOU, BEAUTY? YOU HAVEN'T SAID ANYTHING.

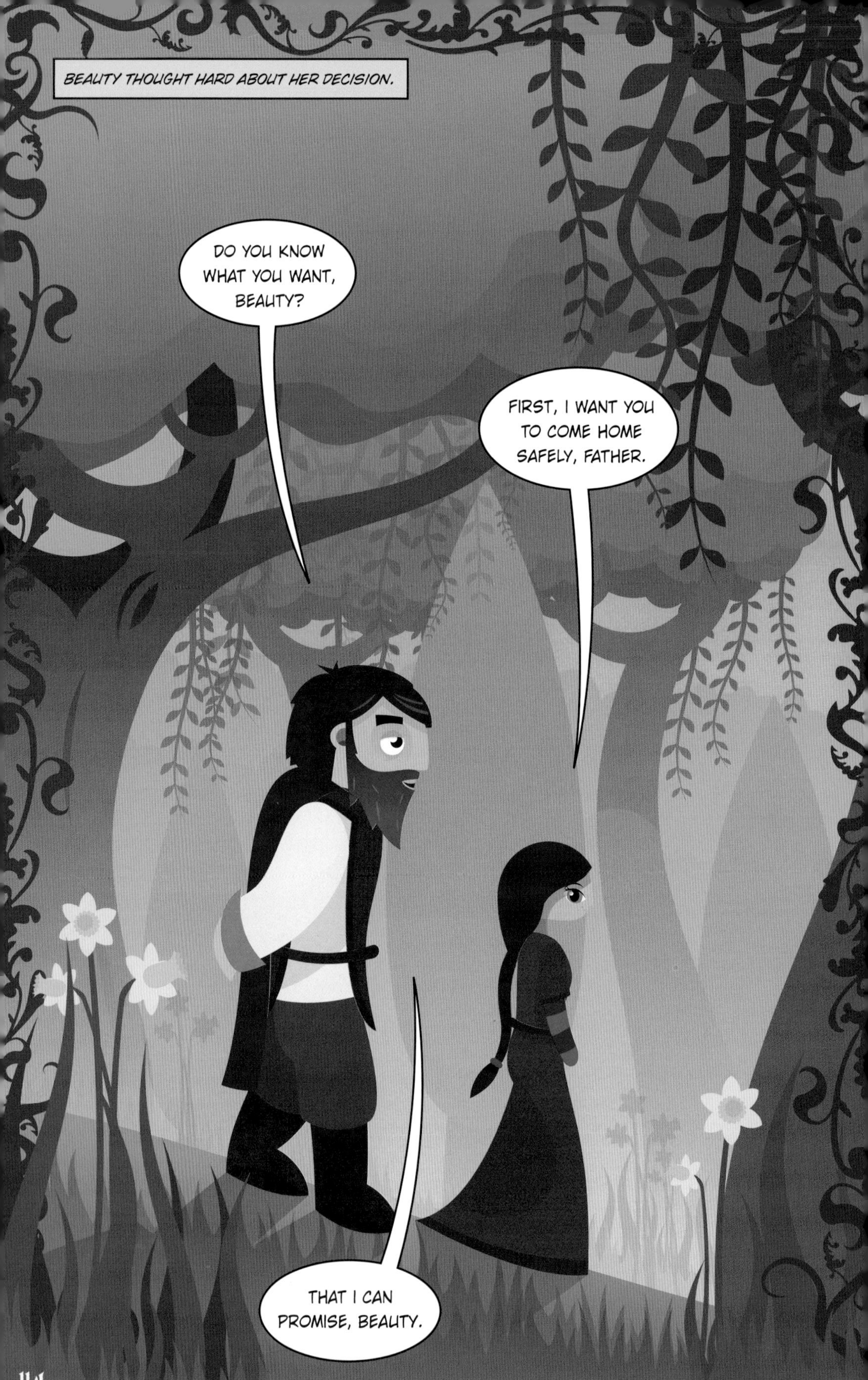
BEAUTY THOUGHT HARD ABOUT HER DECISION.
DO YOU KNOW WHAT YOU WANT, BEAUTY?
FIRST, I WANT YOU TO COME HOME SAFELY, FATHER.
THAT I CAN PROMISE, BEAUTY.

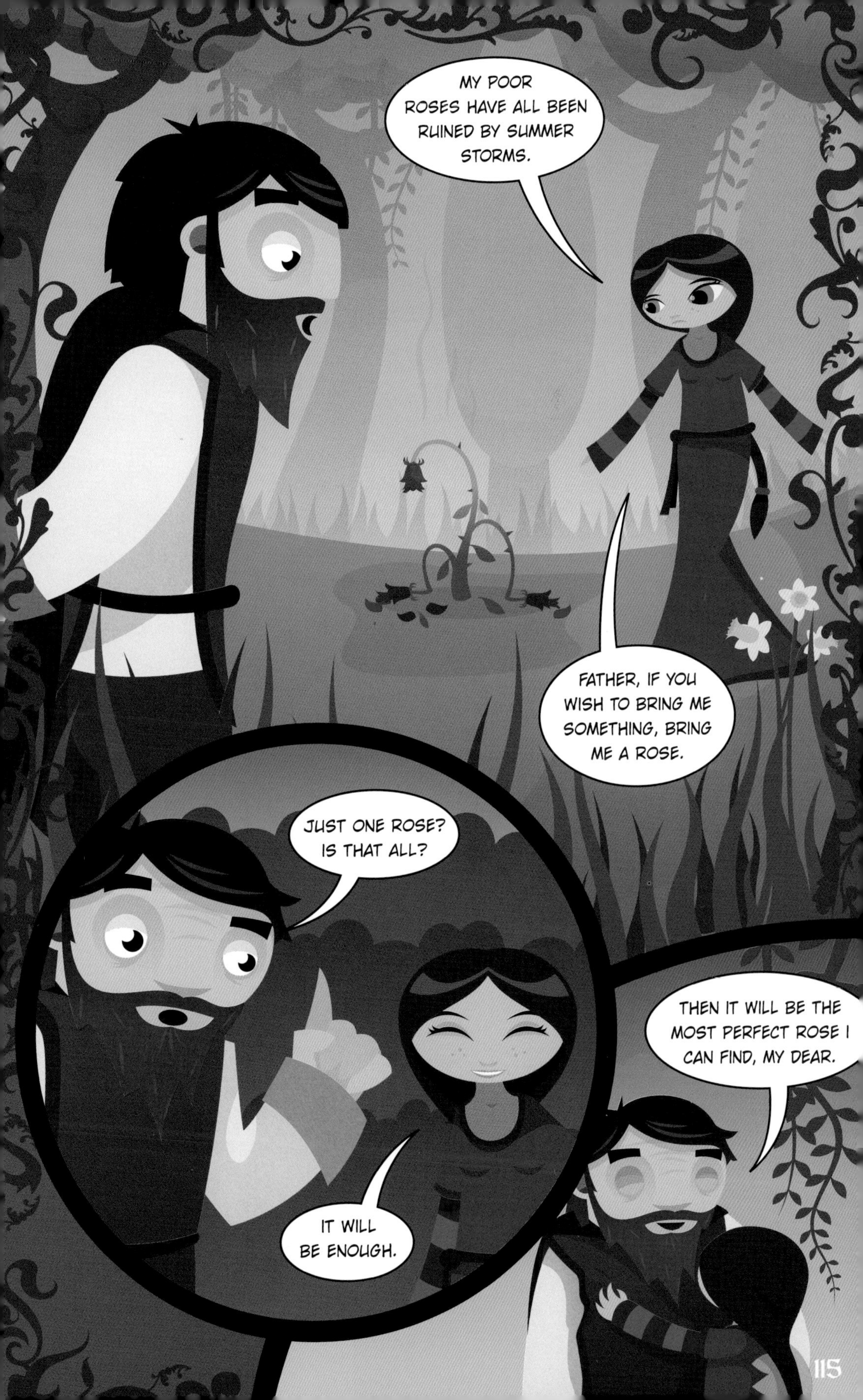
MY POOR ROSES HAVE ALL BEEN RUINED BY SUMMER STORMS.
FATHER, IF YOU WISH TO BRING ME SOMETHING, BRING ME A ROSE.
JUST ONE ROSE? IS THAT ALL?
IT WILL BE ENOUGH.
THEN IT WILL BE THE MOST PERFECT ROSE I CAN FIND, MY DEAR.

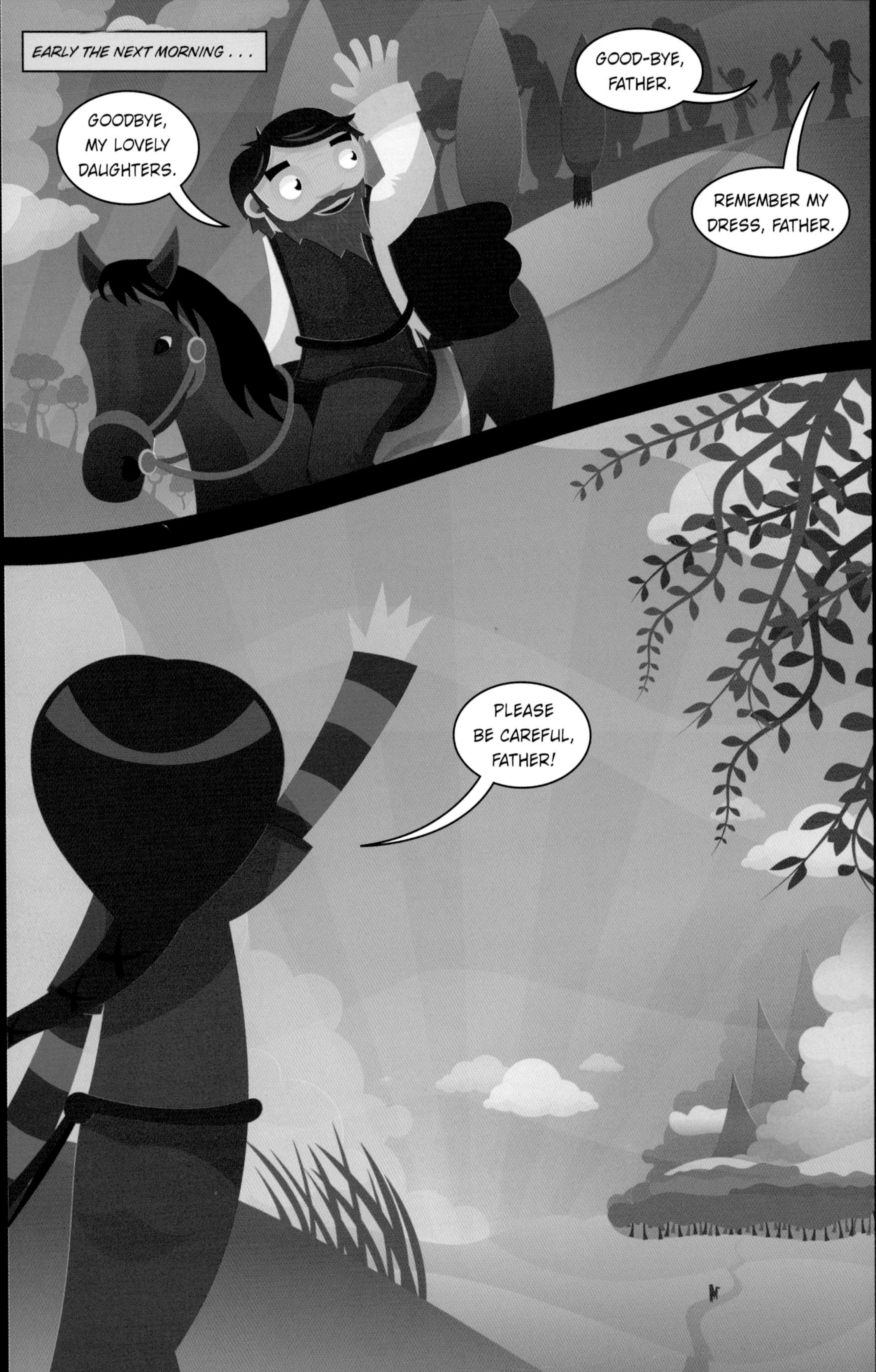
EARLY THE NEXT MORNING . . .
GOODBYE, MY LOVELY DAUGHTERS.
GOOD-BYE, FATHER.
REMEMBER MY DRESS, FATHER.
PLEASE BE CAREFUL, FATHER!

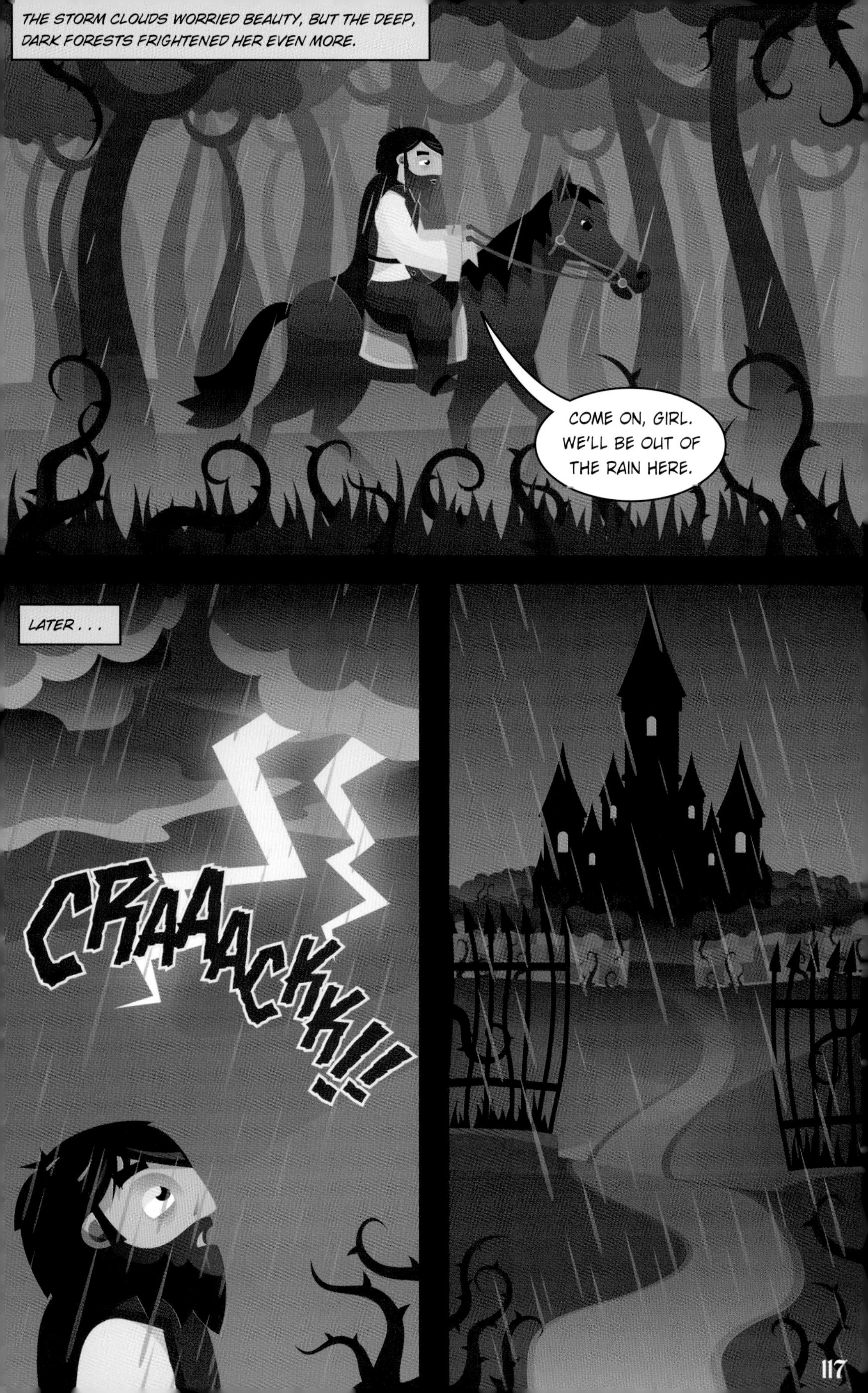
THE STORM CLOUDS WORRIED BEAUTY, BUT THE DEEP, DARK FORESTS FRIGHTENED HER EVEN MORE.
COME ON, GIRL. WE'LL BE OUT OF THE RAIN HERE.
LATER . . .
CRAAACKK!!!

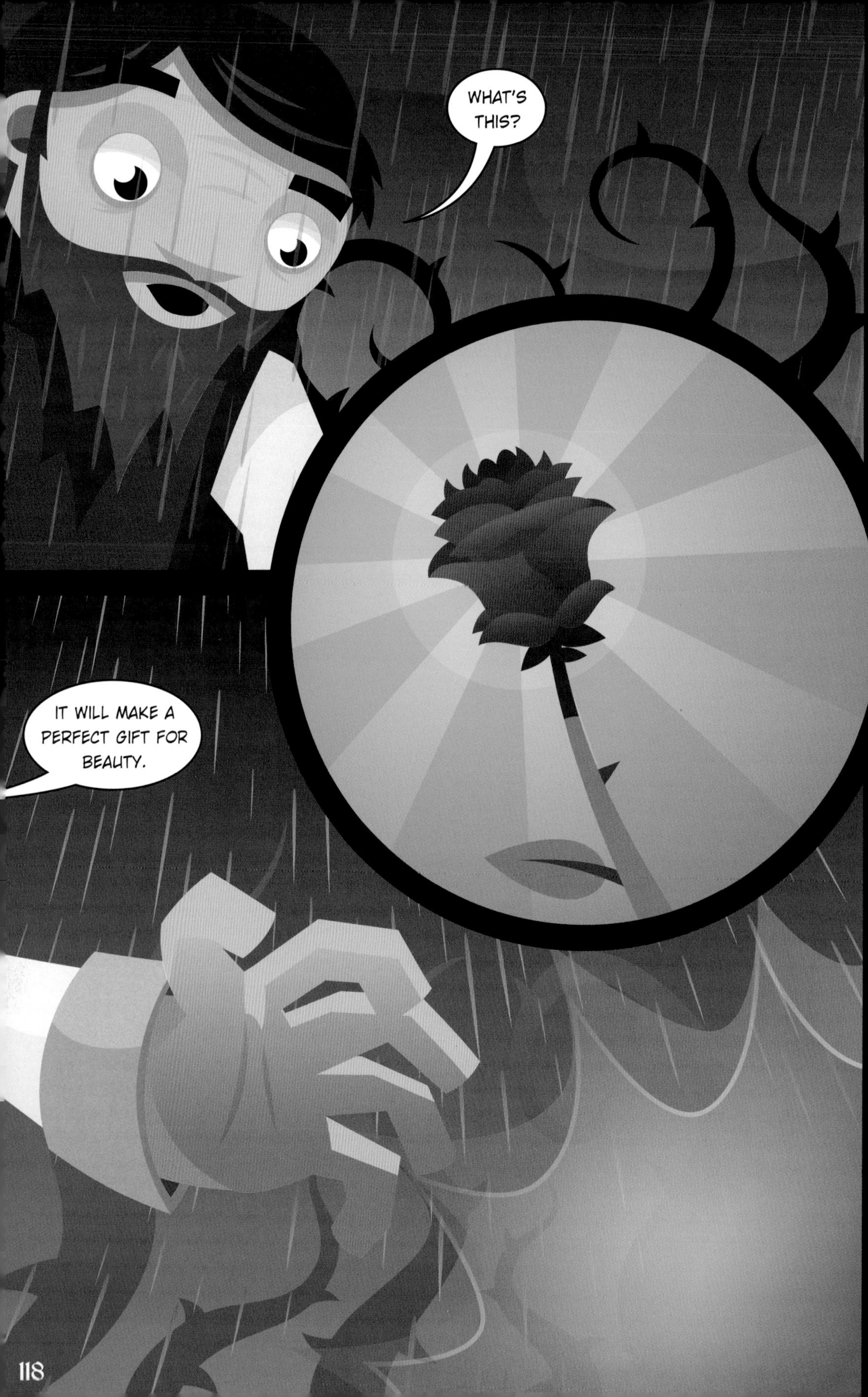
WHAT'S THIS?
IT WILL MAKE A PERFECT GIFT FOR BEAUTY.

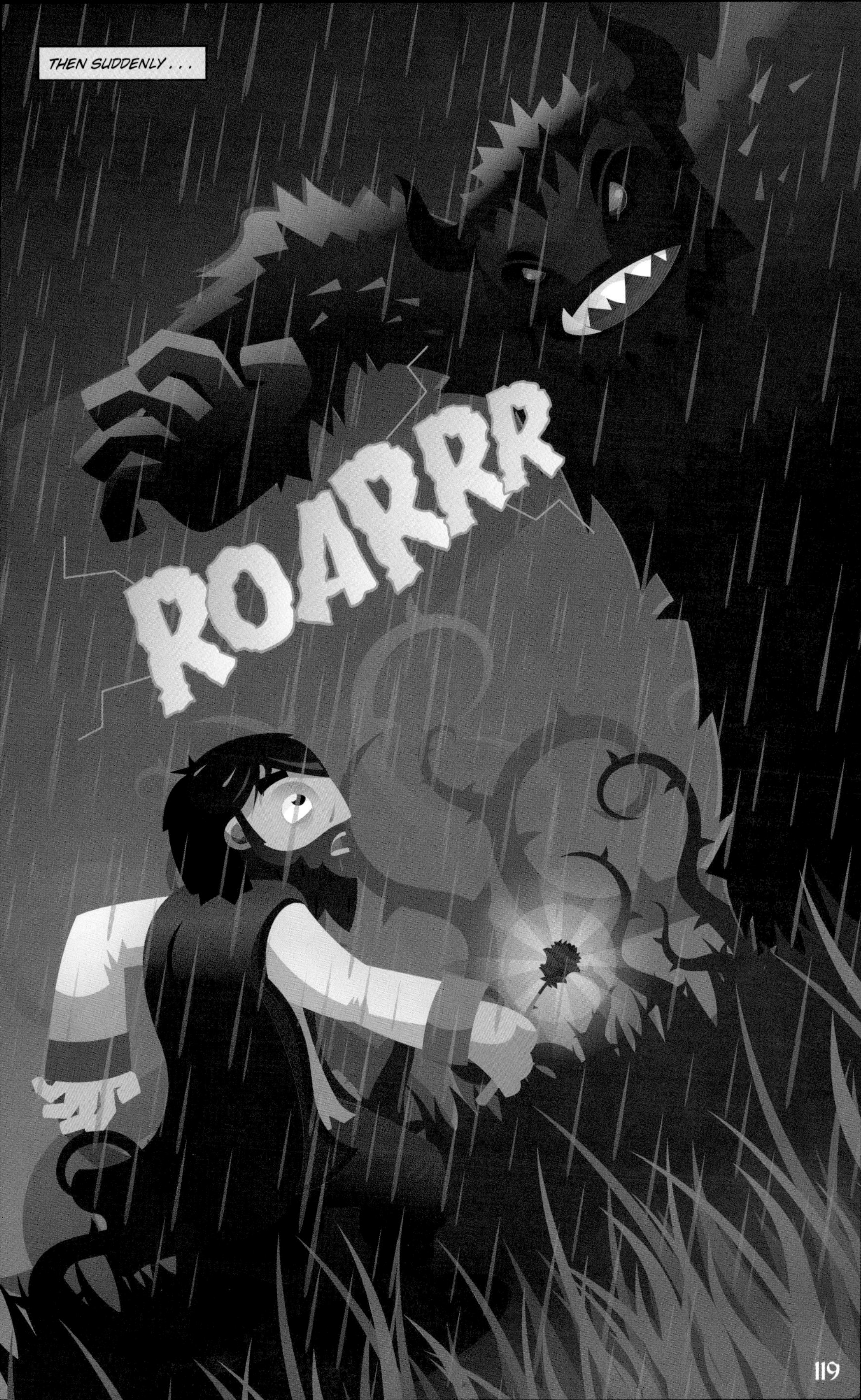
THEN SUDDENLY . . .
ROARRR

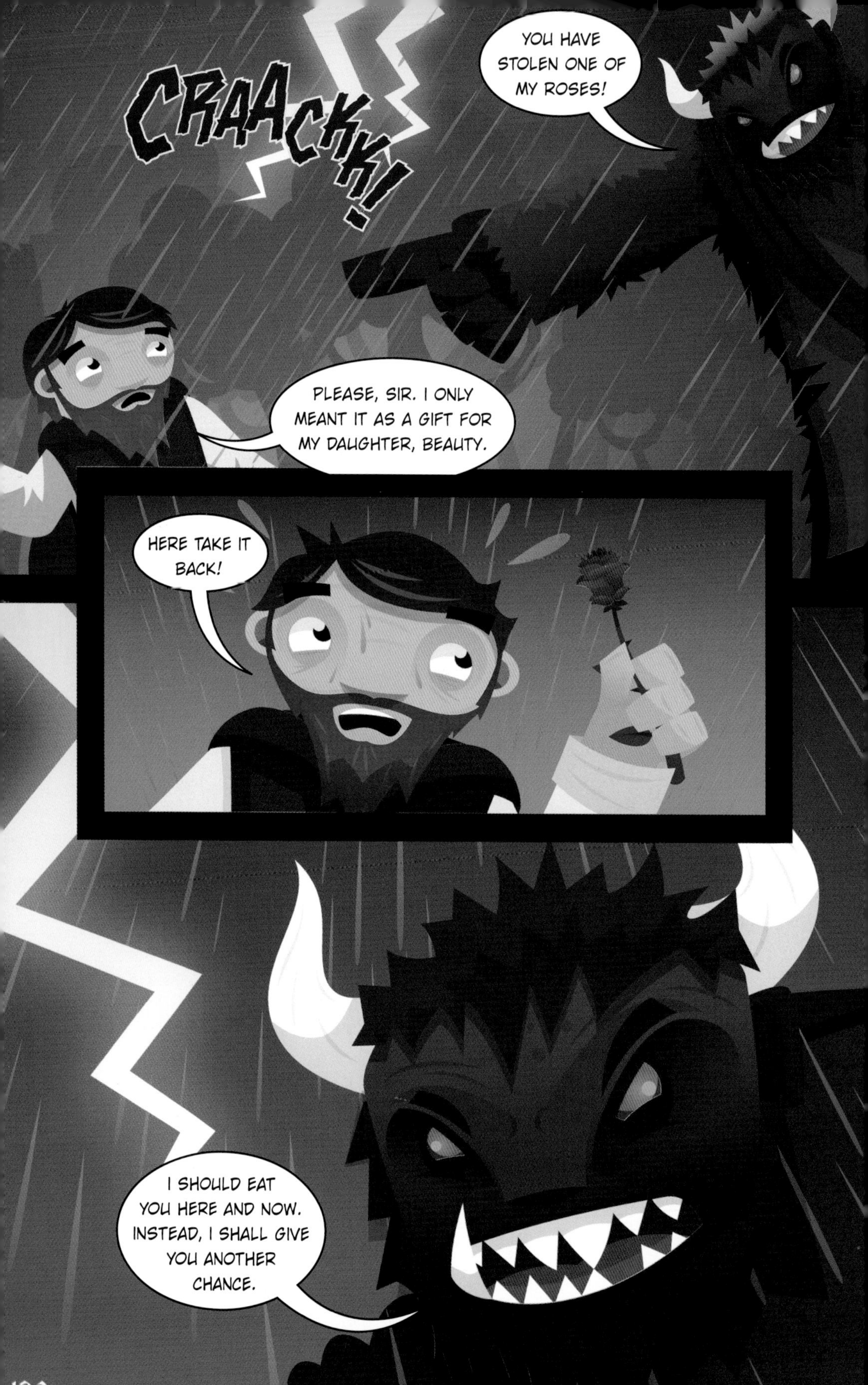
CRAACKK!
YOU HAVE STOLEN ONE OF MY ROSES!
PLEASE, SIR. I ONLY MEANT IT AS A GIFT FOR MY DAUGHTER, BEAUTY.
HERE TAKE IT BACK!
I SHOULD EAT YOU HERE AND NOW. INSTEAD, I SHALL GIVE YOU ANOTHER CHANCE.

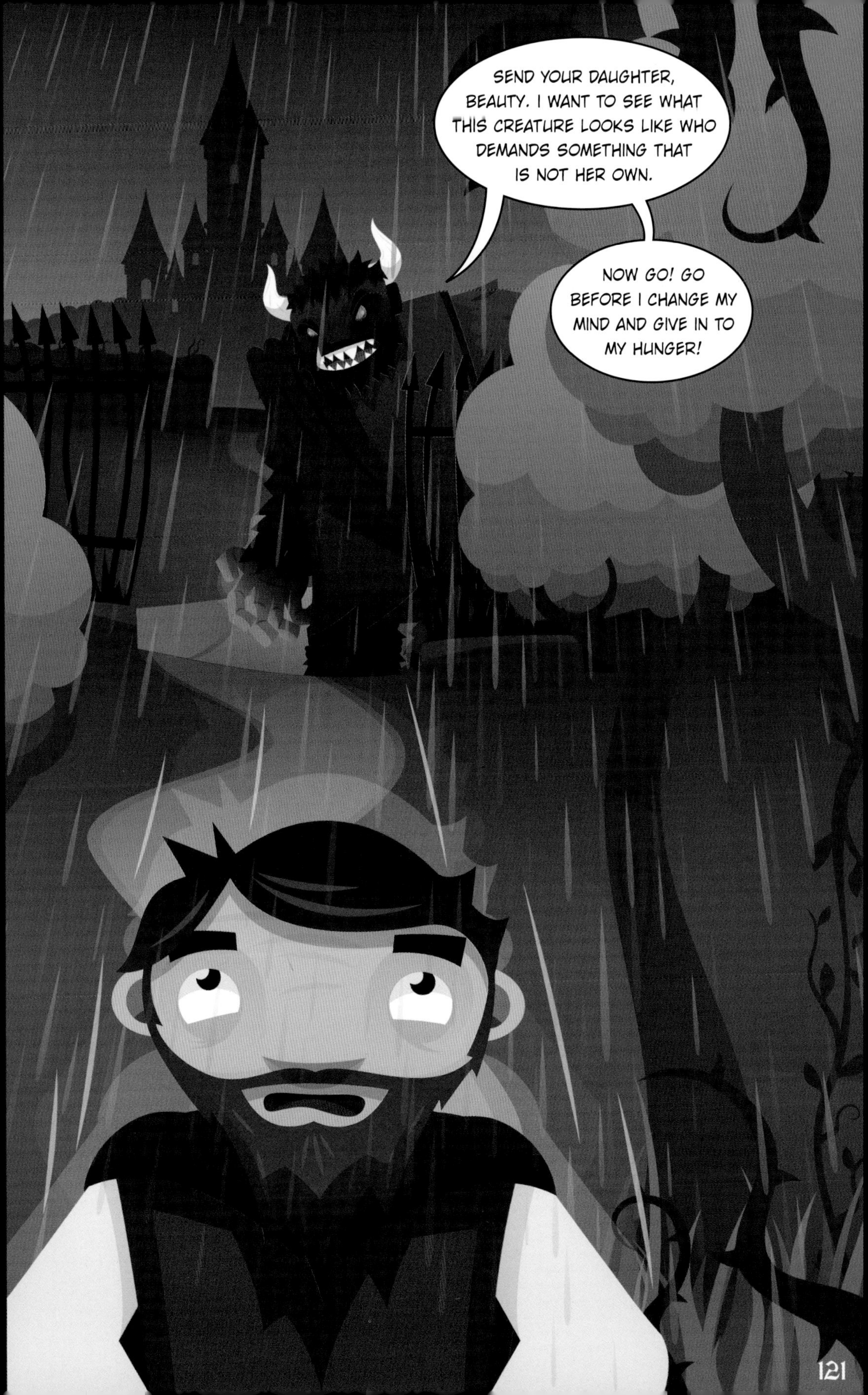
SEND YOUR DAUGHTER, BEAUTY. I WANT TO SEE WHAT THIS CREATURE LOOKS LIKE WHO DEMANDS SOMETHING THAT IS NOT HER OWN.
NOW GO! GO BEFORE I CHANGE MY MIND AND GIVE IN TO MY HUNGER!

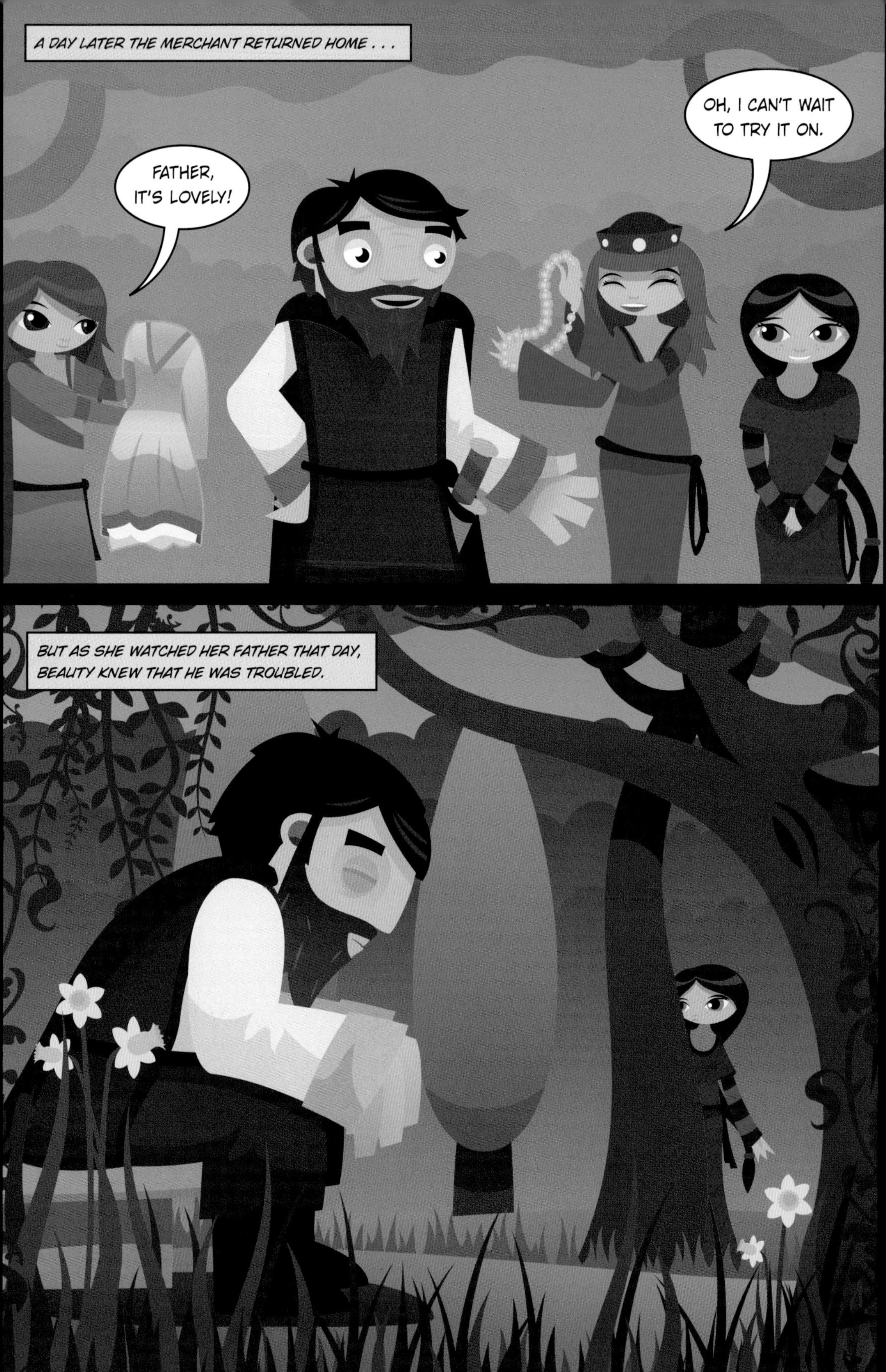
A DAY LATER THE MERCHANT RETURNED HOME . . .
FATHER, IT'S LOVELY!
OH, I CAN'T WAIT TO TRY IT ON.
BUT AS SHE WATCHED HER FATHER THAT DAY, BEAUTY KNEW THAT HE WAS TROUBLED.

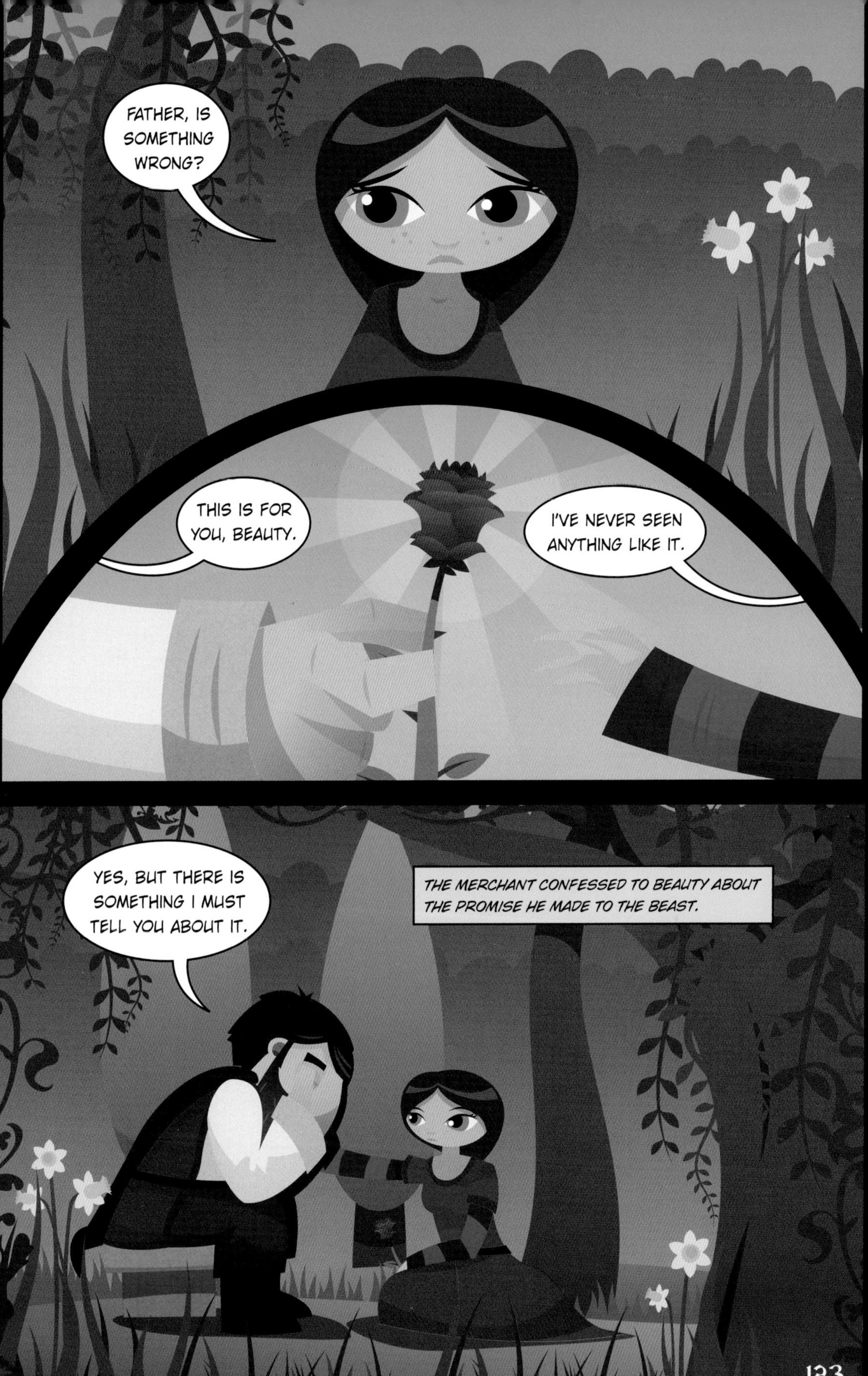
FATHER, IS SOMETHING WRONG?
THIS IS FOR YOU, BEAUTY.
I'VE NEVER SEEN ANYTHING LIKE IT.
YES, BUT THERE IS SOMETHING I MUST TELL YOU ABOUT IT.
THE MERCHANT CONFESSED TO BEAUTY ABOUT THE PROMISE HE MADE TO THE BEAST.

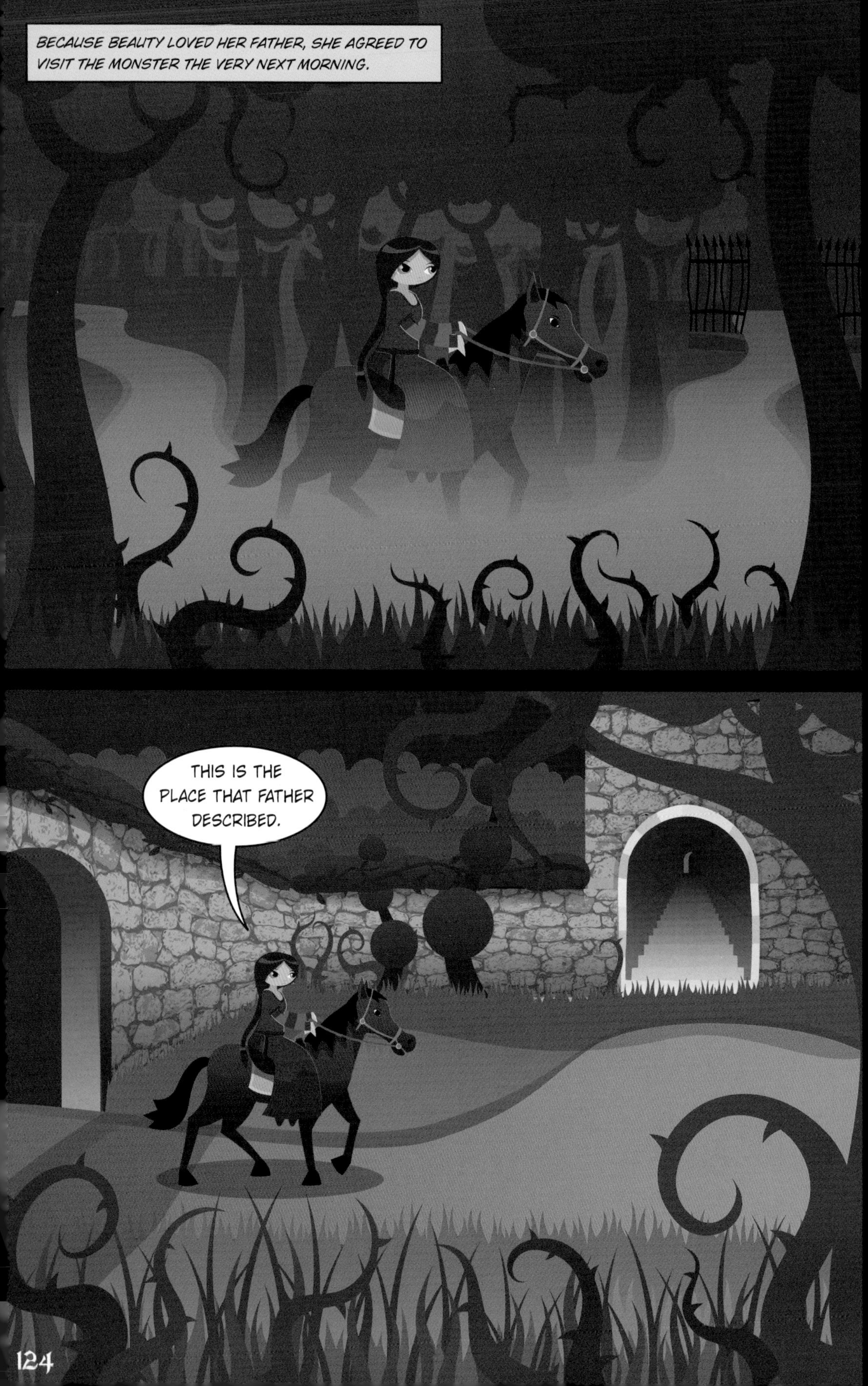
BECAUSE BEAUTY LOVED HER FATHER, SHE AGREED TO VISIT THE MONSTER THE VERY NEXT MORNING.
THIS IS THE PLACE THAT FATHER DESCRIBED.

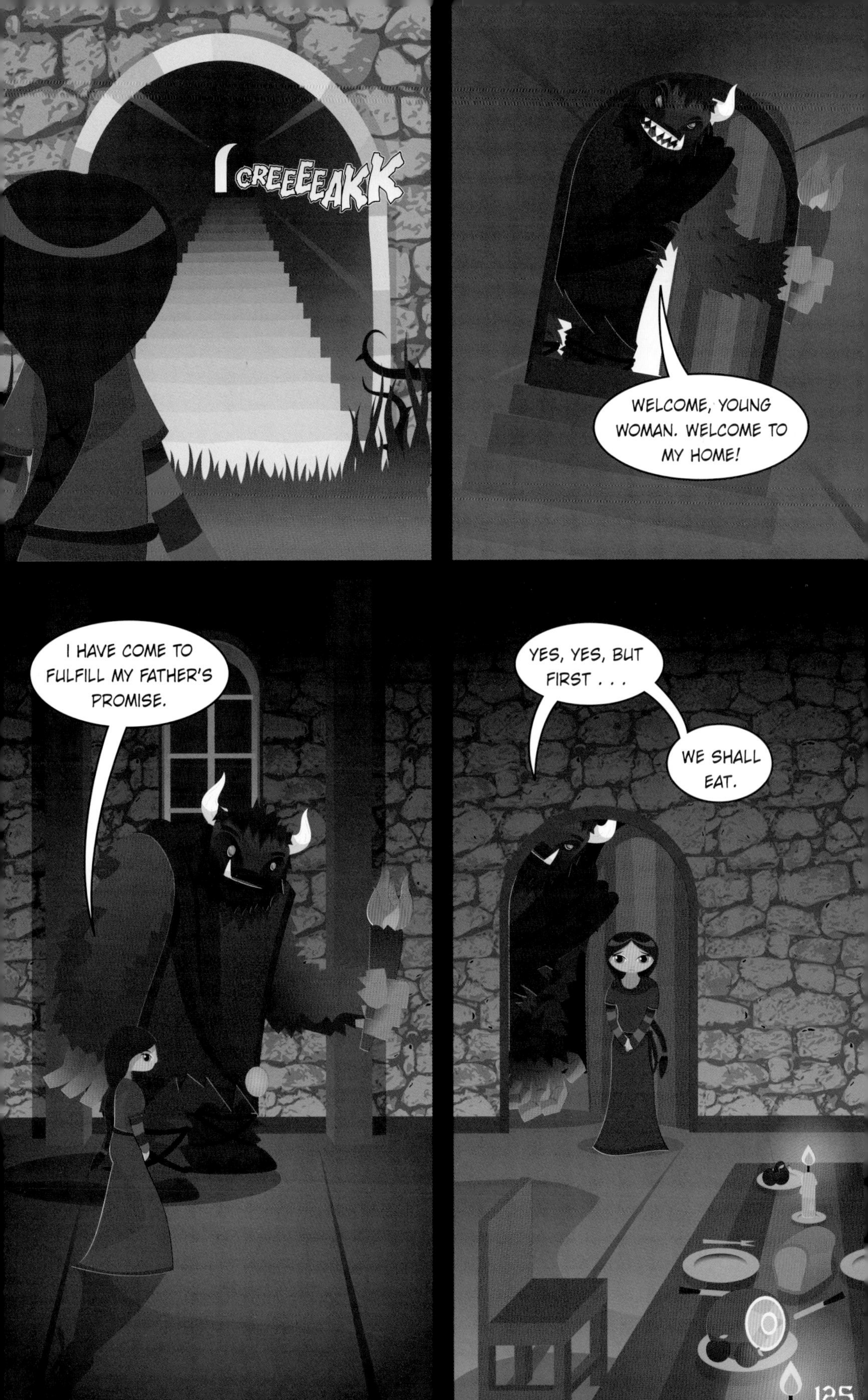
CREEEEAKK
WELCOME, YOUNG WOMAN. WELCOME TO MY HOME!
I HAVE COME TO FULFILL MY FATHER'S PROMISE.
YES, YES, BUT FIRST . . .
WE SHALL EAT.

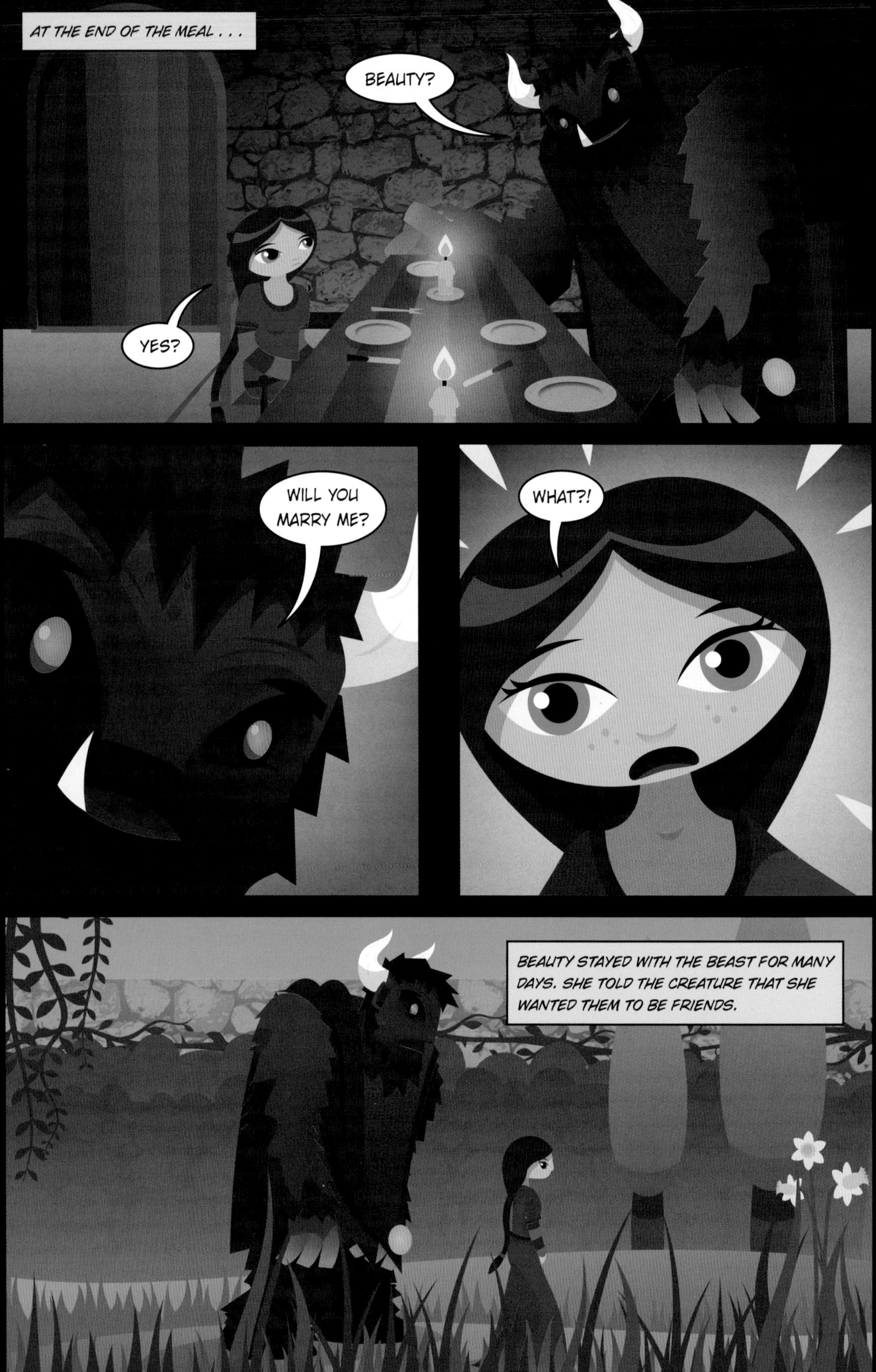
AT THE END OF THE MEAL . . .
BEAUTY?
YES?
WILL YOU MARRY ME?
WHAT?!
BEAUTY STAYED WITH THE BEAST FOR MANY DAYS. SHE TOLD THE CREATURE THAT SHE WANTED THEM TO BE FRIENDS.

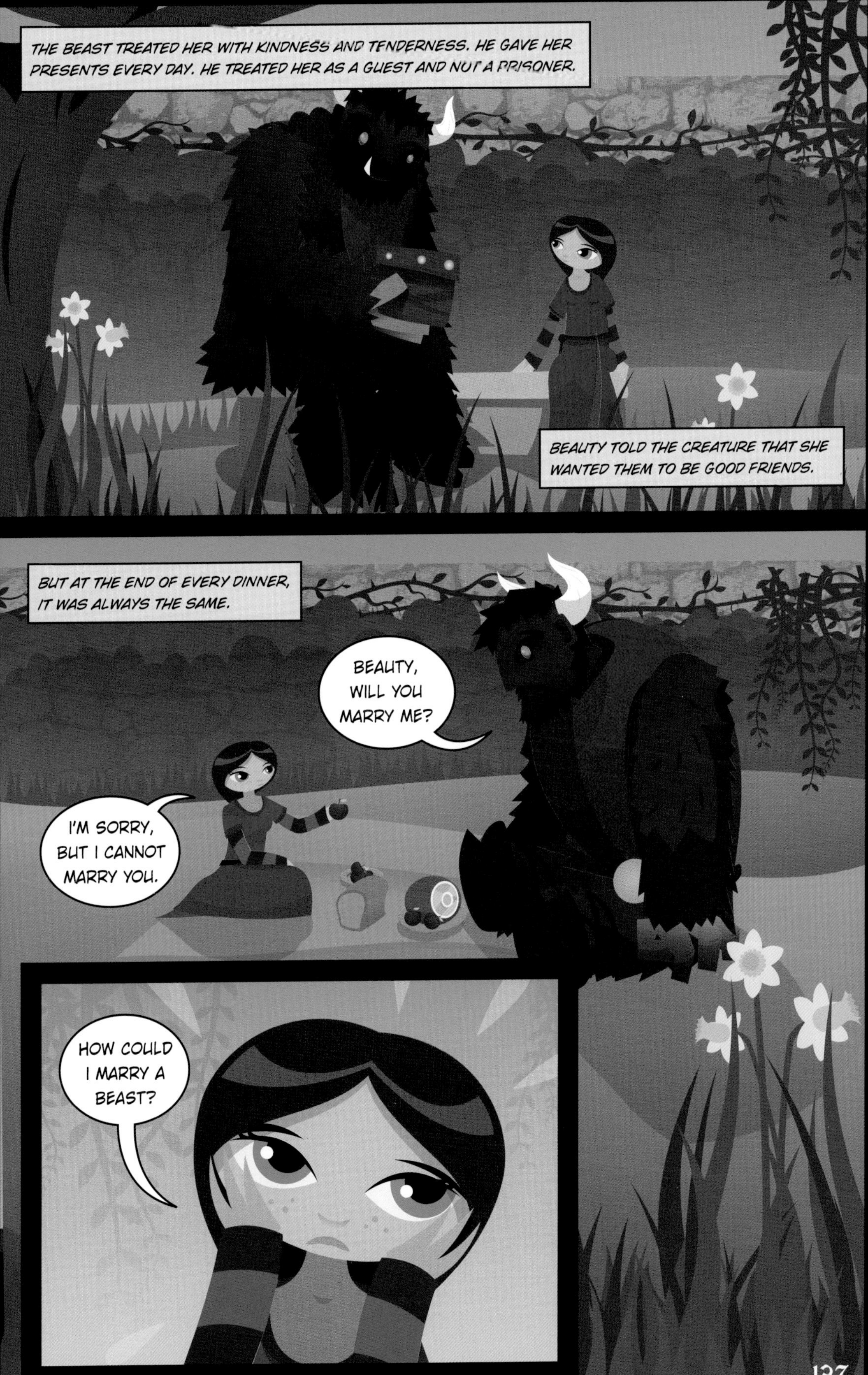
THE BEAST TREATED HER WITH KINDNESS AND TENDERNESS. HE GAVE HER PRESENTS EVERY DAY. HE TREATED HER AS A GUEST AND NOT A PRISONER.
BEAUTY TOLD THE CREATURE THAT SHE WANTED THEM TO BE GOOD FRIENDS.
BUT AT THE END OF EVERY DINNER, IT WAS ALWAYS THE SAME.
BEAUTY, WILL YOU MARRY ME?
I'M SORRY, BUT I CANNOT MARRY YOU.
HOW COULD I MARRY A BEAST?

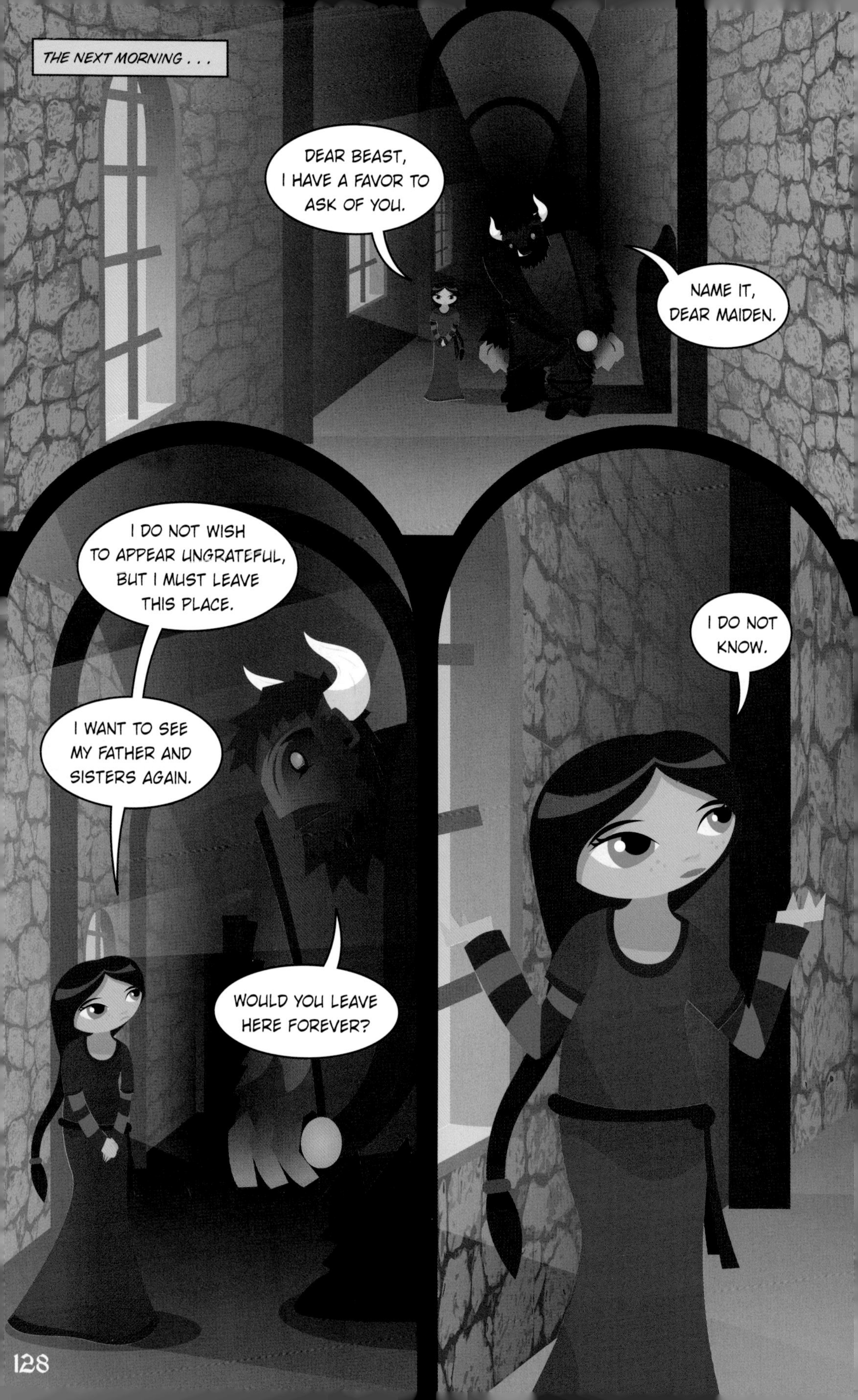
THE NEXT MORNING . . .
DEAR BEAST, I HAVE A FAVOR TO ASK OF YOU.
NAME IT, DEAR MAIDEN.
I DO NOT WISH TO APPEAR UNGRATEFUL, BUT I MUST LEAVE THIS PLACE.
I WANT TO SEE MY FATHER AND SISTERS AGAIN.
WOULD YOU LEAVE HERE FOREVER?
I DO NOT KNOW.

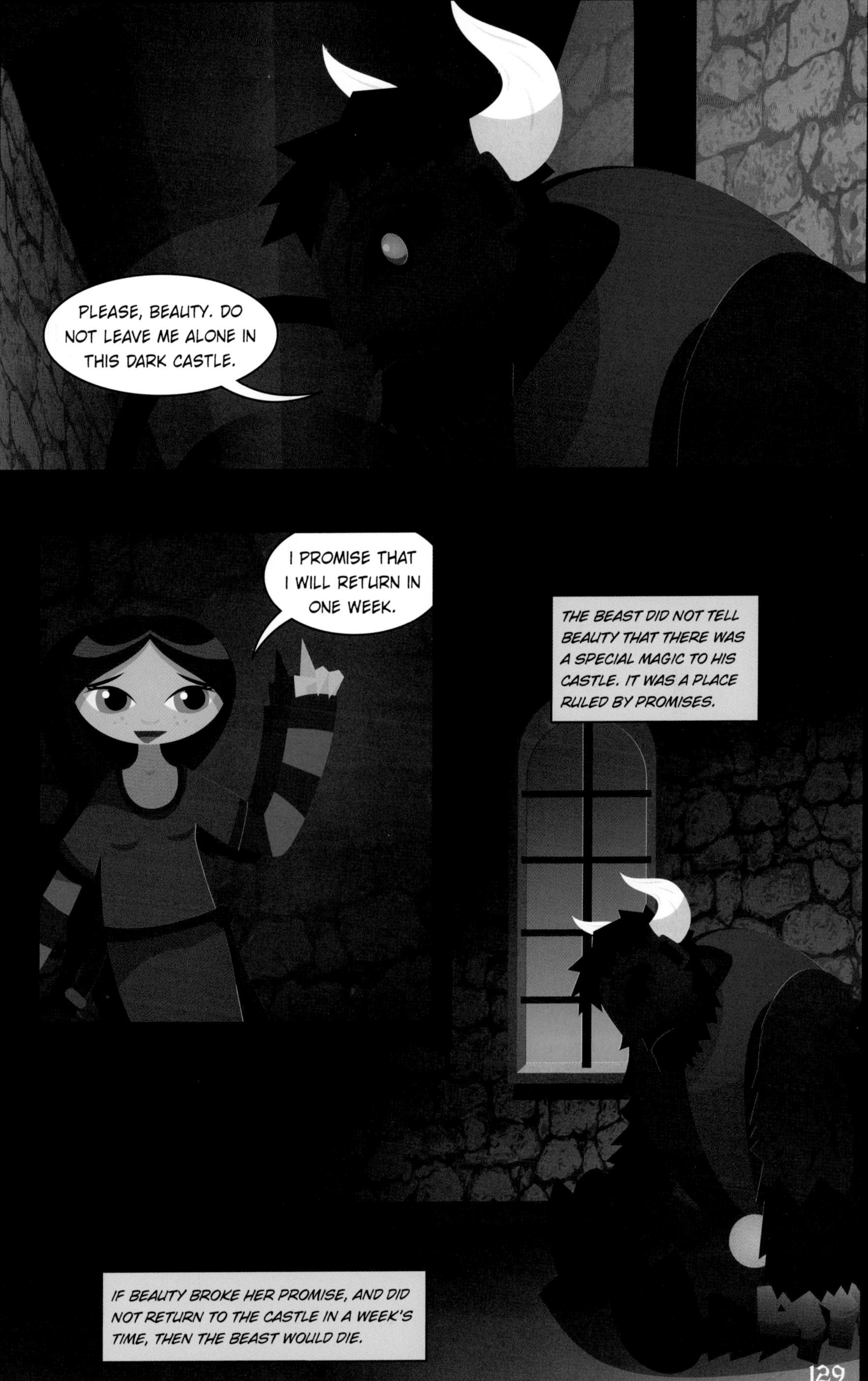

PLEASE, BEAUTY. DO NOT LEAVE ME ALONE IN THIS DARK CASTLE.
I PROMISE THAT I WILL RETURN IN ONE WEEK.
THE BEAST DID NOT TELL BEAUTY THAT THERE WAS A SPECIAL MAGIC TO HIS CASTLE. IT WAS A PLACE RULED BY PROMISES.
IF BEAUTY BROKE HER PROMISE, AND DID NOT RETURN TO THE CASTLE IN A WEEK'S TIME, THEN THE BEAST WOULD DIE.

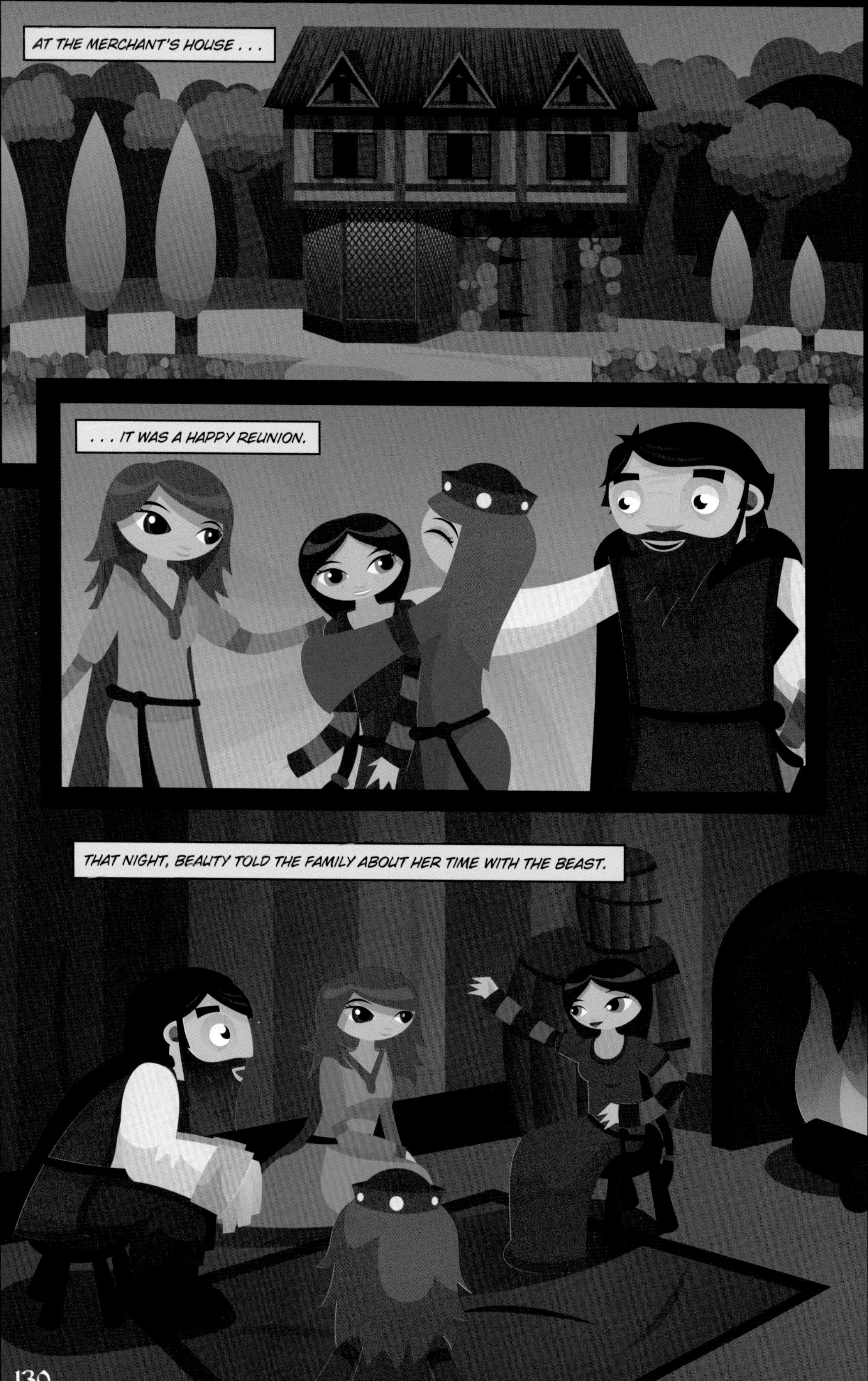
AT THE MERCHANT'S HOUSE . . .
. . . IT WAS A HAPPY REUNION.
THAT NIGHT, BEAUTY TOLD THE FAMILY ABOUT HER TIME WITH THE BEAST.

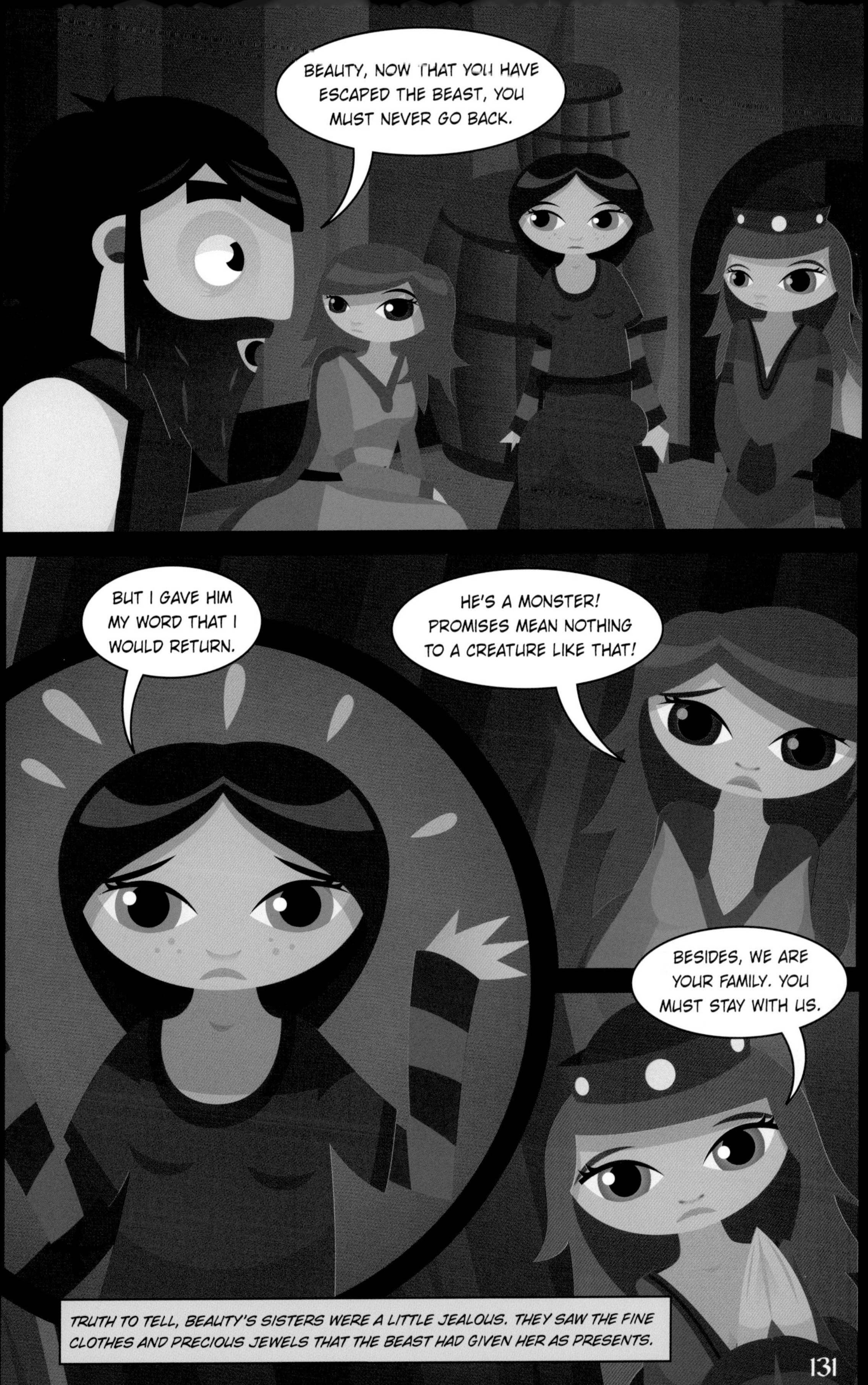

BEAUTY, NOW THAT YOU HAVE ESCAPED THE BEAST, YOU MUST NEVER GO BACK.
BUT I GAVE HIM MY WORD THAT I WOULD RETURN.
HE'S A MONSTER! PROMISES MEAN NOTHING TO A CREATURE LIKE THAT!
BESIDES, WE ARE YOUR FAMILY. YOU MUST STAY WITH US.
TRUTH TO TELL, BEAUTY'S SISTERS WERE A LITTLE JEALOUS. THEY SAW THE FINE CLOTHES AND PRECIOUS JEWELS THAT THE BEAST HAD GIVEN HER AS PRESENTS.

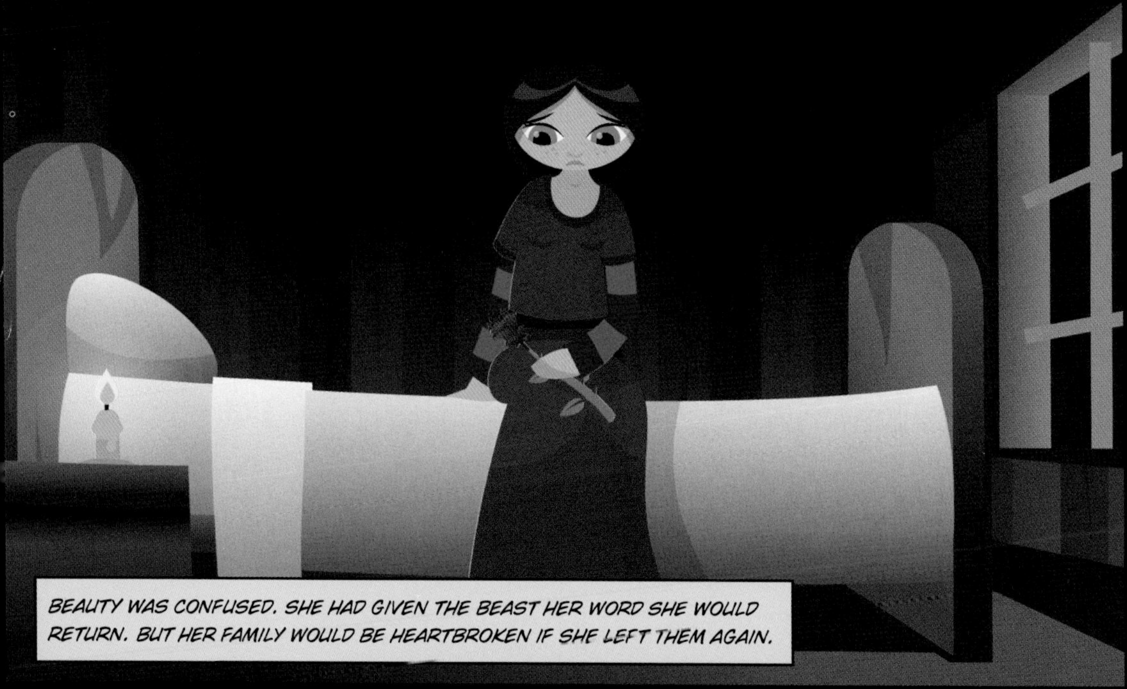
BEAUTY WAS CONFUSED. SHE HAD GIVEN THE BEAST HER WORD SHE WOULD RETURN. BUT HER FAMILY WOULD BE HEARTBROKEN IF SHE LEFT THEM AGAIN.

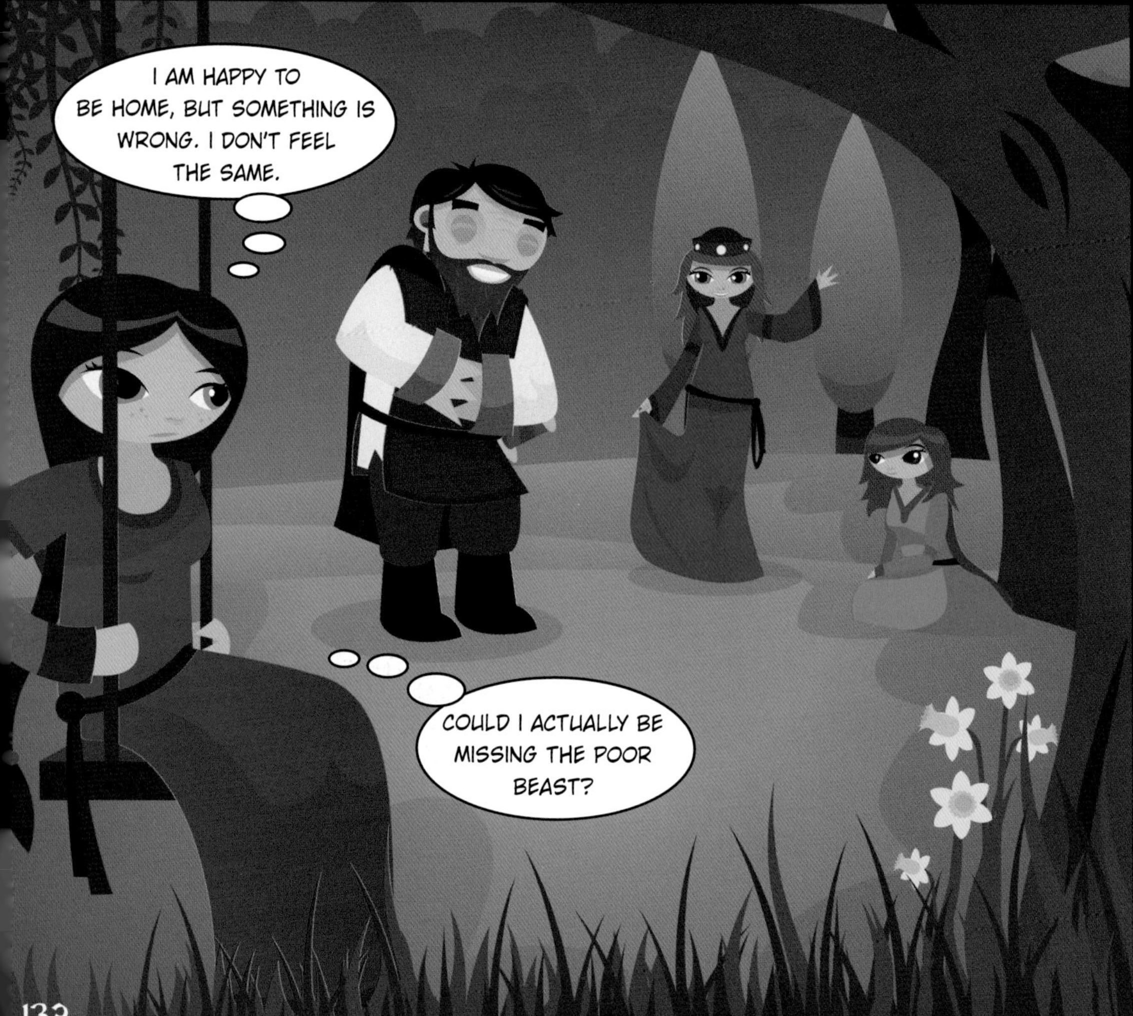
I AM HAPPY TO BE HOME, BUT SOMETHING IS WRONG. I DON'T FEEL THE SAME.
COULD I ACTUALLY BE MISSING THE POOR BEAST?

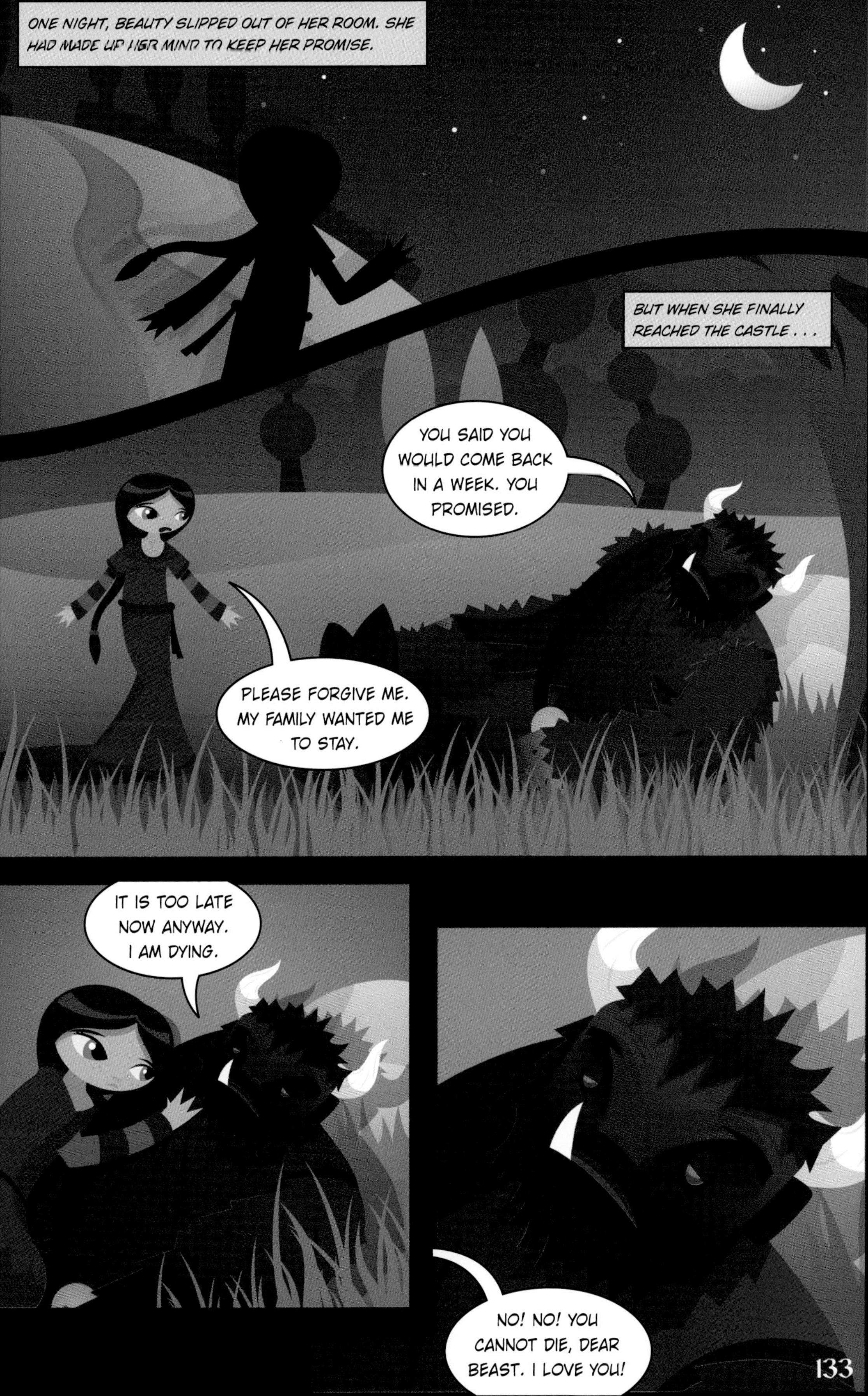
ONE NIGHT, BEAUTY SLIPPED OUT OF HER ROOM. SHE HAD MADE UP HER MIND TO KEEP HER PROMISE.
BUT WHEN SHE FINALLY REACHED THE CASTLE . . .
YOU SAID YOU WOULD COME BACK IN A WEEK. YOU PROMISED.
PLEASE FORGIVE ME. MY FAMILY WANTED ME TO STAY.
IT IS TOO LATE NOW ANYWAY. I AM DYING.
NO! NO! YOU CANNOT DIE, DEAR BEAST. I LOVE YOU!

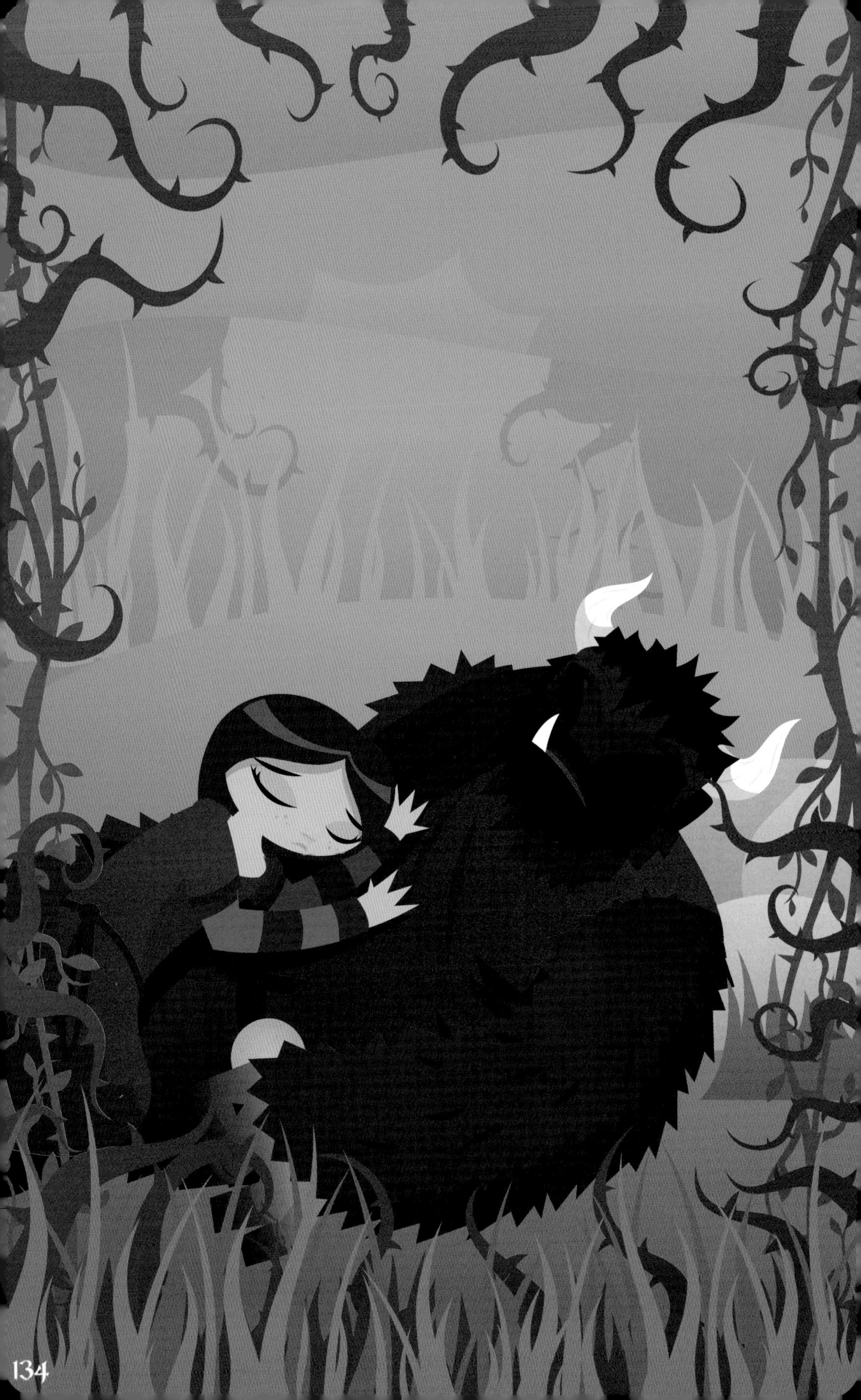

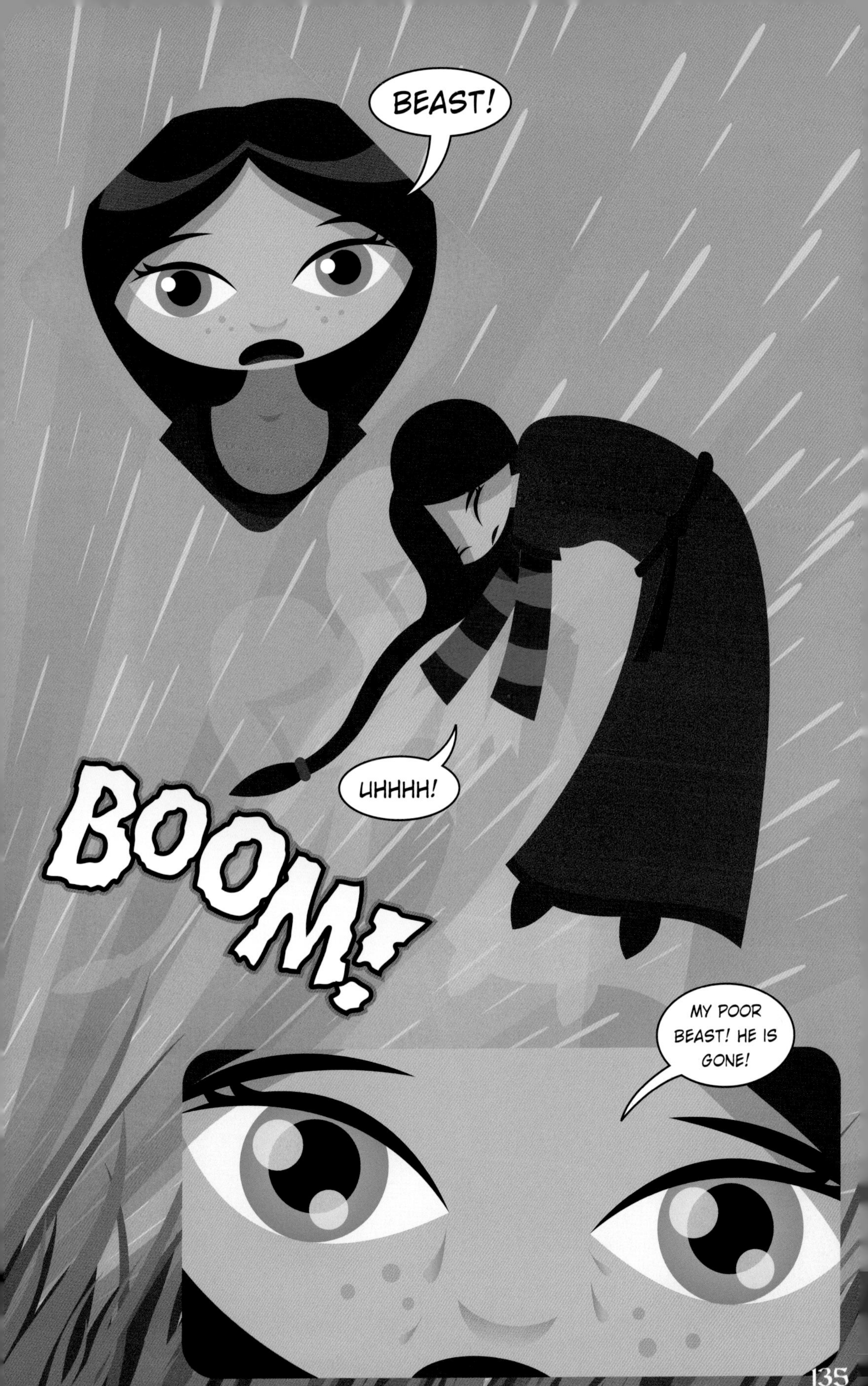
BEAST!
UHHHH!
BOOM!
MY POOR BEAST! HE IS GONE!

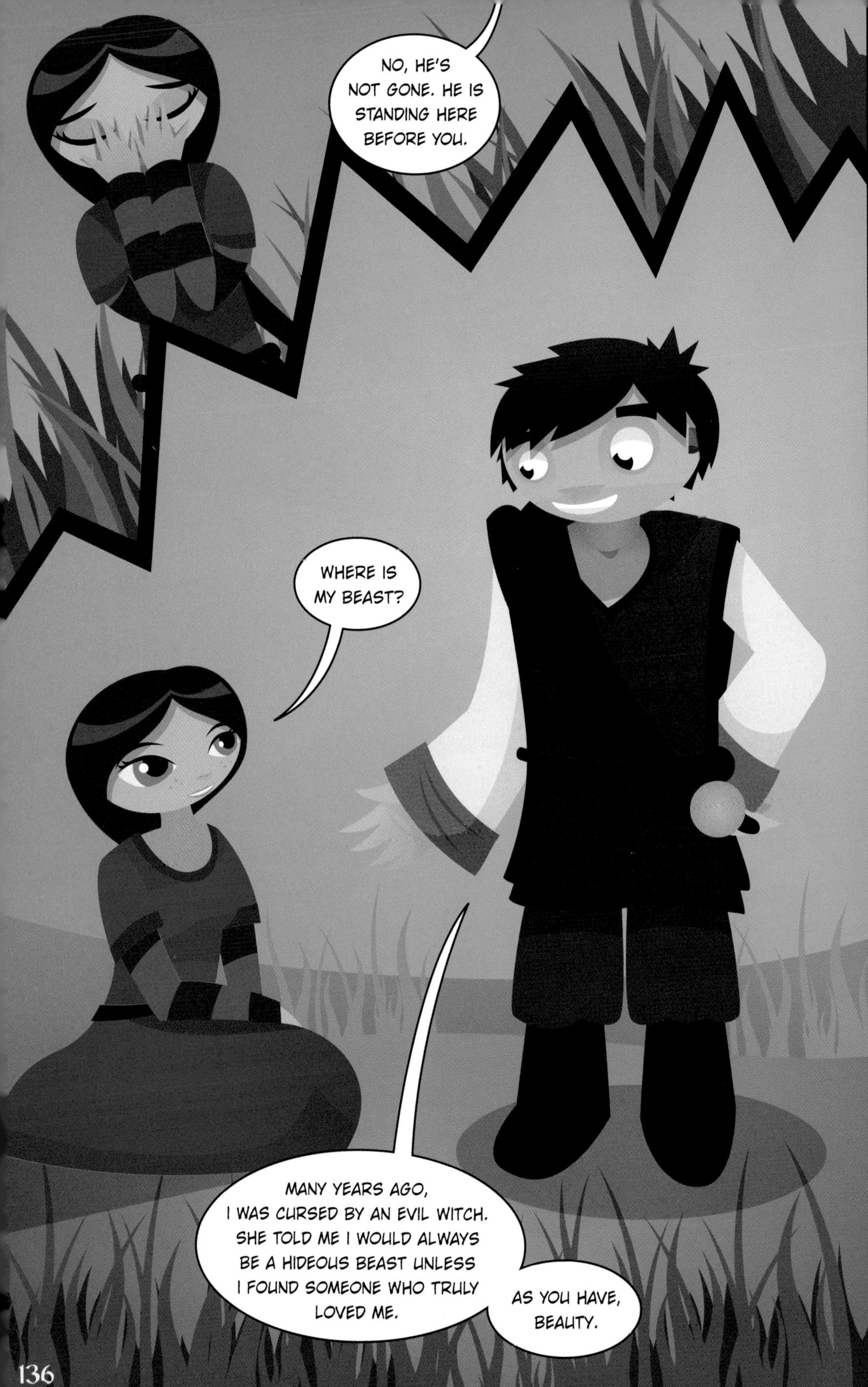
NO, HE'S NOT GONE. HE IS STANDING HERE BEFORE YOU.
WHERE IS MY BEAST?
MANY YEARS AGO, I WAS CURSED BY AN EVIL WITCH. SHE TOLD ME I WOULD ALWAYS BE A HIDEOUS BEAST UNLESS I FOUND SOMEONE WHO TRULY LOVED ME.
AS YOU HAVE, BEAUTY.

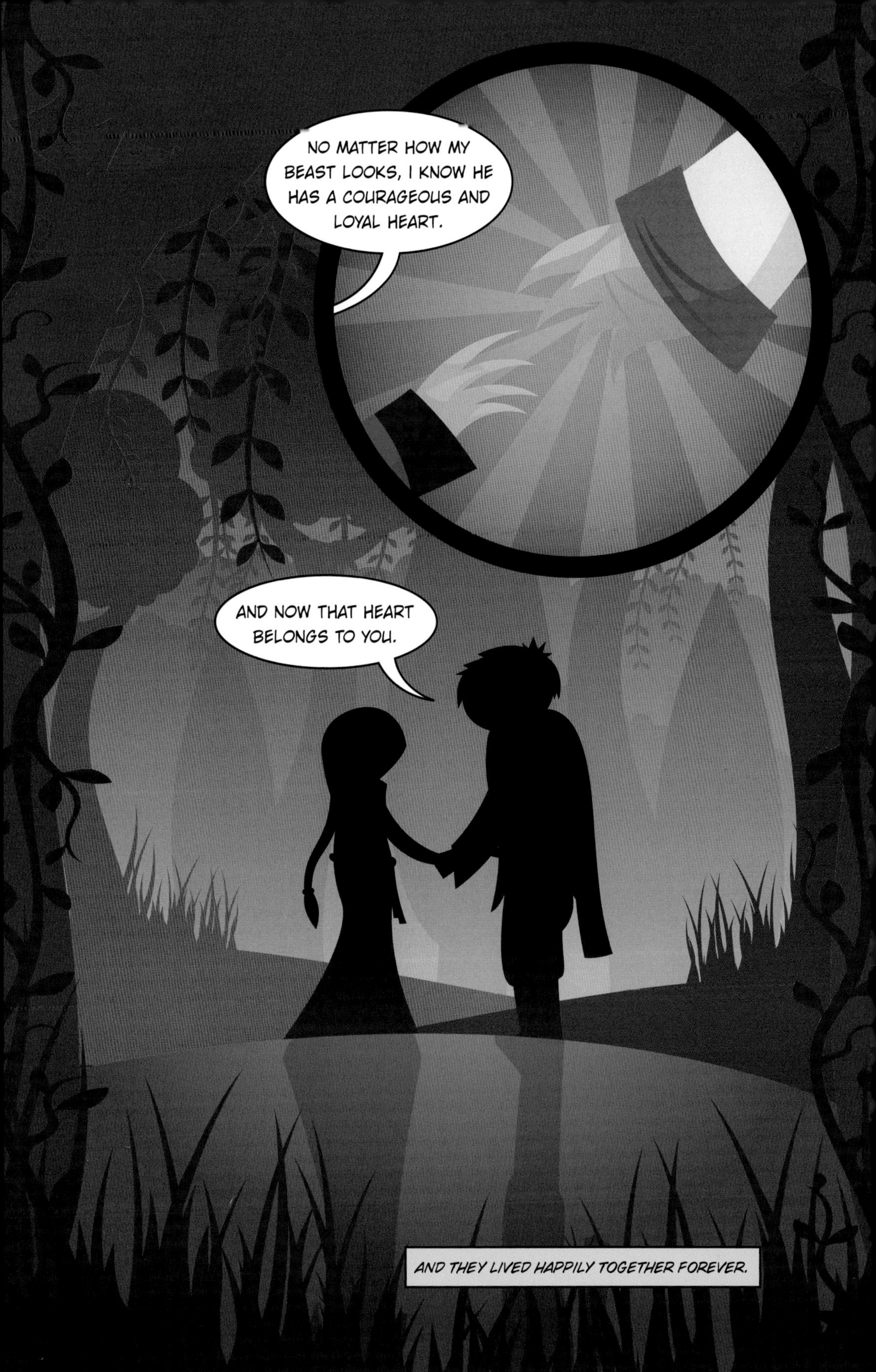
NO MATTER HOW MY BEAST LOOKS, I KNOW HE HAS A COURAGEOUS AND LOYAL HEART.
AND NOW THAT HEART BELONGS TO YOU.
AND THEY LIVED HAPPILY TOGETHER FOREVER.

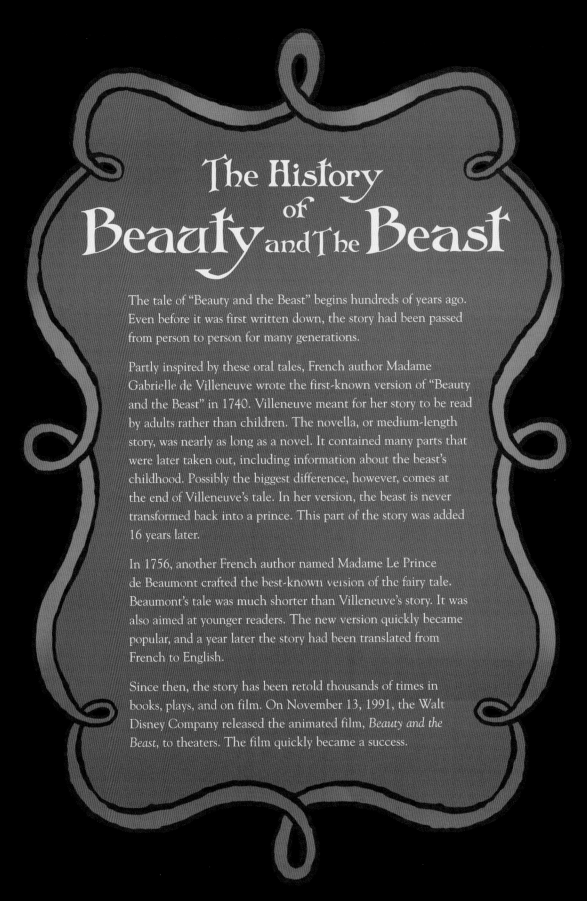

The History
of
Beauty and The Beast

The tale of "Beauty and the Beast" begins hundreds of years ago.
Even before it was first written down, the story had been passed
from person to person for many generations.

Partly inspired by these oral tales, French author Madame
Gabrielle de Villeneuve wrote the first-known version of "Beauty
and the Beast" in 1740. Villeneuve meant for her story to be read
by adults rather than children. The novella, or medium-length
story, was nearly as long as a novel. It contained many parts that
were later taken out, including information about the beast's
childhood. Possibly the biggest difference, however, comes at
the end of Villeneuve's tale. In her version, the beast is never
transformed back into a prince. This part of the story was added
16 years later.

In 1756, another French author named Madame Le Prince
de Beaumont crafted the best-known version of the fairy tale.
Beaumont's tale was much shorter than Villeneuve's story. It was
also aimed at younger readers. The new version quickly became
popular, and a year later the story had been translated from
French to English.

Since then, the story has been retold thousands of times in
books, plays, and on film. On November 13, 1991, the Walt
Disney Company released the animated film, *Beauty and the
Beast*, to theaters. The film quickly became a success.

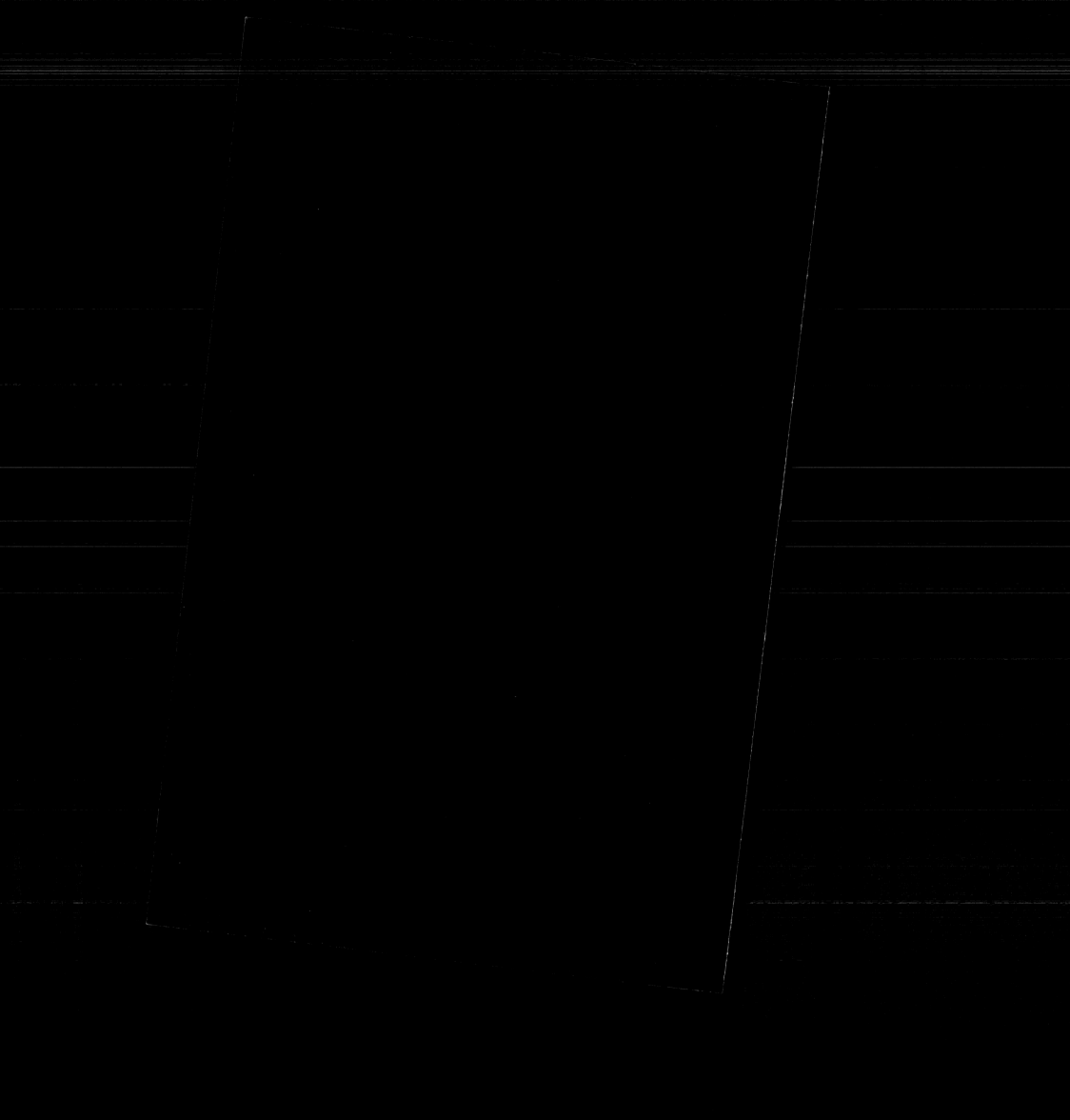

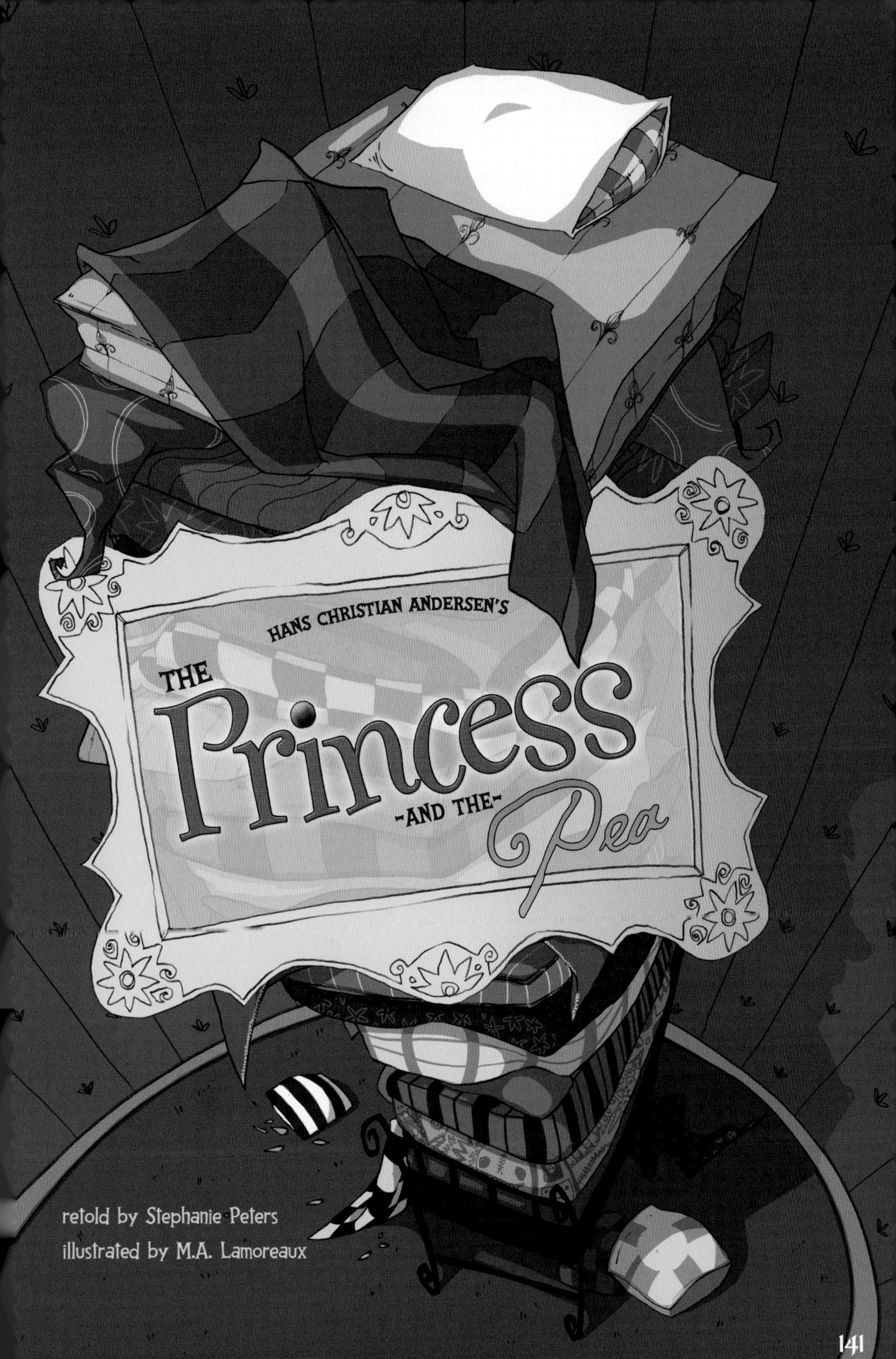
HANS CHRISTIAN ANDERSEN'S
THE Princess -AND THE- Pea
retold by Stephanie Peters
illustrated by M.A. Lamoreaux

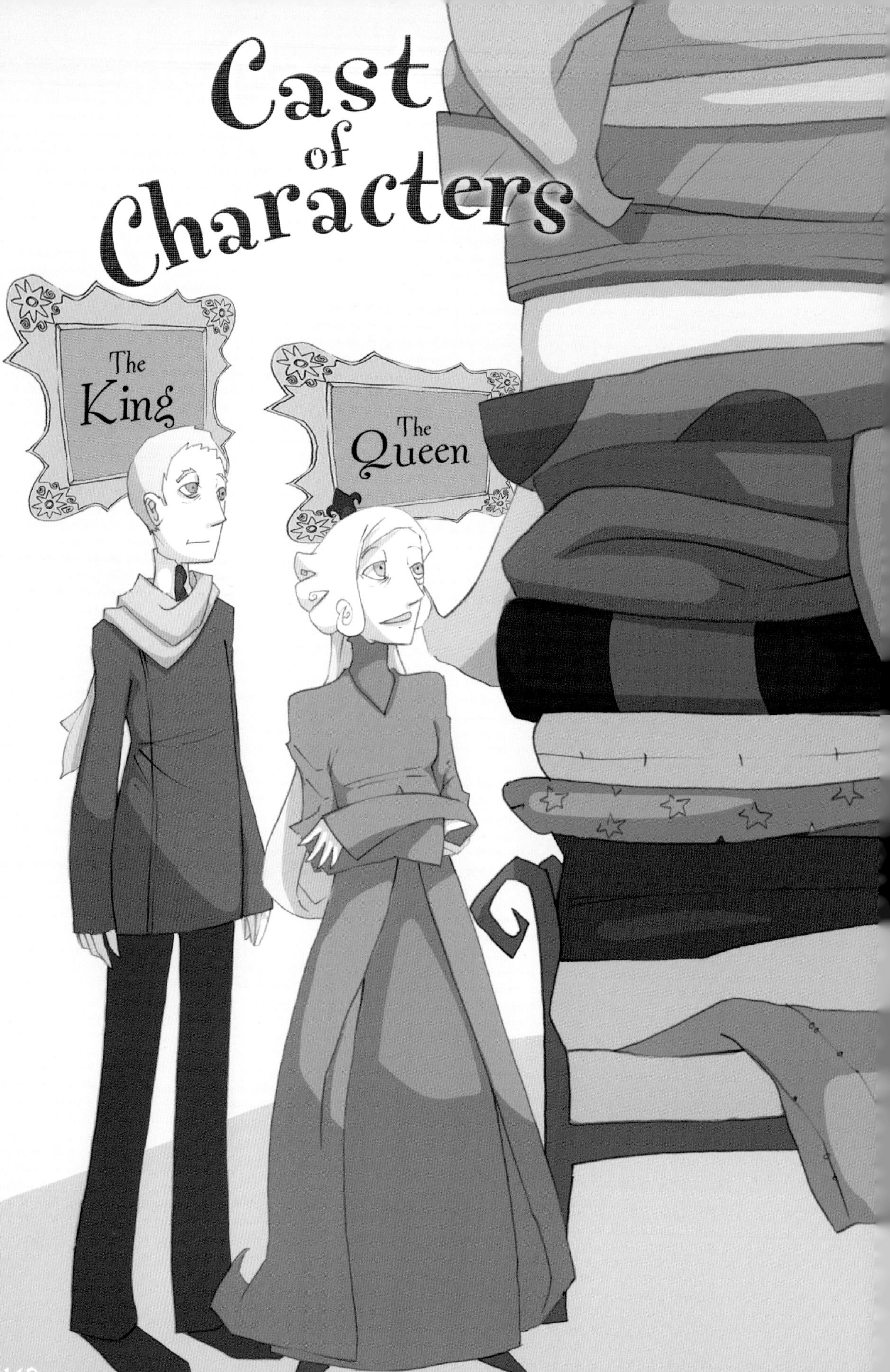
Cast of Characters
The King
The Queen

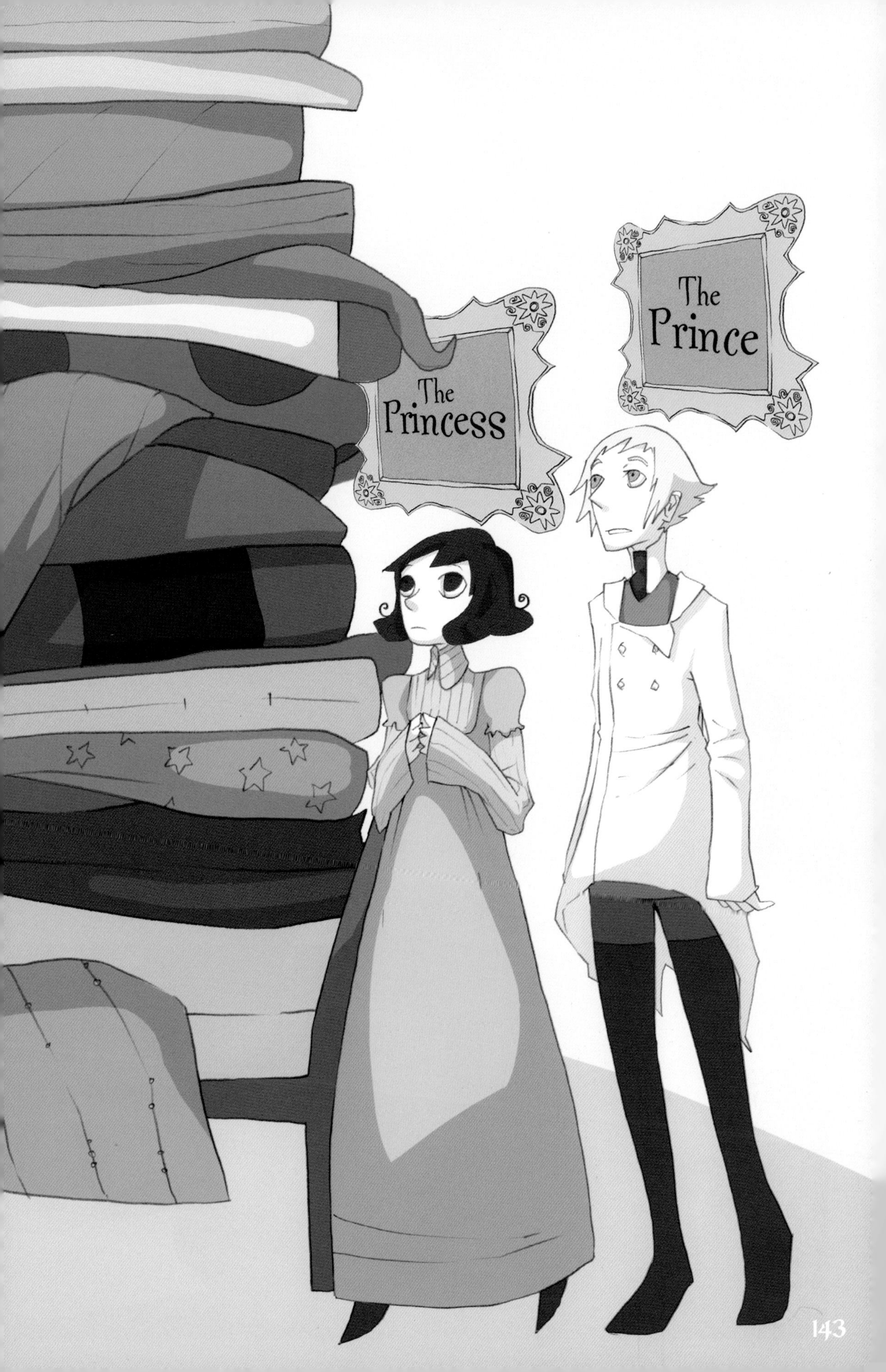
The Princess
The Prince

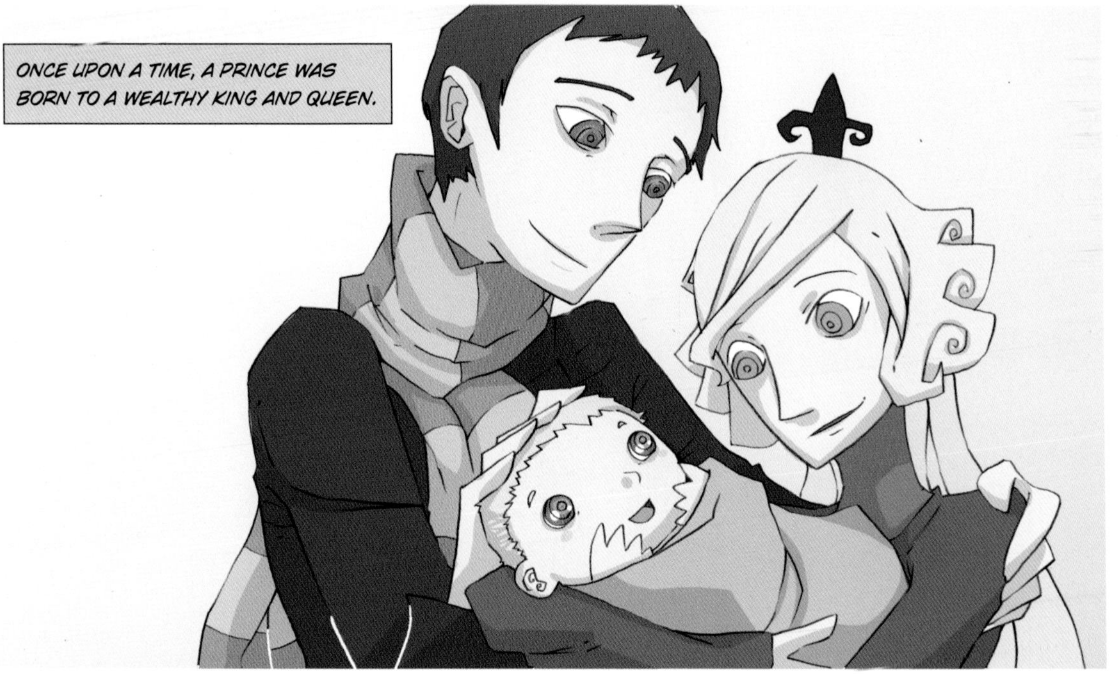
ONCE UPON A TIME, A PRINCE WAS BORN TO A WEALTHY KING AND QUEEN.

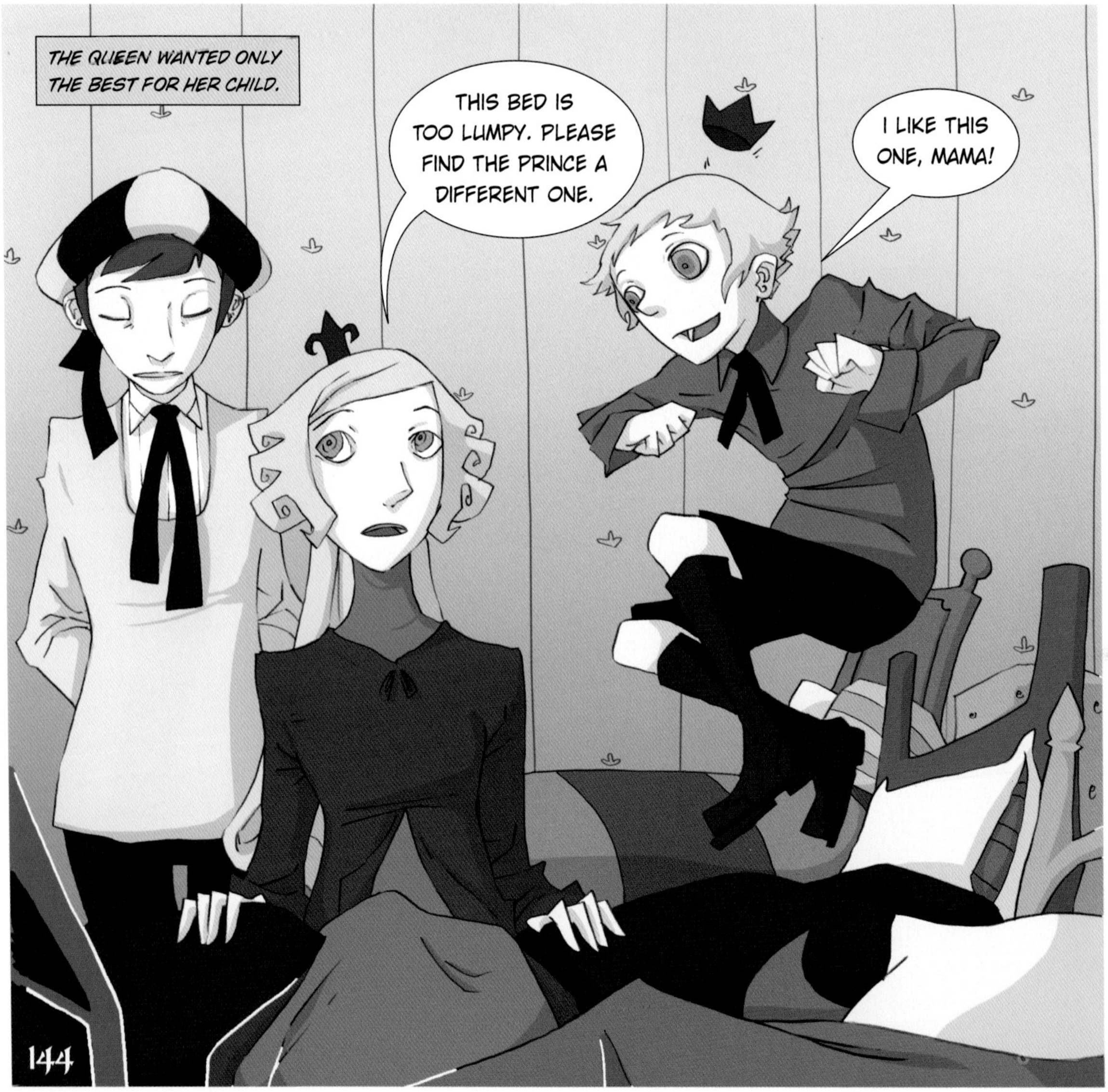
THE QUEEN WANTED ONLY THE BEST FOR HER CHILD.
THIS BED IS TOO LUMPY. PLEASE FIND THE PRINCE A DIFFERENT ONE.
I LIKE THIS ONE, MAMA!

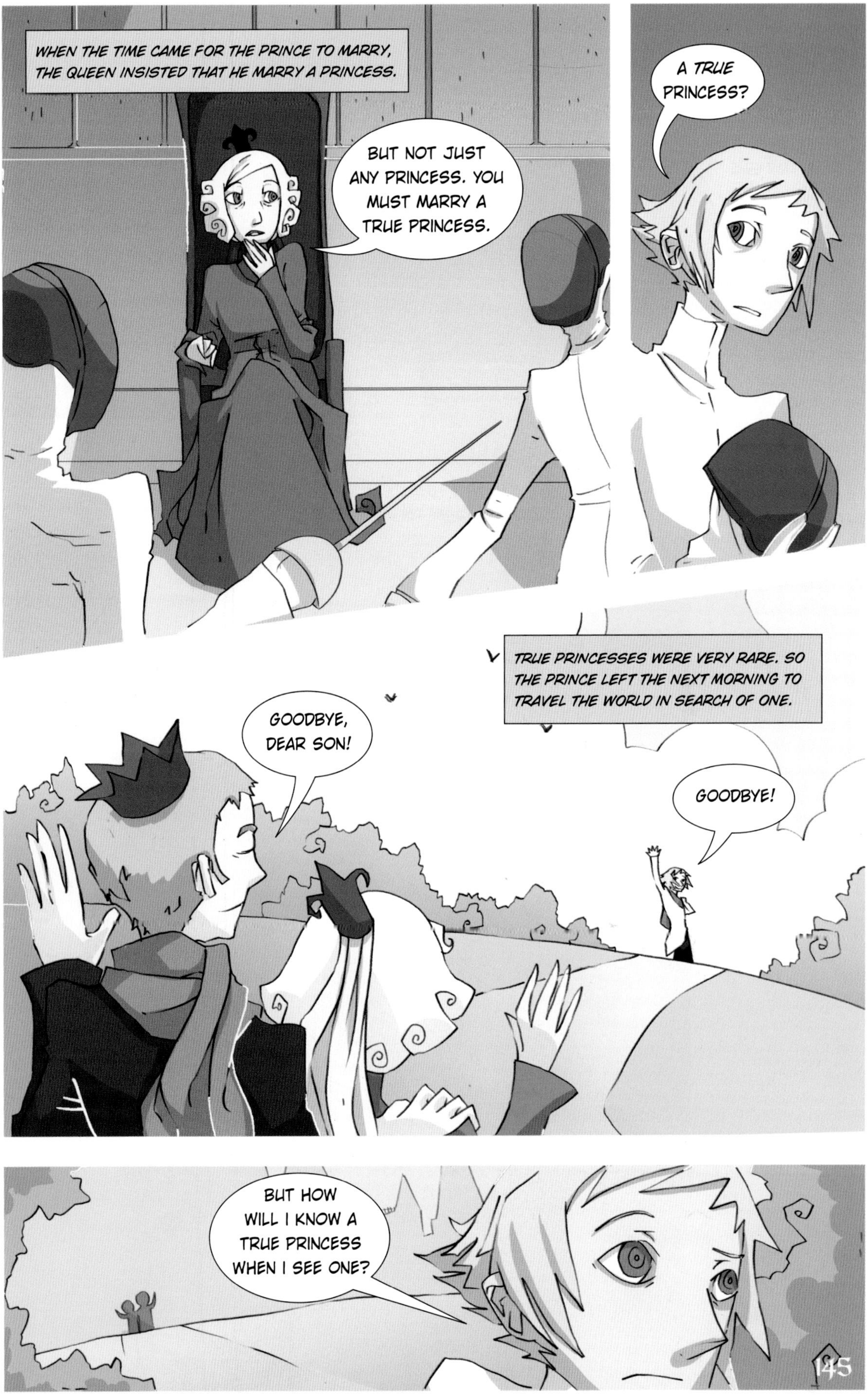
WHEN THE TIME CAME FOR THE PRINCE TO MARRY, THE QUEEN INSISTED THAT HE MARRY A PRINCESS.
BUT NOT JUST ANY PRINCESS. YOU MUST MARRY A TRUE PRINCESS.
A TRUE PRINCESS?
TRUE PRINCESSES WERE VERY RARE. SO THE PRINCE LEFT THE NEXT MORNING TO TRAVEL THE WORLD IN SEARCH OF ONE.
GOODBYE, DEAR SON!
GOODBYE!
BUT HOW WILL I KNOW A TRUE PRINCESS WHEN I SEE ONE?

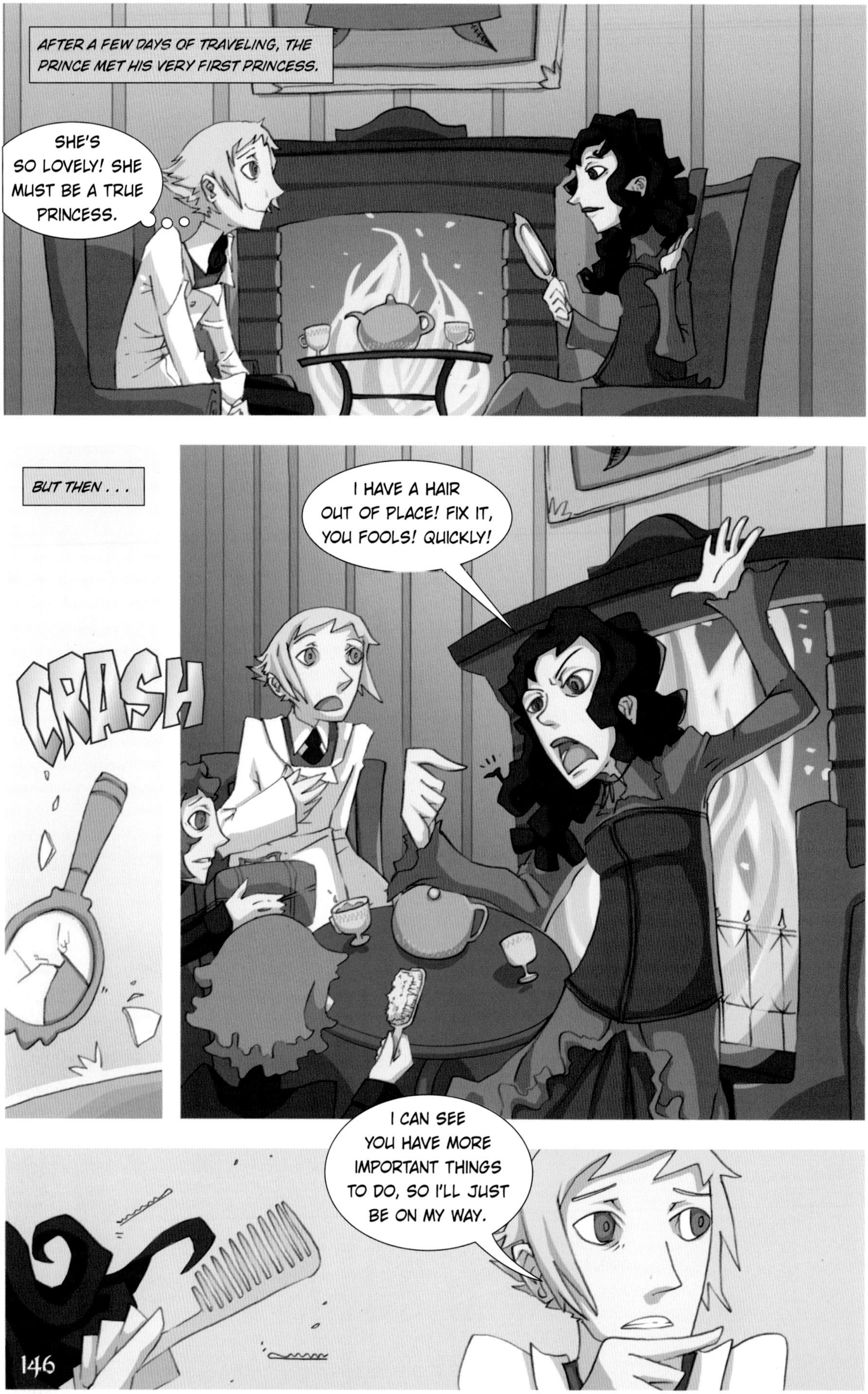
AFTER A FEW DAYS OF TRAVELING, THE PRINCE MET HIS VERY FIRST PRINCESS.
SHE'S SO LOVELY! SHE MUST BE A TRUE PRINCESS.
BUT THEN . . .
CRASH
I HAVE A HAIR OUT OF PLACE! FIX IT, YOU FOOLS! QUICKLY!
I CAN SEE YOU HAVE MORE IMPORTANT THINGS TO DO, SO I'LL JUST BE ON MY WAY.

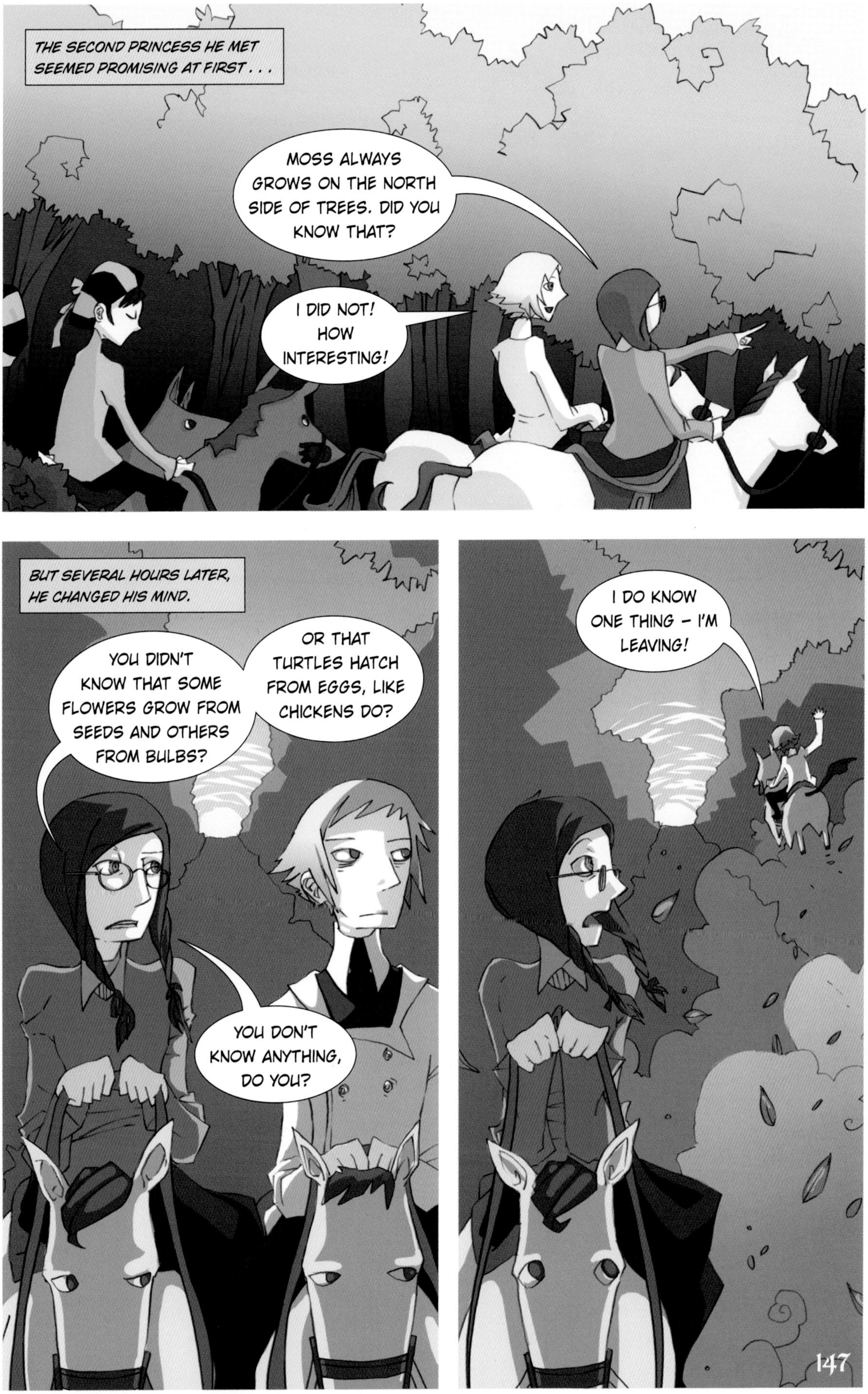
THE SECOND PRINCESS HE MET SEEMED PROMISING AT FIRST . . .
MOSS ALWAYS GROWS ON THE NORTH SIDE OF TREES. DID YOU KNOW THAT?
I DID NOT! HOW INTERESTING!
BUT SEVERAL HOURS LATER, HE CHANGED HIS MIND.
YOU DIDN'T KNOW THAT SOME FLOWERS GROW FROM SEEDS AND OTHERS FROM BULBS?
OR THAT TURTLES HATCH FROM EGGS, LIKE CHICKENS DO?
YOU DON'T KNOW ANYTHING, DO YOU?
I DO KNOW ONE THING – I'M LEAVING!

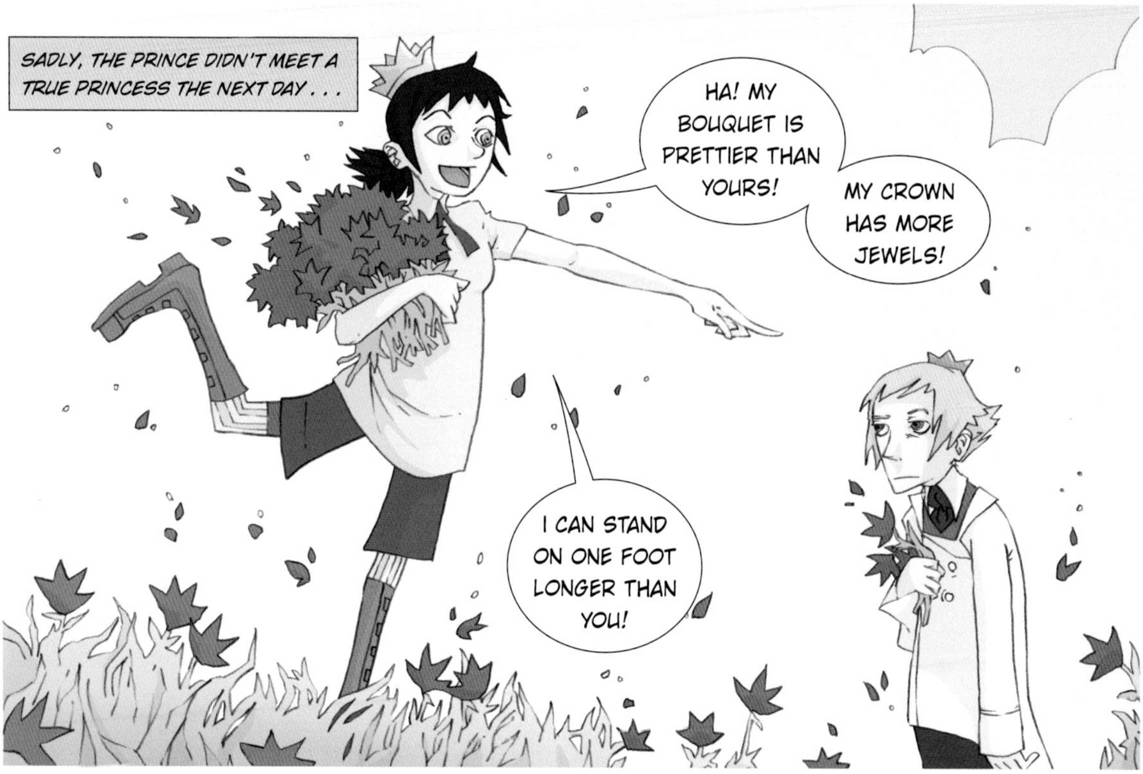
SADLY, THE PRINCE DIDN'T MEET A TRUE PRINCESS THE NEXT DAY . . .
HA! MY BOUQUET IS PRETTIER THAN YOURS!
MY CROWN HAS MORE JEWELS!
I CAN STAND ON ONE FOOT LONGER THAN YOU!

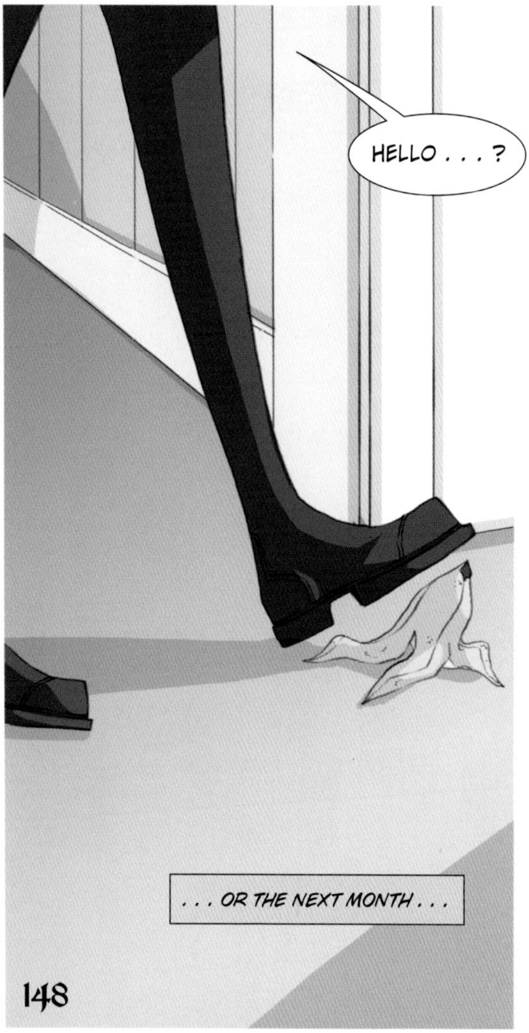
HELLO . . . ?
. . . OR THE NEXT MONTH . . .

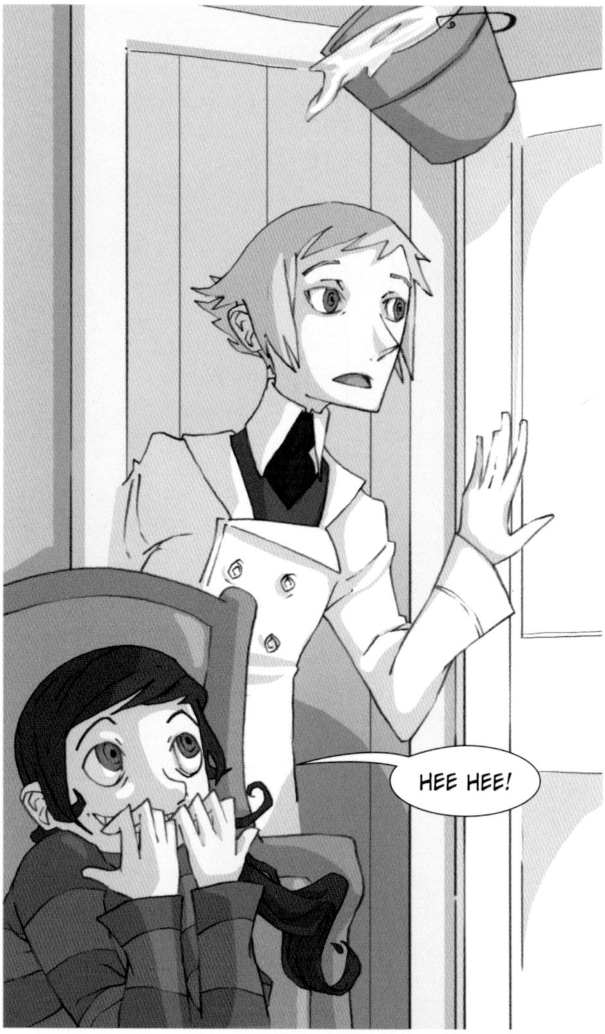
HEE HEE!

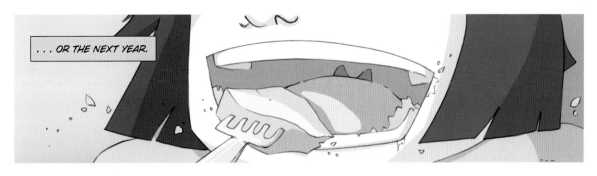

. . . OR THE NEXT YEAR.

AHEM . . .

MUNCH MUNCH

MAY I TRY SOME OF THIS?

DON'T TOUCH THAT!

OR THAT!

IT'S MINE! IT'S ALL MINE!

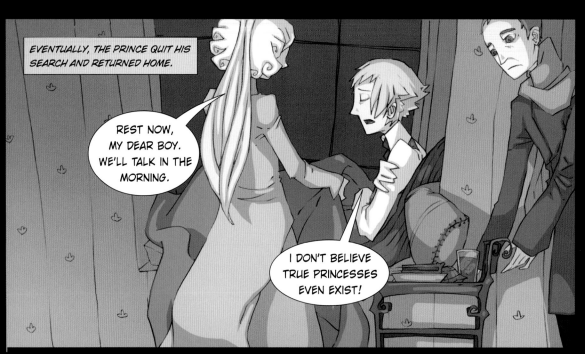

EVENTUALLY, THE PRINCE QUIT HIS SEARCH AND RETURNED HOME.

REST NOW, MY DEAR BOY. WE'LL TALK IN THE MORNING.

I DON'T BELIEVE TRUE PRINCESSES EVEN EXIST!

THE PRINCE HADN'T BEEN ASLEEP FOR LONG WHEN A BRIGHT FLASH WOKE HIM.

CRACK

AH!

I WOULD HATE TO BE OUTSIDE ON A NIGHT LIKE THIS!

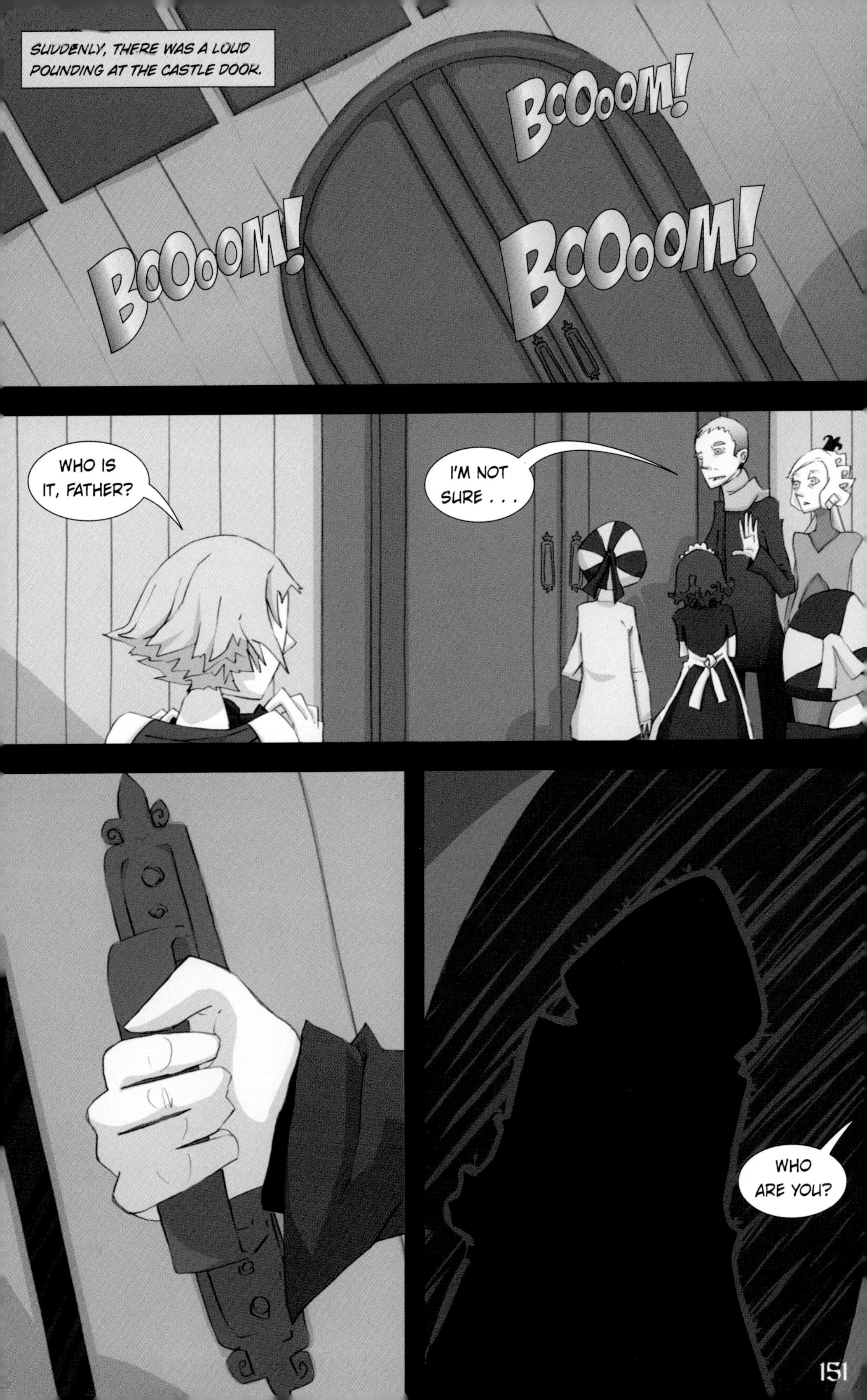
SUDDENLY, THERE WAS A LOUD POUNDING AT THE CASTLE DOOR.
BOOOOM!
BOOOOM!
BOOOOM!
WHO IS IT, FATHER?
I'M NOT SURE . . .
WHO ARE YOU?

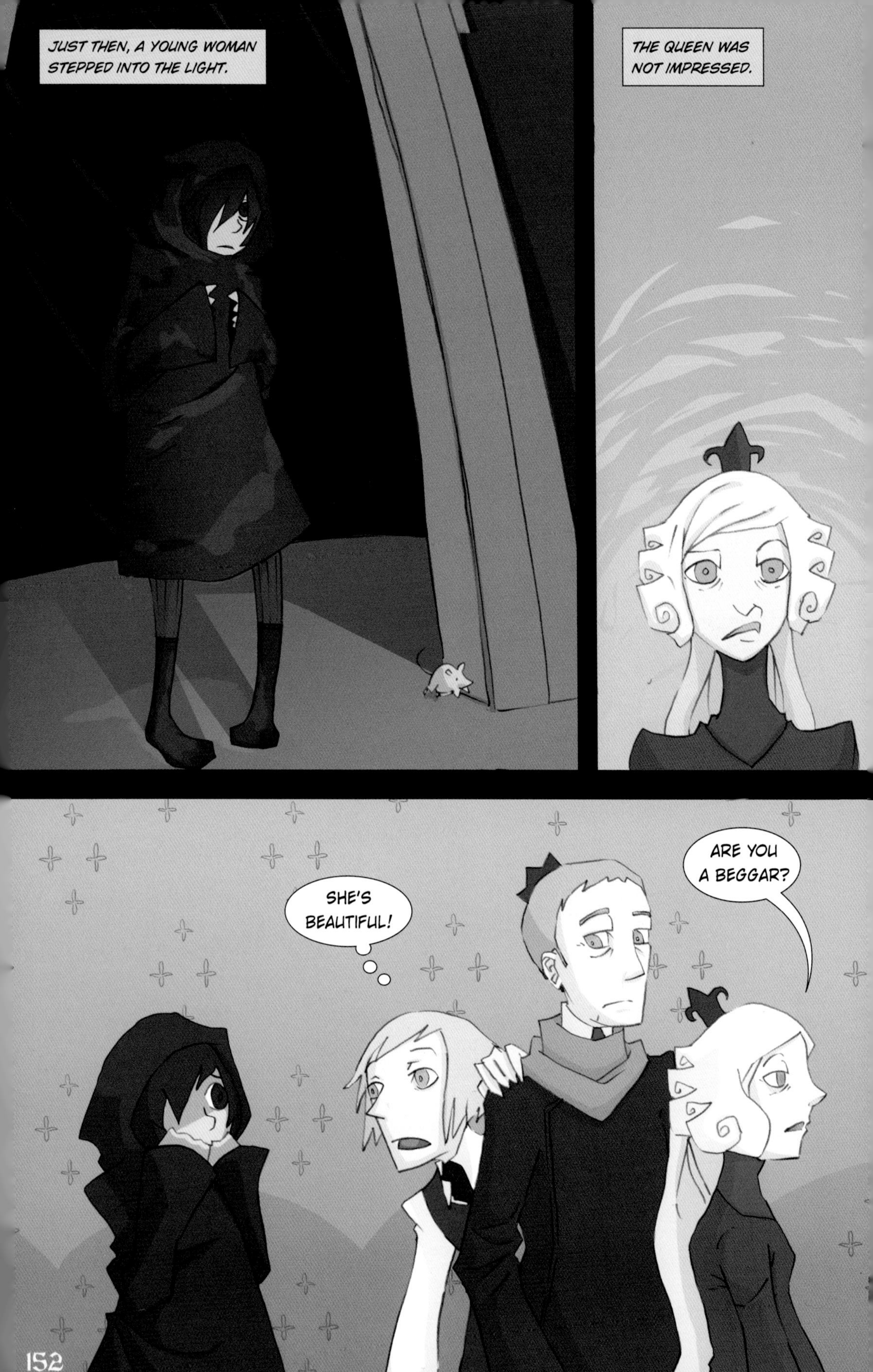
JUST THEN, A YOUNG WOMAN STEPPED INTO THE LIGHT.
THE QUEEN WAS NOT IMPRESSED.
SHE'S BEAUTIFUL!
ARE YOU A BEGGAR?

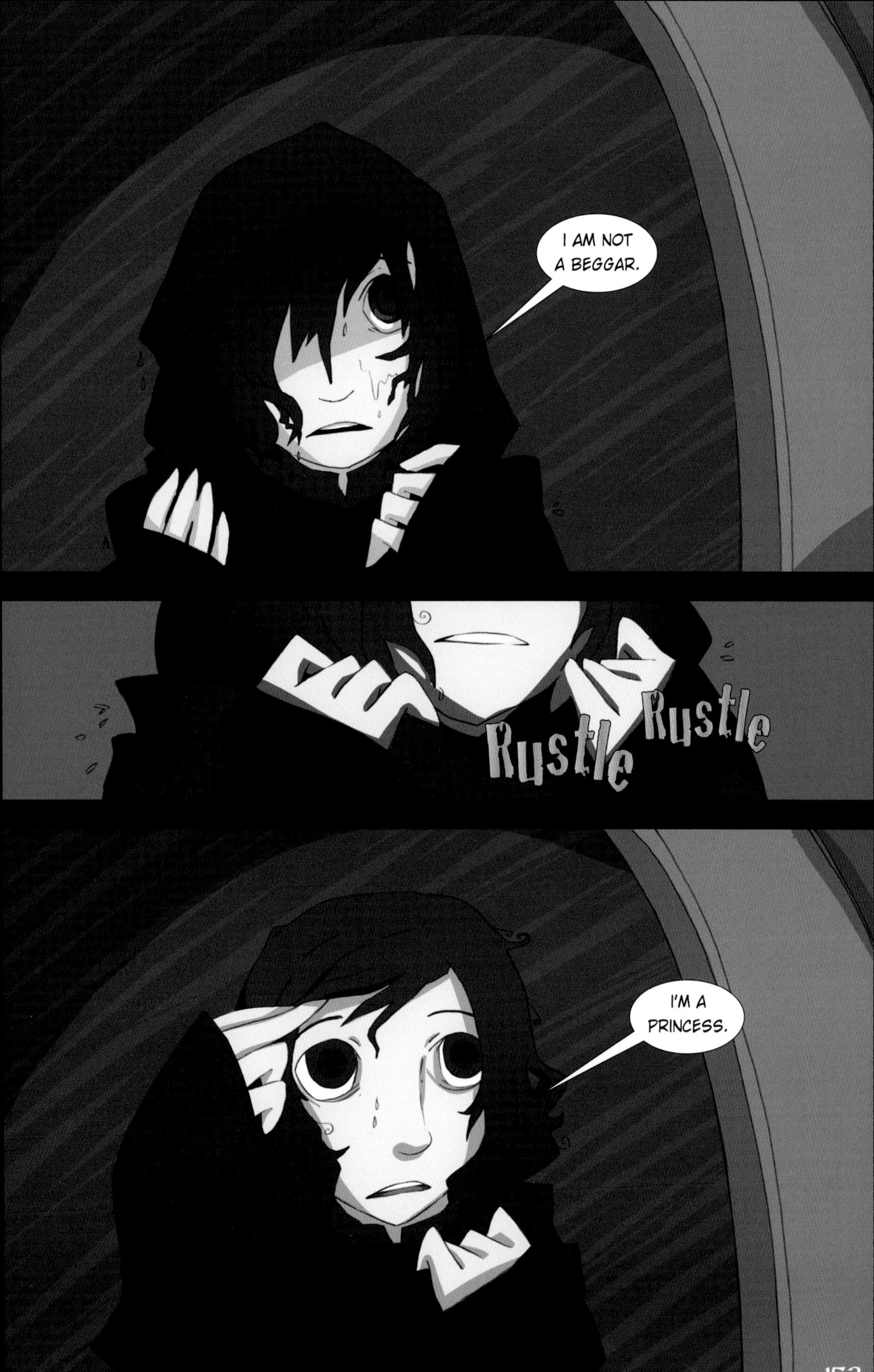
I AM NOT A BEGGAR.
Rustle Rustle
I'M A PRINCESS.

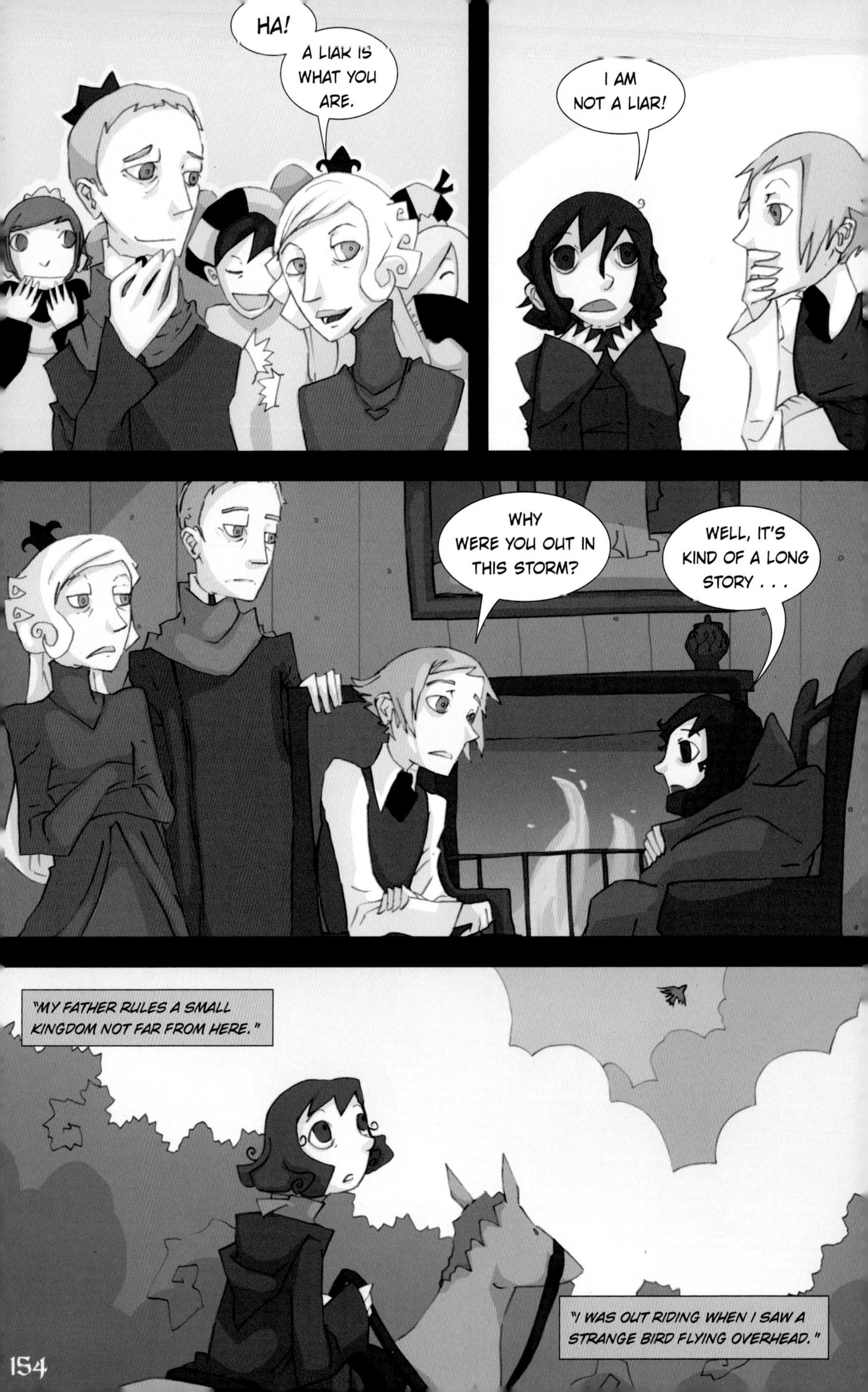
HA!
A LIAR IS WHAT YOU ARE.
I AM NOT A LIAR!
WHY WERE YOU OUT IN THIS STORM?
WELL, IT'S KIND OF A LONG STORY . . .
"MY FATHER RULES A SMALL KINGDOM NOT FAR FROM HERE."
"I WAS OUT RIDING WHEN I SAW A STRANGE BIRD FLYING OVERHEAD."

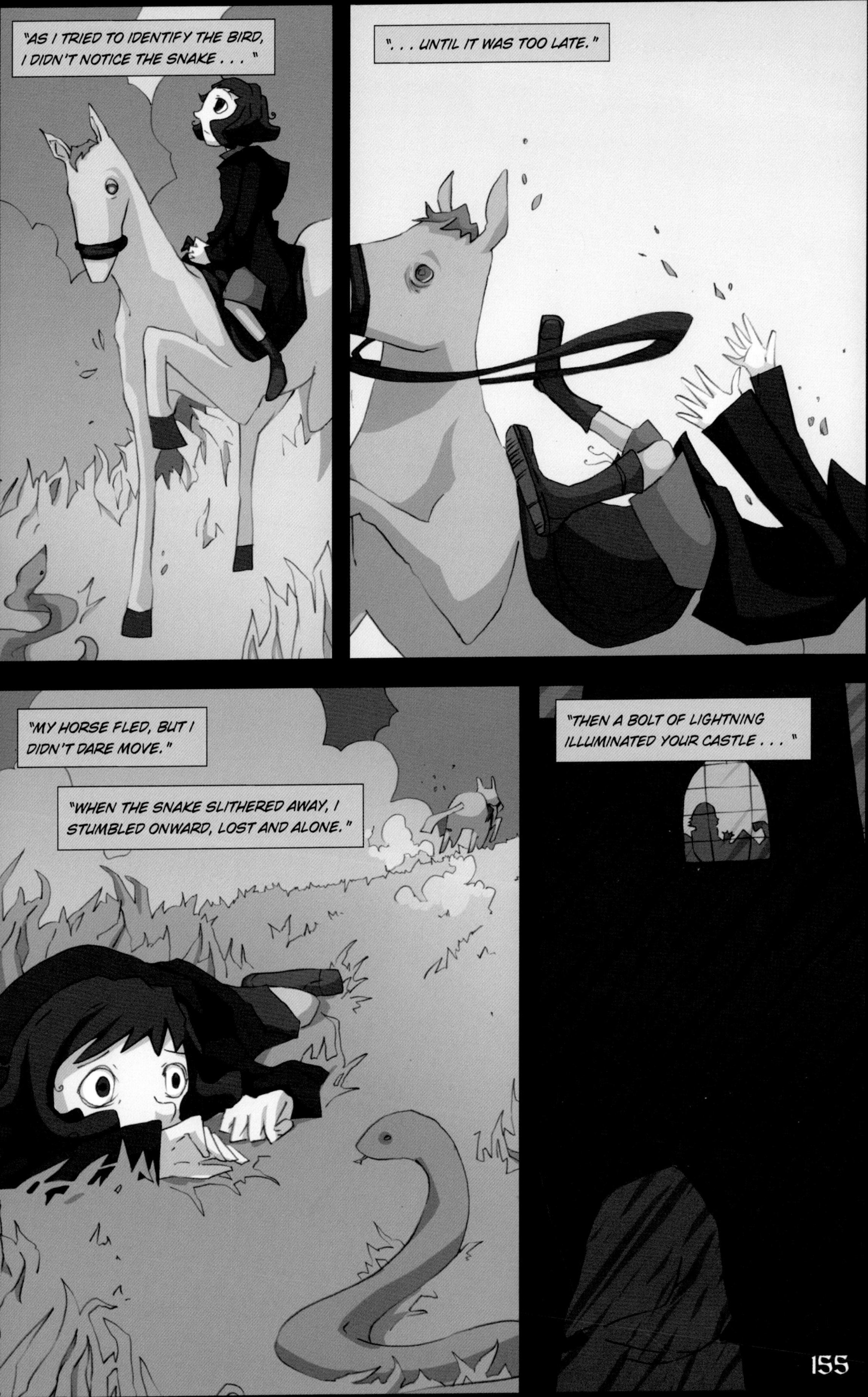
"AS I TRIED TO IDENTIFY THE BIRD, I DIDN'T NOTICE THE SNAKE . . . "
". . . UNTIL IT WAS TOO LATE."
"MY HORSE FLED, BUT I DIDN'T DARE MOVE."
"WHEN THE SNAKE SLITHERED AWAY, I STUMBLED ONWARD, LOST AND ALONE."
"THEN A BOLT OF LIGHTNING ILLUMINATED YOUR CASTLE . . . "

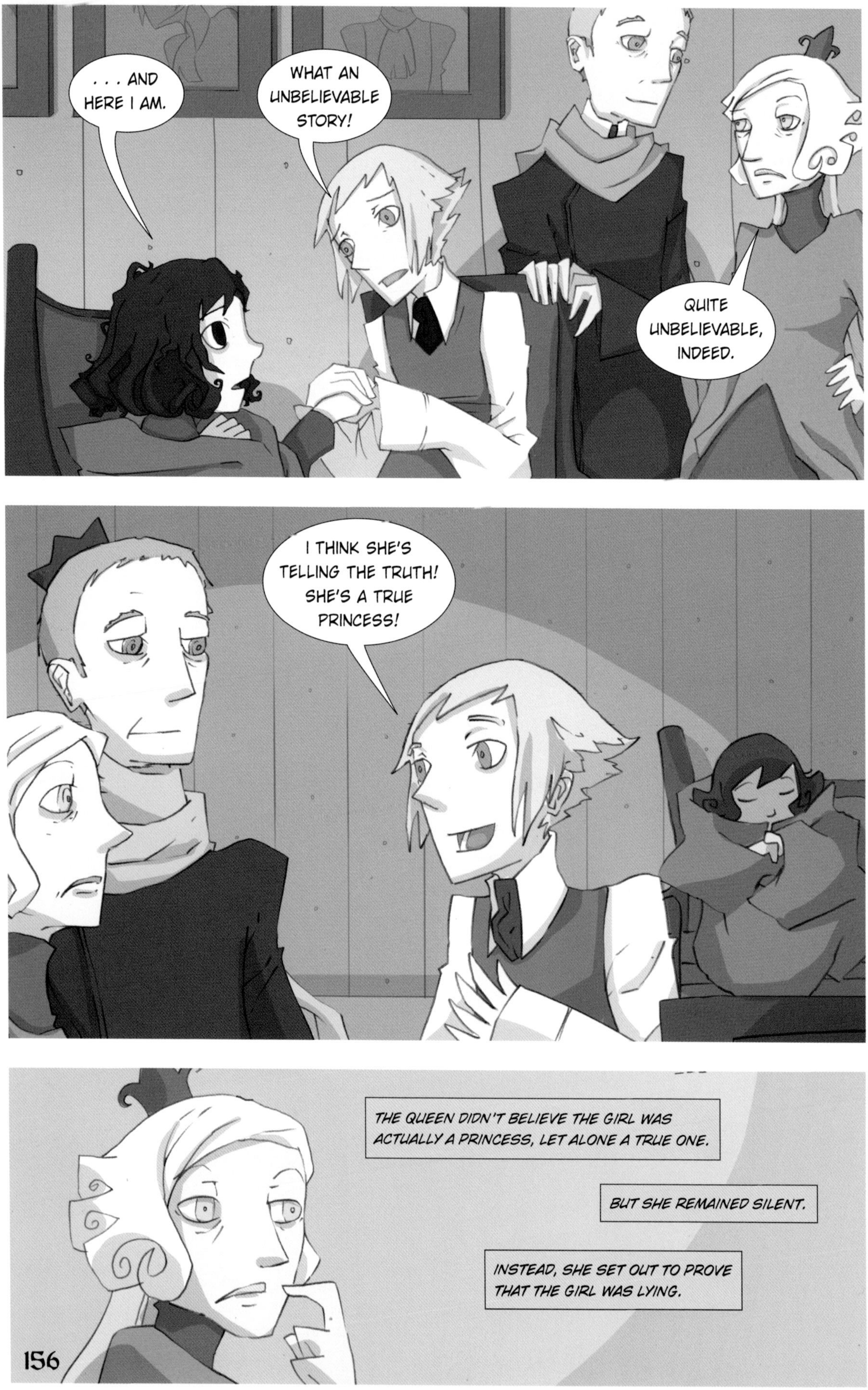
. . . AND HERE I AM.
WHAT AN UNBELIEVABLE STORY!
QUITE UNBELIEVABLE, INDEED.
I THINK SHE'S TELLING THE TRUTH! SHE'S A TRUE PRINCESS!
THE QUEEN DIDN'T BELIEVE THE GIRL WAS ACTUALLY A PRINCESS, LET ALONE A TRUE ONE.
BUT SHE REMAINED SILENT.
INSTEAD, SHE SET OUT TO PROVE THAT THE GIRL WAS LYING.

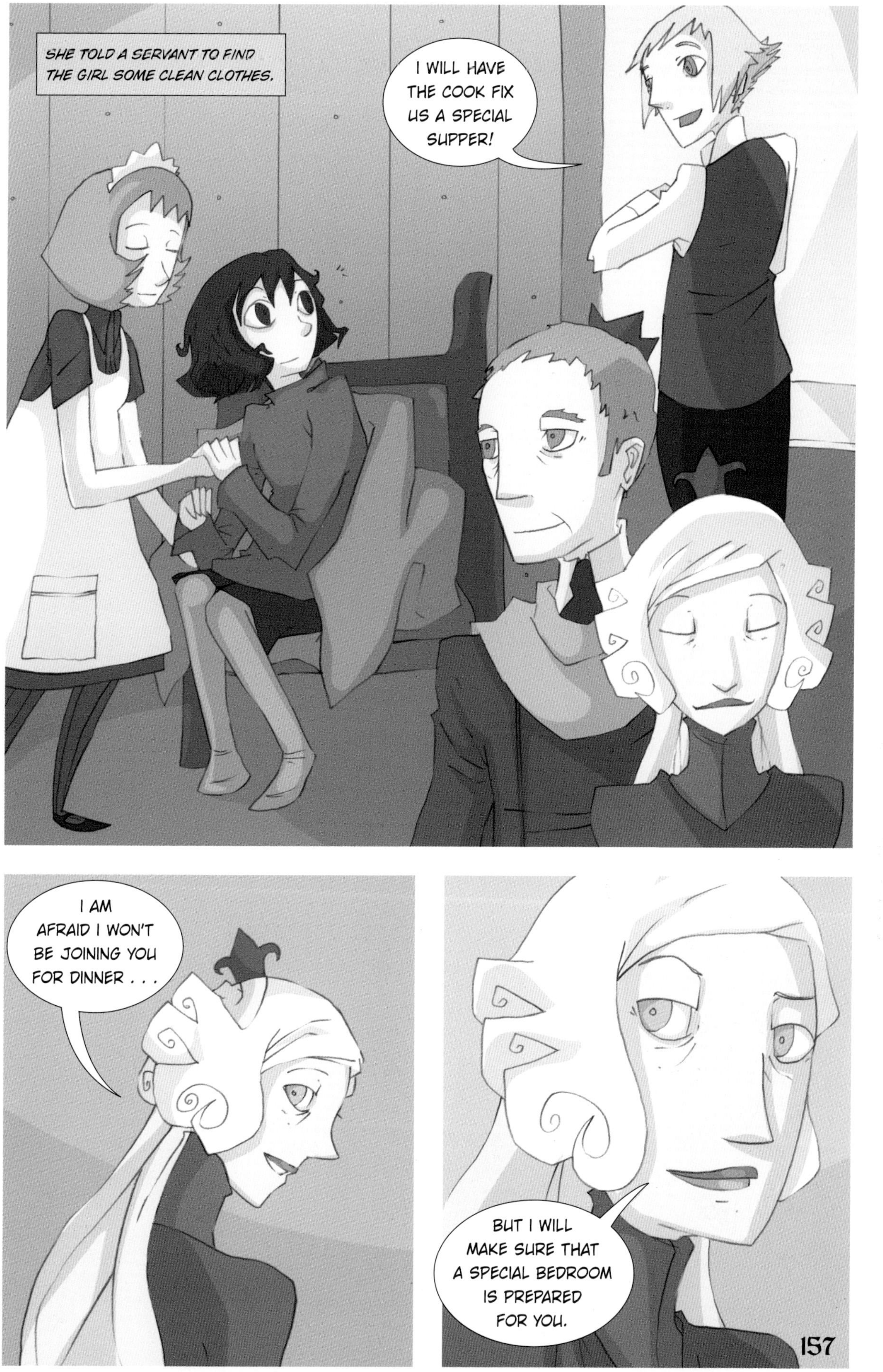
SHE TOLD A SERVANT TO FIND THE GIRL SOME CLEAN CLOTHES.
I WILL HAVE THE COOK FIX US A SPECIAL SUPPER!
I AM AFRAID I WON'T BE JOINING YOU FOR DINNER . . .
BUT I WILL MAKE SURE THAT A SPECIAL BEDROOM IS PREPARED FOR YOU.

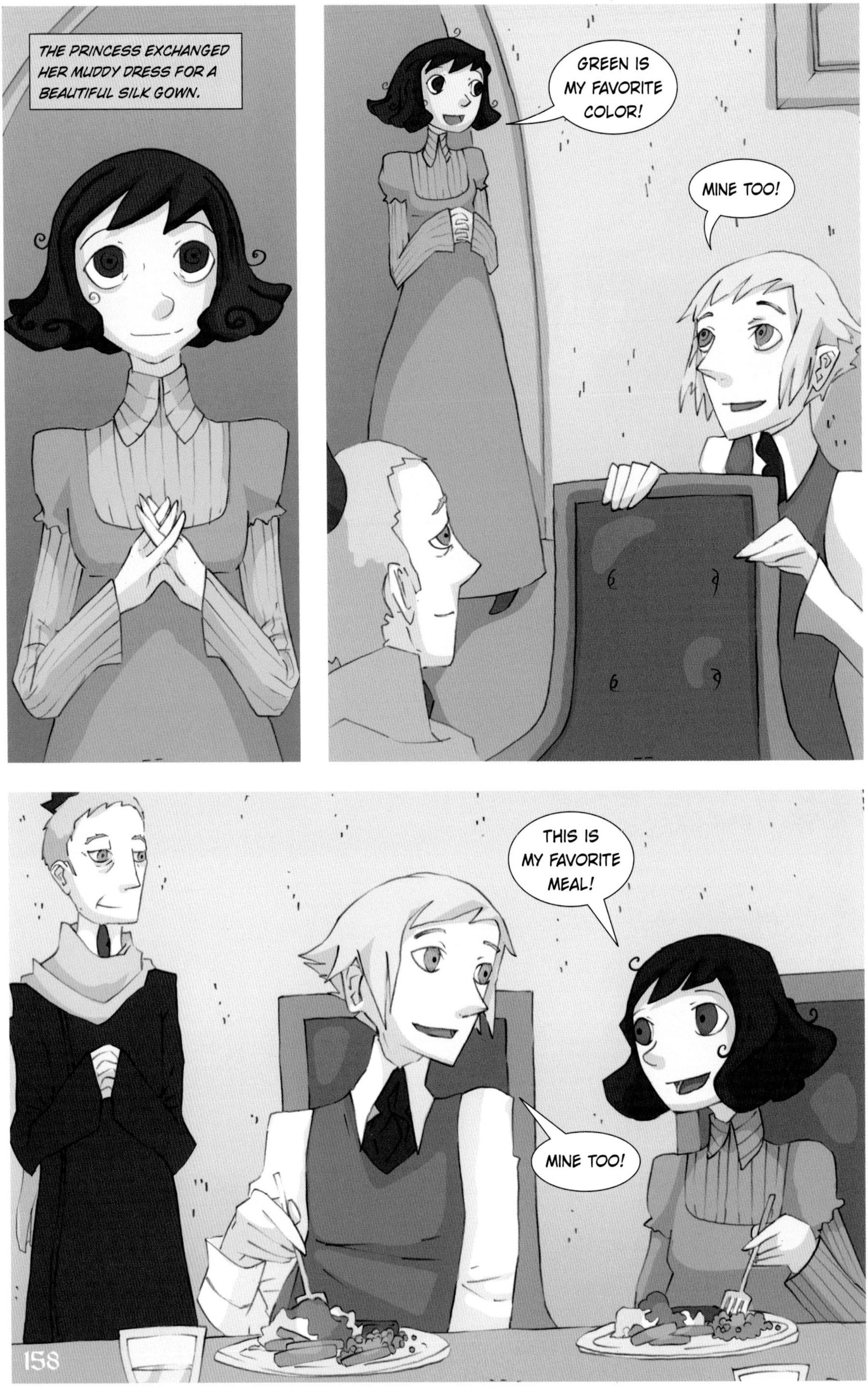
THE PRINCESS EXCHANGED HER MUDDY DRESS FOR A BEAUTIFUL SILK GOWN.
GREEN IS MY FAVORITE COLOR!
MINE TOO!
THIS IS MY FAVORITE MEAL!
MINE TOO!

AFTER DINNER, THE PRINCE READ TO THE PRINCESS WHILE THE KING DOZED.

THIS IS MY FAVORITE STORY!

MINE TOO!

IT FEELS LIKE I'VE KNOWN YOU MY WHOLE LIFE.

ME TOO.

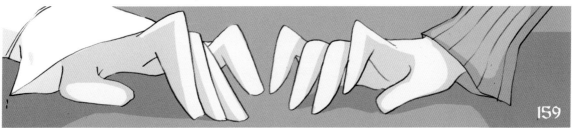

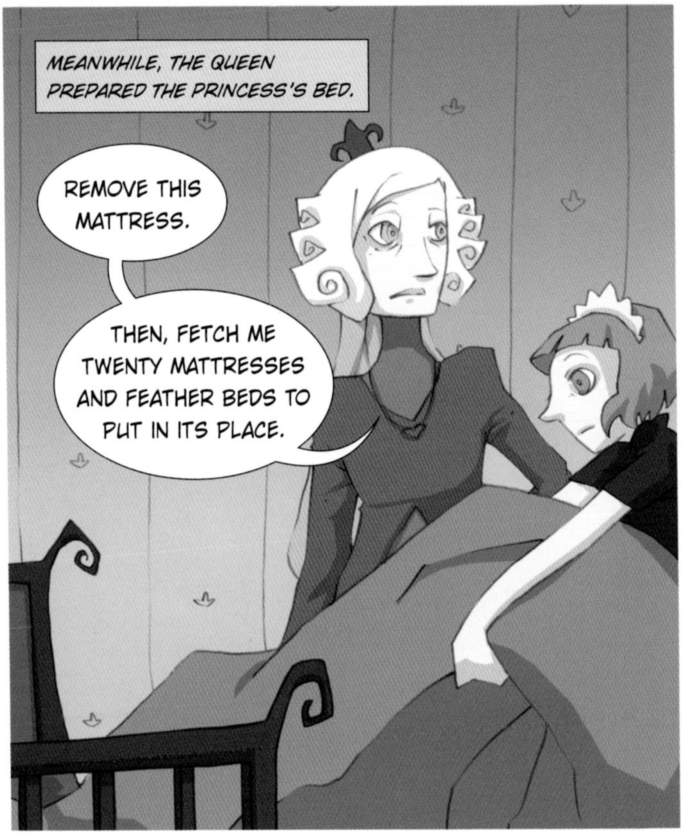
MEANWHILE, THE QUEEN PREPARED THE PRINCESS'S BED.
REMOVE THIS MATTRESS.
THEN, FETCH ME TWENTY MATTRESSES AND FEATHER BEDS TO PUT IN ITS PLACE.

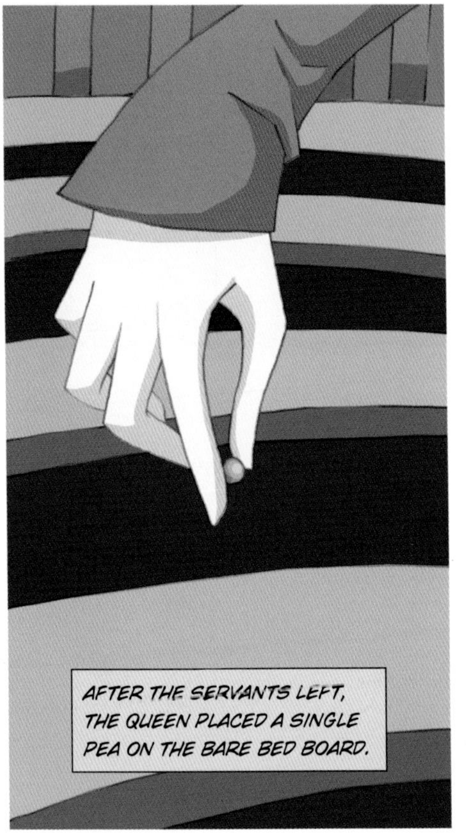
AFTER THE SERVANTS LEFT, THE QUEEN PLACED A SINGLE PEA ON THE BARE BED BOARD.

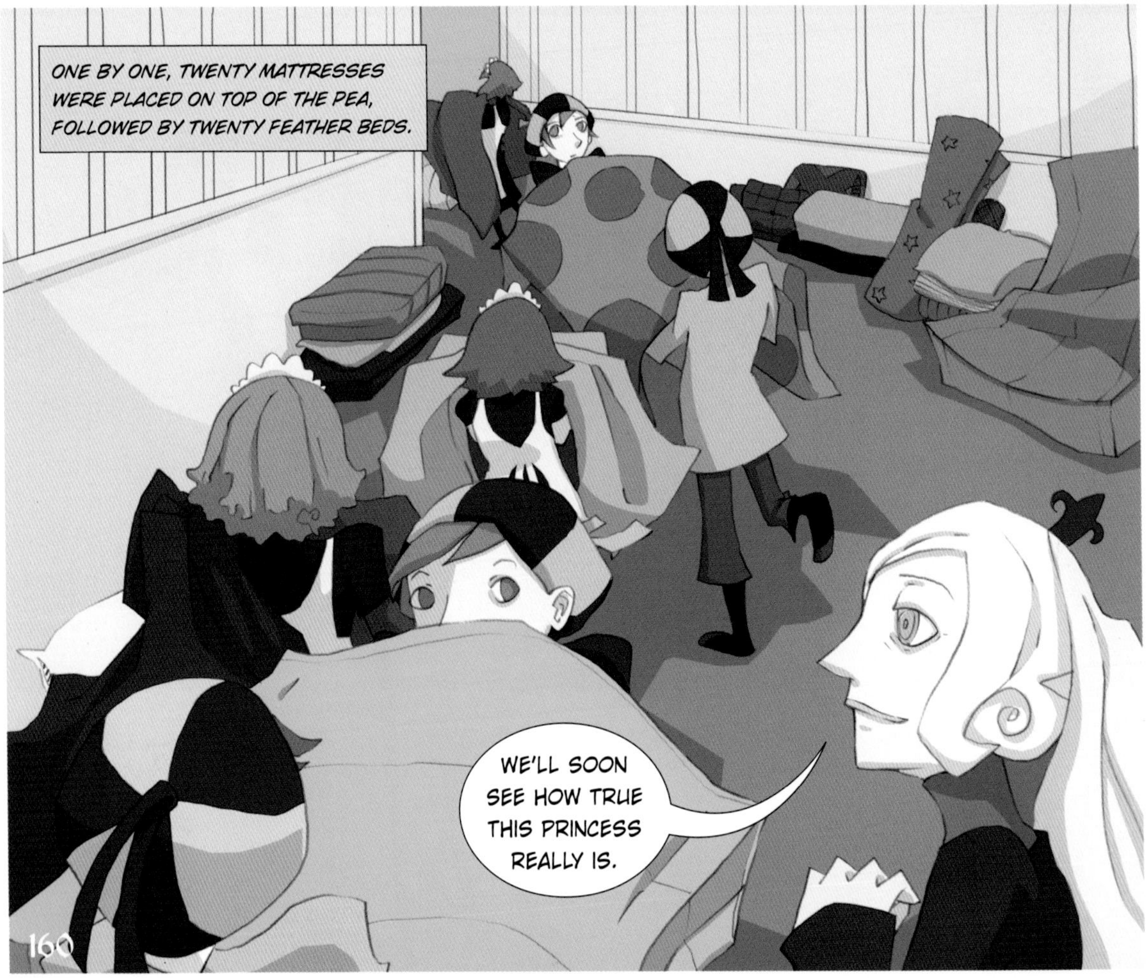
ONE BY ONE, TWENTY MATTRESSES WERE PLACED ON TOP OF THE PEA, FOLLOWED BY TWENTY FEATHER BEDS.
WE'LL SOON SEE HOW TRUE THIS PRINCESS REALLY IS.

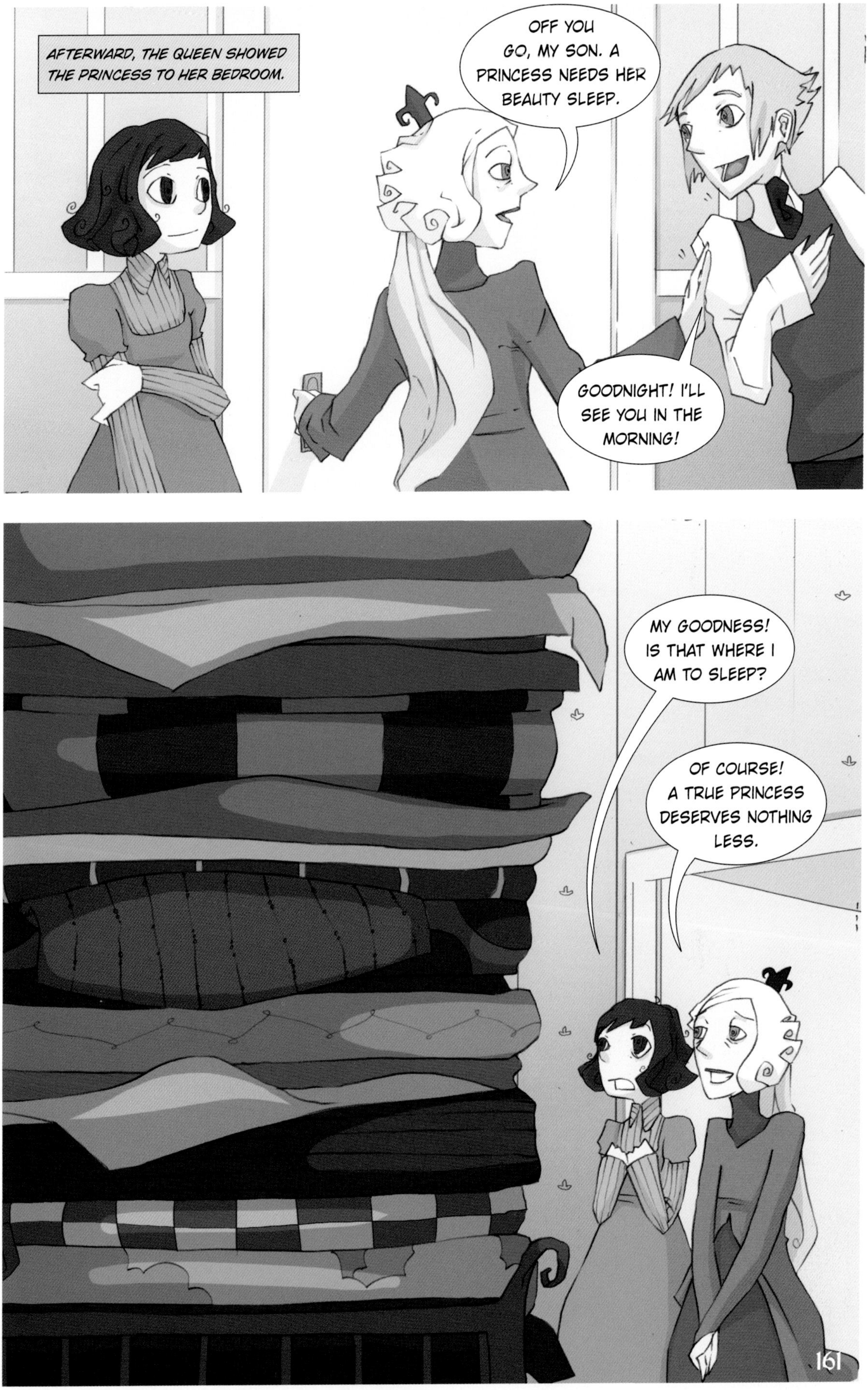
AFTERWARD, THE QUEEN SHOWED THE PRINCESS TO HER BEDROOM.
OFF YOU GO, MY SON. A PRINCESS NEEDS HER BEAUTY SLEEP.
GOODNIGHT! I'LL SEE YOU IN THE MORNING!
MY GOODNESS! IS THAT WHERE I AM TO SLEEP?
OF COURSE! A TRUE PRINCESS DESERVES NOTHING LESS.

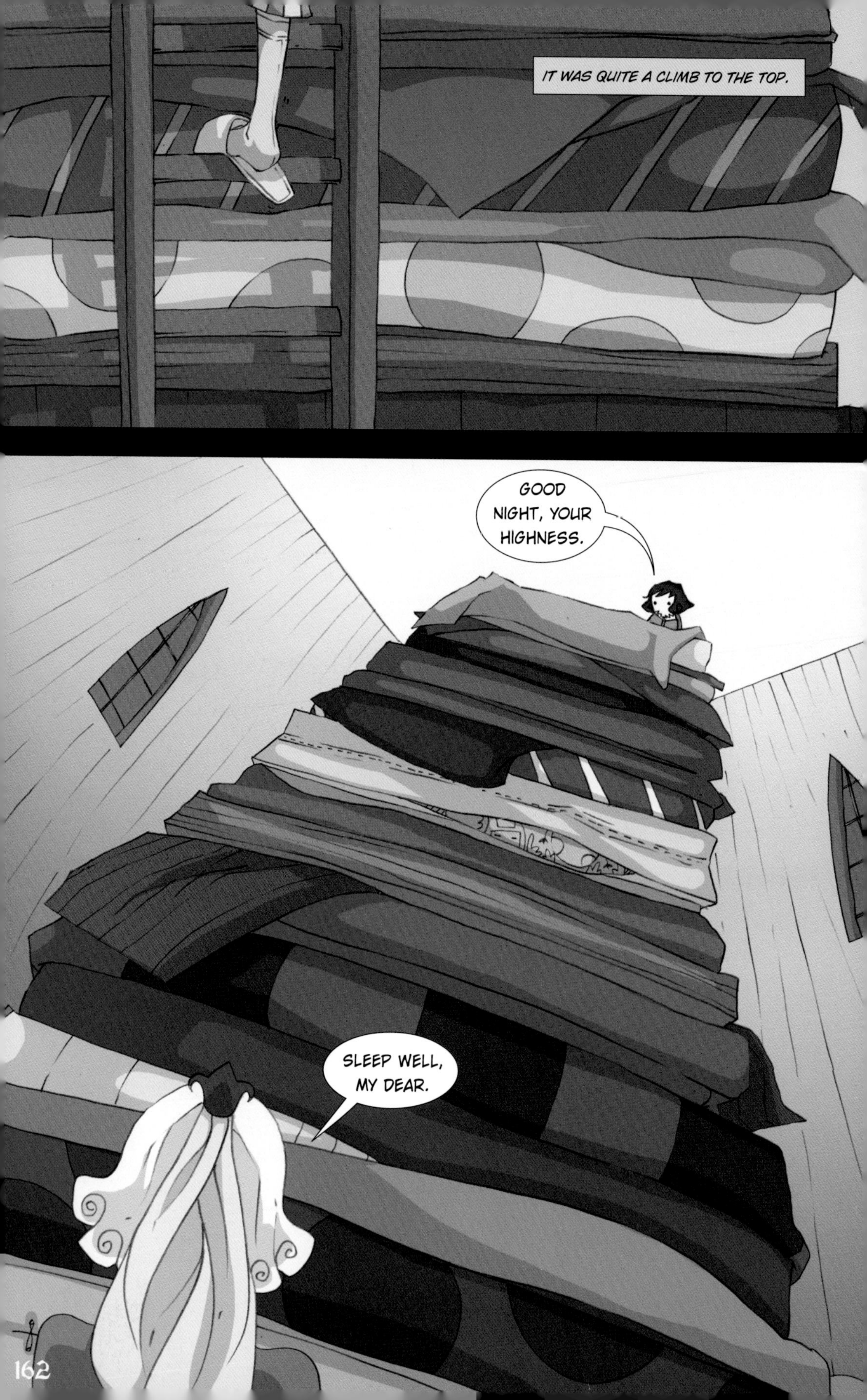
IT WAS QUITE A CLIMB TO THE TOP.
GOOD NIGHT, YOUR HIGHNESS.
SLEEP WELL, MY DEAR.

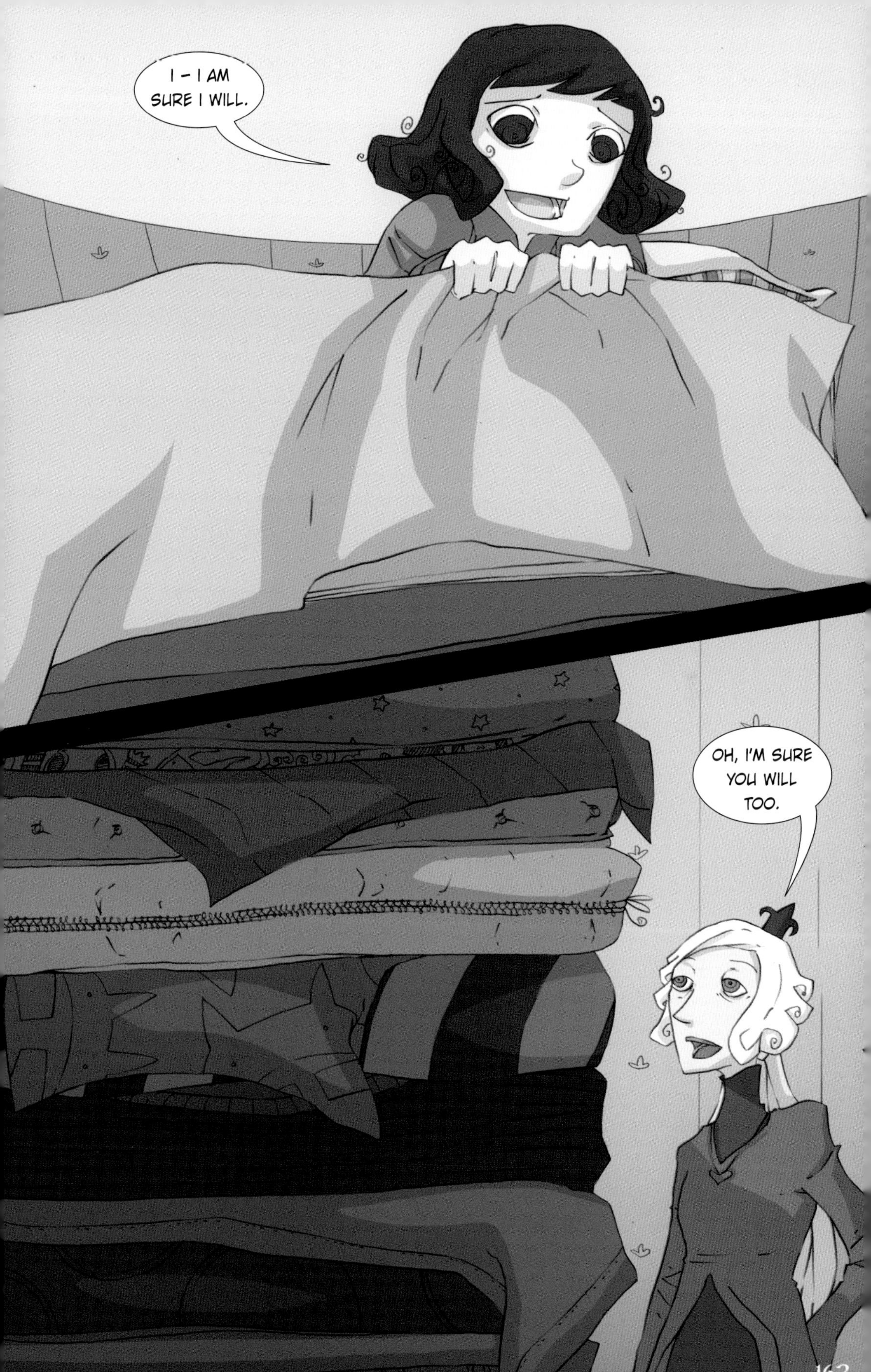
I – I AM SURE I WILL.
OH, I'M SURE YOU WILL TOO.

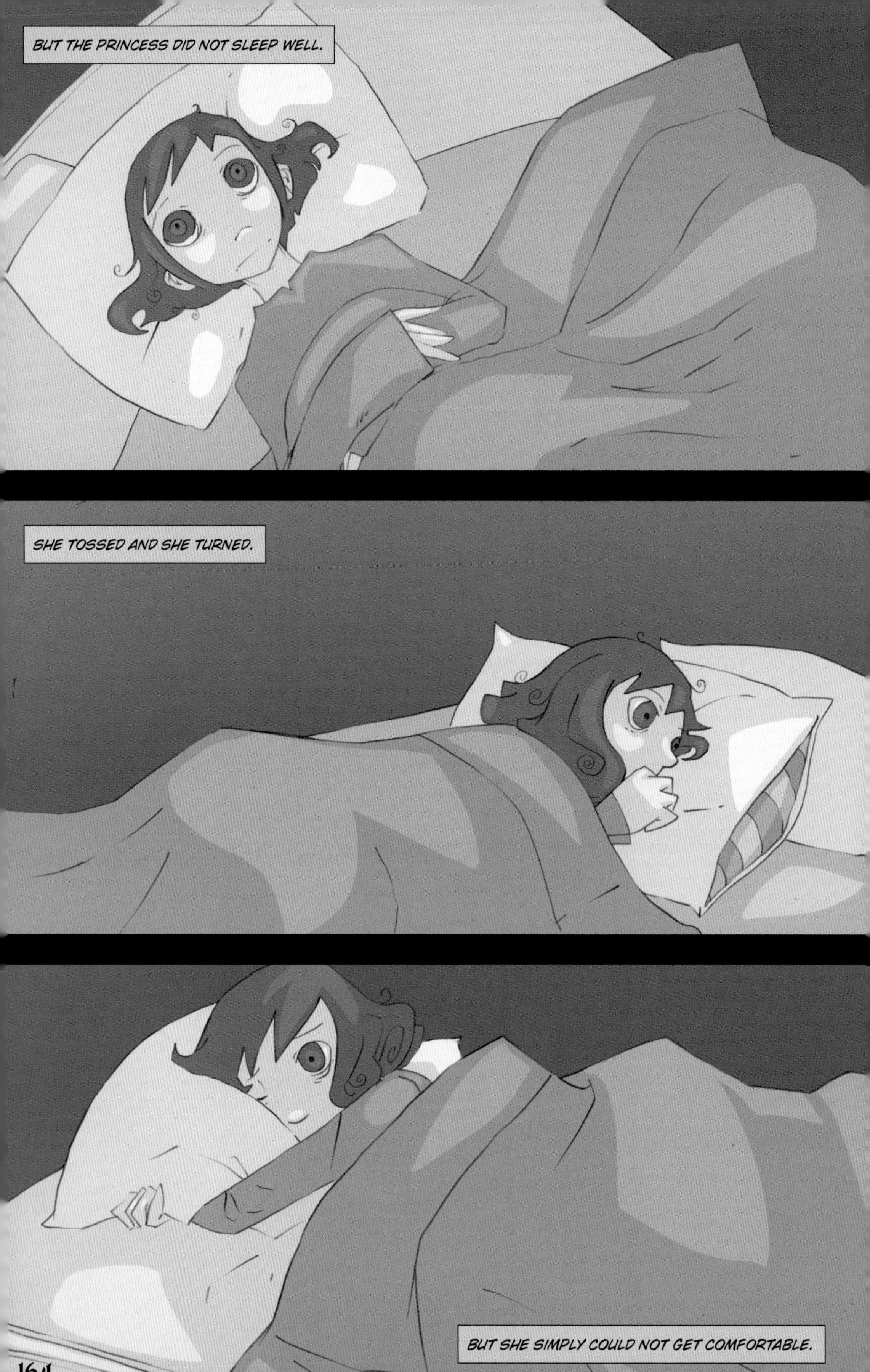
BUT THE PRINCESS DID NOT SLEEP WELL.
SHE TOSSED AND SHE TURNED.
BUT SHE SIMPLY COULD NOT GET COMFORTABLE.

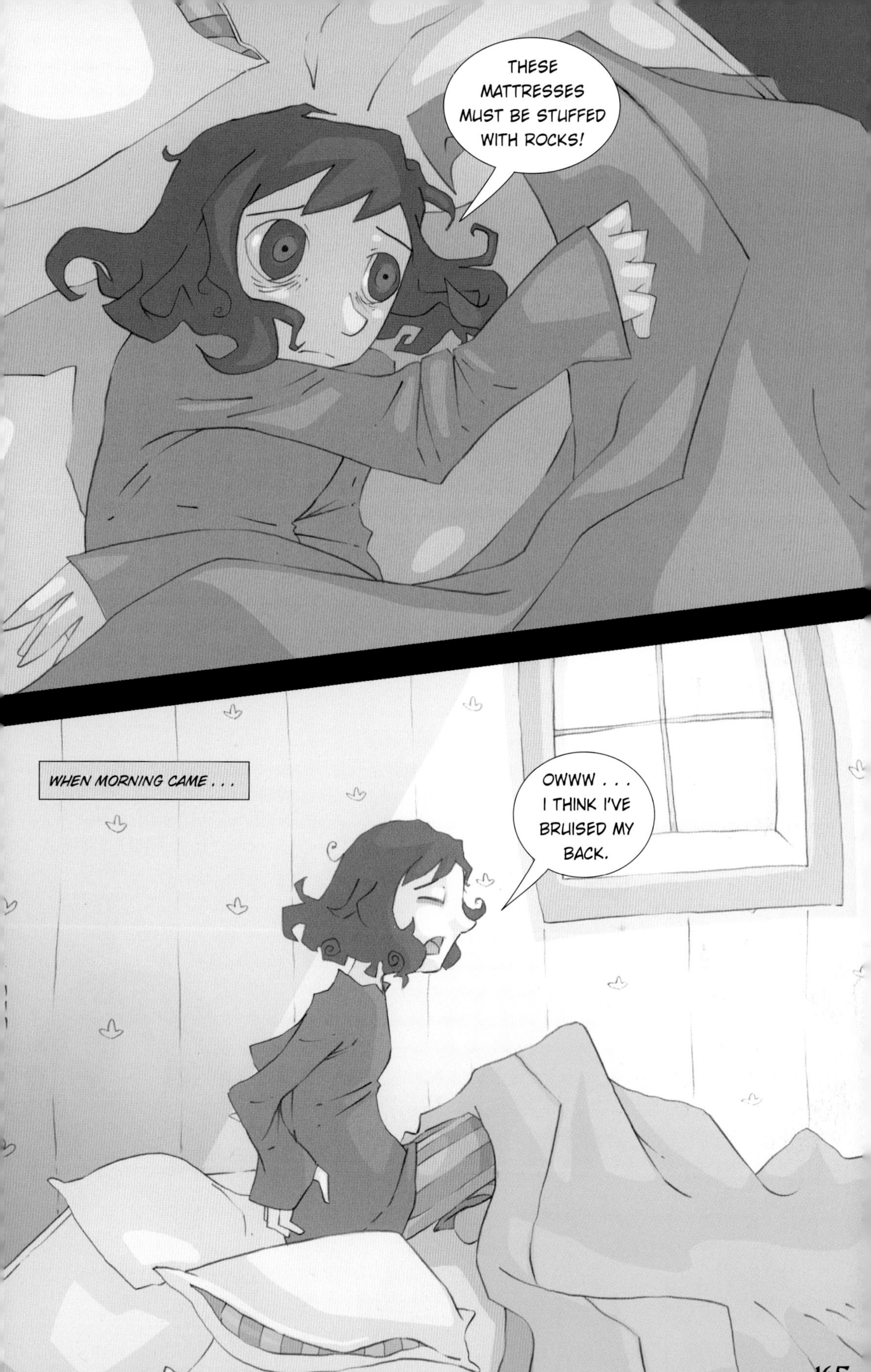
THESE MATTRESSES MUST BE STUFFED WITH ROCKS!
WHEN MORNING CAME . . .
OWWW . . . I THINK I'VE BRUISED MY BACK.

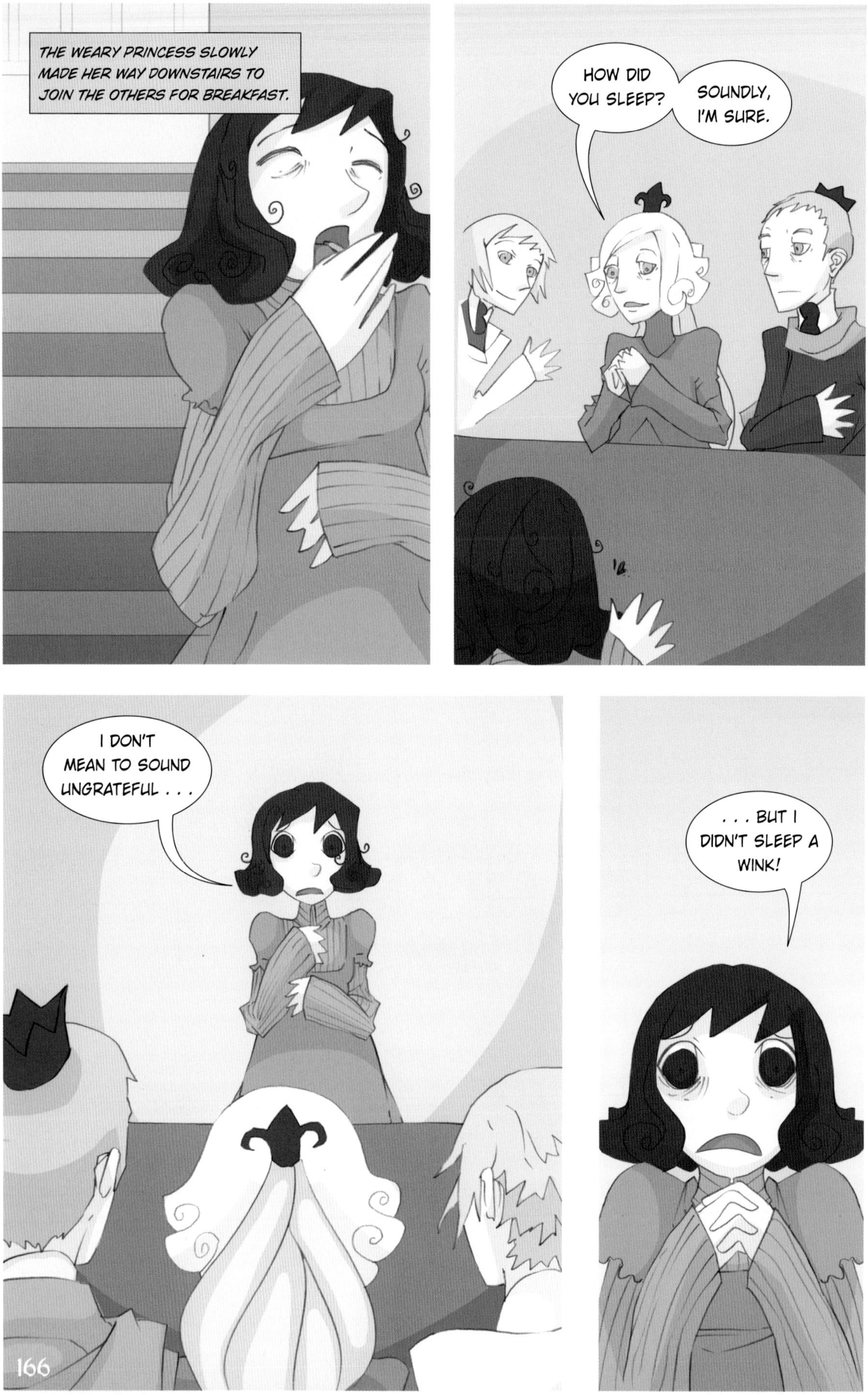
THE WEARY PRINCESS SLOWLY MADE HER WAY DOWNSTAIRS TO JOIN THE OTHERS FOR BREAKFAST.
HOW DID YOU SLEEP?
SOUNDLY, I'M SURE.
I DON'T MEAN TO SOUND UNGRATEFUL . . .
. . . BUT I DIDN'T SLEEP A WINK!

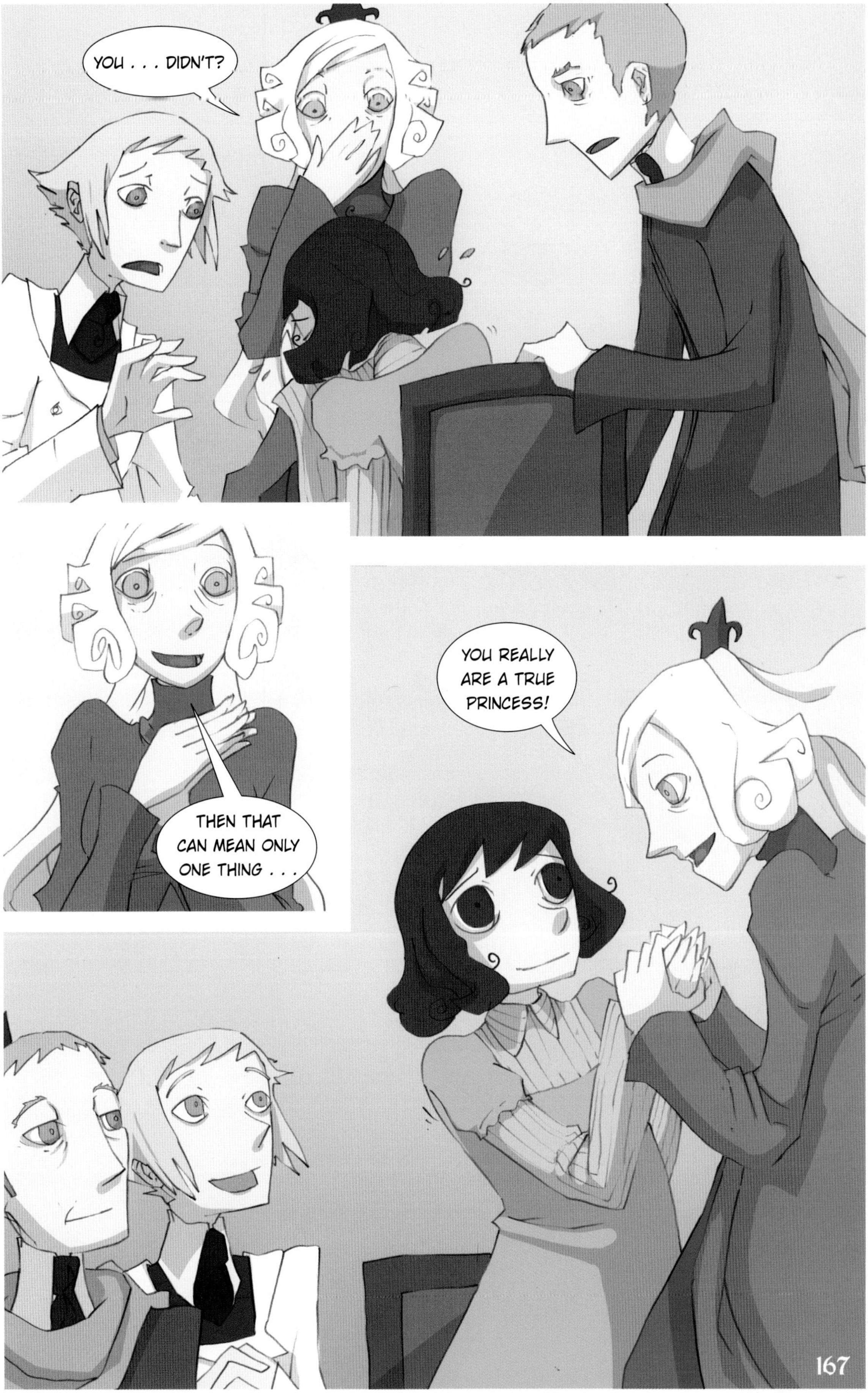
YOU . . . DIDN'T?
THEN THAT CAN MEAN ONLY ONE THING . . .
YOU REALLY ARE A TRUE PRINCESS!

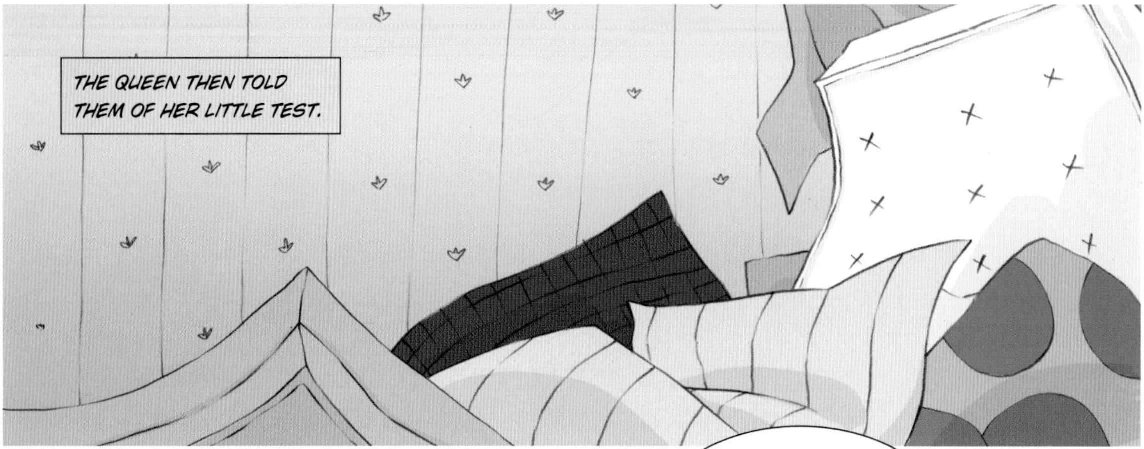
THE QUEEN THEN TOLD THEM OF HER LITTLE TEST.

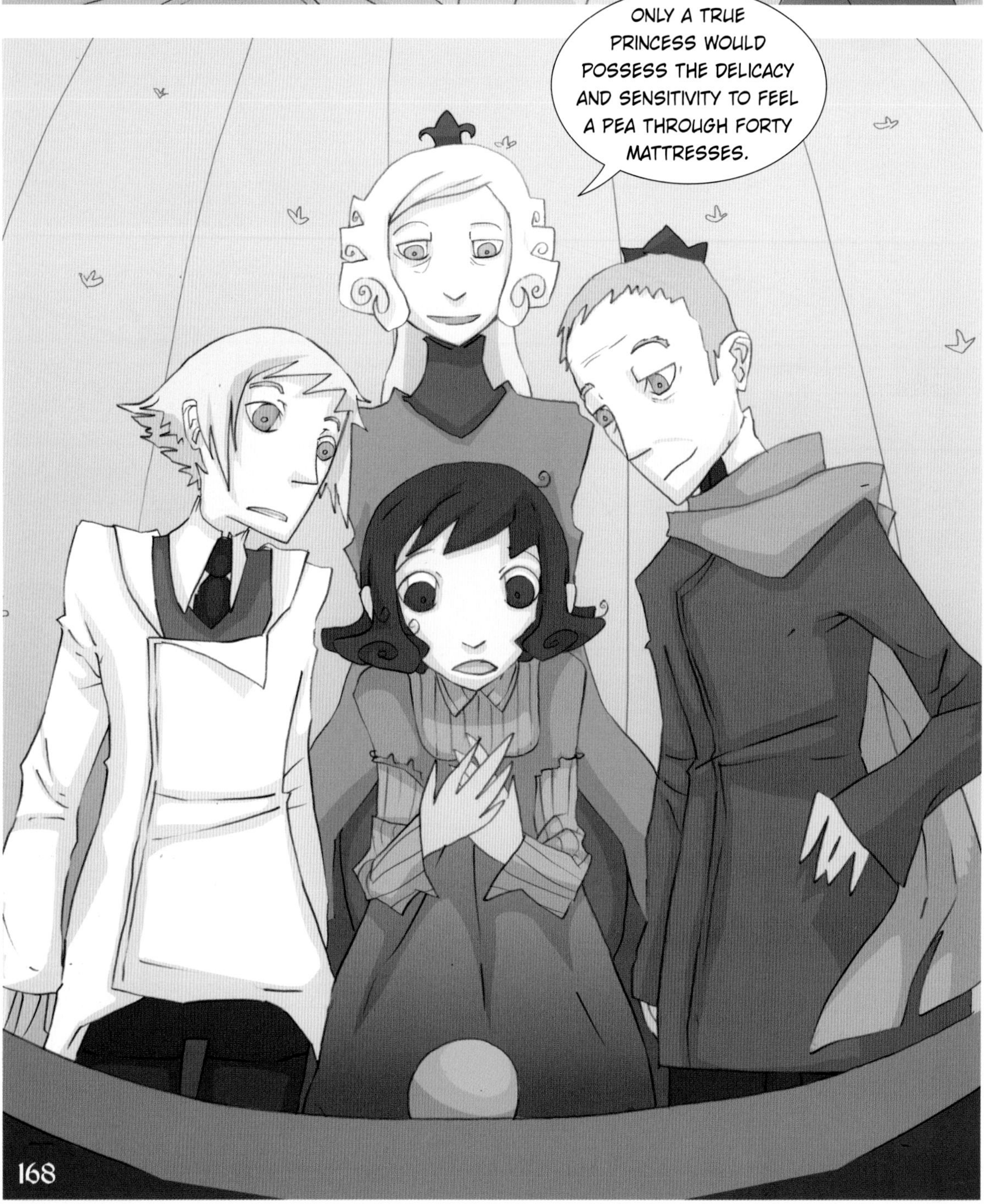
ONLY A TRUE PRINCESS WOULD POSSESS THE DELICACY AND SENSITIVITY TO FEEL A PEA THROUGH FORTY MATTRESSES.

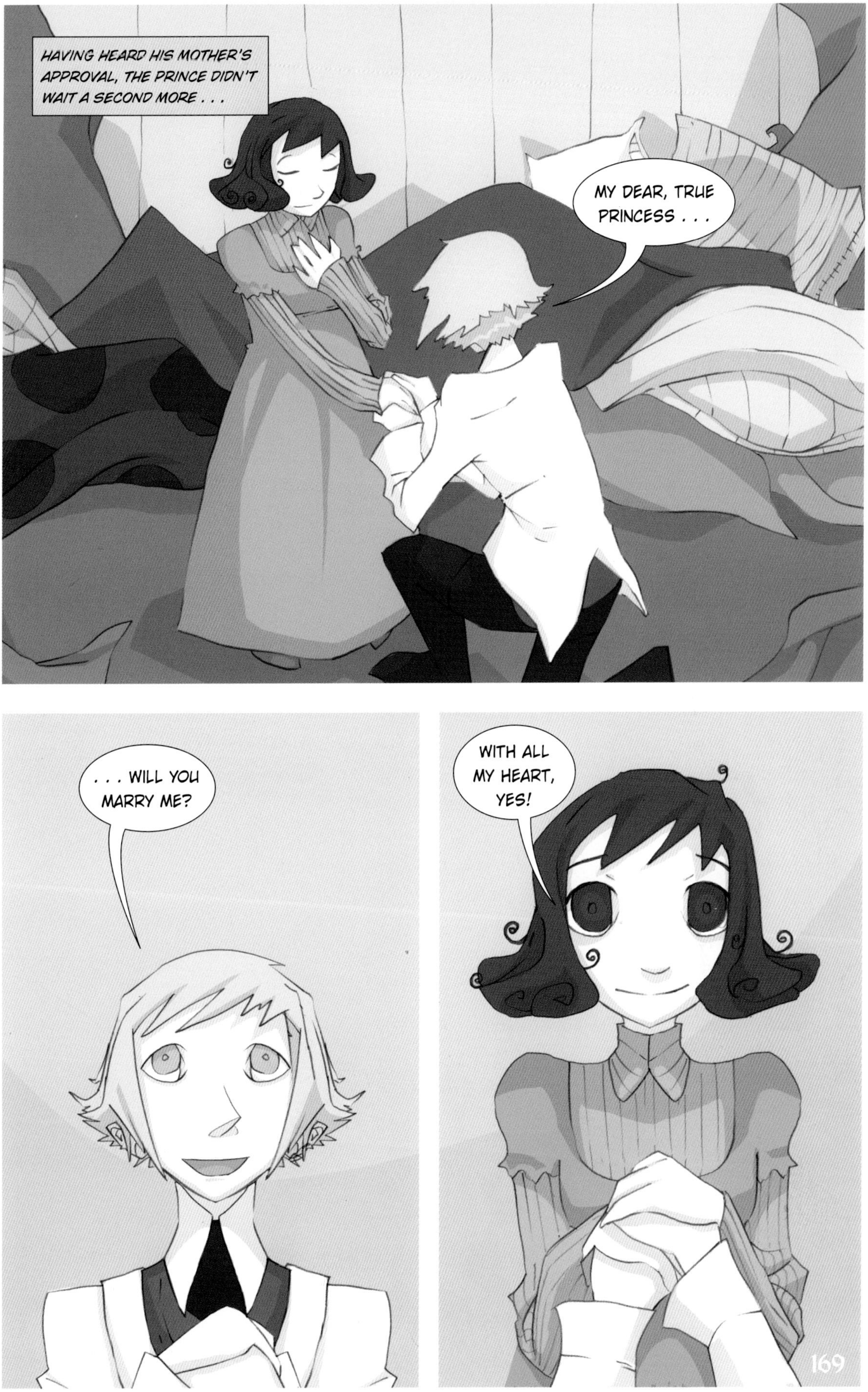
HAVING HEARD HIS MOTHER'S APPROVAL, THE PRINCE DIDN'T WAIT A SECOND MORE . . .
MY DEAR, TRUE PRINCESS . . .
. . . WILL YOU MARRY ME?
WITH ALL MY HEART, YES!

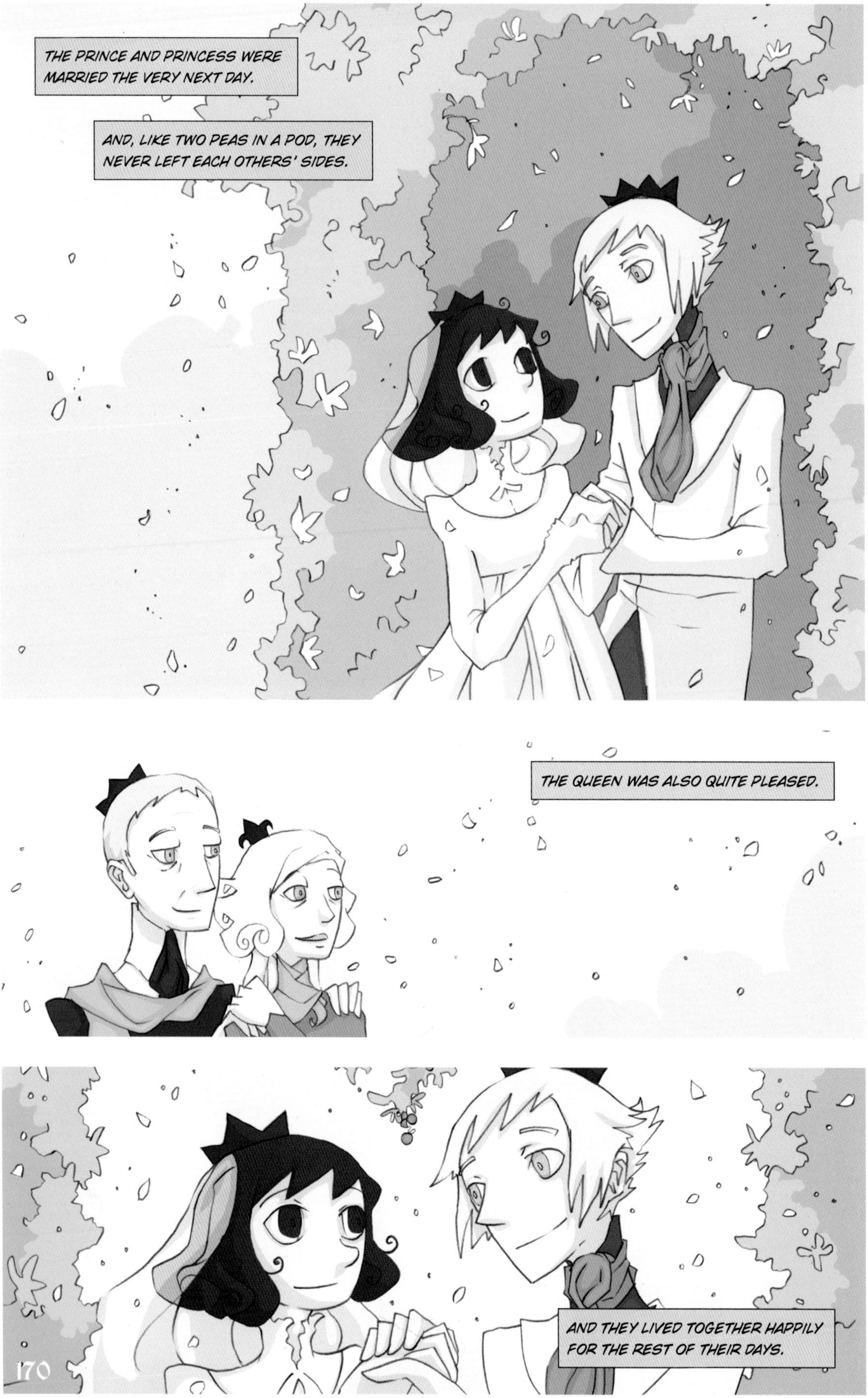
THE PRINCE AND PRINCESS WERE MARRIED THE VERY NEXT DAY.
AND, LIKE TWO PEAS IN A POD, THEY NEVER LEFT EACH OTHERS' SIDES.
THE QUEEN WAS ALSO QUITE PLEASED.
AND THEY LIVED TOGETHER HAPPILY FOR THE REST OF THEIR DAYS.

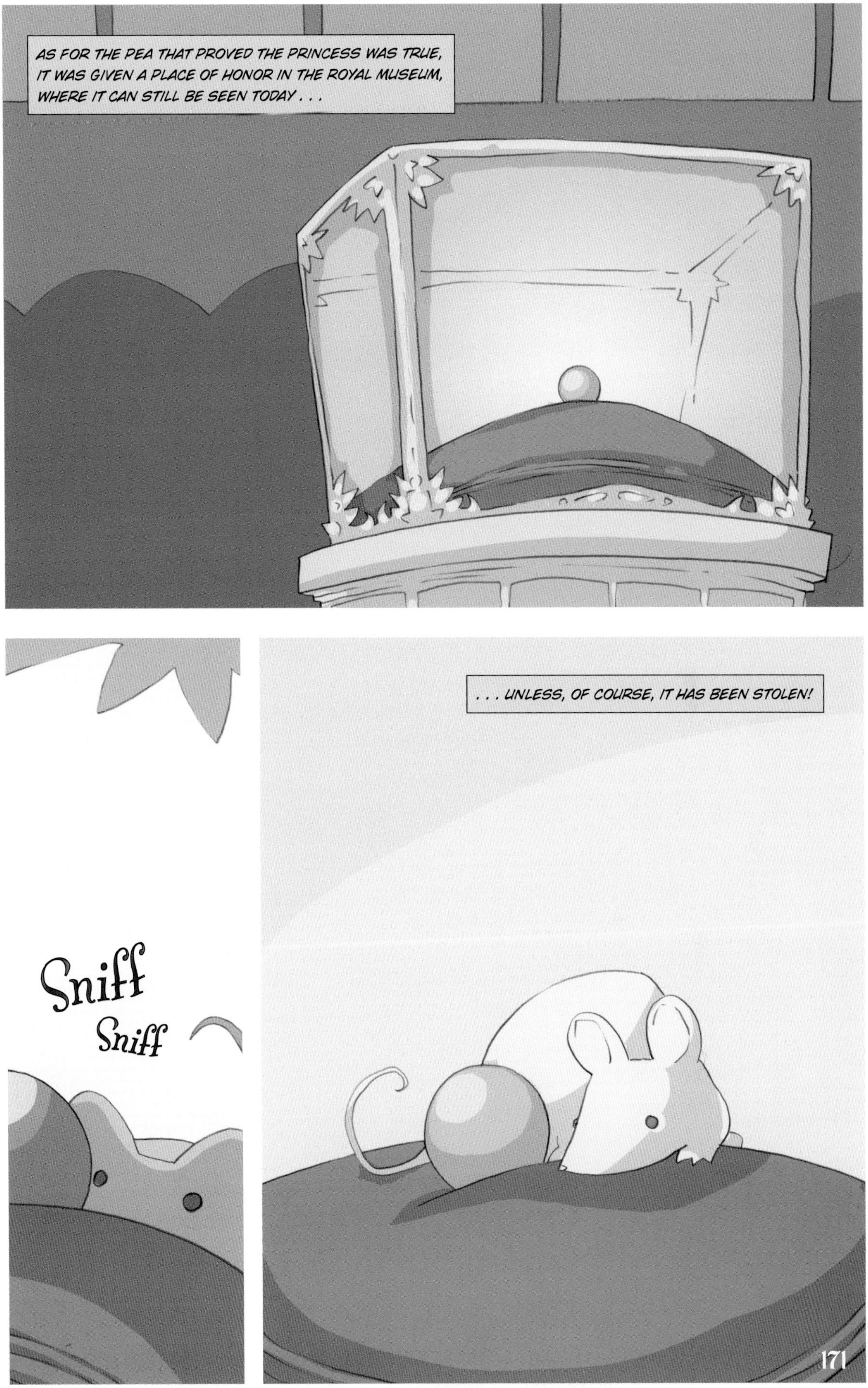
AS FOR THE PEA THAT PROVED THE PRINCESS WAS TRUE, IT WAS GIVEN A PLACE OF HONOR IN THE ROYAL MUSEUM, WHERE IT CAN STILL BE SEEN TODAY . . .
Sniff
Sniff
. . . UNLESS, OF COURSE, IT HAS BEEN STOLEN!

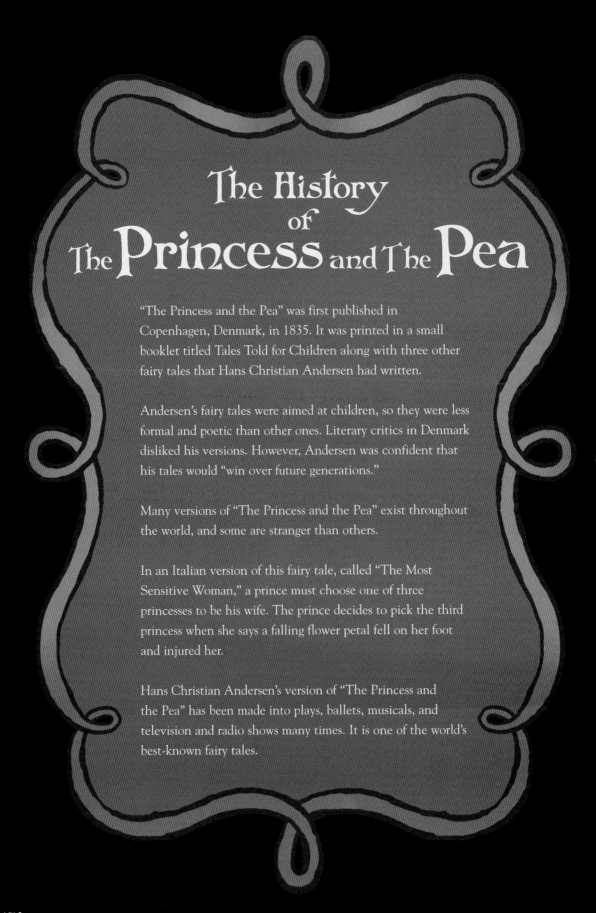

The History
of
The Princess and The Pea

"The Princess and the Pea" was first published in
Copenhagen, Denmark, in 1835. It was printed in a small
booklet titled Tales Told for Children along with three other
fairy tales that Hans Christian Andersen had written.

Andersen's fairy tales were aimed at children, so they were less
formal and poetic than other ones. Literary critics in Denmark
disliked his versions. However, Andersen was confident that
his tales would "win over future generations."

Many versions of "The Princess and the Pea" exist throughout
the world, and some are stranger than others.

In an Italian version of this fairy tale, called "The Most
Sensitive Woman," a prince must choose one of three
princesses to be his wife. The prince decides to pick the third
princess when she says a falling flower petal fell on her foot
and injured her.

Hans Christian Andersen's version of "The Princess and
the Pea" has been made into plays, ballets, musicals, and
television and radio shows many times. It is one of the world's
best-known fairy tales.

about the Authors

Stephanie Peters

After working for more than 10 years as a children's book editor, Stephanie Peters started writing books herself. She has since written 40 books, including the *New York Times* best seller *A Princess Primer: A Fairy Godmother's Guide to Being a Princess*. When not at her computer, Peters enjoys playing with her two children, hitting the gym, or working on home improvement projects with her patient and supportive husband, Daniel.

Martin Powell

Martin Powell has been a freelance writer since 1986. He has written hundreds of stories, many of which have been published by Disney, Marvel, Tekno Comix, Moonstone Books, and others. In 1989, Powell received an Eisner Award nomination for his graphic novel *Scarlet in Gaslight*. This award is one of the highest comic book honors.

Michael Dahl

Michael Dahl is the author of more than 100 books for children and young adults. He has twice won the AEP Distinguished Achievement Award for his nonfiction. His Finnegan Zwake mystery series was chosen by the Agatha Awards to be among the five best mystery books for children in 2002 and 2003. He collects books on poison and graveyards, and lives in a haunted house in Minneapolis, Minnesota.

about the Illustrators

Jeffrey Stewart Timmins

Jeffrey Stewart Timmins was born July 2, 1979. In 2003, he graduated from the Classical Animation program at Sheridan College in Oakville, Ontario. He currently works as a freelance designer and animator. Even as an adult, Timmins still holds onto a few important items from his childhood, such as his rubber boots, cape, and lensless sunglasses.

Sarah Horne

Sarah Horne was born in Derbyshire, United Kingdom, on a cold November day. Since then, she graduated from Falmouth College of Arts in 2001 and from Kingston University with a master's degree in illustration in 2005. Currently, Sarah lives and works in Wapping, London, and spends many hours sipping tea while working at Happiness At Work Studios.

Erik Valdez y Alanis

Erik Valdez y Alanis was born and raised in Mexico City, Mexico, and has been drawing since age 2. He has done illustrations for books, magazines, and CD covers. Today, Valdez has focused on comics including, most recently, *The Sleepy Truth* for Viper Comics. When he's not working, Valdez loves traveling, really good books, and chocolate cake.

Luke Feldman

Luke Feldman is an illustrator, animator, and designer from Australia. For more than 10 years, he has worked on high-profile projects for large corporations such as Microsoft and Coca Cola. He has also worked closely with the Australian education department, developing animations and interactive games for children.

Michelle Lamoreaux

Michelle Lamoreaux was born and raised in Utah. She studied at Southern Utah University and graduated with a BFA in Illustration. She likes working with both digital and traditional media. She currently lives and works in Cedar City, Utah.